CW00523569

DAMONE RA

A Rock and Roll Betrayal.

BY

Damone Ramone

AND

Frank Lord,

AUTHOR OF "KILLED TO DEATH: DETROIT, ASSEMBLY PLANTS, MURDER."

SEVERELY

DETROIT BERLIN PRAGUE MINSK

Damone Ramone

Cover Art: Rahul Bajad

Cover Design: Sean Foyle

severelybooks.com

damoneramone.wordpress.com

ISBN: 1523945397
ISBN-13: 978-1523945399

DEDICATION

To Beert S. and to the fans that love the "Ramones" music that they believe was written by them but was actually written by me, specifically the first four albums.

CONTENTS.

Part V.—A DIVERSION OF THE HEART FROM GOD

Part VI.—BACK TO THE FRONT.

Part VII.—THE END OF THE SEVENTIES.

Part VIII.—THE LOST DECADES.

Part IX.—TERMINUS.

Damone Ramone

ACKNOWLEDGMENTS

Heartfelt thanks to: Peter Ellsberg. Your ability to shoplift alcohol has made 1970 to the present bearable, sometimes magical. You are the definition of "sophisticated." David Ellsberg for his willingness to argue his bullshit beliefs and for letting me watch his television, not withstanding the premier of *Little House on the Prairie*. The security guards at the Brighton Beach Public Library who knew I was sleeping beneath the books in the donation bin, but turned a blind eye. Danny Fields for always coming through. Curzes for his brilliant piece *Misery*; the work provided the perfect posture for me to emulate while modeling for the cover of this book and for demonstrating my worldview. Alex Askaroff for his Elias Howe biography. The Burmese Socialist Programme Party for the 1962 Constitution and for 1963's *The System of Correlation of Man and his Environment*.

PREFACE.

THE BREAKING POINT.

I reached it in 2002. It was unexpected. I thought I had nearly reconciled with what my brothers—the Ramones—had done to me. Despite decades of misery, I had ultimately come to believe that whatever problems we'd had, they meant nothing compared to the majesty of the music; it had taken on a life far bigger than the concerns of any one Ramone. The world didn't need the sordid truth or a bitter whiner lashing out in a self-serving manner that would spoil the music, the fans' memories, and the experience of hearing my Quartet Cycle as interpreted by the Ramones for the first time. In sum, I couldn't let the fans down since they were actually my fans by proxy, so I remained silent.

That was my mental state the day I heard they were going to be inducted into the Rock and Roll Hall of Fame. When I heard the news, I experienced a euphoria I'd not felt since September 4th, 1991: the day I won twenty-four dollars playing *Lucky 7*. What a wonderful moment, because in addition to winning twenty-four dollars, I had also managed to slip a half-pint of mint schnapps into my pocket.

When they were inducted, Dee Dee, clad in a smart purple sport coat, thanked himself. Johnny couldn't hide his happiness, finally receiving the mainstream recognition he had always craved. He didn't forget to thank those that had helped them on their nefarious path, like their first "manager" Danny Fields. Marky looked vibrant, the perennial twinkle of humor in his eye shining

1

just as brightly as it had when he was a mischievous youth. There was more thanking, endless thanking, including their personal laundry lists of so-called "influences."

But it was Tommy who broke me. It's one thing to steal hundreds of works of art from your own brother and claim them as your own. It's crossing the line however to stand on stage at the dénouement of a wildly successful criminal career and mock the victim in front of millions:

"We were truly brothers."

Whatever his intent, it can at least be said that Tommy stated a truth—a rare thing for my brothers. The crucial Ramones truth that was turned on its head until the world believed it wasn't so: *We were truly brothers.*

Because we are: Johnny, Joey, Dee Dee, Mickey, Tommy, Marky, Tyler, Terry, František. And me: Damone. We also have a sister named Ramona. The *actual* Ramones: by name, by law, *by blood*. The story that has been sold to the world since 1974 is completely untrue, a gimmick: the Colvin-Hyman-Cummings-Erdelyi-Bell fantasy. This falsehood made them all wealthy and famous; they built a metropolis of lies in order to steal my ideas and cut me out financially. Potency has been torn from me, leaving only a calm sea of impotence.

My brothers took advantage of my insularity and idealism, my enslavement to the solitary endeavor of creating. They took advantage of my lack of practical skills, my ritualistic barriers, my masturbation issues. Even sewing—the one area outside music where I illustrate utility—was used against me during those dark years, although it should be noted that sewing and music were inexorably linked within the realm of my particular genius. This will all be explained herein.

My own brothers plundered my life and abandoned me on an island in the night. They sailed into a dark fog, and then onward into a universe of rapturous fans, unbridled masturbation and lovemaking, photo shoots, world travel, and the steady thwack of stolen greenbacks going bang and crack as they stacked their accounts full of ice cold cash. Horrible, cringe-worthy alliteration? You didn't seem to mind when it turned up as *She's a Sensation*[1].

By this point, I frankly don't expect to be vindicated by the revelations herein, but by becoming a textile magnate I will at least be comfortable. Perhaps you've already noticed that the bankers, lawyers, and ad-men on Park and Madison are looking a little more battened down in the midsection. Why? Tail-Sinkers.

The Tail-Sinker is a system that keeps the dress shirt neatly tucked in, even when the working gentleman rises from his desk after a long day or arrives at work after a frenzied commute.

The Tail-Sinker consists of strategically placed rings sewn at intervals around the interior perimeter of the dress shirt: six on the rear shirttail, two on the front, and one on each gusset. These rings are made of polyurethane alloy. For the British market, the alloy will be reinforced with titanium tendrils designed to support ultra-heavy tail-sinkers, an elite feature I plan on marketing in a joint venture with Thomas Pink.

Thin, adjustable steel cables hang approximately two feet down the pant leg from each ring, depending on preference and height. A lead sinker slightly larger than a golf ball hangs from each cable. The weights guarantee a clean tuck.

I will eventually offer customized options for the sinkers: engravings and gold plating. As the line's popularity expands, I envision solid gold sinkers hanging from silver cables under the tuxedo pants of wealthy rappers and rockers as they walk on stage to collect awards. Induction into the Rock and Roll Hall of Fame, for example.

The function of the Tail-Sinker is self-evident, and therein lays the idea's simple brilliance. Like any clever advancement, the Tail-Sinker has the all-important, "Why didn't I think of that?" quality that defines all truly great inventions, like the wheel, the six-pack ring, one tap for hot and cold…the music of the Ramones.

---

[1] Original title: *Brutal Goons of the Diaspora.* This was the only Ramones "song" plagiarized from my quartets that appeared after *Road to Ruin*—a creative Kaliningrad if you will.

Damone Ramone

DAMONE RAMONE.

Part I.

YOUTH. THE DEATH OF INNOCENCE. REBIRTH.

CHAPTER I.

MONTEZ.

Our father, Victor Montez Ramone, was born in Cuba on Christmas Day in the year of grace 1915. His father was a fugitive German anarchist and his mother was a Puerto Rican immigrant that became the fastest cigar roller in Margarabomba and later all of Cuba. Victor Montez[2] was a long, underweight baby, but otherwise healthy. Montez's father Rheinhold was said to have been so overjoyed that he assaulted the attending doctor in an explosion of exuberant fury. Exiled to Cuba and far-removed from the political tumult of World War I Berlin, he repackaged his adversarial rage into joyous violence. Our mother told us this family legend as a bedtime story: Grandpa punched out the doctor's left eye and shoved it in his mouth. He hopped from left foot to right while humming the *Ode to Joy* with the doctor's eye partially visible through his pursed lips like a Cyclops gag-ball. Of course we didn't believe the story, or at least not until we saw the

---

[2] It was credibly supposed that Montez had fabricated the family name Ramone—reason unknown.

rotted remains of the doctor's eye in a large locket[3] our father always wore.

Still, doubts and contradictions remained. According to Joey, Rheinhold was a myth. Joey claims that Montez's father was actually the anarcho-syndicalist Rudolf Rocker. Joey claims when Rudolf Rocker was living in England, he travelled to Cuba to invest in a sugar racket, and Montez was conceived during the trip.

Johnny, on the other hand, vehemently denies Joey's assertions. Johnny claims the Rudolf Rocker story was a fabrication Joey concocted because he supported Rocker's politics, and he wanted to be descended from someone politically like-minded, especially someone named Rocker. Based on Joey's subsequent Jeff Starship persona, perhaps Johnny's assertion was at least partially correct.

According to Johnny, Montez's father was one Rheinhold Vomhof. Rheinhold infiltrated anarchist organizations as a double agent, but he ultimately went on to take part in the Beer Hall Putsch. Our mother agreed that our grandfather's name was Rheinhold, but she said he was a Jewish Weimar liberal and vehement anti-fascist. That's how it was in our family—you were left to piece together the truth to the best of your ability, with supposition inevitably playing a part.

To be fair, each version of the family story had a kernel of credibility. At the same time, each version was heavily colored by personal agenda. Johnny, for example, couldn't allow any version of the past that clashed with his contemporary beliefs. Joey tended to improve or romanticize the details—he was a dreamer and idealist, and embellished his version accordingly. Tommy scrupulously researched every version, but he kept his findings to himself to avoid conflict. Dee Dee and Marky were apathetic and neutral respectively. Mickey leaned toward Tommy's research-based conclusions on the rare occasions Tommy shared them. Our sister Ramona's thoroughly characteristic assessment was: "Our family

---

[3] Precisely. *Locket Love* was their idea of an "homage" to the tale, if one considers bringing immeasurable dishonor to something an "homage." My brothers, of course, have never been plagued by such subtleties.

history? Fuck-ups speaking bullshit over there instead of American over here."

Tyler, Terry, and František were bereft of faculty,[4] and consequently did not concern themselves with our ancestral past. On the other hand, there were occasions when we'd be sharing family legends, and František would ease into a grin like the air in the room was slowly being replaced with nitrous oxide. Granted, his grin wasn't necessarily tied to any one situation; one time I accidently discovered him in the lavatory easing his thumb slowly in and out of his anus while raising his thick leg with his free hand, all the while with that same smile. One never knows, really, the inner workings of an inscrutable mind. To be clear, František was no idiot, and I mean that outside the previously described act, since later tests verified that particular activity was not entirely devoid of merit.

Our family was more or less in agreement regarding Montez's mother. An incredibly fast cigar roller. A disciplinarian. A Puerto Rican-Cuban-Italian Sephardic Jew. She raised Montez in a Catholic sect similar to Opus Dei, but it was even stricter regarding the sins of comfort, something I think had a lot to do with Montez's later obsessions with silky undergarments and plush mattresses.

Our mother's name was Szilarda. She was born in the Hungarian Soviet Republic, a nation that existed for less than four months in 1919. She came from Jewish and Gypsy parents, although nobody knew who was the Gypsy and who was the Jew. Our family was pervaded with a Gypsy ethic to a point, wanderers begetting wanderers, and a consequence of that was a sloppy and mysterious family history. For instance, Szilarda supposedly met Montez in the 1930s while he was wandering Europe while on leave from the Spanish Civil War. Szilarda's father was one of the Lenin Boys, a group of homicidal dandies that served as secret police in the short-lived Hungarian Soviet Republic. Along with his wife and the baby Szilarda, he had fled Hungary when the

---

[4] Retards.

Romanian army invaded to put an end to the communist experiment. He resettled the family in Spain. When Szilarda was a teenager, she could have met Montez in Italy, Czechoslovakia, or Spain itself—it wasn't clear. It was also unclear what Montez had been doing in Spain during the Civil War.

And we were unlikely to ever find out, because the Spanish Civil War was a hands-off topic in our house, and a perfect example of why we had to sift through shadowy, contradictory versions of our past. Obviously Montez, Szilarda, and Johnny knew more than the rest of us, but Montez was aloof and Szilarda laconic, so none of us learned much from them. We were also kids with kid concerns like surviving in the house and making something of ourselves in the playgrounds and streets of New York City.

But Johnny was the most substantial obstacle between our family history and us, despite being the oldest brother. He knew more than he revealed, but the hidden details often made him nervous or angry. Whether at dinner or on our boat, if the conversation drifted into uncomfortable territory for Johnny, it was the best way to end up with a bloody nose if you were responsible.

Regarding the Spanish Civil War, Montez had definitely been involved. I went through a period—abruptly cut short by Johnny—where I regularly interrogated my brothers about our parents so I could understand myself better. Now, I'm not inept at self-discovery, to be clear; through masturbation alone I've learned things about my heritage that facts only serve to verify. That being said, the greater truths I've learned through self-manipulation are sometimes enhanced by the solidity of a traditional fact. Picture a country you know well, impressionistically speaking: the smell of the local cuisine, the street sounds, the chants and songs of religious ceremonies—but it's a broad, sloppy impression. One day you sit down at a table with a blank sheet of paper and some paint, and a few hours later you have that country's flag. That's how I view facts.

We lived on the coast near Fort Tilden, Queens in a house now long demolished. A bank of dunes separated the big house from the vast, desolate Fort Tilden Beach. My favorite room in the house was the sunroom. Located on the fourth floor, it offered fantastic views of the sea. There was an old stand-up piano against the wall that was there when Montez bought the house. Nobody in the family used the room except Joey and me, so we installed an old couch and made the room into our private lounge. It was ideal because it was beyond the shrieking madness of the lower floors. We would frequently retreat to the room to smoke and talk while the rest of the family was busy with the urban rioting otherwise known as dinner or the fascist invasion otherwise known as Johnny coming home from work.

One evening we were thus engaged, relaxing on the couch enjoying the sea breeze and the fading sun. Joey reached into a multitude of pockets in his coat and pants and pulled out seemingly endless small bottles. He piled around forty between his legs. He poured them one by one through a funnel into a nearly empty Windex bottle. When the bottle was full of brown liquid, he took a deep pull and handed it to me. It tasted like vanilla-infused gasoline. A few minutes later I was in a mental condition infinitely superior to the one I'd inhabited prior to imbibing. It turned out Joey had stumbled on a veritable gold mine by enrolling in 8th grade Home Economics. He'd pilfer the vanilla and almond extracts and make cocktails like the one we were now sharing.

We passed the Windex back and forth. Joey was talking about Montez traveling to Andalusia in the 1930s to join the Popular Front to fight Franco and his fascists. He painted a picture of Montez and his comrades sitting around an open fire in a dark Andalusian desert singing Socialist anthems. Thanks to Joey's elaborately detailed story and the extract cocktail, I was transported to Spain and was sitting around that fire. But Joey stopped talking. He looked as if a ghost had appeared behind me, and then he scrunched his face as if something stank.

A fat pink Wiffle bat hit him square in the face, and then three times in quick succession on the top of his head. "Shut the fuck up," yelled Johnny. "Dad was never in any Popular Front, he wasn't even in Spain then. Why you telling lies to Damone? Damone, you listen good, dad wasn't in Spain, and if he was he would have fought for the Falange like any normal person. And you'd better believe that or you get the bat too."

Joey rolled up in a ball on the floor and started crying. Johnny poured the rest of our cocktail out the window. He told me to get the fuck out.

That was the first time I saw the pink fat bat, a tool of discipline that went on to be Johnny's favorite, his very own all-American version of rubber bullets and water cannon, its pink flash calling us to order more often than I prefer to recall. Our father Montez liked things a certain way, but he was very hands-off. Johnny was like the sergeant major of the house while Montez was the remote general, so when Johnny went on a bat-swinging tear, you couldn't be sure if he was carrying out Montez's orders or acting on his own. On the other hand, when he was working one over with that pink motherfucker, one didn't really think about the nuances of causality.

Ramona was exempt. For instance, one Saturday night we were all sitting around the living room except for Johnny who was at work. Because our house was so far away, it was such an inconvenience to go into the city that we frequently stayed home trying to invent entertainment, even when we weren't getting along. On this particular night, we raided Tommy's room where he had an extensive toy train set with bridges and tunnels, miniature towns, forests and fields. We disconnected the electric transformer that powered everything and brought it downstairs. Tommy was extremely nervous that we'd break it and angry that we had raided his room, but we always got our way if we ganged up on him.

We took steel SOS pads and jammed the wires into them, and then we turned the transformer all the way up. Sparks sprayed everywhere. The room filled with smoke. It reeked of burning metal and soap. We shut off the lights. White and blue sparks blasted into the darkness. Everyone said, "Oooooo," and "Aaahhh," as if we were at a fireworks display or a particularly arcane peepshow.

But we quickly grew bored and had to add variations, like hooking the transformer up to ourselves. Marky, always up for anything, began by attaching the wires to one of his fingers and turning it all the way up. His hair didn't stand on end, but he howled. When Ramona reached over to shut it off Marky said, "No, not yet," and he went on shocking himself for several minutes. He turned the transformer off and said to me, "Try it, you'll like it."

I must admit I was jealous because it was always Marky that thought up the most novel diversions such as hooking one's self to train transformers, so I felt I had to top him. I went to the kitchen and filled a bucket with water. I brought it to the family room and set it on the floor. I put my left hand into the water and threw the transformer in with the right.

I jerked like a marionette controlled by an epileptic. I was overwhelmed by an unrelenting agony that was also spiritually uplifting. The problem was after it started getting old, I couldn't will my arm to pull itself from the bucket. I screamed for help. Ramona grabbed my shoes and yanked me out. The room erupted into applause.

Marky had to reclaim his throne: we refilled the bucket. He took off his pants. He removed his underwear. He stepped into the bucket. He raised a jar of glue to his nose and huffed madly. He ordered us to throw in the transformer. As soon as the transformer disappeared into the water, Marky popped out of the bucket. He was fired out as if from a gun, barely bending his knees.

Ramona said, 'Look who's here." Our brother František was standing in the doorway naked. This was not surprising; nude cameos were a specialty of his. We'd be halfway through dinner— we all ate together at a long table—and František would appear in the doorway naked, smiling. It was helpful because our family argued constantly during family meals, and František's fleshy exhibitions always broke the tension. I suggested he did it on purpose, but Johnny and Ramona would laugh and say he doesn't even know who he is.

František was next in the bucket. Marky hypothesized that František wouldn't pop out so easily since he was significantly heavier. Ramona stood behind him and held the glue jar under his nose. He was grinning broadly and lolling his head so much that Ramona had difficulty holding it steady, granting its excessive largeness. Marky suggested choking him a little before throwing in the transformer, but I intervened and said there was really no point to that unless František was also masturbating, which he was not. In fact he was quite limp.

But he was definitely high on the glue by the time we threw the train transformer into the bucket. When the electricity hit him, it was like he had entered a room he had known all his life. Instead of jerking and jolting like the rest of us had, he bounced. It resembled dancing more than electrocution. It was like he was grooving to music only he could hear as he moved up and down, shaking his gelatinous body. He was grinning like never before, as if he were attempting to relocate his cheeks to the top of his head.

His hands were particularly hypnotizing. He held them out. His right fingers trilled with delicate accuracy. His left made longer, steadier jabs. His right hand danced back and forth, typing and jumping. It was bizarre because the movements were so precise, and precise movements were not the hallmark of František who had once, for example, exploded right through the dry wall into the front room like the Kool Aid guy one night when the rest of us were sitting on the floor playing Monopoly for Seconals.

Joey nailed it: "Look, he's playing the piano! František, you're playing the piano, right?" František didn't respond, but with the smile and blind eyes of one lost in artistic reverie and his dancing hands, it was clear that was precisely what he was doing.

Johnny walked in. At the time he was working as the assistant manager of an oil change shop on 21st Street near the Queens Library. He liked to stop somewhere after work and watch baseball in peace, so he often didn't get home until quite late.

He ran to the kitchen. He returned with the pink fat bat. He smashed me in the face. I fell to the floor. He pummeled Marky, Joey, and Tommy. All of us silently took it except Tommy who held up his hands and said, "Johnny, stop and think for a minute, is this really rational?" The rest of us told him to shut his mouth just as the bat connected with his forehead. But when Johnny raised the bat to hit Ramona, she didn't flinch. She said, "You hit me with that thing, the fat end will be going in and out of your mouth while I control it with the small end sticking out your ass. Got it?"

Johnny froze and locked eyes with Ramona. He turned away. Ramona smirked and lit a cigarette. Johnny yelled, "You're all idiots!" He stormed upstairs.

We remained on the floor. We simultaneously turned to František who was still standing in the bucket getting shocked. Dancing, smiling, and playing that invisible piano without a care in the world.

Our mother Szilarda was the musical one in the family, the inspiration for all of us in many ways. The house was often filled with the sound of her accordion—mournful Gypsy, Magyar, and Klezmer songs. She also had an extensive record collection that included folk, classical, and jazz. Supposedly she was also the source of our extensive library, although we had never seen her buy a book. Tommy claimed that Montez had been a voracious reader in his youth, but gave it up when cynicism set in. In any case, the library allowed me to read extensively on many topics, as did Tommy, Mickey, and Joey. The others were less interested.

Szilarda had dark skin and hair, a complexion best represented by Dee Dee, although all of us have black hair and if we spend time in the sun we get quite dark. The exceptions are Johnny and František. Our mother wasn't František's birth mother—that was acknowledged. František was born in Czechoslovakia. Montez had spent time there in the Fifties. There were the usual disagreements about why he'd been there; Joey said he was helping to build a socialist utopia, whereas Johnny and Ramona insisted that he helped lay the groundwork for the Prague Spring. Ramona said Montez preferred Czechoslovakia to other Eastern Bloc countries because Czech women are the most beautiful in the world, and he would have done or said anything to enter the land of the long-legged, including pretending to be a communist. I wasn't so sure about that, based on Montez's later exhibitions. Ramona never changed her opinion though—she wrote off Montez's later behavior as a breakdown under the weight of responsibility, a revolt against all bourgeois mantles, but I didn't really see what that had to do with wearing women's panties. But more on that later.

We ultimately decided Johnny was also Szilarda's biological son, not withstanding some incongruities. First, it should be clarified that the respective birthdates of the Colvins, Bells, Cummings, Hymans—they were all entirely false, or colloquially stated, bullshit; the false dates were part of the intricate plot against me. To be fair, I retract *bullshit*, because although I am betrayed and angry, I'm not one to deny a caper well done, even when I am its primary victim and have had every shred of hope sodomized and burned to oblivion. On the other hand, I want to make sure I successfully portray two things when I explain what really happened—I'm outraged, but I'm also an artist of integrity. If something is done well, I'm man enough to admit it. In sum, they—in collusion with criminal mastermind Danny Fields—neatly accounted for everything, and all the Ramone birthdates were falsified.

Clearly the Ramones inherited excellent genes in many respects, but their collective genetic strength was most obvious in the fact that they simply did not age. If you observe my brothers on the cover of their 1976 debut and compare it to how they looked in the 2000s, they haven't changed in any notable way. Even if their haircuts and clothes had evolved, their remarkable preserved youth would remain unchanged as if there was a family portrait hidden in our Fort Tilden attic in the Dorian Grey tradition.

Nobody illustrates this better than Johnny and Montez. In the 1960s when Montez was already in his fifties, he looked like he was in his thirties. When he had his hat and sunglasses on, he passed for twenty-six. Johnny took the lion's share of that gene—his real birth date is March 18th, 1930. When he appears on the cover of the first Ramones album, he's already forty-four years old.

Our mother was the same; you'd never think she'd have been of child-bearing age in the early 1930s, yet there was never any hint that Johnny was the product of an illicit union. One trait we all shared was a love for digging into each other's affairs looking for something we could ridicule like a cucumber and some lightly scented lotion under a mattress, but nothing turned up in this case.

Joey in particular pursued the theory that Johnny had a different mother. I remember sitting with him in the sunroom smoking and staring at the ceiling while we thought up insulting new nicknames for Johnny once we got proof.

But nothing concrete ever turned up. However, everybody in our family except Johnny, Mickey, Tyler, Terry, and František had some command of the Hungarian language. The others were too young or too impaired to learn it, but Johnny had no such excuse. Tommy—and of course Szilarda—spoke it fluently. Tommy could read and write in Hungarian or English with equal proficiency. He had an extensive collection of Hungarian literature. To note, Tommy's inquisitiveness went far beyond Hungarian—he was a true intellectual. Tommy was also the only brother that made any effort to learn Czech, which was far superior to English when it came to getting anything across to František. Ramona knew a few words, I can't remember them exactly, but one of them would cause František to masturbate furiously, and she used to shout it out in public: on buses, in the subway, in restaurants. It sounded something like *chair-knee-pee-voe*. Montez rarely disciplined any of us himself, but in that case he'd personally beat Ramona once he got František to stop, which was no mean feat. Ramona was never phased by a slap however, no matter how harshly delivered—she'd merely laugh, and during the next family excursion she'd do it again. If you're ever in the Met, look for the anomalous highlights in the tree in the bottom left hand corner of El Greco's *View of Toledo*: František.

To wit, we all spoke and understood Hungarian to some degree except Johnny. Whenever Tommy and Szilarda would speak Hungarian at dinner, Johnny would turn to the person next to him and ask, "What'd they say? What are they talking about?" and that person would have to translate. Ramona claimed it was second-generation immigrant rejection of ethnicity, that Johnny could speak it but refused to, but I wasn't so sure. Whenever he asked me to translate he seemed truly agitated, as if he was paranoid he was being talked about.

My Hungarian is passable, but any native-born Hungarian can discern my American inflections. I'm the third youngest in the family—the twins are the youngest, followed by Mickey, and then me—so we understand it, but speak poorly. On the other hand, if we ever consort, I'm perfectly capable of getting us hookers and drinks in Pest, so in the non-academic sense perhaps I'm fluent.

When Danny Fields and my brothers put their plot into action, they wiped out our Hungarian, Gypsy, and Hispanic background, retaining only a nod to Hungary via the renamed Tommy "Erdélyi Tamás" Ramone and a hint of Judaism via Tommy and Joey. They did retain some of our original birth years, but they changed the days—we are all a little older than you'd think. Johnny was the only case where they changed the year substantially, which makes sense when you consider it from Field's business perspective—you don't want the kids to know their favorite guitarist is older than their father. Johnny was a bit like Groucho Marx in that respect, who if I'm not mistaken was already forty when they filmed *Coconuts* in 1929.

The published and widely accepted Ramones "history" states that Fields didn't co-opt the Ramones until 1975. Right. That's how good they are. Fields not only was there from the beginning to conceive of and orchestrate the great deception, he was part of our life for years before that working as a deckhand on Montez's boat. When Fields dropped out of Harvard in 1959, it was to go work with Montez. In a single summer, Danny made so much money working for Montez that becoming a lawyer or a doctor like his father[5] supposedly was would have been a step back. Deckhand on a drug runner's boat, and he has the giant anchor tattooed on his back to prove it.

So details on one Victor Montez Ramone who was born in Cuba in 1915 and later settled on the coast of Queens in the hinterlands of the Rockaways are sketchy. But by the 1950s, Montez and Szilarda had built a more or less normal domestic existence in the big house near Fort Tilden. According to Szilarda

---

[5] My research verified Field's Harvard attendance; however, his East Coast origins, although I could not disprove them, are unlikely; he frequently referred to having lived in a trailerpark in the American Southwest. It stands to reason his familial origins shared this geography, and in all likelihood, the same socioeconomic characteristics.

and Johnny, Montez went on fewer political adventures as the 1950s progressed. In the 1960s, he became increasingly focused on the family business: drugs.

I don't relish dredging up these facts. Based on how I feel about our sordid past, I can only imagine how Johnny must have felt as he became increasingly conservative over the years. It's no accident that his conservatism placed particular emphasis on an anti-drug position—as kids, we were essentially employees of the Montez cartel. Perhaps that was part of the reason Johnny went along with the plot against me: to whitewash his shame over our past.

Conversely, I've been told that I sound proud when I recount the facts, but it was what it was: a well-managed, efficient, and highly productive corporation with Montez—literally—at the helm. It was a classic feast-or-famine operation, but volatility in that business is innate: vermin in the coco; war in the poppy fields; management shakeup at a drug company, and so forth. But when it was on, it was on—we'd sometimes do seventy sea runs in one month, two or three a night, seven days a week—absolutely, and without any *ifs* and *ands*. If your name was Ramone, then you were on that boat at your post at midnight, two in the morning, three. Even František and the twins pulled their weight. If it was November and the sea was raging, we were still out there doing runs. No chowder in the boathouse, no looking out the window the day of the run to check for rain. Pulse, high speed diesel, the connection: it was on. From the mid Sixties through the early Seventies, if you sparked up, popped a pill, or snorted a line, I guarantee that one in ten times that product came across the water on the *Havana Banana*. If you purchased drugs in Washington Square Park or Tompkins, one in five times: Montez. During the summer of '69, Washington Square Park, nine times out of ten: Montez.

CHAPTER II.

THE DOLDRUMS.

The problem is that the drug business is seasonal, and not just because of the predictable ebb and flow of the marijuana or poppy crops. Any number of complications could affect cash flow. First, drug people aren't reliable. They don't always show up—tardiness, arrests, deaths. Second, although we were a disciplined crew there could be problems beyond our control—engine problems; bribed police patrols not following the agreed sea routes; missions aborted at the last second by cagey suppliers; getting lost on foggy nights; political unrest in supplier countries.

The net effect was highly unpredictable revenue patterns. We could be thundering along week after week, hauling in bushels of cash every night, and then it would just stop. We'd sail to the rendezvous point, cut the motor, and drift across the silver streak of a full moon. We'd wait in absolute silence for hours, but nobody would come. As a family and as a well-oiled operation, we were highly intuitive, and we always knew by a sixth sense if we were experiencing a one-time delay or if we had entered the doldrums. In the case of the latter, I felt a long silence in my soul that was far deeper than the silence surrounding me, followed by the dread of wondering how we'd get through the dry spell. We'd all hit this moment more or less at the same time: Montez would nod toward Johnny in the darkness and Johnny would order us to our posts, the motor would roar into life, and we'd head back to the Rockaways.

When I was little and I noticed the portions getting smaller and we'd stop going on family excursions, I thought it was because everything cost enormous amounts of money. When things were good there was always piles of loose cash strewn around the house, but during the doldrums the bushels of money would be gone and we'd be restricted to ever-smaller portions of rice and beans. In reality, Montez was just bad with money.

Really bad. I didn't know until years later the precise frivolities and extravagances he would blow money on, but Montez's need to spend went far beyond wanting or lusting after flamboyant goods and services. He was simply a compulsive spender; not in the sense of compulsive shopping in order to feel good or occupy an empty soul, but rather in some perverse manifestation of a cleanliness obsession where racing toward complete insolvency made him feel clean, neat, and deeply satisfied.

In the meantime, we'd be starving, the phone would get shut off, and then the heat. The mailbox would be stuffed with collection letters that seemed to exponentially increase in number overnight as if they were having orgies and producing endless offspring. At night, we'd lie in our beds listening to Szilarda scream at Montez in Hungarian laced with Spanish and English curses. It was always the same theme: Montez's profligate spending and pathological disregard for his bread-winning responsibilities.

During the doldrums the house would drown in sorrow and rage. At night the sound of Montez and Szilarda fighting was counterpointed by the tearful bellowing of František; he hated it when they fought unlike when we fought among ourselves and František would point, drool, and laugh at the fiercest beatings as if he was watching a Three Stooges episode. But when our parents did the same he couldn't take it, and Ramona would have to cradle his bald head in her lap, rubbing his meager fringe and sweaty gray pate until he sobbed himself to sleep. František's howling even got to Johnny, who one night took a ball of red playdough and a ball of blue and pressed them into František's big ears. It seemed a dubious proposition, but Johnny kept pressing the dough into his head with both hands while he told František everything would be okay. Johnny fed him some of the blue playdough, and František finally fell asleep with his big blue tongue hanging out like George "the Animal" Steele.

But on most nights, Johnny wasn't around to hear the fighting. During the doldrums he'd always manage to get some job somewhere, and he always volunteered for night shifts for the pay premiums. He'd work anywhere and he apparently was an excellent worker in all his odd and sundry professions. The same places would hire him back again and again even though once the drug trade revived he'd quit. He never burnt bridges, he was up front about how he could suddenly get "reinstated" at his other job, and he worked hard so he always got good references.

He worked in several auto repair and muffler shops in Queens on 21st Street, or he'd find work in Jersey in some foundry, or he'd flyer Forest Hills, Kew Gardens, and other nice neighborhoods presenting himself as an independent plumber. He was such a good plumber, that even when the drug running was hot he'd fix the occasional burst pipe or broken toilet for his loyal customers. In that way, he managed to keep himself busy and avoid the dark mood that hung over the house. On the downside, when he was around he was always exhausted and volatile, liable to go off on someone with his fists or the pink bat without any provocation.

The rest of us hung around the house waiting for Montez to get his act together and hoping that whatever issue had caused the doldrums would blow over so we could go back to sea. It was strange, because when we were working we were always on the verge of collapse from the relentless hard labor in all weather and Johnny's dictatorial ways. He ran things like a cruel English boatswain charged with a gang of unruly sailors that had been forcibly pressed into the King's Navy. But when the doldrums came around, we wanted nothing more than to be back on the boat, experiencing the thrill of that first voyage after a long dry spell when Johnny would shout orders in the darkness and the *Havana Banana* would nose out into the moonlit sea.

Hunger and cold can make you crazy, but they also make you smart. We all developed different methods to survive the lean times, and by blending meager household income with our own schemes, we always managed to get by. School was a gold mine in this respect. We all became bullies to varying degrees, but mainly for food and money rather than sadistic delight alone. Dee Dee lorded over a simpering congregation of nerds and sissies that he'd rob daily. I understand Dee Dee later had a reputation as being the "true punk" of the Ramones, a violent and crazy character, but he really did have a big heart underneath his menacing exterior. During the doldrums for instance, he'd ask us what we wanted to eat, and then he would force one of the kids he regularly brutalized to have his mother make it. He'd seize it the next day and bring it back to us—it was essentially take-out you'd order a day in advance.

Mickey and I became master thieves, breaking into lockers or walking around parking lots trying car doors to steal loose change or the occasional grocery bonanza. Ramona would seduce middle-aged men and squeeze them for money. She made her older married boyfriends take her to nice restaurants in the city. She'd bring home doggy bags that she'd toss in the middle of the living room when she came home, and we'd pounce and tear at the delicious restaurant food like a pack of starving hyenas.

Joey lived out of dish tubs—at school, he'd volunteer in the kitchen and he'd bring piles of uneaten food back home. He got the occasional dishwashing job for the same reasons. One summer he worked at Le Grenouille on 52nd Street, arguably New York's quintessential French restaurant. For three weeks we feasted on kidneys, steak frites, and quails. He got fired when Raquel Welch came in and he kept pretending to drop things near her table. Dishwashers weren't even allowed on the floor at Le Grenouille let alone under movie stars' tables.

Marky worked at a country club, and they fed him there. He used to pour drink dregs into a cooler hidden in the staff coat closet, and when he got home at the end of the night we'd have a cocktail party, pouring the drink de jure from the little drainage tap at the bottom edge of the cooler.

Generally, after having to work as a military unit when the drug trade was hot, we'd all fend for ourselves as lone scavengers during the lean times, helping each other just enough to keep spirits up and stomachs full. We always remembered to set aside some of the spoils for Tyler and Terry. František did surprisingly well on his own—he went to a special retard school, and when he'd come home his pockets would be stuffed with mashed potatoes and Brussels sprouts, which he adored. He'd dig into his pockets and scoop up the food. We'd get on our knees and eat directly from his outstretched hands, usually me from his left hand and Joey from his right. One of my first sewing jobs in fact was adding extremely broad, deep pockets to František's baggy pants so he could increase the size of his payload. Granted, he occasionally used the extra room to achieve other things.

The one brother that didn't fair very well during the doldrums was Tommy. None of us were Lucky Luciano, but we did what we had to do. Truth be told, we enjoyed our light criminality. But Tommy was just too straight. These days Tommy leans toward corpulent. That's his natural state, inherited from Szilarda. But during the doldrums, Tommy just couldn't bring himself to steal, let alone bully someone for their lunch money. That's why he got so skinny—he didn't have enough food. Over time, getting by with very little became habit: even when things were good he'd continue to eat very little and hoard food in his room. It always backfired, because during hard times the first place the rest of us would go was Tommy's room. If he protested, we'd simply push him out of the way and rob his vast store of provisions. That's why he's so thin in early Ramones photos. For the rest of us, it was our natural physique inherited from Montez, but with Tommy it was genuine malnutrition.

One time Marky, Joey, and Dee Dee beat him up because they couldn't find a gallon of cooking wine they swore they'd seen in his closet. Tommy denied ever having it, so they punched him in the mouth, giving him fat lips. The following week, František brought home a sack of institutional potato flakes, and we ate them every night for a month. We constantly reminded Tommy how lucky he was because he could still eat the potatoes through his puffy lips. Mickey asked him if he'd mind singing *Under my Thumb* to entertain us. Even Johnny got in on it, asking Tommy if he was John Howard Griffin.

Johnny's reference to Griffin was revelatory. There were other illuminating incidents. One night he joined us for dinner during particularly bad doldrums. We were eating fried eggs, huge greasy piles of them from an egg tray stolen from a truck. We didn't like Johnny joining us for dinner because his perpetually terrible mood dominated the room and we'd end up eating dinner in silence. But this time Joey spoke up, which was bold on its own, but he also seemed to be ridiculing Johnny in some way. He said, "Hey, Johnny," but Johnny ignored him. He said it again:

"Hey, Johnny! Johnny. Johnny. Johnny."

"Shut the fuck up, Joey."

"No, please Johnny, I really need to ask you something. This is real serious."

"What?"

"Are you a *Midnight Dancer?*"

"What, asshole?"

"A *Midnight Dancer*. Are you a *Midnight Dancer*, dancing at midnight in your tights in the middle of your room at night?"

The rest of us nearly shat ourselves except Marky who laughed along with Joey. We knew they were on to something, because Johnny seemed more nervous than angry. Joey pulled a book from under the table and read aloud in a fake English accent that veered wildly between Cockney and Queen Elizabeth's:

*"Beat the drums of tragedy for me. Beat the drums of tragedy and death. And let the choir sing a stormy song…to drown the rattle of my dying breath…*fuck, grab it Marky!"

Johnny leapt from his chair, knocking it over and very nearly overturning the huge rectangular dinner table—it jumped and the yolk-covered plates slid toward the edge. Ramona yelled, "Cool it, Johnny, you fucking rock head, that's food yer fucking with!"

Joey threw the book to Marky and yelled, "Page 57!" In his haste to reach Joey, Johnny fell on his face, giving Marky time to read in his Queens[6] accent:

---

[6] My brother Marky was *not* from Brooklyn.

"Beat the drums of tragedy for me and let the white violins whir thin and slow, but blow one blaring trumpet note of sun...to go with me to the darkness where I go..."

"You're going to darkness all right, you fucking prick!"

Johnny knocked Marky to the floor and kicked him. Joey yelled, "Marky, don't be so mean to Johnny, don't make fun of him for his special fantasy...his *Fantasy in Purple.*"

I expected Johnny to kill Joey and Marky, but instead he grabbed the book from the floor, wacked Tommy in the back of the head with it, and stormed off to his room. Even though Marky had just gotten his ass kicked, him and Joey laughed and laughed—I'll never forget Marky laughing while blood poured from his mouth into his eggs.

Collateral damage to Tommy's head was frequent—one of us would misbehave, and it would be Tommy that took the beating. But lest Tommy appears a wimp or pushover, do not be deceived: at the end of the day, Tommy was and is a Ramone. Even back then he would prove it on occasion.

For instance, around 1960 a Canadian grocery chain opened a branch on Queens Boulevard. It was called McCoy's IGA and they were always hiring. One summer Tommy got a job there stocking shelves, unloading trucks, and cleaning up.

This was during a particularly bad spell of the drug doldrums—we were supposed to have met a French freighter off Governor's Island carrying a large load of heroin, but it turned out to be one of those nights where we sat for hours at sea looking across the black waves at the New York lights. The ship never came.

Johnny was livid for weeks. If that wasn't enough, he was also having problems picking up additional work, so he was hanging around the house working everybody over. Since Tommy had the IGA job, Johnny rode him constantly to steal burger meat, steaks, and hot dogs, but Tommy never brought home the amounts Johnny demanded.

One day when Johnny was yelling at him, Tommy said, "Hang on, John. I have an idea. See, they lock the front door at closing time, but the shipping and receiving doors are still open. At closing time the place is full of cash that the owner takes to the bank.

This McCoy guy, he's Canadian so he doesn't know to make several trips throughout the day so he's never holding too much cash, see? I could let you guys in after we close, and you could rob the place. What do you think?"

Johnny picked me, Joey, and Dee Dee to do the job. Tommy was our inside man. The store closed at seven. Tommy would let us in through the shipping dock. Tommy would signal when he was alone in the stockroom. Once inside, we'd put stockings over our faces, burst into the store with squirt guns that we had spray-painted black, and take all the money.

On the big day, we waited in the alley for Tommy's signal. After fifteen minutes he came out, looked around, and went back in. Johnny asked what time it was and Joey said seven. "Really?" Johnny asked, "It seems like it should be earlier than that. What, was that the signal?"

"I think it musta been, John," said Joey. I wasn't so sure. On the other hand, maybe fear was distorting our perceptions. Johnny finally decided that Tommy had given the signal and we missed part of the gesture because of where we were standing.

We pulled ourselves onto the shipping dock. We entered the stockroom. It was empty. We pulled nylons over our faces. Johnny hissed at Joey that he was a fucking idiot because instead of a single nylon he had stolen a pair of tights from our mother's underwear drawer, and the other empty leg dangled from the side of his head like a snout or a weird deformed ear.

"What's the difference, Johnny?" Joey asked.

"The difference? Someone could grab that and pull it off your head, you idiot."

"No way, man. They're gonna be way too scared."

"You talking back to me? I oughtta..."

"Later, guys. We need to do this thing," I said.

The three of us lined up behind a big metal door and counted off in whispered unison while Dee Dee stayed behind to keep watch:

"One...two...three!"

We burst into the store.

It was still full of people. Either they were closing late or our timing was off. When Joey burst through the door in his sloppy, long-limbed version of running, he lost control and careened from the stockroom across the back aisle, right into a pyramid of Folgers coffee. The cans crashed down and rolled across the floor.

People were initially confused and a little boy laughed at Joey, but then the customers saw Johnny and me with nylons over our heads holding guns. They screamed. Johnny pivoted from right to left, pointing the squirt gun at shrieking mothers and weeping children while Joey sat among the purple Folgers cans rubbing his head. Johnny yelled at Joey to get the fuck up. Johnny reached into the meat cooler, grabbed a package of bloody red meat, and then he ran back through the stockroom. He leapt off the shipping dock into the alley. The rest of us followed. We ran off, scattering in different directions as we had planned.

Fortunately we weren't apprehended. It turned out Joey, who had wanted to synchronize our watches, set them all an hour ahead. It was a harrowing and risky endeavor, and all we had to show for it was the package of liver Johnny grabbed during our getaway. We watched in silence while he fried it for Tyler and Terry.

That fiasco got me thinking that there had to be a better way. I couldn't do a thing about the unpredictable drug business or Montez's stellar profligacy, but I could do something for myself if I could just figure out what.

CHAPTER III.

THE IMPERIALS.

My mother was a first-rate seamstress. She was miraculous with alterations, and her original creations were indistinguishable from the trendiest Paris designer's. If you've ever lost an enormous amount of weight and then brought your suits in for alteration, you've likely been told it can't be done; the pants pockets would end up on your ass, for instance. Most tailors will admit that you're better off buying a new suit because it would cost less than the virtual reconstruction required for them to take it in.

To this Szilarda would wave her hand and say, "They can't make big suit small suit? How this? I measures, and okay. We see us in two days." When the client returned, the suit fit better than when they'd bought it. If they had lost their midsections, Szilarda would reshape the suit accordingly, helping them to exhibit their new physiques in the most flattering manner. She'd also throw in bits of flair that ensured her client's loyalty. For instance, if the pant lining was covered in urine stains she'd replace it free, and when she returned the suits they were always pressed with deadly bluesman creases.

The money Szilarda made was meaningless when the *Havana Banana* was making nightly runs—it was just something to keep her occupied like playing the accordion. But when the doldrums set in, Montez would spend more and more time hovering around the sewing room door, whispering to Szilarda. At first she'd whisper back, but with each day of the dry spell, she'd respond with escalating force until all it took was the sound of Montez ascending the stairs for her to start screaming. My mother is the only person I've seen slam a door *open*, yanking it with such rage and ferocious speed that a loud, deep pop accompanied the appearance of her angry face. The Hungarian oaths that followed set Montez's face aflame: *Baszom a Kristus Mariat!*

Of course he was simpering around looking for a handout. She'd give him some money in the beginning hoping he'd spend it sensibly, but he would immediately run off and spend it on some mysterious pursuit. Johnny said that he was betting at the OTB, but I wasn't so sure. I'd ask Tommy about it, and he'd confirm dad was blowing it at the OTB or at some deli where he'd play the numbers and sit around outside on milk crates speaking Spanish with old Puerto Ricans. But I never saw him at the OTB or at the deli.

One night I was upstairs when my parents clashed with particular ferocity. Bodies slammed into walls and furniture crashed to the floor. I went to their bedroom to break it up if necessary, but when I looked through the open door and saw Montez careening backwards after a shove from Szilarda, I let sleeping dogs lie. Montez was wearing nothing except a gold lamé Speedo. Szilarda yelled in Hungarian, "Those are what you buy, you perverted faggot!" I didn't tell anyone—I just hoped we'd get back to sea soon and the rest of it would all just go away.

In the meantime I had discovered Szilarda's sewing machines. She had an Imperial 562 which was relatively new and an Imperial 703 which was a big black steel antique. Marky and I had gone in the sewing room one day looking for something to do, and we turned on the 562 and tried to sew scraps of cloth together. We didn't do very well with that, but I noticed how much the machines vibrated, the 703 in general and the 562 when it was set on embroider.

The next time I went to the sewing room I went alone. I took the old 703 off the sewing table and set it on the floor. I fired it up. I got down on my haunches and pressed my hungry organ against the wheel-shaped back of the machine, swiftly getting hard from the twirling vibrations. One thing led to another and I ended up naked in a push-up position over the 562—set on embroider of course—while I blew my load all over the top of the sewing machine.

Needless to say, since I didn't have access to Johnny's stereo where I had hoped to press my naked manhood against the woofer while blasting Charles Mingus's *Let My Children Hear Music*, I started spending substantial time in the sewing room getting off on the two machines. Luckily the door locked, so I could experiment extensively with different layers and moods in order to get the most out of the extractions. When I combined my advanced methods with some things I picked up from František's playbook, the effects were explosive.

One day Szilarda said, "Damone...I need must talk at you of something." Of course my immediate thought was that I had made a mistake during one of the sewing machine sessions; perhaps I had left a giant viscous load on top of the black 703 where it would be especially noticeable. I waited for the hammer to fall. "You gonna been sewing with my nice machines, I know this. No, you don't worry, is okay. Good for you try the sew, but you no show me what you been there doing?"

"Um, I don't want to show you because everything I do comes out so horrible."

"Horrible? Maybe shows this to me, and we do the fix?"

"No, I threw them all out. I got so angry when I looked at them finished, I didn't want anyone to ever see what I had done so I threw everything out."

"I know problem. You must start at the starting."

That's how Szilarda started teaching me how to sew. She was adamant that I couldn't use the machines until I learned how to sew by hand. My first lesson was threading a needle. Szilarda's teaching method was via excessive repetition: even after I had illustrated beyond a doubt that I could thread a needle, she made me do it 100 more times while she watched. When I had that down, she made me sew a button and remove the same button 100 times, and so on.

This was intensely frustrating because my penis had developed clear-cut expectations regarding the sewing room, and they weren't being met. Every time I snuck up there and fired up the Imperials, Szilarda would show up two minutes later, and unfortunately she had a key to the room so locking her out was pointless. Of course I got myself off regularly in other ways, but once I had a taste of those sewing machines nothing else came close. Now I look back and laugh a bittersweet laugh, thinking of everything I achieved in subsequent years with masturbation, and how the era of the Imperials was relatively quaint by comparison. But at the time, not being able to blow one out while the 703 pounded away beneath me was a tremendous cross to bear.

I learned sewing very quickly, both because of and despite Szilarda. She insisted that I didn't sew without her supervision until she felt I had mastered the fundamentals. She didn't want me developing bad habits, and I commend her for that. It was similar to Picasso drawing representational nudes as a young man before he moved into Cubism—you can't break the rules until you learn them.

But I sewed on my own anyway. I cruised the fabric, yarn, and porn shops for a variety of materials that I could use, ironically, to relieve myself until I once again had unfettered access to the Imperials. I bought vinyl, rubber sheeting, and even coarse burlap to create a surrogate for what I imagined grinding the underside of my cock against prickly Dominican pubic hair would feel like. Using these materials, I started making alternative vaginas by the dozen. I'd sew vaginas across the entire spectrum of texture and tightness, and then I'd put them between the box springs and mattress of my bed, lubricate myself appropriately, and fuck my bed doggy-style as it were.

I have to say, although not on the same level as the Imperials[7], the vaginas and occasional assholes I made were a respectable alternative. As happens in any household, my brothers figured out what I was doing and what the tight little pockets in my room were for, and they started using them. I only caught them in the act once, but I was always finding vinyl vaginas where I hadn't left

---

[7] Yes, I did later combine these technologies, but found the hybrid effect to be more novel than functional relative to construction costs.

them, often filled with semi-dry gobs of jizz, a hygienic laxity which was in complete contradiction to my MO: I was absolutely dogmatic about wiping out my loads with tissue immediately after the final convulsions had subsided and I had taken a few moments to collect my thoughts. I also found my vaginas in my brothers' bedrooms; lying on dressers, sticking out from under the bed, or strewn haphazardly on the floor with their underpants near a few crusty editions of Playboy, magazines obviously salvaged from some Queens garbage can; dismal, rain besotted planks that had to be pried open with an oyster knife.

But as I mentioned, I only caught them red-handed once. I was walking up the stairs to the sunroom to drink some vanilla extracts after school when Marky yelled, "František, get the fuck out of here, I'm busy. Stop! Put your clothes back on and get out of here...Jesus Christ, the fuck are you doing?"

I entered Marky's room. Marky's back was to the door—never a good move. He was on his knees naked, fucking the back of the bed. A long strand of orange yarn dangled from between his mattress and the bedspring; the yarn was a special feature so one could hang the vaginas from a coat peg. In this case I had used orange yarn to identify an especially brilliant model I had made that consisted of contradictory strips of cloth—rubber to burlap and back again—designed to stun the penis with a variety of sensations which could be measured out depending on how fast one chose to thrust in and out of the vagina. It had gone missing a few days earlier. I was enraged because I hadn't even used it ten times yet before a thief made off with it.

Now here was Marky thrusting away. At least two weeks had passed, so even estimating conservatively, based on the quality of that vagina and Marky's general masturbation habits, I could safely assume he had used it to achieve orgasm anywhere from thirty to fifty times. On the other hand, I was flattered because despite the fact that František was in the room conducting his own affairs without compunction and I was also there observing them both, Marky continued to steadily thrust away into the vagina I had made. I was proud—I had created something irresistible.

Meanwhile František was naked from the waist down beneath one of Szilarda's sweaters, a fluffy bright yellow number he was wearing inside out and backwards, and he was doing his damndest to fuck Marky's bed from the side. The problem was that although he understood the concept of the tight slit between the mattress and the bedspring, he didn't comprehend that Marky was using a device and extensive lubrication as he pumped away. František just assumed like anyone would that Marky was humping the slot bareback so he did what he thought was the same thing. He'd shove his cock into the slot and thrust away, but his smile quickly became a frown and he squealed when the roughness chafed his swollen member. But instead of giving up, he thrust back in again only making matters far worse. He kept doing this over and over, getting more and more frustrated, swiftly moving toward a rare František tantrum, which was the absolute worst. We'd have to tackle him and inject him with a sedative until he cooled down: František commanded a formidable retard strength that far exceeded that of his colleagues. Johnny eventually got several used tranquilizer guns from the zoo that helped significantly, but this particular anecdote predates that wise prophylactic measure.

Marky was yelling at František to get out while he continued his bed-fucking. I was delighted: the first vagina I had made was nothing more than a sandwich bag filled with canola oil and now I was creating vaginas of such quality that a guy simply couldn't stop fucking even while one brother watched and another brother was fucking the same bed only a few feet away while tears flowed down his bright red screaming face and blood dripped from his wounded turgidity. It was an impressive spectacle indeed, but I had to put an end to it for humanitarian reasons. I ran to the bathroom and filled a glass with water. I took it to Marky's room and threw it in František's face. I repeated the process until František forgot about what he had been doing. He sat down on the floor—cross-legged, head up, eyes closed, tongue out, smiling—and waited for the next dousing. Marky had finally shot his load and had disengaged my vagina, pulling it out by the orange yarn. He tossed it and said, "Here, take it. So yeah, it was me that took it. Whatcha gonna do, tell mom?"

I retired to my room and looked at the vaginas I had made. They covered my closet wall. I had made over a hundred, and they spanned a rainbow of textures and looks. Every one of them was excellent, and the more I made the better I got at it. The last twenty or so were simply marvelous—I could state with absolute confidence that any one of them could guarantee extrusions, even from old men that hadn't performed since the New Deal.

Proudly recollecting Marky's adoration of my device, I considered selling it to him. Then it occurred to me I could sell all of them, and not only to my brothers. I approached Marky and said, "Look, clearly you enjoyed my device. It's yours for three bucks." He said, "Really man? Wow, I appreciate that Damone. That thing is magic, man. Three bucks is a bargain."

I raised the price to five dollars—still a bargain, because they flew off the shelves. I sold them in Union Square as "change purses." I'd camp out on Friday night to ensure I got a high traffic spot among the painters, sculptors, and vegetable salesman. There was some initial confusion about the item I was selling. A lot of people believed they were change purses; I sold a substantial number to women who thought they were cute, oddly long purses. I suppose from a marketing perspective there was a subliminal phallic message that attracted them to my creations, but I knew I wasn't going to make it strictly on off-label use. The real money would come once I effectively communicated my message to the male demographic. My first step was creating a logo: VV for Vinyl Vagina. True, they weren't all vinyl, but I was confident everyone would understand VV was just a branding strategy irrespective of the vagina's constituent parts.

I developed a staged series of signals to convey the product's true function. I'd begin discreetly and move toward less ambiguous displays as each situation warranted. If a gent was clever, he immediately understood when I held a VV aloft as if I was selling live trout, so when I'd then say something like, "Looking for some loving companionship?" it merely served as verification.

If that didn't work, I'd adjust my pitch based on how quick on the uptake the individual appeared to be. Say I was dealing with a guy who didn't get how the dangling pocket I was waving around could be used for "loving companionship" but he didn't look like a complete idiot either. In that situation, I might add some verbal cues: "You know, a place to slide your lonelier parts in…and out…in…and out. Get my meaning?"

I admit, a lot of the time they did get my meaning, but it didn't necessarily result in a sale. There was definitely a certain amount of risk in promoting the product, especially if I misread someone perusing the wares. I'd be ratcheting up the message, and they'd get this shocked look and I'd know right away that I had made a mistake. Luckily in the city most people expected things like that even if they weren't in the market for handmade sexual relief, so generally they'd just tell me to fuck off, call me a sicko, and move on.

That was tolerable, but occasionally some blowhard with a chip on his shoulder would have a point to prove—I noticed it happened a lot if they were with their wives or girlfriends—and he'd knock my stand over and maybe even rough me up a bit. This sometimes happened when I misjudged the guy as an idiot and had decided to move to my last-resort marketing plan. I'd tell them to hang on, and then I'd turn around and make some adjustments, ostensibly to my belt, but then I'd whirl around with my erection sticking out of my zipper whilst clad in a Vinyl Vagina. I know, you'd think that would get me a punch in the face, but you'd be surprised—when you think out of the box, in the vast majority of cases you're rewarded. It's when you sit back and just hope things work out that you get the worst return: nothing.

I made good money. It eventually got around what my VVs were for. To my customers' credit, it took balls to approach the stand and buy one, especially for connoisseurs that wanted to make a studied selection. And I was ready for the connoisseurs: as I developed a better understanding of each client's singular quirks and general longings, the better equipped I was to accurately sate their desires. I took great pride in making each VV unique and better than the last. I tested every single one myself before I would even consider selling it, and I had incredibly high standards that I continually forced myself to raise. I think if you do something, the only way to do it is to push yourself beyond your limits, to suffer really, in order to achieve any notable reward. And not just from creating sex toys, but from whatever it is you do with passion, and by "reward" I don't mean money—money is just the icing on the cake when you work on something with commitment, the equivalent of a trophy or plaque. The real satisfaction comes from doing good work and from the respect you earn by doing something well.

Now remember, during the initial phases of VV production, I was under Szilarda's strict tutelage, did not have access to the sewing machines, and was making everything by hand—old school needle and thread bullshit, hours and hours of it. Between her boot camp instruction and my new business, I was already a crack tailor by the time she let me fire up the old Imperial 703 again. But I was so consumed by my endeavors that finally being able to fuck the sewing machines again had taken a backseat to improving and expanding my craft. Now when Szilarda asked me to show her what I had been working on, I could produce shirts, pants, dresses, suits—and I was prolifically creating VVs on the side. When I took a few minutes to unload a white one on the back of the 703, I felt like I had earned it.

Don't forget I was quite young then despite the maturity of my endeavors. It was a family trait—every Ramone was industrious and independent at a young age. Discipline in our house varied wildly—it was strict when Johnny was around, lax when he was away. But neither environment taught intimacy, so even though I was mature enough to find merit in vibrating sewing machines and to work with discipline to make money, I still didn't understand the murkier regions of the heart.

So when Ramona started acting weird during the summer of '64, that's all that I discerned: weird. My mother and Johnny likely knew what was going on, but the rest of us just thought she'd gone goofy. That summer the Shangri Las had released *Remember Walking in the Sand*. Admittedly[8] it was decent for a pop song, but Ramona became completely obsessed with it. She'd hide up in her

---

[8] In hindsight you might consider that adverb to be a gigantic concession, even a contradiction; I must however grant special status to the number due to its hallowed place in my musical and personal genesis.

room listening to it over and over for hours, every single night. She'd lie in bed in her Catholic schoolgirl uniform staring at the ceiling, smoking cigarette after cigarette. She kept the 45 player next to her bed so she wouldn't have to move to restart the song— the needle would drop with a pop, there'd be that moment of crackling fuzz, and then the damn thing would start up again. If anyone interrupted her smoky reveries, she'd fly into a rage—she even told our mother to go fuck herself when she showed up in the doorway, and with such psychotic conviction that even Szilarda backed off. I thought Ramona had gone completely insane. Remember, this was 1964; a daughter telling her mother to fuck herself was not yet *de rigueur*.

The sewing room was next to Ramona's bedroom, so when I was working that song was constantly thumping through the wall and seeping under the door. Even after I left the house, I kept hearing the song in my head, not unlike how I'd continue feeling the roll of the sea long after leaving the *Havana Banana*'s deck. Even now, if I hear it on the radio it will haunt me for several weeks before it recedes from my mind. But I owe that song a lot, because it set the alchemy in motion, the magic brew that eventually transmogrified into what you now know as the music of the Ramones.

At the time I was spending an increasing number of hours in the sewing room because I was trying to expand my own business while I helped Szilarda with hers. We were having a dry summer. Szilarda had to keep the Imperials pounding away while Montez did whatever he did that sucked up all our money. She'd get steady jobs doing alterations or making dresses, and I'd help. Initially, I did the basics and she'd handle the artistry, but I was a natural and swiftly became her equal.

I was also diversifying my own product line. I started creating hip shirts along with the VVs, working late into the night so to do. And in the background, beneath the steady rhythmic thumping of the Imperials, there was the constant steady drone of the Shangri Las singing about a romantic summer long over, mortifying in the past, replaced with life's first sad wonder. The blend of sounds stretched across the relentless hours had a hypnotic effect as I worked. I'd be startled as if woken from a dream when Szilarda would tap me on the shoulder or Ramona would finally fall asleep and the loud silence produced by the absence of *Remember Walking in the Sand* would snap me out of dreamy journeys. I'd look around and there'd be shirts, pants, and brilliant new VVs that I had no recollection of producing.

One evening I was sewing a bright orange pantsuit when I was overcome by an eerie sensation that something was hugely different. I focused as I sewed until it hit me: Ramona had finally changed records. Interestingly, after all that time wishing she'd do exactly that, I found the change to be disturbing. That constant, reliable drone had become an almost organic part of my psyche—even when I was out in the city surrounded by yells and honking horns, that smooth thudding drone kept playing, not so much in my head or ears, but in my bones and soul. It was bizarre, but the sound had somehow formed a magic tendril between me and a parallel universe. And now it was gone, replaced by a new alien presence that destroyed the perfect symbiosis that the old drone had achieved.

So as I sewed I listened to the new song, but I couldn't tell what it was. It didn't have the steady predictability of rock, but it also didn't have the wild chaos of jazz. It was something different, a dark cacophony of clashing tones that oscillated between the cold Scottish Highlands and some ancient civilization of Oman. Although the change distressed me, I listened in fascination as the mysterious dark music danced among the pounding of the Imperials, provoking a contradictory mix of feelings in me; on the one hand, the steady reliable pounding of the Imperials made me feel powerful, full of intense forward motion; highly organized purpose; brutal energy. On the other hand, the wild, unpredictable tones of the mysterious pipes filled me with existential uncertainty defined by purples, blacks, and blues, not unlike the family of feelings Szilarda's accordion expressed when she'd pump out the sad madness of the Balkans or the funereal lament of the Carpathian Romany.

I stopped sewing. Ramona stopped the record. I drifted in a strange contemplative aftermath, a peaceful moment filled with a swelling sense of greatness around the next corner. I left the sewing room to find out what Ramona had been listening to.

Her door was wide open and the lights were off. Ramona was no longer in her room. It seemed odd, because I hadn't heard her leave, and I have an incredibly heightened sense of hearing—I could tell who was in the house, where they were, and what they were doing most of the time. I ran down the stairs thinking I'd catch her. When I turned the corner of the final landing before the family room, I ran directly into Joey. He staggered backwards, spinning his arms in a desperate attempt not to fall, eventually careening into a giant threadbare couch against the wall.

"Damone, you dumb jerk, why don't you watch where you're going?"

"I'm sorry, Joey. I was trying to catch Ramona before she left."

"She's not here, she left hours ago to Coney to stare at that guy."

"What guy?"

"Who do you think? That guy she kissed like a million years ago on the beach, he's a dad and shit over on West 8th Street, and now she's all psycho sitting outside his house or riding the Wonder Wheel like a million times in a row."

"She's not here?"

"What'd I just say?"

"Joey, will you come upstairs to mom's sewing room for a sec? I want to show you something."

"I already know how to do that, I seen you do it like a million times already. I don't really like it."

"No, not that. I want you to listen to something."

We went upstairs. I sat down at the sewing table and fired up the Imperial 562. To make it more natural, I resumed work on a huge project of Szilarda's: a massive pile of blue bridesmaid dresses she was altering for a Bensonhurst wedding. Sure enough, as soon as I started the 562 I heard the weird music in the background, pipes of Pan and funeral organ music bounced off funhouse mirrors. I sewed for five minutes until Joey yelled, "What the hell is this?"

"Did you hear anything weird?"

"No."

"Listen again. Don't listen to what's in front, listen to what's behind, above, and below the immediate sound of the sewing machine."

I resumed sewing.

"You're drunk or something," Joey laughed.

"No, listen again, but listen past the sewing. Relax, and listen for other sounds beyond what you hear."

I started the machine again. To his credit, Joey closed his eyes as he sat cross-legged, concentrating on the pounding of the 562. I sewed for 10 minutes, actually making some decent progress on the fattest bridesmaid's dress. I stopped.

"Anything?"

"I don't think so, Damone. I mean, I started having some weird thoughts but I didn't hear any music."

He got up.

"Damone, can you turn the machine on again for a sec?"

I did.

"Okay, now turn it on and off one more time."

"Did you hear something?"

"Maybe. Turn it off and on again real quick."

I did.

"Anything?"

"No, sorry man. But thanks, now I'm gonna go."

At least the guy made an effort. Nonetheless, the fact that only I could hear that amazing music darkened my mood. Although I was busy at that time sewing and doing other things, I made a note to think about ways I might be able to break through that wall, figure out some way to decode and transmit all those strange wonderful sounds that danced on top of the roaring Imperials.

CHAPTER IV.

THE BRUBECK WARS.

As a reward for completing my apprenticeship and to help support both of our businesses, my mother bought me an Imperial 919, which was a real killer when you put it up against the 703 or 562. There were likely better machines out there, but Szilarda got an excellent deal on the 919 from a 36th Street sweatshop that had been shut down for employing foreign children.

The 919 was a sweet ride—with a feed-dog drop for darning, high capacity spool pins, and a button-hole maker built in, that baby was tricked out. It took everything to an entirely new level—both me and Szilarda took to the machine like it was a third arm, and we started whipping out larger volumes of high quality work in a much shorter time.

Unfortunately, just as we were making some tracks with the 919, Montez figured out that in addition to Szilarda's seamstress money, I was also making a few bucks during the doldrums selling VVs and clothing. He started coming around the sewing room, knocking on the door, asking me how I was doing, what I was working on. Now I'm not saying Montez was a bad father—he had his faults, but I really think he did the best he could—but it was very unusual for him to ask personal things about any of us like how we were doing. It made me nervous.

Sure enough, the next time he visited the sewing room, he paid a few compliments to whatever it was I was working on—I was working with a lot of silk and calico at the time—and then he just stood there in the door, shuffling around. He was wearing white pants, white loafers, a blue and white Hawaiian shirt, sunglasses, and a white canvas sun hat. He had recently grown a dark pencil moustache that suited him quite well. He filled the door with his tall bony body, jiving around, touching the door jams, reeking of cheap cologne.

"Um…what is it dad? Did you want to ask me something?"

"Damone, the bank is closed today and I need a few dollars to go to the store. Do you have any money I can borrow for the next day or so? Maybe five, ten dollars?"

"Sure."

I took out my wallet.

"Damone, you need to clean out this wallet, yes?"

"Been busy, dad, but I know."

I didn't appreciate people commenting on my fat wallet. I handed him a ten.

"Thas eet? I need money to shop for the family."

"You asked me for five or ten. I thought you'd be happy I went with the high number."

"Everyone needs to chip in Damone. I spoke to your mother earlier and she told me to tell you to give me some money."

"That's all I have."

"Check your wallet."

"I did. That's all I have."

"I saw more."

I opened it for him, pushing the pocket that actually had money in it over to the side so it looked like it was a one-pocket wallet. With all the old movie tickets and receipts in there, the reality of my wallet was fairly well obfuscated. It worked: after staring at me from behind his sunglasses for a few seconds, Montez left.

I heard the front door shut. I ran downstairs and then outside. He was turning down the lane in front of our house. It ran parallel to the beach behind the ridge of dunes. It passed some abandoned stone buildings before ending in a parking lot near an abandoned factory.

Following Montez down the shady lane was easy enough. Crossing the big field between the abandoned factory and the bus stop was harder. I waited until he was a distant smear of blue and white before I risked crossing.

Then there was the bus—almost impossible. I could take cuts, get on first, and then slump in my seat, or I could get on last and hope he was looking out the window. Either way seemed unlikely to work, but if he saw me I'd say I was also going to the city.

Montez was smoking fifteen feet from the stop. I ducked into the bus gazebo. I caught glimpses of Montez out of the corner of my eye—he was smoking quickly and jiving around like he had to urinate. Fortunately this bouncing state seemed to distract him from his immediate surroundings; his attention was focused on the highway where the bus would emerge before looping around to the stop.

When the bus appeared, Montez threw down his cigarette as if the bus had already stopped and he was about to board even though it wouldn't be arriving for a few minutes. I leaned against the gazebo wall.

When the bus rolled to a stop in front of us, Montez bolted for the door, but a fat lady grabbed him by the arm and yelled, "Hey! Know what a line is, asshole?"

I had never seen Montez confronted in that way; I was curious what he'd do. Not much—he got in the back of the line.

I was in front thanks to where the bus stopped, and there were about twenty people behind me. I was second in line, so assuming Montez didn't recognize the back of my head, I'd at least get in without him identifying me.

I wasn't sure whether to sit in the uncool front because hip Montez would be looking past me for a rear seat, or to head straight to the back and curl up with my face in the corner. I noticed an empty brown paper bag on the floor. I put it over my head and sat down. I shoved my fingers through the bag to create eyeholes.

Now instead of nobody looking at me everybody was looking at me as they filed in. Nobody did anything except a couple kids who laughed until their father wacked them on the head and told them to shut up. The seats filled up around me but nobody sat next to me.

Montez walked down the aisle. He didn't even notice me as he headed toward the back. I knew he'd try and get as close to the backend as possible because that's where he was the most comfortable. The bus pulled from the stop.

We crossed the Marine Parkway Bridge to Brooklyn. We rode up Flatbush Avenue while the usual stream of Italians, Hasids, Arabs and Blacks got on and off. Montez got out at the BMT station. I removed the bag from my head. I paused to give him some distance. He turned the corner. I followed his white hat as it descended into the station and bounced through the crowds.

I watched him through the window of the adjoining train car as we rode from Brooklyn to Manhattan. After a transfer, he got out at 34th and 7th Avenue. I followed him to 8th. We entered a neighborhood that my brothers and I frequently visited because we had a booze buyer and the neighborhood hosted a burgeoning porn industry. This included some of the very first stroke-booths, something a man with my cultural interests and hobbyist's fascinations found delightful and brilliant. It didn't occur to me that my father might also have an interest in these early manifestations of facilitated masturbation.

Looking back, I mock my naïve surprise, as if the first wave of the Great Parsing wouldn't hold equal fascination for all men, no matter their age, race, color, creed, or obscure proclivity. I consider myself one of the key architects that influenced the accelerated evolution of masturbation in recent decades as it moved from a desperate, ill-defined, persecuted and lonely pursuit into the intricate, micro-analyzed art form it is today, full of glorious segments and sects where every man can find brotherhood in micro-societies that are welcoming, fair, and wonderfully public and private at the same time. But back then I wasn't so clear on things, and my discovery of the segment and sect that called forth the extrusions of Montez was rather a shock.

He went into a deli called FizzBots on 41st Street. I assumed he was buying smokes or lottery tickets, but after fifteen minutes I figured whatever the hell he was doing in FizzBots must be his secret endgame.

I was trying to decide what to do when a familiar gruff voice said:

"Hey...little Ramone...little Ramone...what gives? You need sodas?"

A middle-aged man with a greasy black fringe looping around his head approached. As always, he was filthy and unshaven with stains all over his clothes that increased in density and darkness until they reached the black hole of his crotch, the center of Frank "Peepshow Charlie" Denardo's universe. God knows why he didn't wear black pants instead of the same filthy tan suit he wore all the time. Denardo was a Bowery bum, a filthy grinning wine drunk that bought kids liquor in exchange for peepshow money.

"Hey Charlie. Nah, but you might be able to help me with something else. See that deli? My dad has been in there for over twenty minutes, and I'd like you to go find out what he's doing."

Peepshow didn't say anything; he just stood there grinning like an idiot looking back and forth from me to the deli while drool oozed from his mouth.

"What? Why are you looking at me like that? Will you do it?"

"That's FizzBots."

"I can see that. Go find out what my father is doing and I'll give you enough money to keep you jacking off all day."

"Kid, I don't have to go in to tell you what he's doing, but I will if you insist. That's FizzBots."

"And?"

"It's a sissy place."

"What?"

"Sissy place. You know. The gays and the fairies. Old man FizzBot nearly lost everything a few years ago. Nobody wanted to shop there anymore. Why would they? His wife is Mildred, Mildred with the scarves, and after he started putting on the sissy shows in the back she really came to life, and we thought she'd fly the coop, kid. She's a Catholic. Or so I hear, you never know for sure what's going on in this neighborhood."

"Surely you jest."

"Sorry, kid. If your old man ain't up front buying a paper, then he's in back looking at the dancing boys."

"Jesus Christ."

"How about that money you mentioned?"

I fumbled with my wallet and gave him money.

"Thanks, little Ramone. Ever been to Playville? They got flexible Annette? She lets me hand the wine bottle over the booth. Hey kid, I know it's hard but don't dwell. You and your brothers seem like good kids, so the man's done his work. Leave off. He isn't hurting anyone, and he's the same guy as always. Just keep your mouth shut and forget it, kid. Trust me, you got harder things in life coming your way. Come on, I'll buy you a few beers to drink it off."

I took him up on his offer, returning to Queens with a twelve-pack and a pint of Seagrams. I was hoping to spend some time talking to Joey or even to Johnny, but when I got home nobody was there except Ramona—before I could even see our house I heard *Remember Walking in the Sand*. When I rounded the corner I saw the clouds of cigarette smoke coming from her upstairs window. Knowing there'd be no solace from that quarter, I sat in the sunroom alone slamming beers and whiskey until I was mollified, and then I went to bed.

I opened my eyes to blackness and overwhelming thirst. Rather than rushing to sate it, I lingered in the dark, half of me in pain and half of me in pleasure. The disturbing memory of discovering my father's interest in off-off Broadway mingled with the horrific fuzzy dryness of my mouth and the overall thump of my nocturnal hangover. On the other hand I could hear the Atlantic crashing onto the beach; this gave me hope, so I licked my palm and began to masturbate my cares away, massaging the gelatinous lump into a more workable format.

I graduated from the start-up phase to a nice plateau of dips counterpointed by thrusts in the fantasy narrative, my dancing hand corresponding to the lurid montage racing through my skull, profuse images which I firmly believed were composed of eighteen-karat destiny in those sweet days before the strokes were poisoned by the more recent montage where strings of regrets are dealt with in a humiliating parody of rectification in an unreachable past leaving nothing but the increasingly curdled grey blotch on my swelling belly and me down in the basement unrolling balls of paper searching for some long-faded phone number; but back then it was all ahead of me, and as I stroked away I ceased to care about anything other than the light at the end of the tunnel, so bright and full of promise.

I was lingering in the night, postponing looking for a wipe of some kind, contemplating the probability of not rolling over in my sleep and simply letting the slick pool of ejaculate evaporate into the gentle sea breeze coming from my window when a beautiful sound filled the house. Someone was playing the piano in the sunroom, and the mellifluous rolls of fingers up and down the keys melded sweetly with the night, with my relief, my slackening worry, the soft background of waves and breeze coursing across me, the evidence of my success verified by the somewhat colder spot on my belly where the Atlantic winds worked their wonders, taking the little beings I had spawned out through the window on endless journeys over city and sea.

I recognized the music. It was *Summer Song* by the Dave Brubeck Quartet, the version from *Jazz Impressions of the U.S.A.* At first the rendition was an immaculate facsimile of the recorded version, so similar that at first I thought one of my brothers had acquired some futuristic hi-fi system that could transmit sounds with a purity unknown in those days. But as the mysterious player delved further into the piece, he illustrated a virtuosity that far exceeded Brubeck's; he was not only doing Brubeck's part, he was also weaving in Paul Desmond's sax part, instantaneously transcribing the miraculous alto sounds to the piano, somehow without losing a single cool wheeze of Desmond's smoky interpretations; at the same time, the thump of the double bass supplied a rock solid foundation, and there were even the clicks and pops of Morello's understated drum work. I sat up, doubting my own ears—maybe there was more than one person up there, a musical gang of burglars so passionate about jazz that they decided on an impromptu recital instead of heave-hoeing into the night with our Zenith. Whoever was up there manipulating the piano was constructing aural illusions of such solidity that one could almost see translucent figures of Brubeck's quartet floating through the rooms playing their instruments.

I heard someone coming up the stairs from the depths of the house. When the person passed my floor, I could hear athletic breathing breaking into snarling crests of sputtering hostilities, syllables devoid of edges, but clear of meaning nonetheless: an angry Johnny Ramone on the offensive.

He continued toward the 4th floor and the sunroom. I lay in the dark in a state of apprehensive despair as his fading footsteps disappeared under the blanket of virtuosity that was ringing through the house, a blanket, I was sure, soon to be torn away and thrown in a heap to be burned while Johnny defecated into the flames. Sure enough, the wonderful sounds jump-cut to a cacophony of rage. Johnny yelped obscenities and smashed furniture. František's wails sounded like a buffalo baying at the moon on top of the mangled piano, the beautiful music replaced by the sound of drunken delinquents jumping on the keys.

Silence. Johnny descending the stairs, calmer now, but breathing heavily from the exertion of derailing spontaneous genius. The house was quiet for five minutes, and then František started bellowing again. I thought how lucky we were to live way out on the beach where nobody would hear him and call Social Services. I got up, swiftly brushed my hand across my belly and headed upstairs to offer consolation.

Ramona was already there, cradling František's head in her lap and rubbing his bald head. He had stopped bellowing and was now sobbing. Ramona was speaking Czech to him. His crying subsided. I stood in the doorway. Ramona looked up and said, "I got this. And you listen up, Johnny's not getting away with this. He's in for it."

I was also surprised that Johnny had been so hard on František. Usually all of Johnny's toughness was directed outward when it came to František—one time for instance Johnny beat up an entire family because he had seen the father make some snide remark into his son's ear about František, as if a man of his age hadn't done the same thing with a lollipop dozens of times. Johnny walked up and delivered a fist to each face: first the husband, then the wife, then the eighteen year old, then the twelve year old, then the baby carriage, kicking it over into a lawn where a sprinkler was running.

But this was a particularly bad doldrums and Johnny was working multiple jobs, hard jobs, to keep the money coming in. He also had some problem with one of the employers, something about a bonus if Johnny did whatever to some number of cars in one week's time, and now he was refusing to pay. Granting that, I thought if John had a big stick up his ass, he should keep it up there all nice and snug and not make everyone else in the world miserable too.

Needless to say, the next night when I was in bed and the magical sounds of *Summer Song* once again split the night, I was delighted by František's defiance, but also terrified because I knew Johnny would be roaring up the stairs even madder than before. Granted, on that second night I couldn't be sure if František was defying Johnny or had completely forgotten about the previous evening, but as it turned out he was perfectly aware of what he was doing.

Johnny raced up the stairs. When he passed my room he said, "That crazy motherfucker is in for it this time." But the music kept on going; in fact, it grew louder as František gave *Summer Song* the *Hammerklavier* treatment, pounding away at the keys. Johnny was yelling and pounding on the sunroom door. "Knock knock," said a voice outside my room.

Joey smiled down at me. I quickly pulled up the sheet.

"What's going on?" I asked.

"I shown him how to lock the door—Johnny is so pissed."

The pounding and yelling continued. Then Johnny stopped, leaving only the sound of *Summer Song*. The peace was short-lived: Johnny roared, timber exploded, František screamed, a baby elephant pounded the piano. Shattering glass. František yelling. A loud cry from Johnny. And then silence.

When he passed my room he was breathing heavily and pinching his nose. His shirt was covered in blood. Joey and I headed upstairs to check on František.

He was sitting on the sunroom floor. His face was wet and he was rubbing one eye, but he was smiling—he had stood up to

Johnny and got a good jab in to boot. If I had been Johnny, I wouldn't have had to get punched before I thought twice about going head to head with František—you don't fuck with a guy who can run straight through a wall unless you've got the advantage of surprise and the tranq gun. But that was Johnny, rushing into fights without thinking.

But the door was destroyed. This put František at a huge disadvantage. I predicted there'd be no midnight serenade the following night, so while a full moon bathed my nudity in funereal blue, I embarked upon what I considered at that time to be a particularly intricate fantasy involving a girl that lived near the bus stop that wore red shorts. The scenario was supplemented with an imaginary stack of Playboys: I'm sitting at a table looking at a centerfold while she is under the table licking my cock. The stack of Playboys is next to her. The narrative hinted at future complexities, because it was imperative that I started the fantasy by imagining myself riding the Q35 bus, rolling into the stop already warmed up from the motor's vibrations. When I get off the bus, she is in the yard standing among daisies in her red shorts. At the time I didn't know why, but the session was indescribably better if it started that way. It also included us walking across the big field to our house before she got under the table and licked my dong.

This was the beginning of brilliance and slavery, the first manifestations of an internal order of stroking that could lift me on wings of ecstasy or shackle me to cumbersome rituals that left me exhausted and spiritually destroyed by the time I finally achieved a few sad spasms and a stain. Needless to say, after what my brothers eventually did to me, my brain chose to permanently retreat into highly detailed rituals that made the *Art of Fugue* look like a cave drawing in reaction to the PTSD and the impotent anger, but more on that later.

But I was wrong—the girl had just unzipped my pants and was pulling down my underwear when *Summer Song* kicked in. A moment later, Johnny ran up the stairs swearing. This time, *Summer Song* stopped before Johnny got to the fourth floor. When he got there, his war cry was cut short. Sweet silence. Two minutes later František started *Summer Song* again from the top. Johnny passed my bedroom ten minutes after that, shuffling in half-inch increments and cradling his privates as if František had performed an abbreviated gender reassignment.

In the ensuing weeks, things got more and more over the top. We learned that in a family where hard-headedness was universal but Johnny wore the crown, there was an ascending will of steel that appeared to be challenging him for the throne. But no matter how many times they went into combat, neither could prevail. Night after night the carnage escalated, swelling in volume, growing increasingly complicated and causing ever-larger amounts of collateral damage.

One night the battle raged for over an hour. It sounded like the house was collapsing. It concluded with *Summer Song* and no sign of Johnny. Dee Dee, Joey, Mickey, Ramona, and I went upstairs to assess the damage. The piano was halfway out a window that had been dramatically enlarged by random gaping holes. František was playing while straddling a chunk of missing wall, one leg outside, one leg inside, grinning and sweating. The combination of holes looked remarkably like a silhouette of Johnny.

Another night we heard a few mangled notes from *Summer Song* followed by chimps wearing chain-mail battling each other along piano strings, and then the sound of two cars ramming into each other over and over. When we went upstairs in the morning there were somehow two standup pianos in the sunroom instead of one, both badly damaged, and about twelve-hundred unopened boxes of Werther's candy strewn about. František was sitting on top of the original piano eating his nine-hundredth-odd Werther, based on our inventory of empty boxes.

On another night Johnny shot up the stairs wearing a New York Jets helmet along with his regular black leather jacket and jeans. He stopped *Summer Song* a few minutes later with relative ease. He went back downstairs. Twenty minutes later, František played Franz Liszt's *Piano Sonata in B minor*. I lay in my bed completely enraptured by the piece, wishing I could create such things. The next day Ramona told me she had gone upstairs when the sonata was over and she found František on his knees weeping harder than she'd ever seen him weep before. Out of a thirty-seven-night war, that was the only instance where František played something other than Brubeck's *Summer Song*.

František soundly trounced Johnny on night thirty-seven because Mickey, Dee Dee, Joey, and I had taken him to the Bowery where we paid Peepshow Charlie thirty dollars to help us teach František how to use a can of mace. Peepshow pretended he was an assailant, and František would mace him in the eyes, hence the whopping payment to Peepshow. That day was one of the highlights of my youth with my brothers, all of us laughing together while Peepshow rolled around on the concrete screaming in agony with his hands over his eyes, and then agreeing to let us mace him two more times before we were satisfied that František was ready to go.

The next morning we were having a convivial breakfast together, letting František eat a mountain of Werthers covered in maple syrup, when Johnny walked in. We expected the worst, and I think at that point we all looked to František to see if he would defend us. But Johnny was docile, looking at our breakfasts through red-rimmed eyes, smiling at František's when normally he'd have knocked it off the table and beaten us for feeding him too much junk food. Instead he said, "Good morning." We said good morning back and looked at one another. He asked where Ramona was. We told him we didn't know, probably upstairs, but he said, "No. She's not there. She's gone. All her stuff too. You guys know where she might be?"

We said no. He hung his head. He tossed a letter into the garbage very obviously as he left the room, like he wanted one of us to retrieve it and read it, which is exactly what Joey did. He read aloud:

Johnny,

I am sick of your crap with František. I can't believe you are such a loser that you need to win over František. I am real glad he kicked your ass every night for the last month. I am leaving this stupid loud house to go

*live in Manhattan. Tell mom and dad not to worry, I'm moving in with
a real nice guy that has a job.*

Ramona

That night when František started playing, Johnny didn't show
up. The sea breeze blew, *Summer Song* played, I masturbated with
confident languor, and I got a good night's sleep for the first time
since before the war.

Two nights later, well past midnight, a hard rapping on my
doorframe waked me. I sat up. Johnny.

"Get up, Damone. You guys need to come downstairs and help
me with something. Jesus Christ, throw on pants first. What's the
matter with you?"

I pulled on jeans and went into the hall. My brothers were
already heading downstairs, Joey rubbing his eyes wearing his
Yankees pajamas followed by an energetic Dee Dee hopping down
the stairs naked. We met outside in front of the house where
Johnny was standing with his fists on his hips next to a fat guy
with a beard. A truck was in our lot. Johnny and the fat guy
opened the back of the truck. Moonlight bounced off the gleaming
black lacquer of a grand piano. We were dumbfounded. When
Johnny yelled at us not to just stand there but to get moving, we
hopped to with delighted obedience, thrilled to assist in the
dénouement of his contrition.

The agonizing labors commanded by the slave-ship brutality of
Johnny diminished our collective enthusiasm not at all as we
somehow got the gleaming black monstrosity up into the sunroom.
Mickey sat down, about to imitate a concert pianist. Johnny
knocked him off the bench backwards.

"You idiot, that's a surprise for František in the morning. I had
to tranq him good to give us time, so don't fuck it up. Now get to
bed."

The following night we lay in bed waiting for his reaction,
expecting the dancing ascendance of an unfettered *Summer Song*
played by our triumphant genius. Instead I heard a sound like the

foghorns we'd hear during drug runs in the dense mists of New York Harbor that others feared but we embraced. The deep tone sounded like a tuba blended with Himalayan throat music. The tone slowly crawled up the scale. It was still immensely low like a sound coming from an alien throat the width of a volcano, but it was discernibly creeping up in register. I sat up, completely forgetting about what I had just been doing.

As the tone got higher, I realized it was František and not a device that was delivering the hypnotic drone. There was no break in the sound's constancy; it was one long slab of throbbing tonality reaching gradually toward the sky as it moved upward on what was clearly a rigidly scheduled journey. It was as if František had multiple lungs and throats that had split the tasks of inhaling and throat singing.

The journey took nearly forty minutes. I was paralyzed in a state of terror and joy, as if I was on the Cyclone for the very first time sober. My bones felt like delicate bundles of needle-thin icicles that the slightest movement would shatter, condemning me to flaccid death.

During the final five minutes, the tone was ultra-high like a test of the emergency broadcast system, screaming on and on, but unlike the finite tests, this tone got even higher and louder. I wanted to plug my ears, but I didn't want to miss what I was sure would be an ethereal, revolutionary climax.

The sound got so high that it sounded like a man stuck in a wet rubber bubble desperately trying to get out, zipping vibrations that began to fade as the tone journeyed beyond what man was capable of hearing. And indeed, after a silent half-minute the sound of distant gulls grew into a roar as the screaming birds gathered above our house, and then a vicious pack of rabid wild dogs emerged from the darkness, leaping and growling for meat beneath our windows.

But just as quickly as they appeared they disappeared. There was fifteen seconds of silence, and then František's victorious hands thundered down onto the keys into the piece we recognized as his declaration of both victory and reconciliation, the three gigantic opening chords of Tchaikovsky's Piano Concerto No. 1 in B-flat minor, Op. 23.

Ridiculous, you say, criticizing this choice from the self-righteous mountain of hindsight, picturing that shameful display of those morally bereft Englishmen with their pianist trapped in a sack? Let me enlighten you: František's decision came not from himself, but from the other-worldly disc jockey, the towering muse that I am quite sure is the tallest sister of the Northern Lights, the magical great beyond that all music comes from, occasionally choosing to isolate one sad brilliant medium to send forth sound into the miserable world of chronically embittered flesh. That one family should be both cursed and blessed with such close coastal placement to one of this dimension's thinnest walls is the ongoing topic, the theme really, that over time has inspired the greatest and most loyal of loves and some of the most pathetic and duplicitous hatreds. But of course genius in the short term is fiercely rejected and relabeled as madness, but this is merely the dying gasp of resistance against the inevitability of its reign, the feeble screeches of the infuriated little people, but ultimately the truth is to what we all shall bow. If you doubt me, go drop a needle on *I Just Want To Have Something To Do* and let the giant waves crash over you, and then tell me how those three crushing chords could ever be ridiculed no matter how primordial their form. Go ahead. I'll wait.

But the problem with every Pax Romana is that although peace reigns, boredom ultimately prevails, and now the midnight reliability of František's rendition of *Summer Song* faded into our collective landscape, a brick in each night's redundant passing, each black swath reminding us ever more sharply that these doldrums were long and hard. Granted, Marky was occasionally able to derail František's single-minded obsession with *Summer Song* based on theories he had about the night when František performed Liszt and then collapsed into abject misery. But Marky admitted that whatever he did up in the sunroom to induce the occasional different piece was unreliable, working at best one of ten times. On those wonderful nights, we got tiny glimpses into the gigantic sub-arctic ocean that was František's savant madness—although none of us could recall ever hearing what he played before (our mother and Tommy had to identify the pieces), he nonetheless did smashing renditions of Debussy, Beethoven, and Satie. Outside a preference for French composers, there were no obvious markers in his choices or sources; the only thing that was clear is that if we could break down the ferociously reliable mechanism that drove him back to *Summer Song* again and again, we could bust the polar cap, melt it wholesale, and expose his raw genius to the world.

I respected Marky's work in this area—he illustrated a scientific probity intertwined with familial intuition based on his life not only in proximity to František, but as one of many Ramones. Marky watched the expansion of our orbits and compared it to the staid centrality of František, who outside of some minor aging, was exactly the same in every respect from the moment Marky—and the rest of us—started existing.

I have to say that in that respect, Marky was the first one of us to add self-assessment to his life, although it was collective in nature—he assessed the Ramones as a single unit comprised of complementary parts driven by similar mechanisms rather than himself as an individual sharing origins with people that could just as well have been strangers from distant parts of Queens. Nonetheless, this thinking represented a move into an externality other than simply being a Ramone brother experiencing either orgasm or impotence. By thinking of all of us as a large serving platter, he was able to slightly increase the ratio of other pieces per rendition of *Summer Song*; on the other hand, he could never successfully isolate that singular element that ignited František's derailment into more diverse repertoires.

For instance, one night Marky claimed to be "on to something." Indeed, just after midnight František lit into Sergei Prokoviev's entire cycle of piano concertos. František miraculously created a pseudo-orchestral largeness by adding dots and dashes here and there, specks of sound that stimulated the mind to create an orchestral accompaniment not necessarily composed of sound, but of the emotional knowledge of the piano being ensconced in a greater universe. František played for several hours without respite, urinating liberally on the piano bench before completing the concertos and collapsing backwards onto the sunroom floor. He woke up fifteen minutes later, wept bitterly for three hours, and then retreated to a vegetative state for roughly the same amount of time. When he finally emerged he was back to his old self, smiling contentedly at his right thumb which he held directly in front of his right eye for the entire day.

The next night however Marky could do nothing to stop the inevitable roll of *Summer Song*. After getting a glimpse of how good things could be—I had never heard Prokoviev before—it was very difficult to return to the wind-chime optimism of Brubeck's sweet reflections. None of us would ever admit it, but it seemed we might be driving on the same road Johnny had been, just in far slower cars. Marky suggested to me that we retreat to the beach to listen to the sea and slam a bottle of Muscat he had stolen from the country club.

We had only been on the beach for five minutes—the Muscat was already gone and Marky had just heaved the bottle into the dark Atlantic—when a piercing tone stabbed through the ocean's roar, three long shrill blasts of the boatswain's pipe: Johnny calling us to order. It was time to go back to sea. The doldrums were finally over.

CHAPTER V.

BEATEN ON THE MADELEINE DE BREST.

We left the beach and ascended the wall of dunes. From their peak, we saw a souped-up Ford pickup roaring into our driveway on gargantuan tractor wheels: Danny Fields. The truck's foglamps blinded us. The truck was so tall that Danny had to weld a ladder to the passenger side so the weaker among us could get in, whereas he simply heaved himself in and out with an orangutan's powerful grace. He jogged to our house and went inside.

We followed him in and joined the others at the long dining room table. All the lights were off—the only illumination came from a single candle on the floor under the table. From now until Johnny blew the whistle signaling the end of the run, we would operate in stealth mode from both reflex and discipline, always erring on the side of silence and darkness.

Montez sat at the head of the table, hat pulled down, sunglasses on, arms crossed over his chest. Johnny sat to his right, Danny Fields to his left. František sat at the other end of the table grinning and sucking his thumb. The rest of us took our places along the table's length.

Montez never spoke, but it was clear he was in charge. There was no more of the shuffling, scratching, or face-touching that hinted at his double-life—only stillness, dignity, and quiet command. Johnny spoke on his behalf, having already organized everything with Montez several days before calling us to order. When the entire family was there except Szilarda and the conspicuously absent Ramona, Johnny began.

"Okay, shut up everyone. Dee Dee, stop fucking around with Tyler and look at me when I'm talking. This is a Roxbury Reversal, and if we finish early, we'll do an Edward the Second to get ahead. Get ready. We got a lot of work to do. And if I catch anyone sneaking booze on the boat, I'll drown you."

Montez, Johnny, and Danny encrypted our complicated routes into simple codes that we all knew backwards and forwards—we performed our individual roles with speed and exactitude. For instance, František, who served as sea cook, knew that a Roxbury Reversal meant we'd be on the *Havana Banana* for a minimum of four days and he'd plan accordingly. The rest of us knew our respective watches and chores, and roughly how much product we'd be moving.

We only rendezvoused at night. During the day we stayed below decks like vampires, anchored in a marina or among the islands of Jamaica Bay. To assuage curious sea patrols, we sometimes used Tyler, Terry and František as feints to create the appearance of innocuous good times at sea for a family of retards and half-wits. Usually the sight of Montez pretending to teach a drooling Dee Dee and a bellowing František how to cast a fishing rod while Tyler and Terry sweetly gazed on was enough to send them on their way.

The secret codes reinforced a distinct line of authority between the inner circle of Montez, Danny, and Johnny and the rest of us—the inner circle had a second set of codes that revealed more details and the precise route. These upper-level codes included an arcane system of measurements that was awe-inspiring in its obfuscating complexity, a system where Imperial Admiralty Miles were swapped with International Sea Miles and then tossed in a gristmill of archaic Carolingian Klafters, Lachters, and Russian Arshiny until Einstein would have to bang a mermaid to create someone that could figure the shit out.

Nonetheless, our sheer experience gave us fairly clear expectations about what was ahead. There were exceptions: Joey never bothered with the codes, choosing to live by daily orders rather than the long-term plan. Dee Dee didn't know the codes, but nonetheless he was always one step ahead of the rest of us, carrying everything out with swift accuracy as if his bones had memorized everything so his brain could soar freely.

A Roxbury Reversal meant we'd dock at Broad Channel, which is the peninsula-island between the Rockaways and Howard Beach. The *Havana Banana* got moved around regularly among marinas to ice down the trail, a task where every Ramone's predilection for patterns really came in handy. Everyone had a heightened objectivity about patterns because we resided in them. So when we needed to violate as many of them as possible for the drug business, we were great at it, paradox though it may be. For instance, we'd hit the second hand shops and buy outfits that we'd wear only once, including hats and glasses and sometimes fake beards; we'd take assumed names for the outbound journey which we'd change for the return voyage; we'd always land in a different marina from the one we left, and so on.

The Roxbury Reversal meant we were going to meet a French freighter, either the *Dupetit-Thouars* or the *Espadon*. We'd sail westward through the islands of Jamaica Bay, round Breezy Point, and then sail east. We'd wait for the freighter about twenty miles south of Long Beach. Waiting tended to be the unpredictable part of the voyage. Sometimes everyone was on time and we'd set our course by the lights of the waiting *Dupetit-Thouars*, or in the case of the light-wary *Espadon*, we'd navigate the final half-mile by the sound of the crew singing old French sea songs on the deck of the darkened ship, turning off our motor at intervals to listen among the black waves.

But most of the time we had to wait. Usually Montez built in two extra hours, so we'd end up waiting for three to four hours on average. Of course there were anomalies—one time when Montez had some sort of stick up his ass we stayed out there for sixteen days. I remember all of us passing around one shitty can of warm grape Fanta under burning sun on day fifteen, Johnny following the can from person to person to make sure that nobody had more than a drop on their tongues—good times. Another time Christ only knows what happened, but Montez gunned the boat all the way to Bermuda—I think he was coked out of his mind—and we had to pull all sorts of bullshit shenanigans bordering on piracy to get fuel, and then on the way back Joey and Johnny got in a fight because Johnny tore down a bunch of mop handles and bed sheets that Joey thought we could use to sail north to save fuel.

This time it seemed like business as usual. When we reached the rendezvous point, we cut the motor and lights. We drifted in a calm sea under starry skies. There were several dots of light on the horizon—incoming and outgoing ships. If a third of us agreed which dot was the freighter, we were almost always correct. This time we were unanimous—we all looked toward the same light without pointing or saying a thing.

Forty-five minutes later it reached us. Lights, voices, a low drone. I heard Danny say, "That's not our ship, John. Something isn't right." Johnny asked if he was sure. Danny just looked at him with his piercing blue eyes.

"So…what do you think we should do?" Johnny asked.

"Wait and watch. Do we have money or is this some sort of credit deal?"

"I hear you, but we actually have the cash. Swiss Francs in Terry's underpants. You have no idea what I had to go through to keep it away from Montez. These last few days were ridiculous. It wouldn't have surprised me to see Montez running a lemonade stand."

"Or holding one up."

They chuckled quietly, and then Danny said:

"Nonetheless, let's clear it with your old man just to make sure we have his blessing."

Danny went to the bridge to confer with Montez. The *Havana Banana*, by the way, was one of the most Christ-awful heaps of shit on the high seas, an ancient hulk of a tug that looked worse than some tugs I once saw dredged from the bottom of New York Harbor—it looked like it was made of sheets of sun-dried dog shit. Granting that tugboats lasted fucking forever—80 years or something—ours had to have been in the War of 1812. In fact you could never even know; there were so many rebuilds, renamings, replacements of this or that, that the boat began to resemble an old Brooklyn apartment building that was once an eighty room flop house, then a debtors prison with one huge room, then a two family, then a condo, a coop, a grocery store, and on and on until you were living in an architectural Frankenstein.

That's what our fucking boat was like, the so-called "new" boat. The old boat was newer than the new boat, but of course Montez had to trade the first one in during one of our many Ramones Depressions. So when I tell you we were in rough weather or Montez sailed the thing to *Bermuda*—we are talking about some serious shit, pants-shitting terror on the high seas. And I'm telling you, not three days before Montez had to trade in the old new boat for the *Havana*, I saw three caskets in my parents' room lying next to each other on the floor. Of course I needed to take a look, expecting a *Tales from the Crypt* situation with skeleton women in evening wear, their long blond hair still growing. So I lift the lids, and all three coffins are stuffed with cash. Not willy-nilly crumpled ones and filthy pennies, but neat stacks of laundered hundreds. The fact Montez boiled ninety lobsters that night is totally irrelevant to how much money was there, and you really can't fill enough cathedrals, stadiums, and homeless shelters to their ceilings with vomit when you think about how bad my father was with money. Two days later we all had to share a single can of refried beans, and then the next day we were all looking at the latest lifeline—the far more "practical" ship, the *Havana Banana*.

Danny Fields returned and joined Johnny on the foredeck. They whispered near the bow. It was game-on. Montez flashed a light four times from the bridge as the freighter got close—the ship towered over us. One tap and the *Havana Banana* would be finished. We managed to get close enough for Danny to catch a line and tie it to a bullring.

Normally we didn't board the ships—we'd hoist one package up, one package down, and leave. But we'd gotten over-chummy with the French; we'd frequently board and spend an hour on deck drinking wine with them. So when the sailors smiled and gestured us aboard, we weren't surprised. Nonetheless, seeing *Madeleine de Brest* painted on the black hull instead of a familiar name made me apprehensive.

For Johnny and Danny it was a foregone conclusion—we would not board. Danny Fields yelled, "No," followed by a profusion of

French. The sailors yelled back and continued to gesture for us to board. One of them waved wine over the bulwarks, a bottle in each hand.

Johnny was agitated, pacing and sneering, but then a familiar face peaked over the bulwark, a bony face with deep eye sockets and spiky hair. It was a Dutchman from the *Dupetit-Thouars* named Beert. He yelled:

"Johnny, come up and see us, you fuckers, there is a bunch of guys you know. The *Dupetit-Thouars* is in Marseille for repairs, and we split crews. Come up and have a drink!"

Danny and Johnny shared a smile. The rest of us relaxed. I was shocked when Johnny yelled some things in French, and then the sailors threw down a rope ladder. Johnny noticed my expression and said, "Danny taught it to me, it's all I know. I've been waiting to blow Beert's mind with it, you know his French sort of sucks is what Mersault says."

"Impressive, John."

"These French are a bunch of faggots, just go use their bathroom and see how their fucking toilet works. These fuckers think they have this culture and they can't even build a toilet right."

We lined up to use the ladder except for Danny Fields, František, and Dee Dee—they effortlessly climbed the mooring rope. The rest of us needed the ladder except Johnny, but Johnny always had to follow Joey because Joey's long legs would continually slip off the ladder and Johnny would have to grab his white tennis shoe and put it back on the rung. On more than one occasion Joey had lost his grip and we had to fish him out of the ocean. Tommy went last because although he was good at climbing, he went slowly and cautiously. Mickey stayed on the *Havana* with Tyler and Terry.

When I got on deck I saw some familiar faces, but there were far more unfamiliar faces; hard looking bastards with hostile smiles. There was even a skinny old black guy with a fucking eye patch and a white beard, looking like he'd just arrived from the 17th Century. But Beert was there, hugging us and handing us bottles of wine and cognac that we attacked full-throttle. Business-related drinking was the only exception to Johnny's no-liquor-at-sea rule, so we always took full advantage. We all thought his rule was unfair since everybody on every other tug was always drunk. So every time Johnny turned around to shake someone's hand, the rest of us pounded all the liquor we could without vomiting over the bulwark. František slammed two bottles of champagne in seconds while we tried not to laugh. Johnny turned around and said, "What the fuck is so fucking funny?"

I personally didn't care about Johnny and his rules on these French boats, because whenever Johnny hob-knobbed with French seamen, he'd get all non-Johnny: he'd become this guy who nobody back in Queens would recognize, laughing at the Frenchmen's moronic jokes and resting his hand on their shoulders while he talked, an entire non-Johnny routine that made me want to spew. One time on the *Espadon* I actually saw him spin wine around in a glass—he saw me see him, so he pretended to not like the wine and he spit it out, but not until after he'd already buried his nose in it like a true connoisseur.

Danny Fields on the other hand always played it cool, leaning against the bulwark nursing a glass of wine, waiting for people to approach him, occasionally checking out one of his own flexed biceps, nonchalant in a sleeveless camo sweatshirt and Browning baseball cap. Except for pounding every drink in sight, I tried to be cool like Danny, but I could never achieve it because all my brothers just saw me as Damone the jerkoff-king, and although that garnered some respect, it did not quite put me on Danny's level. Maybe if my brothers had caught Danny in the bath pulling a heavily lubricated Christmas bulb out of his ass while wearing surgical gloves they wouldn't think he was so cool either, but that's how it went for me growing up.

I had a nice buzz and we were having fun. Marky got on his knees and we spewed wine into his mouth from ours. He made ridiculous sounds and wagged his tongue. But then I heard loud swearing. I turned around. Two sailors were wrestling Johnny. One had him in a headlock. Joey was fighting another sailor with huge goofy karate kicks, and unbelievably he connected with the guy's head: his adversary fell to the deck. František attacked the sailors choking Johnny, practically ripping their arms off their bodies. One of them landed a solid punch in František's face that did absolutely nothing. František grabbed them and tossed them around like he was a giant uprooting flimsy trees.

Tommy on the other hand wasn't fairing well. He was trying to ward off three sailors with a round life-preserver, and it ended up being more like a game of monkey in the middle. A sailor grabbed it from him and tossed it over his head to the others. They laughed as Tommy leapt about trying to get it back.

A scream. I spun around. Dee Dee leaning back, smiling, a bloody knife in his hand. Beert pressed his hand to his former cheek in wonder as blood sprayed from new flaps. Before he fully registered his problems, Johnny delivered a football hit that flipped Beert into the sea.

This was all happening on the broad foredeck. I was concerned about reinforcements emerging from the superstructure that towered behind us, so I ran sternward to face any danger head-on, leaping from the foredeck onto the crate-covered cargo deck. It occurred to me it might be wise if I stopped somewhere in the middle and climbed onto the freight to get a better view.

I was climbing between two crates when someone grabbed my ankles and yanked me to the deck. I hit my head and saw stars. The sailor kicked me several times in the chest, once in the face, and then he dragged me by my ankles across the deck as if I was an empty laundry bag.

A trapdoor clanged. He dragged me below decks. My head bounced down the steel staircase as the powerful sailor dragged me into a dark passageway. Other French vermin were howling and leaping in the passage. I rolled up in a ball, but I got a boot in the face nonetheless. Everything was fading. It was over, over before I even got close to achieving the prolific output I had intended with my burgeoning explorations of sound and my fierce pursuit of perpetual ejaculation; it had been my vision to create veritable arks of brilliance, my dense rich semen acting as ballast, my fertile dreams rising above the deck in vibrating masts, superstructures of color and light surrounded by winged songstresses from electromagnetic wormholes with galaxy-sized stamens, my filthy stinger with its overwhelming excretions rallying to the sound of bugles as my creations bypassed both filament and style, my furious little tail-wagging beasts thrashing about in tempestuous oceans of goo, hurling themselves downward, downward into holy ovules; but now, now this, this petty darkness. The world would never know me.

"Get up, Damone. Come on. Get up."

It was Danny Fields. I rolled over and opened my eyes.

"Come on Damone, we have to go. We need that second leg tonight, so let's go."

"What happened? Where are my brothers?"

"On deck. It's all over now. We gotta go."

"Did anyone die?"

"You kidding? Just a fight among seafaring men, Damone. Nothing to write home about."

"Is that the money?"

Danny was holding a brown grocery bag.

"The drugs. Come on, let's get out of here."

"How did...I don't get it. You got the drugs?"

"Er...yeah. That's why we came here."

I was dumbfounded, dizzy. I can't say I even felt relief, so baffled was I at this sudden reversal in the dynamic toward death. Danny seemed unfazed, as if we were running late because the others had been lingering over their wine rather than facing certain death on that God-forsaken steel carcass of Gallic doom.

We joined the others on the foredeck. Beert was leaning against a bulwark, touching his cheek, drinking wine from the bottle. The other sailors were milling around. The fight was clearly over. Danny approached Beert.

"What the hell are you doing, don't touch it! What did I tell you? Leave off!"

Danny had apparently stitched up Beert's face. Dee Dee raised his hands and said, "Hey, I'm sorry. Real sorry."

A French sailor said, "Forget it, but you should go now."

We slid down the mooring rope to the *Havana Banana*. Everyone manned their posts with the usual Ramones speed and discipline, but unlike the others who seemed amused by what had transpired on the *Madeleine de Brest*, I was destroyed. My body somehow did what needed to be done, which was miraculous because I felt like rolling up in a ball below decks and crying in the very tip of the bow among the ropes and filth.

Meanwhile my brothers and Danny Fields actually seemed to have enjoyed themselves. They were laughing and executing their tasks with unusual vigor. I couldn't comprehend how I could be psychically demolished by what was surely a near-death experience for all of us while the rest of them went unscathed. Once we were steadily cruising, Marky noticed what I suppose was the white mask of terror I wore, the grim result of my existential bullwhipping. I started to doubt the reality of what had transpired, so when Marky asked me why I looked so dreadful, I asked him what happened. I claimed to have been too far away to know. I tried to sound nonchalant.

"Ah, they started talking about soccer, I don't know why. Johnny says to Beert that American football is a real game and soccer is for sissies. Beert says soccer is the biggest sport in the world, you know, like because a lot of people do something that makes it cool. So Johnny says it's a prerequisite that you have to be a homo to get on soccer teams and that's why everyone plays soccer in Europe, right? One thing led to another and Beert shoved Johnny. You know the rest. Anyway, we're all cool now."

"All *cool now?* Dee Dee cut half that guy's face off, Jesus Christ, you're telling me we're cool now?"

Danny and Johnny joined us. Danny said, "Is something wrong Damone?"

"No, no, I'm fine. I was just saying to Marky that I couldn't believe we ended up on good terms with those guys after Dee Dee cut him. It was pretty bad."

"Come on, Damone," said Danny. "Did you have a look at that crew? What Dee Dee did to Beert was just a shaving cut. He's going to be *proud* of that scar once it heals up white and rigid."

They laughed and returned to their posts. I wanted nothing more than to be back home in my room with the door locked. Unfortunately, since it was too close to sunrise to finish the second leg, Montez had decided that instead of returning to port we'd anchor among the islands of Jamaica Bay until the following night. That meant we'd be stuck in the bowels of the *Havana Banana* for over twenty hours. I felt like I had entered a special hell, such were the agonizing sensations that coursed through me, violent waves of an eviscerating, freezing anxiety that set every nerve ablaze in unholy blue fires. My mind raced through countless justifications and negotiations with what had happened, thinking perhaps that I was the sole Ramone that had just faced death, a mouse-like plaything of some psychopathic French savage, while the others had merely been involved in a harmless drunken scuffle. But then I'd recall Dee Dee's blade dripping blood under an icy moon, his animal grin of murderous conquest, and all my false constructs were flushed down the toilet once more. I was confronted with an idea that was swiftly growing into a stiff certainty: I was the only one that truly understood the meaning of death, the true chaotic whirlwind of the universe. In this crucial respect, I had surpassed all of them except for Danny Fields, who had surely crossed this dark border many years earlier and had moved on to a staid acceptance of all miserable conclusions, hence his seemingly endless collection of chronically cool exteriors.

I knew then that my inner universe of doomsday fantasy had emerged victorious and would henceforth command the captain's chair. But why me? What is this injustice, that I should be cut down by the overwhelming firepower of morbid imaginings while my brothers continued to frolic in a blissful denial where mortality is only a cockroach's fate, a cockroach's and Mrs. Portawayzee's with her walker and elephantine left calf? But such was the cast of my destiny; unbeknownst to me, those violent horrors would never be diminished, but would be pounded into a long unbreakable tendril, a tendril otherwise known as the rest of my life.

But from this depth-charge of despair came the most critical explosion of enlightenment, the cleansing realization that would define my objective greatness despite my subjective misery, no matter how loud and all-pervasive that misery attempted to be. I realized then that in the face of such an unreliable existence where such a great wholeness as the entirety of my years could be stomped out in one blistering senseless second, that I was subject to a racing stopwatch that would stop at a time I did not control, and if I intended to travel to the secret universe and return laden with brilliance to share with the entire world, then I had to act immediately. At that moment under my blanket in one of the bunks that lined the sleeping quarters of the *Havana Banana*, those towers of bunks all gently shaking in the night, including my own, Damone Ramone, composer…was born.

Part II

CREATION. PERFORMANCE. TREACHERY.

CHAPTER VI.

CHICKS WITH DICKS SLEEP LATE.

We returned to Broad Channel a fortnight after the incident. During the ensuing two weeks at sea, I came to a surprisingly comfortable reconciliation with my spiritual death by pulling forth a discipline I had hitherto never possessed, a fierce discipline that allowed me to compartmentalize my agony behind an unyielding Great Wall of willpower, leaving me impervious to the sucking vortex of the whirlpool which sought to pull me in and spit me out as nothing more than a simpering, yellow-bellied worm of existential cowardice.

Instead, a new man placed his sneaker on the shores of Broad Channel, a man who illustrated a cold, hard veneer in complete opposition to the blithering, shook-up little woman who had been so utterly emasculated by those French monsters. Now to be sure, there was no end to the torment they unleashed; the best I could do was create a psychological demilitarized zone to contain the ocean of weakness which had drowned my true will. I replaced my organic sense of self with an artificially constructed one, the new will characterized by an almost demonic impermeability, artificial superimposition though it was. At the same time, my true self, the gentle flower that was my burgeoning young soul, was reduced to what was surely the universe's best example of utter obliteration, as all sense of trust, permanence, and a future of modest possibility was fire-bombed forever out of existence.

But the bug-eyed coward imprisoned within me mattered not; what mattered was the flurry of activity I had committed to inside the vehicle of the new me, the new me that stripped itself nude of all commitments, connections, and interests—anything that would interfere with the sexual congress of one, the solitary calling of creation. I would show them, show them that it was me that was the creator, savant even, that would take the Ramone name and use it as a battering ram to strike back with white-hot vengeance at global anonymity, replacing it with the first truly international language, a language consisting of two proper nouns that everyone from the lowliest fish monger in Sri Lanka to the Queen Mother would know and respect: Damone Ramone.

When we returned to the house at Fort Tilden, I wasted no time with napping or nourishment, but instead raced up four flights of stairs with a deer-like athleticism I did not know I possessed. But the stunning revelations were only just beginning.

When I shut the sewing room door behind me, I did not know that my decisive insertion and downward yank of the deadbolt I had installed several weeks earlier was my kissing of the sword, my oath to see through the sequestration from beginning to end, the brutal solitary confinement that would define my life, even if it compromised my sanity and body and eradicated the love of my family—a love I no longer relied upon since my transformation at sea.

I looked around the room at the sewing machines that would be my mediums, slaves to the transmogrification of my heavenly imaginings. I succumbed to a surge of pleasure when I pictured the looks on my brothers' faces when I finally premiered my work. But then I was taken aback, fearing that the mechanical limits of the machinery at hand, state of the art though it was, might compromise my work by being unable to express the total spectrum of my brilliance. I resigned myself to a slight adulteration, taking solace in the fact that all true creators that came before me suffered similar pangs. Imagine, I thought, what it would be like to create symphonies that one would never hear, having to trust their expression to the crude hands of strangers and their interpretation to waxy pits bookending craniums devoid of all introspection; these agonies I could not imagine, likening them to being an illiterate writer or a quadriplegic choreographer. By comparison, my concern over the loss of the thinnest of musical margins mattered naught, and to worry further over it belied my ability to masterfully convey my work with these instruments most expressive, machines so seductive that I could never resist their erotic charms. Reassuring myself in this way I forged on, making note that the counsel of past creators would be available to me throughout the endeavor, their wise tutelage serving as bedrock to all who know with implacable certainty that they are artists.

I turned on the Imperial 703 first out of respect for its dignity and age. It responded in kind, filling the room with its steady throb and the mystical sounds beyond it. I no longer had to search for that critical secondary effect, the giant tower of dark melody that instantly shot up from the aural foreground: the reliable, perfectly timed piston of the Imperial 703.

I fired up the 562. I set it on embroider. The resultant tonal shift caused an explosion of desire that made me feel as if superheated porcupines were mating inside my heavy scrotum. The effect was amplified tenfold due to the backdrop provided by the 703. When I walked to the sewing table to start the 919, my knees were shaking; I staggered against the crushing power of this St. Vitus Dance of lust. I doubted that I would have the fortitude to turn the final machine on. I prepared myself to collapse face-down on the floor while hot geysers burst forth through the inadequate dyke of denim as I deliciously shamed myself without even the slightest digital ministration.

But miraculously, I defied the pounding mandate to masturbate, my new steely will making me a steadfast dissident against the totalitarian demand to which I normally always surrendered. I moved across the room step by step, and successfully turned on the 919. I pulled the paddle reverse lever. I paused, knowing that the next maneuver would forever condemn me to the Foreign Legion of Loneliness: dropping the feed dog. My very biology took charge, and I thought how each cell that comprised my right arm and right hand was a universe unto itself as I watched them move of their own accord.

Consummation: the feed dogs dropped, the machines engaged as a trio, and the primordial firmament that would evolve into *Chicks With Dicks Sleep Late* entered the world for the very first time.

I knew in that instant that the untamed hoard of roaring noises that dwarfed the meager sounds allotted to mortals was well within my power to tame, that the aural hieroglyphics were mine to decode and share at will. I paused and considered the nuances dancing above the sewing machines' roar, considering what adjustments would refine my already nearly perfect composition.

First, I removed all my clothing. I could not afford the slightest inhibition to movement: I was swiftly learning that composing was not merely a mental task, but also called forth sweat and gristle. I swiftly stripped, allowing myself a moment of levity when my erection slapped upward into my belly as I yanked my pants down, a sort of life-giving catapult as it were. Next, I placed the Imperial 919 on the floor with the other two machines. I made a triangle with the 919's snout facing the Atlantic's frothy white expanse. As I expected, there was a spontaneous interlinking of fibers no thicker than needles of neutrons, but composed not of earthly particles but of minute subtleties of sound. In order to free my soul to fire upward to the triangle's zenith, the sharp spike of the obelisk, I placed both my hands on the 919 and prepared to place a foot on each of the other two machines. Once situated, I intended to arch my back until my erection pointed directly at the hot, hard core of the Earth.

But then I realized I was testing the limits of the mortal coil by expecting these three delicate machines to withstand that sort of treatment: imagine, for instance, if Antonio Stradivari had embarked upon the creation of a tone poem composed of the sounds made by wearing his violins as shoes and running however expressively through the streets of Cremona. Alas, I needed to rethink my course.

I stood up. I felt as if a reward for my labors was not out of order. After all, although I was only at the cusp of my endeavor, the immense effort to get to this point was immeasurable. I felt as if my soul was not a small thing locked in the head or heart, but a tangible body that exactly doubled my filthy earthly one with its stenches and squirts. This spiritual body had burst forth to join the musical comet rocketing from the sewing room. The sense of it wrenching free from my body, in addition to lifting the sewing machine from the table to the floor, had left me exhausted. Furthermore, my mania of self-longing still pounded me with seductive demands. Weakened by my enterprise, my legs failed me; rather than resist, I allowed gravity to pull me to the floor as if a large, heavy woman had wrapped her arms around me and was using her heft to pull our coupling to the bed. Oh, humble bed! Wonderful stage of consummation!

But unfortunately there was no bed in the sewing room, so I careened wildly around in a hopeless attempt to gain control over my descending stagger, one hand swinging over my head suggestive of a bronc rider, the other thoroughly engaged in its piston-like journey toward the pearly blossom. I crashed into the wall and fell to the floor, my ruby red scepter barely avoiding a terrible accident as my pelvis stretched itself between the floor and the wall, ensconcing the stick of life safely in the corner. My body convulsed of its own volition, leaping up and down like a lowrider full of screeching Puerto Ricans I once saw stopped at 7th and B. My hand raced in a far faster rhythm than my thumping pelvis which was banging so hard into the corner that I later bruised rather badly.

The ropes were tossed from the ship. My pelvis accelerated its pounding until it sounded like a washing machine during a spin cycle gone horribly wrong, the out of control pounding sending the lady of the house racing toward the basement to stop the leaping machine. It had been my intention to execute the ejaculation with little or no fanfare; clearly the creative surge had unleashed an erotic force that my projections simply couldn't have accounted for. I was squealing like a sack of piglets tossed into a bonfire, so I was not surprised when I heard someone racing up the stairs to destroy my moment of respite, so badly needed before I resumed work on my composition. The unwelcome interloper pounded on the sewing room door.

"Damone! Open the door! What the fuck is going on in there?"

It was Johnny.

"Go away! Leave me alone. I'm working."

"The rest of us are trying to sleep, okay, so stop fucking the floor or whatever you're doing."

That that philistine should feel entitled to degrade me was too much, particularly during a revelation that should have had me capering with delight: for the ying of creation to achieve its effective ebb, it was necessary to counterpoint it with the yang of deeply introspective self-love in order to achieve the necessary flow. Needless to say, I was furious that this moment of key foundational discovery had been perverted by his substandard presence.

"Disappear, untoward vermin!" I screamed. "Get out now or I'll show you who I am! I shall destroy you, sir."

I slumped into the corner gasping; this series of varied extrusions was threatening to wipe me out before I even started the second movement of my piece. It seemed however that my bold expression of rage had worked—Johnny was silent, a stunned silence I imagined, at my unexpected display of cutting audacity.

He eventually said:

"Go ahead Damone, play the big man behind the locked door. I'll get you later."

"*Later?* What of it? There is no *later*, not for you, not for me, not for any of us! Now go before you upset me any further! I'm not aloof to a fearsome rebuttal, should you force my hand, and I assure you sir, my well-practiced hand a rebuttal can deliver!"

I stepped outside of myself and proudly listened to the unerring righteousness and crushing force of my new voice.

"Damone, why are you talking like a homo? I swear to God, I'll punch you in the mouth. Between you and 'Jeff Starship' downstairs, this place is turning into a fucking nuthouse."

But I ignored him as my rage subsided and the concept for the Second Movement of *Chicks With Dicks Sleep Late* began to form. I thought of how marine life cycles are bound to the tides, these movements in and out, and how human beings and their respective cycles of life and love were commanded by the same tides. I was sure based on my own contemplative immersions that this was correct—not because of evolutionary theory, mind you, but because the sea made me flush with intuitive guarantees of nearly all of my leisurely reflections. I was slightly perturbed however by the precedented nature of my concept, considering the similarity of my intended colorations to those of Debussy's *La Mer*, so I therefore fired a projectile into the heights of brilliance to which I had access unfettered. I penetrated an alluring angle and hauled it back, easing it out through the magic portal of transcription so that even a purely functional boor like Johnny would kneel to the flowing beauty of my musical portrait, despite only having access to its diminished, corporeal rendition.

The Earth, this algae-covered spinning stone, was simply too quaint to provide the backdrop to the Second Movement. I therefore created a planet the size of three Jupiters with only one continent and one citizen. The continent was tiny, roughly analogous to Rhode Island or perhaps Transnistria, whereas the sea was massive. The lone citizen stood in the continent's center. Eleventeen Eleventy moons raced around the planet, and the planet orbited its sun 136,000 times a second. The planet's rotation included arrhythmic motions that were completely divorced from 3rd Dimension orbital relationships. Sometimes it spun one way, sometimes the other; sometimes it moved steadily, sometimes in stops and starts.

On an oceanic planet subject to such unique and powerful forces, the drama of the sea was the main attraction. It was also the sustenance for the planet's single inhabitant—his nourishment was the ongoing visual display. From his position he could see the spread of the sea when the tide came in—which was every ten seconds—and he enjoyed its choppy green expanse. When the tide was out, the entire ocean retreated to the opposite side of the planet. It became a massive aquatic protrusion that leapt far into space, its tip just managing to gently and briefly kiss the planet's most visually arousing moon, a large, densely atmosphered satellite surrounded by mists of yellow and orange. The cold blue-white tip of the ocean would extend itself until it no longer looked like leaping water, but like something strained and rigid. The tip would just manage to enter the very top layer of the warm, wet mists, and then it would race back to the surface of the planet and disperse over its surface. Simultaneously, the single inhabitant's long, slender organ would move in an equal and opposite direction across immeasurable distances into the adjacent galaxy where it would penetrate the only female of his respective species; he would penetrate her, and with each convulsion of the massive ocean he would achieve orgasm, firing his genetic imprint into a mate he would never know or see. Their only bond was at the pleasure point, and their only feelings were ecstasy and fear, because they knew at some point the mating would be complete, his organ would return to its planet of origin, and there'd be nothing left for either of them. Their solitary residencies were mirror images, and at the culmination of the life cycle neither would be aware of the birth of their child because the offspring of this species come not from the gravida, but simply appear on some other distant planet, also to reign as sole citizen.

That was the intergalactic love story that spawned *Me Specifically or White People Generally?* Opus 2 of the Cycle. In addition to the mental process, there was a correlating physical aspect that put me through my paces and still gives me some back trouble to this day, but its relevance is miniscule; it was nothing more than an incidental effect resulting from the profusion of imagery pouring forth.

I apologize to the non-musicians for this segment. It delves into complicated musical abstractions in great deal, but it's important that the background of at least some of these works is explained, because it will help you understand why their later perverted, looted forms caused me such great distress. Hearing one of "their" songs was so devastating, that to this day I still have to close my eyes during the love act and fantasize about masturbating in order to successfully satisfy my partners, while simultaneously picturing what their reaction will be when I confess immediately after withdrawal that that's what I had been thinking about behind my tight, strained wince, because in addition to dreaming of masturbation, I also have to have that foretaste of horrible embarrassment and intense humiliation that always accompanies the terrible scene when I reveal my turgidity's source.

As you can imagine, my relationships invariably falter after consummation, and my condemnation to loneliness is one of the greatest crosses to bear in the totally ruined life that their cold-blooded thievery left me with. So when I paint you a picture of a young Damone Ramone holding his head in his hands and weeping upon hearing *Cretin Hop* for the first time, you will understand the source of my bottomless anguish and permanent psychological mutilation.

But at the time it never would have occurred to me that my moment of creation would ultimately lead to treachery; on the contrary, during the composing of *Chicks With Dicks Sleep Late*, I had no tangible concerns beyond getting the most from my instruments, emptying the bucket out the window, and sating my nervous longings. That such pure activity could be plagiarized and commoditized was simply not part of my landscape; it was something done to toothless bluesmen by privileged Englishman with flowing locks and Viking pretensions perhaps, but not to a Ramone by other Ramones. But it did happen. It happened within the walls of the family domicile, a place that had lulled me into a haze of false security, a naïve trust that left me wide open for a broadside of reality at its most cynical and avaricious.

Those miserable days were all ahead however; my chief concern then was laying down the Cycle. My goal for the piece was to write 100 quartets, each exactly one minute in length, divided by rests of exactly 10 seconds. Each quartet would be further subdivided into movements. I was tormented from the start by some impossible reconciliations grounded in the very structure of timekeeping itself. I could not, for example, even begin to understand why whoever assigned increments to the respective designations of time assigned 60 seconds to each minute: why in the name of God didn't they assign 100 seconds to a minute and 100 minutes to an hour? The sheer injustice of these absurd correlations being forced on the world was unbearable to me. In the early stages of composing, I spent just as much time writhing on the floor, arching my back, futilely trying to sooth my burning brain which was trapped in an oven of dysphoric white fire—as I did writing the piece. It was only through rigorously applied prostate massage executed with the discipline of General George S. Patton that I managed to drive a wedge between my obsessive concerns and the imperative to complete the task. I forced my agonies into the bowels of my mind, and I forged on.

Although the first few pieces were originally composed as trios, I later went back and rewrote them as quartets so they'd be in synch with the rest of the piece starting with the fourth movement of the fourth quartet, *Purge the Dong.* The transition from trio to quartet is one of the most complex aspects of the Cycle, because it really started as a physical issue: namely, my concerns about placing my full body weight on the three machines. My plan was to somehow climb out the window; I had to laugh even as I considered this, for it was my literal intention to create a rope from the bed things as in some ridiculous prison movie. I would climb out into the night, buy a fourth sewing machine the next day, and then hide in the dunes until nightfall so I could stealthily return to my quarters.

I quickly realized the foolishness of this plan. I didn't believe a rope made from sheets would support my weight, but even if it did, one of my brothers would surely see the rope hanging from the window the following day, inform on me, and then they would all collude on some perverse and disruptive prank. I thought of them at that moment affectionately, savoring the camaraderie based on years of mischievous disasters we all at one time or another caused each other. I never considered these pranks to be the pattern setters for true cruelty, but my historical naïveté is surely clear to the world at this point, available to everyone the globe over if they ever need a good chuckle.

But in the midst of the impasse I discovered a surrogate right in front of my eyes: the 919's case cover. Although the rectangular cover was taller than the 919 itself, its height was more or less in accord with the other machines, and of course its function lent it natural rapport with its colleagues, the task, and the *mise-en-scène.* That such an obvious solution had hitherto escaped me induced a formidable shame. I assuaged my self-recriminations with four seminal dismissals that returned me to focus and ardor.

The top of the case allowed me to realize my vision—albeit in a slightly modified form—of creating a symmetrical shape with the sewing machines, thereby allowing me to straddle them; this placed me within the tower's base. It was a cube-shaped foundation and it vibrated. I conducted inside of it. It supported a glimmering tower of trillions of intersecting needles and sounds that taken together surely formed the original source of the biblical story of the Tower of Babel. The scribe's conversion of the tower into a religious rallying point is secondary to the fact that the writer recognized and clearly understood the very event that led to my masterpiece. What was uncanny however was that some tectonic shift in the ancient Middle East must have occurred at precise enough coordinates with sufficient orchestration to create the same throbbing vibrations that I was creating thousands of years later aided by the predictable exactitude of modern machinery. To think of the probability that some seismic event created the same circumstances back then is utterly mind-bending, the chances so low as to be nearly impossible; yet when I first witnessed the tower rise up and heard the never-ending variations on themes within motifs, I made the connection instantly, almost organically. The one thing I did envy about the ancient context was the amplification of awe relative to the event's having bloomed from a hard, empty crust of redundant nothingness, where sound was almost strictly a horizontal phenomena; to see it not only assume verticality for the first time, but a verticality of such glorious height and eminence must have been simply overwhelming. It made perfect sense to me why such an event would be considered scripture-grade material.

But what I did not expect, and what gave me unutterable delight, was that the case cover did so much more than act as a mere stand-in for a fourth machine; it revealed itself as its own highly nuanced musical instrument, one that supplied thick gorgeous sound. The revelation made me furious with myself for having considered the trio the proper format for my work. No, as soon as I heard what the case added to the overall sound, I fell to my knees before I even had a chance to straddle the quartet. I flailed away at my duplicitous flesh while I formed a paddle with my free hand that I allowed to pummel my shamed face with harsh, sobering slaps until an acceptable absolution was achieved several minutes after *la petite mort*.

After this I had to take measures to collect myself. I shut off the sewing machines and briefly napped, an activity I loathed and resented but recognized as necessary to regain my strength. Once rested, I resumed work—I plugged in the machines and leapt upon them with naked glee. The newcomer supported my right hand, the 919 vibrated beneath my left. The 703 supported my left foot respectively, the 562 my right. If only the founders of the Imperial firm could have seen it: their original vision extended into a far greater vision that lent divinity to their brilliant machines, already so magnificent and productive in the functions of their original conception. From perfectly tailored garments to entire walls of Vinyl Vaginas to one of the greatest musical masterpieces of the Western world, the Imperials had certainly gone above and beyond the call of duty. In this tale of shame and loathing, the Imperials stand faultless—to this day they shimmer with chastity.

This was the moment when the real work of composition began, and created memories to which I hope to return for solace for the rest of my miserable days. Take, for instance, that initial straddle; thinking myself spent based on past results, imagine my surprise when I was greeted with fresh solidity beneath my arched form. As the vibrations coursed to my center, the tower mummified my nerves with tight metallic coils down to the thinnest red tendril until there was nothing but brightness inside of me, brightness and microscopic vibrations that coaxed forth yet another touch-free extrusion, blinding white flashes of viscous precipitation that came to rest on the throw rug in random islands of pearlescent glimmer.

After that, the act of composing nearly became easy as long as I was not interrupted by the outside world. To that end, I was fortunate to find a collaborator, an ally on the outside, without whom I surely would have collapsed from hunger and thirst and the world would never have known the Ramone family at all outside the wastrels and miscreants that purchased our drugs during those anonymous years—not the legacy any family hopes to leave behind, especially one in which natural talent abounds. So when I heard an angry cry from below after emptying my bucket just before dawn one Sunday morning, I never expected that the unfortunate event would create the lifeline I needed if I hoped to see the process through to the last note of the 100th quartet. When I peaked out the window, I expected to see one Ramone or another screaming the poetry of retribution, but instead I saw poor Joey attempting to shake the unfortunate fluids from his long hair.

"Sorry," I said, "I didn't think anyone would be out there this time of day."

"Damone, you're such a dick sometimes, I can't believe it. Instead of going in a bucket, just pee out the window like I do. Dummy. Now I have to wash my hair before bed, man. Thanks. I was out all night and I'm real tired."

"I'm sorry—just use mom's blow dryer and then wash it in the morning."

"Yeah, well—maybe I'll do that. But you're still a dummy."

"Joey, can I ask you a favor?"

"No."

"I haven't eaten in several days. Can you please bring some food outside and I'll lower the bucket for you to put it in?"

"I'll bring some stuff to your room."

"No! I won't have it! You must bring it outside as I stated!"

"Forget it, if you're going to be a dick I won't."

I knew he was right. If I hoped to gain his assistance, I'd have to control the ferocious irascibility that was a natural corollary and defender of the solitude required by the creative act. I said my apologies, and he disappeared into the house. Fortunately my sheets were still tied into the rope I had abandoned as a possible means to enter and exit the room. Although only a fool or a condemned man would rely on the makeshift rope to descend from any notable height, it was more than sufficient for the task at hand—bringing me desperately-needed bounty from below. It's indeed ironic that my good Samaritan, the one that gave me the sustenance to complete my task, was one of the ones to cruelly wrest the fruits of my labor from me and claim them as his own. Such have been the betrayals that have ground me into nothing more than a blotch of foul smelling mud, a loathsome beady-eyed worm that does not even trust the inanimate objects in his room to retain their reliable simplicity. No, it would not surprise me if the dresser or the bed-frame revealed itself as yet another venomous snake, striking at me over and over when my back is momentarily turned.

Joey reappeared, arms full of provisions: bread, peanut butter, grape jelly, cookies, and several cans of meat odd and sundry—spam and pigs' feet and Vienna sausages and miniature Polish hams. When I raised the bucket, its heft alone inspired my stomach to growl.

With Joey's help, I was able to see my endeavor through at a relentless pace, the only breaks henceforth being sleep and masturbation. In the case of the latter, I did not consider it an interruption per say, but more of a rebalancing of my neurons and dendrites in order to clear the blur when there was a momentary loss of focus. In the case of the former, I needed very little—a short catnap, and I could work for two days without another.

As the grueling process moved forward, I was guided by vast internal shifts in perspective and mood that lent individual character to each of the 100 quartets. Objectively, had one been viewing me from a fly's perspective, they would have seen very little change in the execution of my habits, although as the days passed I grew pale and emaciated from lack of nutrition. Although Joey continued to bring food, I was often far too engaged in the task to stop and eat. When I left this state of pure concentration, I would collapse into oblivion until a new idea coursed through me, jerking me vertical with a defibrillated jolt, and I'd be instantly returned to the creative frenzy without the slightest respite outside the aforementioned medicinal rebalancings.

Despite this regularity of habit, every one of the quartets is unique. At the same time, there is a personal narrative arching across the entirety of the composition: the early quartets exude a youthful, defiant panache; the middle quartets reveal a master at the pinnacle of his craft; the late quartets reflect a deep, introspective, often morbid outlook. It is to the latter quartets that I return most frequently; they are the *ne plus ultra* of my creative work. Nonetheless, they are understood by few, and even at the university in Rangoon where my entire Cycle was received with interest, if not admiration, the late quartets were often viewed as cryptic and, perhaps, even egocentric.

I have no idea how many days I spent sealed in the bathysphere. I took no notice of whether it was day or night. Occasionally when I was hauling up food or emptying the bucket, I would see the stars or the thick white goo of the Milky Way, or fluffy cakes of cumulus clouds beckoning me to search for wild beasts in their shapes. I would take inspiration from these things, which lent nocturnal, pastoral, or ethereal tones to many of the pieces respectively. Of course it was the sea that exerted the most powerful influence across the entire Cycle, the sea from which the Ramones sustained their very lives, the sea which provided the crashing background to our springtime frolics and the stern reminder of our meaninglessness during the cold months. Undoubtedly, each quartet bestows a small bite of sea air, and for those capable of transforming colors into sounds and sounds into tastes and words into forms and so forth, there was definitely more than a dash of sea salt to be tasted in every quartet. It is testament to both the tremendous influence the sea had on the Cycle and to the immeasurable power of the sea itself that even in their latter, grossly perverted forms, many of the quartets still retained the sea's bright sparkle despite the horrific stagnant sludge my brothers slathered on top of the music in their attempt to make it "commercial" or "more rock 'n' roll" or whatever other filthy degradations they used to warp my pure artistic intent. My brilliance was downgraded into a vulgar commodity designed not "for the people" but for base mass consumption in the manner of Cream of Wheat—a highly processed grain that can be consumed without chewing, digested swiftly, and easily dispensed into the rivers of shit flowing beneath the city.

Consider, for example, *Rockaway Beach*, a flagrant, hack grafting of *Use The Word Trope And Then Go Fuck Yourself*; their version is nothing more than a perverse attempt to parody the simplicity and clarity of the original while *concurrently* retaining intact the very piece from which it was stolen beneath their mutated melody, both songs somehow expected to come together in something passing itself off as music. Now admittedly, *Rockaway Beach* is absolutely brilliant for what it is; as I said, even in this base form it still resonates with the maritime themes of the original: the sun-kissed shores of Fort Tilden, the green-blue waves, people wandering into the dunes to violate themselves with summer abandon, and so on. I suppose, to be honest, that my assessment is colored by the horrible events they wreaked upon me, but my central point is valid nonetheless: *Rockaway Beach* would never have existed without *Use The Word Trope And Then Go Fuck Yourself*, and for that I have received nothing—no credit, no money, not even a thoroughly discreet nod in a remote location. Nothing. And I would have been accommodating had they approached me back then to reach an agreement whereby I would have licensed the Cycle for transcription into its thundering offspring; not only would I have been amenable, but there would be even more Ramones albums in the vein of the first four masterpieces. Instead they chose the heinous course, and once *Chicks With Dicks Sleep Late* had been thoroughly mined, they were left to their own devices. Here I laugh, to think that their collective panic resulted in the astoundingly bad decisions that followed: Phil Spector, synthesizers, humiliating cover art and the authentic fake Ramones—Elvis and TJ.[9] I must say, it's commendable you all had enough brass not to come crawling to my door for some scrap of brilliance that you would have pounced on like wild dogs. So at least I have that, the slow and continually reiterated savor of the moment where the ship ran out of steam. Ha! There you all were again, twiddling your thumbs on the dark sea, waiting for the freighter that would never come. Maybe you should have covered *Piano Man*.

---

[9] Richie's status is ambiguous. It's been suggested that he was adopted and then immediately abandoned on the police station steps, or that he was our biological sibling but he was kidnapped by one of Montez's brothers and brought up as a cousin and was never told we were his brothers and vice versa. He did not attend family events in either case, so I was not aware of his existence until he appeared as yet another band member glomming off my work.

But at the height of my creative output I was not subject to a single practical concern, let alone advanced concepts of moral decrepitude, adoption of false identities, or blood ostracism. In the days before concluding the Cycle, I ceased to bother even with the bucket—neither emptying it nor lowering it for provisions. In the final days, I became the music itself, the thundering roar, the original rock-solid wall of sound that not only made them famous, but also spawned an entire generation of bands. Essentially, my Cycle set the gold standard for the new global definition of rock and roll: a pure, clean, orderly, cutting rock and roll devoid of the bedbugs and lava lamps that had so adulterated it during the late 1960s and early 1970s.

But alas, in those heady days at the end of the innocent decade, I was just as much its subject as those I disdained, the lice-infested denizens of Woodstock with their horrific shoes and their rejection of self-examination as evidenced by their blatant, overwhelming preference for couplings, for I was pure and innocent as well: the perfect target, ripe and ready for my own personal Altamont. If I had only had a hundredth of the cynicism I possess today, I might not have been condemned to spend my days writhing on my belly among filth and vermin with all my extremities of note either hacked off or humiliated into uselessness.

CHAPTER VII.

THE EVERYMAN'S MAY 7, 1824.

Once I was satisfied my Cycle was as complete and durable as possible for evocation in a corporeal setting, I developed a list of prerequisites that had to be met prior to the premier. There were several issues of a technical, social, and emotional nature that had to be addressed. First, in order for the Cycle to be understood as a whole, the timing of each quartet was critical—the absolute order of the Cycle demanded numeromaniacal stringency. Although this rhythmic perfection took care of itself when I played the Cycle in my room, it would not be an easy thing to translate to an audience that did not share the infallibility of my internal clock; in fact, due to the mechanical constraints of the Imperials and the physical constraints of my body, the precise timing of the Cycle had to be left to assumption; this was fine for the solitary performances I executed over and over behind a locked door, but it would not do for the premier. The true exactitude of the piece would have to be delivered with an easily digestible literalness if I hoped to communicate my artistic intent as fully as possible considering the limitations of my audience.

To that end, I needed a way to swiftly and easily cut off the electricity to the sewing machines and then restore it instantly in order to embark on the next quartet. The inherent order of the piece is crucial to enjoying and understanding it: the rests between quartets are just as much a part of the piece's meaning and evocative nature as the most thundering passages of the most aggressive of the 100 quartets (arguably *The Inevitable Framboise*, but if one were to judge aggression based on the excitability of the masses—by no means a valid measure—then the exuberant and optimistic *A Dismissal of Fuckos Has Begun* or the tempestuous *The Secret Co-Morbidities of Sarah* would be deemed the most aggressive). This situation was addressed easily enough: I headed for Tommy's room, confident that he had replaced the toy train transformer that had provided such amusement during lonely evenings, empty nights when singular pursuits left spiritual voids that we filled with the jocular sociability of toluene-infused electrocutions.

As I neared Tommy's room, I began grinding and gnashing my teeth with fearsome delight, for I heard the train accelerating, leaping forward as Tommy manipulated the little stick. I knew if I entered the room swiftly and with grandeur, he would be taken completely by surprise when I wrenched the transformer from his hands, yanked the cord from the wall, and returned to my quarters with one major logistical issue put to rest. But when I saw Tommy's back as he hunched over the little towns, bridges, and forested scenes, I was overcome with a wave of sympathy for this perennially victimized brother of mine, so frequently the object of the bullying and looting the rest of us perpetrated at his expense; he had no choice, really, other than to retreat into a toy world populated by smiling policemen and miniature forests of lurid green. The poor fellow had even taken to wearing sunglasses all the time, but unlike Joey whose artistic temperament was inflamed and distressed by sunlight—even a cloudy afternoon had the fierce blaze of a Skagen summer for Joey—Tommy wore them to hide tears or black eyes in various stages of advance and retreat.

He turned around upon hearing me.

"Damone? Holy shit man, what the fuck have you been doing in there? Everyone thought you lost it for good this time."

"Lost it? It was popularly considered that I might have lost control of my senses? Surrendered my wits to a disease of mind and spirit?"

"Why the fuck are you talking like that?"

"I've been working! How dare you question me!"

"Why are you yelling at me, what'd I do? Jesus, Damone, if I was you I'd go right back in that room again, because Dad and Johnny are really pissed. We've made like thirty fucking runs while you were locked away in there, and we had to cover your work on the boat. Danny too, I seriously think he'll kick your ass next time he sees you."

"Give me your train transformer. Give it to me immediately."

"What? Why? I'm using it, and you guys wrecked the last one."

"I need it for my work."

I yanked it from his hands; he made a feeble attempt to stand as if he actually intended to defend himself against my incursion, but a shove—seemingly gentle but backed by the ramrod of my creative will—returned him to a seated position.

"Damone, I mean it, if you break it you have to pay for it. Want some wine instead? What are you going to do with it? I never stole any of those pussies you used to make."

I answered him not, engrossed as I was in the gentle shower of caresses I was lavishing upon the black box in my hands. UL approved, I noted with satisfaction.

"Damone, you should sit down man, a lot of other things have happened while you were locked in there."

"If you are about to relay news unfortunate, hesitate not; you are in the presence of a newly christened fortitude, a fortitude I have named Sir William the Imperturbable. How dare you laugh at me, sir! How dare you!"

"Sorry, settle down. What are you on, Damone? Jesus. Talk however you want, but you're not going to believe this: dad is a homosexual...what, you're not going to say anything?"

Of course he could not know that foreknowledge was the rock upon which my steely gaze rested; by now this once dreadful piece of information meant nothing to me; it was obscured by the empire of shadow cast by my monumental achievements. Where Montez or anyone else chose to make their ghastly deposits was no concern of mine.

"Mom's a mess. She's sleeping all the time, taking tons of pills. You should have heard her when he confessed, she screamed at the top of her lungs for hours. That was bad enough, but now he's been bringing these two guys to the house. They're all hairy."

"Thomas, if you've said your piece, please allow me to say mine. My sequestration wasn't even remotely a submission to madness; it was, without a doubt, the most creatively fertile period of my life. Once some minor details are attended to, I'll unveil the fruits of my labors. This device is one of the tools I will need in order to make my work accessible to you; otherwise you have no chance of understanding it. Next, we will decide the most convenient evening—and trust me, sir, you will look back in wonder at my offering deference to crass 'convenience' after the point of all of this has been revealed—the most convenient evening for the entire Ramone family to witness a performance that will permanently change their lives. For those that experience anything less, I can only offer pity."

At that point a fist relieved my lungs of their duties for the foreseeable future. I fell to the floor. Somehow Johnny had entered the room, and Tommy for whatever reason did nothing to warn me. Before I could roll up in the ever-reliable ball I resorted to in these situations, I was standing again, yanked erect by Johnny's powerful arms, honed on construction sites and in moving vans.

"Got you, prick. Let's hear your big talk now. No? Got nothing to say? Didn't think so. Not so tough when you aren't locked up in your pervert room. Now you listen good: if I ever hear you talking that way again, like a homo or a book, I'll nail your tongue to the floor. Second, you're getting your ass back on the *Banana*, and you're going to make up for all the voyages you missed. While you've been jerking off, the rest of us have been busting ass to keep this fucker rolling. Did Tommy tell you what we've been dealing with out here in reality while you've been in there fucking carpeting? Dad's a huge homo, and that means from now on I'm not doing the liaison duties alone. Because while you've been jerking off we've been dealing with dad the fairy and his two boyfriends who have practically moved in. And you need to help with mom so she doesn't O.D. on pills. And František—he's been going off every few days, charging around like an elephant breaking everything. I shot him up with enough fucking thorazine to take down a herd of moose, and the fucker just keeps on coming. After what he did to the mailman's jeep we don't get any mail anymore. I swear to God, it's like Wild fucking Kingdom around here. I'm telling you right now Damone, I'm taking the lock off that door and I'm going to shove it up your ass. Say goodbye to ever trying to get out of doing your share again."

He tossed me to the ground like a worthless old rag. I fell to the floor in body, but he had not the slightest notion of how strong I was now. He could break my every bone, but I that had journeyed to the top of the tower could not be touched in any true sense.

"I shall do none of those things, sir!"

I was silenced by a kick to the face. I decided that a downward shift in elocution might not be entirely remiss if I hoped to neutralize this savage with a crude form of diplomacy that even he would understand.

"John, stop…please…I'm sorry…I'm really sorry, man. Please don't kick me anymore. I won't talk like that anymore."

"That's better, dick. Now get up, you've been lying around long enough."

"John, seriously. Don't hit me. Don't hit me, but I really can't do any of that stuff."

"What? Why I oughtta…"

"Hear me out, please. I promise I'll do all that stuff, but first I want to show everyone what I was doing in there."

"You take your cock out, it'll be sticking out of some fatso's mouth at Nathan's next time you see it."

"No, not that. I wrote some music while I was in there, and you gotta hear it."

I prepared myself for additional violence. But he became tentative and his fist remained delightfully absent from my face.

"Music? Whaddya mean? I didn't hear any music coming from there."

"You'll hear it. Once I perform the music, I'll be fine. See, if I get back on the boat now, I'm not going to be able to think straight, but if I play this thing for you though, I promise John, I'll work like you've never seen me work before. In fact, you can tell me something hard I gotta do now, and if I do it you'll say yes, okay?"

"Let Tommy shit in your mouth."

"Seriously, John, please."

"Damone, you listen to me: this is your one get-out-of-jail free card, and I'm only letting you have it because there is seriously something wrong with you, do you understand that? You're sick in the head. Go ahead and do your bullshit, then I swear to God, if you don't start pulling your weight, you'll get to know the pink bat better than anyone else—I'll ram it down your cock hole, and I don't think even you'd like that."

"Johnny, thanks man, you won't be sorry."

"Shut up."

He disappeared. I unrolled my body and sat up. I checked the transformer for damage.

"I can't believe it. I was sure he was going to hit me again."

"He's been a little weird lately. He's been nicer than normal, but when he gets pissed he's worse than normal. And he bought a guitar."

"What? He bought a guitar?"

"Why are you getting all worked up again? Yeah, he bought a guitar. He won't let anyone hear what he plays. If you try and sneak to his room and listen and he catches you, you're pretty much fucked. Marky tried—check out his front teeth, also known as front tooth. Anyway, he said Johnny was trying to play along with records and he sucked."

Unbelievable. Now this was news worth noting, a development so contradictory to physical laws as I understood them that I chose to reserve belief until I was presented with multiple empirical proofs. On the other hand, Tommy was an individual devoid of jest: he spent so much time as its victim that he chose to avoid it entirely rather than master it himself.

But it made no sense—Johnny, surely art's antichrist, going out and purchasing a guitar for some reason, and then actually attempting to produce sounds with it instead of using it as a unique, multi-purpose weapon—bash someone's head in perhaps, and then use the strings to whip, hogtie, or lynch them, but to strum a cheery tune? It was impossible.

For some reason this anomalous piece of news immersed me in a mood most black. I considered returning to my quarters contrary to my promise, return and begin composing a second work that would ultimately only be rumored to exist at all, an orchestral Atlantis that would be performed for a single rapturous student of my work with eidetic proclivities and a keen talent for storytelling. In this way, the mysterious piece would exist alongside my documented biography in the form of a shadow epic, my own musical *Iliad* passed down the generations in whispers in the nocturnal hallways of the world's most renowned conservatories, a veritable Tenth Symphony to wash over all those that only composed a feeble nine, a Tenth that would sever *Titan* from Mahler and graft it permanently to my legend.

I was in danger of being consumed by this new plan; I even began to elongate the increments of time in order to lay the foundations of this massive undertaking. For instance, the First Movement would be comprised of one hundred hours separated by rests lasting one hour, and the Second Movement would be composed of 100 movements each lasting 100 hours with hour long pauses between each increment, and so on. The cycle would end after the monumental One Hundredth Movement, a movement of such tsunami-like force that audiences would become permanently vegetative due to the overdose of effusive emotions, a crushing tidal wave of higher feeling that would lead to their cessation following the One Hundredth Movement's famous conclusion, the One Hundred Thousand Hour Rest. This cessation would be so replete with the illusive satisfaction craved by mankind that the next step into holy eternity would seem like a downgrade.

I was smiling broadly as I pictured the dead audience approaching Heaven's Gate, St. Peter wondering at their long faces, these people that should have been reflecting the Lord's amazing grace for having made all the right moves required by the Father in order to end up queuing for his right hand, when I realized a retreat to the artist's garret would be perceived as cowardly however noble my goals. Additionally, did I not owe the world at least a portion of my brilliance? What if I were to meet my untimely death in the sewing room, the victim of a collapsing beam or corroded artery? No. The show would go on.

Over the following days I made my final arrangements for the premier. I tested the transformer by repeatedly playing the piece, thus ensuring the proper evocations occurred. Once everything was perfect, I scheduled the performance. Some of my brothers laughed in my face, some agreed amicably, and others seemed confused by my request for their presence the following Tuesday evening.

Fortunately Johnny supported the endeavor. To ensure I would resume my seamen's duties as promised, he assumed the role of enforcer to guarantee 100% attendance. He even secured Szilarda and Montez, although I didn't place much stock in Szilarda's reception of the piece: ever since Montez broke the big news, she had given up the accordion and sewing. During conversations she usually nodded off. Interestingly, her primary concern, conveyed in slurred, barely audible Hungarian, was obsessive worry over what the neighbors would say. This seemed bizarre to us since our home's remote location allowed us to carry out endless shenanigans that would have been impossible had we had neighbors. For instance, Tyler, Terry and František would have been seized by the state long ago if any neighbor had heard the things that went on, so her concerns made no sense. Nonetheless, she was clearly traumatized by the thought that someone might be talking about her husband's about-face over a picket fence that existed only in her mind.

Montez on the other hand had lost his sullen cast; he dashed about with verve, and he kept making us wonderful chopped salads for dinner, so at least there was that. Furthermore he'd be bringing his hairy boyfriends Ricky and Steve to my Cycle's premier. At first I was upset that outsiders would be attending an exclusive family performance designed to prove that I was the Ramone who had been cursed to create while the rest of them were perhaps above average, but would never be members of the real club. But I reconsidered when it occurred to me that my brothers might unite in silent defense of their collective mediocrity; they would know intuitively to respond to the piece in an understated way designed to instill doubt in the composer. The presence of audience members devoid of sibling rivalry would neutralize this threat—it would be difficult for my brothers to feign apathy when Ricky and Steve were on their knees weeping with joy.

The performance itself would take place in the family room, the same big room where we watched TV, played games, and argued. The family room's acoustics were excellent; compared to the cramped sewing room, the family room provided a cavernous acoustic backdrop that would increase the power and resonance of the Cycle. When our parents chose the tall white house standing alone in the Rockaways, they had a brood of brothers in mind: the house was stone, the floors were wood, and it was already beat up when we moved in. In other words, the careening and the fighting of the Ramones had been factored into the purchase. František's energy alone was a major factor in the decision to keep it raw.

To create a stage, I dragged pallets from the abandoned factory and built a raised surface broad enough to support the quartet and my athletic conducting style. The latter was a dilemma; obviously during the creative act I was free to do whatever was necessary to complete my piece, but I would not have the same privacy during a live performance. Here my sewing skills came in handy; I made a flesh-colored body suit from women's stockings. It was a tremendous risk; I hoped the inhibiting uniform wouldn't compromise the thrust of the piece too badly, but there were social mores to consider, even in the Ramone household. My intention was to convincingly equate nudity while acceptably muting my manhood, but when I took the outfit for a dry run, my arousal was still blatantly obvious. Even worse, its tight, constricting nature did in fact compromise the piece in a highly noticeable way. I was sure that my family would end up mocking the anemic performance, particularly the early quartets which had a tentative, exploratory quality. When executed properly, this quality manifested as an attractive delicacy; however, this delicacy needed to be supported by strident conducting as to not sound wilted and indecisive.

I was utterly flummoxed. Interestingly, it was the expression of frustration born of this impasse that revealed its solution. In my fury I retreated to the shower, hoping an hour or two under its soothing stream would, at the very least, lessen my blood-curdling rage at my embarrassing failure to solve this problem. In order to facilitate relief from my blazing condition, I applied all of the traditional practices: I swathed the rod of life with aqua-blue dandruff shampoo and began to stroke it without mercy. But the sheer banality of this act only served to humiliate me further; would this end in a regrettable spasm fusing semen with the healing blue elixir, which would then quite predictably be eroded by the hot water blasting down, all of its purgative medicinal qualities swirled down the drain before it could be creatively applied elsewhere to maximize its curative effect? Something had to be done, so I applied a second coat of dandruff shampoo and turned my back to the water, thereby preserving the shampoo's assistive qualities. I instantly had another vision; rather than using my hand (did this faithful device not deserve respite?), I decided to wrap my importance into the vinyl shower curtain itself, thus equating many of the wonderful devices I had made, albeit it in a crude manner. The shower curtain was navy blue, so I was confident my conclusive smear would stand out admirably against the richness of that backdrop, thereby allowing me to admire the aesthetic qualities of the expenditure prior to delving into a variety of reapplications.

This operation was a success, both in body and postscript; once I had completed a sextet of reallocations, I felt much better. In this moment of lucid ease, it hit me: I would perform the piece behind this very shower curtain. I was overjoyed—I clapped my hands repeatedly with such intense force that my chest turned scarlet and water jettisoned hither and thither like transparent fireworks. After this brief celebration, I shut off the water and removed the curtain after forcefully yanking the rod from the wall.

But how would I support the curtain? Once again it was Joey that disburdened me of a thorny problem. Joey, as I mentioned, once attempted to power the *Havana Banana* with sails that he made from bed sheets which he attached to masts and spars made from mop and broom handles. Johnny obliterated the endeavor, ostensibly because it was a waste of time and, in his estimation, would never work. I believe John feared Joey's creativity: he destroyed the makeshift sails in a fit of intimidation wherein he attempted to disguise a child's tantrum as a man's pragmatic, decisive rage.

But that was neither here nor there as Joey began his clever constructions. Within an hour, the stage was surrounded by not one but two shower curtains, thereby giving me ample space; I would now be able to conduct in the most sprawling manner in my natural state. Now I'd show them—with the destruction of this last obstacle, the awe-inspiring breadth of my genius would culminate in an orchestral transmission of power and beauty so startling in its perfection that every one of them would be struck dumb, oh yes, struck dumb at the unimpeachable contrast that separated my genuine greatness from their inept fumblings, no matter the pursuit. They would be meeting me for the very first time in their lives.

On the big night, I was delighted when I heard shouting and scraping in the family room and discovered Johnny ordering the rest of them about, making sure chairs were set up in front of the stage. When I saw how close to the stage Mickey and Dee Dee had placed the first row, I became very upset—they needed to move the chairs back at least ten feet in order for them to be acoustically receptive. Although I had not performed in this particular venue, I had an intuitive sense of these things, and if it was me moving those chairs I would have placed them within millimeters of sonic exactitude. As it was, they had taken the initiative and made mistakes, and I was torn between deference to their efforts and insistence on precise execution of my artistic will.

I chose the latter. I approached Johnny to see if he would force the others to comply with my requirements. I expected him to rebuff this seemingly pedantic request, but I had no recourse. But he said nothing when I relayed my wishes; he simply stared into my eyes without expression before turning to the others and screaming at them to move the seats. I looked on with wonder and delight as they went about the task with quiet obedience.

Although I feared testing the limits of Johnny's strange generosity, I realized that employing my brothers to carry the sewing machines downstairs would allow the artist more time for contemplation prior to the performance. Once again, when I whispered my request to Johnny, he translated it into loud, simple orders that my brothers obeyed without question.

Once the machines and the case were in a rectangle on the stage, I personally dealt with the extension cords and the train transformer in order to ensure synchronicity; I also made some miniscule adjustments to assure symmetry between the machines. In this format, the bowsprit would face the audience rather than the Atlantic Ocean. My head and occasionally my face would also face the audience. There were exceptions of course; for example, during the broadly dissonant *Masturbate Me Immediately Prior To My Surgery*, I faced the opposite direction, and during *Archipelagos of Life Remain Unwiped*, I assumed a multitude of positions in rapid-fire succession.

But these things were not important vis-à-vis my audience. The exhausting histrionics required to create the sounds were not their concern. In this respect, the shower curtains would help the audience remain focused on the music without being distracted by the dull mechanics of its generation.

Mickey and Marky were the last brothers with whom I shared a verbal exchange before I demanded seclusion. They offered me a jug of wine, and my declination was perhaps too stringent; they were initially taken aback, but then they looked at each other and broke into convivial laughter. I was glad; I did not need my audience upset, but to suggest corrupting the artist's body with an intoxicant before a performance was misguided generosity that demanded rebuttal. After several minutes of conciliatory banter, I shook their hands despite their visibly emerging jealousy and told them to leave because I needed 100 minutes of solitude.

I considered how things would be completely different after the premier. I would never be viewed the same way. I wondered if the new circumstances would diminish the familial bond between them and me while increasing it among them because of the union of envy that would surely be an incidental effect of my work. I thought about each of them and their respective talents; once things settled, I would remind them of things they did well in order to reduce the distance between us. I hoped that one day, once they accepted I simply was who I was and that my skills were a blessing unto the world and by no means a curse unto them, that we could perhaps be a family again, although admittedly in a form compromised by eyes that would truly see, not unlike Adam and Eve's after ingesting the forbidden fruit.

In this manner, time passed both quickly and slowly. The performance would begin in less than a minute. I disrobed, and then I thrust my erection into the shower curtain six times in quick succession in the sign agreed upon in advance with Joey, whereby he would hush the audience and dim the bare bulb that hung from the ceiling. Fading light. Silence. I began, and the Ramones bore witness to the tiger's roar that was *Unsuccessfully Muffled Whimper*.

I admittedly had to adjust to live performance; I'm certain my initial self-consciousness colored the piece, but not unfavorably; my initial hesitance only served to make the roar denser as I overreached in terms of power to compensate for my perceived internal doubts. I say perceived, because of course they were unfounded. A few seconds later—four at most—I achieved the cool equilibrium that would carry me through the Cycle.

I disappeared into the reflexive nature of performance: I concentrated but I did not; I thought but I did not; I was aware of my surroundings but I was not. I didn't think about how the audience felt or what they were doing; I thought about how they'd be after the performance, how their pitiable rancor would take the form of artistic criticism far too gossamer-thin to hide its true motivation. They may as well title their critique *I Am Burning with Jealousy*, or *We are the little people: thoughts on something we can't do*. I pictured Tommy chewing his pen while considering *Use The Word Trope And Then Go Fuck Yourself*, scratching away in his diary about the objectionable undercurrent of anti-intellectualism inherent in the piece; I pictured Dee Dee pretending the entire Cycle was nothing but a farce, something vain and worthless in the same manner as, say, Rembrandt's *Nightwatch* or Mozart's *Requiem*. After hacking *Trope* to bits, I pictured an agitated

Tommy engaged in a pathetic attempt to attack the thematic underpinning of *Inevitable Framboise*, a tone poem based on a story I conceived about a couple desperately trying to conceive a child, but each month after multitudinous lovemaking, their hopes are yet again dashed. Of course he would create bogus parallels between *Framboise* and Schoenberg's *Transfigured Night*, choosing to ignore, for example, the fact that I did not write a poem to accompany my piece. Furthermore, he'd conveniently overlook the fact that I find the 12-tone technique and the deluded lechers of the Second Viennese School to be indescribably repellant—to think such flagrant hacks with their so-called music would have either the insane delusion or enough hubris to consider themselves the heirs of the Viennese tradition formulated by Haydn, Mozart and Beethoven literally made me sick: many were the times I forcefully vomited until nothing but acidic yellow puss dribbled from my mouth at the mere thought of one of Berg's or Webern's "compositions."

About halfway through *I Can Only Get Hard If I Play With Myself In A Busy Parking Garage*, one of the introspective late quartets, the physicality of my performance hit a crescendo that defied restraint: my left leg quivered as a prelude to a series of spasmodic jabbings that brought the entire stage set crashing down, shower curtains and all. The artist at the peak of his labors was hence revealed to the enraptured audience.

The Cycle was nearing its conclusion. I was at the apex of a nearly hypnotic madness that fused every eye upon my convulsing form. At that moment I achieved a clarity that resulted in a promise that I would never break: never again would I compromise my performance with concessions to petty, bourgeois morals. Henceforth my performances would be executed exactly as I wished, and if any fool should walk out of the auditorium in a huff because their delusions about God involve strategically placed textiles in order to preserve a false moral order, than so be it. I would scream 'Go!' for what need had I for such myopic tripe? So liberating was this moment, so replete was it with lush rivers of dopamine and grace that as I pounded through *A Dismissal of Fuckos Has Begun*, I could hear angelic choruses singing along with the piece's optimistic message of universal brotherhood once all societies are devoid of business development directors. Prior to *Facial of One*, I joined the audience in a sense because I had no idea what would happen next; my spine trilled in eager anticipation as my soul flitted freely about the room.

I felt as if I could play forever; simultaneously I knew that I was on the verge of collapse. I wasn't sure if I would successfully complete *Facial*. I was straddling the four instruments. My desiccated muscles began to waver. I almost burst into tears at the moment of triumph, imagining my hateful, filthy body betraying me, demanding its break like a sullen secretary working for a spineless boss. Even my escalating rage failed to reenergize me. I contemplated the suicide that would follow the humiliating and hatefully imminent collapse.

But Alas! The muse slid her long fingers beneath me and demanded that I reshape myself anew, guiding me toward a solution that would not only prevent the collapse but would bring the final, darkest quartet to the seemingly obvious dénouement that I had hitherto always failed to execute no matter how many times I tried and no matter how much stretching I did between attempts. The muse wrapped her fingers around my sweaty pallid back and guided me to the top of the 919's case where I repositioned myself into the curl of a frightened armadillo. I jabbed my legs skyward in a spritely manner that illustrated a gymnast's speed and strength. I looked up at the face of my dance partner, shiny and red with confidence: together we would see this through. If the Cycle itself weren't enough to dispense with any delusions my brothers had that they could compete with me, this would set the record straight until The Rapture.

My pelvis dropped, and I achieved the unachievable. I felt my teeth and tongue for the very first time with an appendage whose limitations I had long ago accepted as unwavering fact; yet here it was, not only successfully bridging the gap, but supplementing the feat with unexpected joyous leaping, as if my spine had become rubberized by the radiation of song blasting through it during the other 99 quartets. As the most effusive gushing of my earthly tenure began, strange scraps of thought raced by; I was traveling through space at warp speed passing memories and facts both horrible and beautiful, hearing scraps of sound and seeing disparate images and conflicting ideas race past; a small nightmarish flash of Manfred Mann's version of *Blinded By the Light*[10] sped by, swiftly contradicted by strands of *Katyusha*; beautiful women were interspersed between midgets and giants, and throughout it all, the thick white showers rained down.

When the last clear dribble was accounted for and responsibly sent nether, I could finally relent; I fell into exhaustion's sweet arms, collapsing in a sweaty heap in the middle of the four sewing machines. I was vaguely aware of my brothers clapping and howling and pounding the metal folding chairs on the ground. Such was my success that even the green walls of jealousy came crashing down. In the face of such a performance, their fall was a mandate emanating from the very core of humanness—it was a joy undeniable, and as I lay there between oblivion and light, I gently swirled my tongue on the wooden pallet I was resting against, newly born into an impervious, timeless and fearless condition.

---

[10] Not a false memory. I didn't know the title in 1969 since the song didn't exist yet, but when I heard it six years later I definitely recognized it as the song I heard during my performance. I thought that hallucinatory moment would be the last time, but unfortunately it was not.

CHAPTER VIII.

TREACHERY'S TOLERANT MASK.

In the days following my success, I had to fight against drowning in the warm waters of complacence. I roamed half-blind, lost in pleasant reflections, as if my normally brutal sessions of introspection had been mollified by a reassuring intoxicant. Although we were suffering financially, there were several voyages forthcoming, so the backdrop to my success was a certain tally-ho camaraderie in poverty; although we were hungry and the phone had to be kept off the hook, we were not tormented. Instead we enjoyed our deprivations knowing the coffers would soon be filled. But this was only of relative concern to me; when my brothers addressed me I barely heard them, so wrapped up was I in the silken coverlet bequeathed by success. I wandered the house in a haze, dimly aware of agreeing to certain tasks on the next voyage when asked.

My brothers seemed distant. This did not surprise me. A wedge was being driven between us as they contemplated the divine inevitability of my global success: I who until the premier had been marginalized and ridiculed had emerged as the Ramone family's Bokassa of Brilliance. I could not blame my brothers for their behavior in the face of such a humiliating fact. When I entered a room, they would stop everything and watch me with still reverence. Sometimes they whispered and muffled their shy laughter out of deference to my proximity, likely concluding—not erroneously—that silence now would lead to beautiful music later as my unperturbed mind began planning new compositions.

In their nervous laughter I saw the codification of their fealty, both to me and to their own limits. When I heard it, I would smile broadly and behave as if they were not in the room, but of course they mistook my smile for subtle acknowledgment, and in their excitability they would whisper speculatively or surrender to their giddy nerves with even more irrational laughter of compounding volume and length.

I must admit, I was deeply satisfied with their embrace of servility, and I used their adulation to project how I would be affected when not just a few but tens of thousands and ultimately millions would greet my presence with rapture. I was not displeased with the results; so lifelike were they that I became a slavering addict to masculine expenditures from an imaginary statesman's balcony that overlooked a square of such size that its dark cobbles wrapped themselves clear over the horizon. The endless hats tossed repeatedly into the air by the roaring crowd below made the planet look like a boiling gray sea of worshipful tumult. When I imagined the delight of the lucky ones who stood right below my balcony, laughing and leaping as they touched their faces, praying that the moist droplet disguised as rain might really be a minute portion of my extrusion, and then realizing the veracity of the droplet by means of one sense or another, I felt endlessly regal as the one ordained by song to be the trustee of such fertile largesse.

I was thus engaged at the sewing room window, imagining the sound of the sea was the amorphous roar of a crowd of millions, when I was jerked back to reality by Johnny's gruff reprimand, his larynx no less lethal than the stun gun a police officer once used on František when he lost his temper at the Bronx Zoo and attempted to establish himself as the Alpha Male in the chimp house.

"Damone, Jesus Christ, will you fucking stop that for ten seconds? If you applied as much energy to work as you do to that, you'd be a goddamn billionaire."

Prior to the concert, I would have greeted such an interruption with embarrassed rage; now however I simply turned around and folded my arms across my chest, smiling at Johnny as I waited to become pliant enough to raise my pants to a more socially conservative altitude. Johnny looked down at the slowly descending wand, and then he looked up in faux-disgust as he hopelessly failed to disguise his envy, not at my respectable girth, length, and vermillion splendor mind you, but at the resonating brilliance of my composition which must have been destroying him from within like some raging corrosive.

"How may I be of service, sir?" I asked.

"Pull your fucking pants up or I'll throw you out the fucking window, sicko. I want to talk to you."

I honored his request, pushing my special lever to the side with one hand as I slid my jeans up with the other; I felt the guilt of a parent sending a child to bed without supper as I eased the deflating valve into sad incarceration behind the ascending denim.

"You know, that thing you did, it was the grossest fucking thing I've ever seen, but I have to tell you, sort of fucking hilarious. You know, I hate to say this, but that was exactly the thing that Montez and Szilarda needed to see so they could fully comprehend the miserable fuckin' harvest their efforts have produced."

"I'm not following you, John."

"Shut up, it doesn't matter. Have you heard that Led Zeppelin song *Communication Breakdown?*"

"I know of it, certainly."

"Okay, so you don't. Don't worry about it. Come on, we're going to my room."

We went downstairs to Johnny's second floor bedroom. I noted its spartan emptiness and military cleanliness, and for a moment I commended this talent of the simple. As an artist, my soul was filled with writhing muses and emotional typhoons, and this inner universe was reflected in my bedroom's utter chaos, a Bohemian sloppiness subsequently imitated by Joey.

"Sit down. Listen to this."

He dropped the needle. A thunderous, kinetic roar exploded into the room. When the singer started his womanly howling, Johnny lifted the needle and replayed the beginning. The lone pounding guitar shot razor blades from the large speakers. I had to admit, it had an almost Wagnerian sensibility; upon hearing it I felt invincible and warlike.

Back then, ears had only consumed civilized fare like classical, jazz, folk, and early pop-rock. Unlike ears of today, which resemble Warsaw after WWII by the time a person is five, our ears had never heard sounds like the opening chords of *Communication Breakdown* thundering into our virgin brains, destroying everything in their path. I must say, when my brothers used *Blitzkrieg* to describe their later hybrid plagiarism, it was an astute choice.[11]

Yes, there were other harbingers such as The Who's *Live at Leeds* or certain Kinks numbers, but these were aberrative novelties rising above a sea of sweet harmonies, tepid strumming, and gentle tapping. In addition to that historical backdrop was the fact that I was a rock and roll listener only by default because Ramona was always blasting the latest hits from The Ronnettes and the Beatles. I listened almost exclusively to the music in my head and to my parents' extensive collection of Eastern European folk music and classical.

As I listened to the chain of amplified impacts, physical blows to the instruments and ears, a feeling jetted through me that was similar to when I'd snort a pile of Montez's coke on the *Havana Banana* while we roared across a dark sea, all of us at our posts, Joey leaning over the bow scanning the moonlit waves, his long nose acting as our bowsprit while his long black hair billowed in the wind behind him, our leather-clad figurehead. At those moments I felt as if the *Havana Banana* could conquer the firmament; we would roar up 5th Avenue and the sparks blasting from the hull would send the nocturnal pedestrians scurrying for cover like spot-lit cockroaches as we hammered north to plunder Bloomingdales and The Plaza, shoving handfuls of pure coke up our noses the entire way.

I was dreaming thus and listening blissfully to the Kalashnikovs shooting from the speakers when it hit me what Johnny was insinuating. I went from bliss to fury with no transition, exploding into a rage so intense that my face surely turned as shiny and

---

[11] *Communication Breakdown's* electrification blended with the structure and libretto of Futurist-inspired mechanized warfare lifted verbatim from *The Cuckold's Inspired Vesicle.*

purple as my mushroom did when it was stretched to the point of bursting in the final moment before blessed release.

"How dare you, sir, in the name of all that is good and holy, how dare you! If you do not retract your statement, we shall settle this at dawn with thirty paces, you dirty conniving scoundrel!"

"Damone, shut the fuck up and sit down..."

"Your martial air will not deter me, sir, no! I shall have satisfaction or you shall retract your libelous pronouncements, sir. Must I slap you with the proverbial glove, or do you dutifully agree to honor..."

My rage was prepared to deliver a lengthy address, but it was cured of its effusions by Johnny's quartzite fist. Someone hit a gigantic timpani somewhere and I fell to the floor, my trim ass offering scant protection from wood padded only with Pine-Sol's gleam.

"Damone, shut the fuck up. I'll kick your balls out your mouth. What the hell is the matter with you now? I'm trying to be nice here."

"Fine John, you want to humiliate me by making me say it, fine, I'll say it: you think I based *Chicks With Dicks Sleep Late* on what you were just playing, don't you? Don't you?"

"Asshole, did I not just call you out that you never heard the fucking thing before? What's the matter with you? How could you steal from it if you didn't know it existed until just now?"

I sat there rubbing my head as his words sank in, malingering to buy time so I could think of some way to gracefully escape embarrassment's tightening noose. I pictured everybody at dinner later, every single one of them knowing about this humiliating logical fallacy; Johnny's mouth was already watering in anticipation of letting everyone know forthwith that Damone, yet again, had egg on his face.

"Damone, what I was trying to say is that what you did back there, you might be on to something."

"Forget it John, my back hurts like fuck—I won't be able to do it again for months."

"The sound of the three machines all together, it sounded sort of like that, but in a way even better and faster and more orderly."

I thought he was misconstruing something or again ridiculing me by insulting my most prized efforts, but when he continued I realized that it was actually happening: my most hard-nosed of brothers, Johnny Ramone—was complementing me. It stands as one of the proudest moments of my entire life.

"Yeah, you know, I really like how Jimmy Page's guitar sounds, but there's still something hippyish about it, even before Plant starts singing. Then there's that soloing I fucking hate, it sorta reminds me somehow of that painting in the museum but in song form, the one that František—not the picture of the city he jerked off on, but the other one when he jerked off on the bench in front of it then made us all look at his shirt and he said, 'František paints it too,' for three days straight, and we had to tranq him to get him to take it off?"

"*Autumn Rhythm* by Jackson Pollock."

"Whatever, but do you know what I mean?"

Although I hadn't heard the solo, I had an eerie feeling we were about to see eye-to-eye on something. He bumped the needle up and down across the vinyl until I heard an undisciplined mess of horrific, sloppy squeals vomiting from the speakers. I found it hard to believe that the orderly executioner of the song's impeccably disciplined opening notes was the same person responsible for the shameful mess now ruining my day. Thankfully, Johnny lifted the needle and sat down on his bed. I had been contemplating my increasing resemblance to a unicorn, and how this would be yet another thing everyone would laugh at me about when it hit me: Johnny was comparing a painting to a piece of music. This was just too much, and I again wondered if this was not the set-up to an especially guileful humiliation that would bring me to tears while all my brothers laughed at me and prodded me with sharpened sticks. I warned myself not to allow any of them to film me or photograph me during introspective manipulations no matter what enticements they put on offer. I wasn't going to end up on the cover of *Life* magazine for everyone in the entire country to laugh at.

"See what I mean, Damone? There's no total good songs, just parts of songs that are good. They're all too messy and slow, ya know? I'm taking guitar lessons and it's hard, and at first I was pissed off and was going to beat the shit out of the teacher, but then I heard this and I think I can do it, or something close, but I can't do those solos and I don't want to. I'm going to play something for you, and if I screw it up and you tell anyone, I'll chop off your favorite toy, understand me, asshole?"

"Geez, John, no need to get like that. And oh yeah, when I asked you to not tell what I was doing with Ramona's hairbrush that time, you told everybody, and now you're asking—"

"Whatever. Listen."

He grabbed a shoddy acoustic guitar from the corner.

"See, I told my teacher I wanted to learn *Communication Breakdown*, right? So he shows it to me like this."

He strummed up and down, and it sounded somewhat like the song.

"Hear the problem? It sounds all gay like *Mr. Tambourine Man* or something, right? Now listen to this."

This time, instead of strumming up and down he just went down, banging out chords like he was swiftly peeling a potato. The difference was instantly apparent—it sounded powerful and orderly, just like the song.

"Better, right? See, I had the idea to do this during your shitty concert because those sewing machines all together sounded like what I wanted to achieve, do you understand me?"

"Yeah, John. I do. Um, thanks."

"Yeah. How did you get all three to be hitting at the exact same time?"

"Not hard. Two of them have been playing together for a long time so they automatically achieve emotional accord at the start of a piece. The other is a bit of a novice, but I made some technical adjustments, and then I introduced Tommy's transformer in an approximation a first violinist's role vis-à-vis the conductor, so..."

"Okay, shut up. You got them to work together. Great. I think it's possible to get people to do the same thing, speed it up, make sure everyone does exactly the same things at the same time and no more of that sissified strumming, then I think it'd work. Yeah. Are you planning on putting on another show?"

"Not anytime soon, John. I'm still wallowing in a resplendent exhaustion from linking the composing process to the premier without leaving time to recover between the events, so different in their emotional demands, you understand."

"Yeah, right. I want you to start up those machines again like you did soon. I'm gonna show Tommy and Dee Dee how the sounds connect."

"I've played some things for Joey before, but I'm not sure he understood."

"Yeah, that's a good idea, I'll bring Joey too. He sometimes has something smart to say. Get it together Damone, go beat off or whatever the hell you do to recharge your batteries because you're playing dicks of doom or whatever the hell it's called in your 'program' before we go to sea. That's in two weeks, so I expect an update by Wednesday when you can do this. Understand? What the fuck is that look for Damone, I just fucking told you I liked what you did, that you gave me some good ideas, so it should feel good doing what I tell you to do, okay?"

I nodded assent, but I returned to my room furious for a raft of reasons. First, his fascistic order for me to perform on demand like a simpering lackey made me feel like a beleaguered Shostakovich humiliated every which way by a Stalin who knocked him in and out of the Party's favor like a badminton birdie. Next, his mocking reference to my concert programs made me livid; even though I understood that's exactly what he'd intended, I still surrendered to anger. When I thought of the effort it took to draw the pictures and to write down the name of each quartet and opus number with explanatory notes[12], I grew even angrier. Plus I had to bribe Dee Dee with Tommy's largest bottle of cooking wine so he'd go make copies at the deli so I'd have enough for the audience, musicologists, and the press—another effort belittled by Johnny's mockery.

Finally—and worst of all—was his suggestion that I had 'given him ideas' as if I was some stinking ignoramus of a peasant

---

[12] The notes explained how the Opus Numbers and the chronology of composition didn't reflect each other precisely. Opus 58, for example, was actually the 72nd Quartet I composed.

drunkenly scratching at my one-stringed violin in some horrific shithole outside Szeged, and he was an elegant Béla Bartók in town exercising his classist muscle in order to "explore" local folk music, which he in turn would filter through the immensity of his genius in order to create masterworks of unequaled brilliance "based on" the quaint simplicity of genuine Hungarian village music when the fact of the matter was that Johnny was relying on my cowardice in order to embark on some pathetic musical endeavor that was nothing more than a shabbily veiled attempt to create some simplistic crudities extracted from my masterpiece which he would then pass off as his own.

But as I lay in bed calming down after an especially violent and loathsome series of purgative rituals, I began to see things differently. Even though I had only shown the tiniest tip of my anger to Johnny, I still felt deeply ashamed of that and of the gigantic mountain of grievances that I had luckily managed to keep to myself. It occurred to me how utterly silly I was being to think Johnny's guitar playing—his doomed, laughable attempt to imitate my greatness—was in any way a threat to me. As if that callous-handed cretin would ever be able to approximate one measure of my quartets, let alone reproduce them in their entirety. It was about as likely as the sky falling. In my naïveté, I never considered the possibility that the sky need not move at all, that the very earth might collude with them and rear up, thereby crushing me between heaven and firmament. And then they would all laugh and laugh and laugh: the sky, the earth, the sun, and the Canaanite brothers Ramone.

CHAPTER IX.

THE GENESIS OF MY ANNHILATION AT THE HANDS OF TOTAL EVIL.

A few days later, Johnny, Joey, Tommy, Dee Dee, Marky, and Mickey gathered in the sewing room to listen to selected portions of *Chicks With Dicks Sleep Late* (hereafter referred to as "*CWDSL*"). Due to the sewing room's size, there was simply no way to perform the piece with justice, so I decided to treat my brothers to a deconstruction where we would analyze the different instruments, the historical context, my emotional landscape preceding, during, and after creation, and so on.

This format would educate them, give Johnny the information he sought, and would allow me to truncate the session at any time since they would have no expectations regarding its length. I needed this loophole so I'd have time to create: I was feeling the incipient tickle of a new work emerging from the murky depths.

Of course Mickey immediately perturbed me by questioning the can of powder I had stolen several weeks earlier from Coney Island High's gymnasium. The girls gymnastics team had been using it to powder their hands for a variety of enticing feats they were practicing on high bar and horse. The door to the gym had been opened to let in some fresh air, and the gymnasts and their coach were distracted by the tasks at hand (as I had been during the several minutes I spent cowering in the doorway staring longingly at the can). Seeing my chance, I ran into the gym, grabbed the can, and swiftly turned tail. Their coach, a somewhat mannish woman of notable musculature, saw me and was belching the usual platitudes of petty authority that always seemed to reduce any male illustrating any notable panache to a 'young man.' But I was light of foot and motivated by my deep hunger to possess the can: I bade swift retreat below the Coney Island boardwalk, a region I knew like the Viet Cong did their tunnels.

When I got home, I placed the can next to the fourth floor toilet. Mickey recognized the can, and made the crass inference that I enjoyed the powder because in all likelihood a minimum of fifty teenage girls had dipped their hands in it. Granting that my need for the powder indeed had substantial correlation to a new method of self-induced euphoria, I was nonetheless enraged that Mickey would imply my motives were so commonplace.

I turned and stared out the window, my face crunched in fury. Making matters worse, Dee Dee attempted to defend me by suggesting that Mickey's assertion was absurd, and that obviously I was using the powder for the same reason the gymnastics team did prior to spinning over the horse or walking the high beam on their hands—for the additional friction. In my case, additional friction that would cause a grinding, heating effect that could, in theory, lead to a more powerful termination. Although Dee Dee was driven by noble intent, the introduction of yet another "elephant in the room" application only soured my mood further, for indeed, granting again that the powder enhanced my fervid solitude, how I actually used it was not even remotely related to either of their clichéd assertions.

In my anger I swore to myself that I would never tell them how it should be properly used to achieve additional pleasure; no, I would take that particular method with me to the tomb, notwithstanding that there are perceptive people, perhaps even reading this text, that know full well the method I'm referring to and perhaps hundreds of others that the powder can provide. In general, I think anyone that grew up in that era of shoddy carnal options was blessed with a particularly well-honed creativity regarding autoerotic enhancements. Speaking for myself, my natural impulses so far exceeded the thematic limitations of that era's porn that my compensatory responses nearly equaled my prolific musical output, allowing me to state with confidence today that my satyriasis has evolved into a mature democracy.

Thankfully, The Fort Tilden Humiliation Festival was cut short by Johnny. He told Dee Dee and Mickey that if they continued to bait me they would be facing a brutal session with the pink bat. This pleased me greatly. My pleasure was doubly reinforced when I then remembered a moment hitherto unrecalled during *CWDSL's* premier: I looked up and saw Dee Dee attempting to leave the auditorium during *Pretend We Aren't Related*, quartet 38, only to have Johnny yank him back into his chair. My mood restored by Johnny's support, I returned to the task at hand.

"Gentleman, as you realize, a core component of the work is the conducting. In order for the piece to be fully realized should you ever attempt to conduct it yourselves with different orchestras in different countries, the conductor should practice comprehensive nudity. Now, I understand that even as this enlightened decade concludes, we still strain beneath confining straps of convention. I want to assure you, I've watched myself perform hundreds of times, and once the initial novelty wears off, the nudity appears quite natural and rather secondary, an organic minor element of the piece that perhaps commands one percent of any given audience's attention. Now admittedly, there might be one or two that fixate on the nudity, perhaps due to carnal malnourishment rooted in some hoodoo voodoo religion, but in all likelihood this type of person wouldn't be attending a performance of this piece. I shall now disrobe."

"Where did you get that fucking suit, from the Coney fat man? Jesus Christ, that thing is huge."

"Shut up, Dee Dee—let him do what he needs to do," said Johnny.

"Damone, what the hell do you have on under there?" Tommy asked as I revealed my secondary garment.

"I don't know, Tommy—you tell me. You're rather intelligent, I believe."

"Yeah, I do see what it is, and I want you to take it off right now. Do you know how offensive that uniform is, especially for our family?"

"Fool! This uniform is Soviet, an exact replica of the uniform Joseph Stalin wore during his December 11, 1937 speech in the Bolshoi Theatre! I made it myself. And of course I'm taking it off, have you not been listening to me?"

"I know full well what that uniform is, and I'm asking you to please take it off; do you have any idea what our family has been through thanks to those people? In 1956 alone, our—"

"Shut up, Tommy, before I 1956 your fucking face," Johnny said. "He said he's taking it off, he's taking it off, so what's your problem? We get it, the Soviets are bad. I agree. Now shut the fuck up and let Damone talk."

To be fair, a great deal of my anger had nothing to do with Tommy's condescending self-righteousness regarding the uniform I was wearing underneath said large suit; I was trying to organize the wild cloud of ideas I had regarding my Second Symphony, and it was not going well. The unfortunately loose motif was a variation on a theme, not unlike how Vaughn Williams so brilliantly developed on Thomas Tallis. For my piece, I intended to blend certain literary elements drawn largely from Marinetti's Manifesto with incredibly unique permutations based on themes from Bruckner's Seventh Symphony. A critical aspect of the symphony that was clear to me was that unlike *CWDSL*, the piece would have to be performed not only dressed, but with modern clothing covering up any high-tier dictator's uniform from the post-Marinetti age; so for example, I might indeed wear one of the offensive uniforms Tommy so adamantly opposed, but I would under no circumstances dress like Napoleon. The only qualifiers were that the uniform be precisely rendered and post-Marinetti. The first problem was that absolute fidelity to the original uniform was critical (Who would know? *I* would know); therefore, many of the uniforms ended up being rather thick, so getting modern clothing over the top of them proved to be quite difficult. My intention had been to wear the traditional Ramones family outfit of jeans, t-shirt, and black leather jacket over each uniform, but it was impossible to squeeze it all in, not to mention that finding a pair of sneakers large enough to fit over Admiral Horthy's parade shoes was not an easy thing, even in New York. Therefore I had to find giant street clothes that both covered the uniform and were compatible with whatever footwear the respective dictator favored; consequently, I ended up in the giant suit I was wearing at that moment in the sewing room.

But the Second Symphony faced an even greater impasse: although the piece would not require nudity, it did require the unrelinquishable act that served as the ambassador between my art and my life, and needless to say, wearing two suits of clothing was leading to every manner of personal access problem. By the time I achieved flesh-on-flesh and moved forward, the music was so lost that the utter precision the piece demanded was rendered out of the question. For indeed, although not meant to be offensive in the manner Tommy presumed it to be, the piece was meant to question certain assumptions of the European right regarding Bruckner with an intent to undermine their base assertions. At the same time, the ironic concessions of the piece were offset by a very real demand and respect for discipline and precision, an icy total order that would create yet another careworn 'Cathedral of Ice.' But in this instance, the dictatorial urge would be sublimated to a divine perfection of sound, particularly acute in the haunting andante. You can imagine the extent of my surprise when years later in 1974 in a homeless shelter, I witnessed an oddly precise rendering of my unexecuted intent in the impressive visual displays running concurrently with the performance of the *Snow Miser Theme* from the film *An ABC Special Presentation*. The way that the composer rolled some of the darkest themes of the 20th Century from *Snow Miser* into the opposing yet complementary *Heat Miser Theme* was so extraordinarily clever that I was almost glad I never completed my Second Symphony. I did have occasional bouts of paranoia in the middle of the night that my Second Symphony's foundation was yet another thing my brothers stole from me, stole and sold to the composer[13] responsible for the aforementioned film's score. In the end however, it was this genius composer's excellent final product to which I surrendered any unpleasant

---

[13] The great Maury Laws.

feelings; even if there was a derivative element, I have to admit the piece stands on its own, and no matter how awful things were in the ensuing years, I made sure to never miss the film when it was shown, which was invariably around Christmas for some reason.

Fully nude now, I walked around the sewing room several times, doing several rough approximations of an ice skater's double axel (I admit, I was attempting triple or better, but that sort of athleticism was not my suite) in order to more swiftly acclimate my brothers to my nudity. I postulated that the lack of a stage and the inadequate distance between audience and performer might make the nude element more noticeable than it had been during the premier. As I expected, my brothers engaged in a certain amount of childish mirth as I capered about the room twirling and leaping; I accepted it graciously within the confines of the situation, and in fact hoped that they would do what they needed to do in order to get it out of their systems.

After ten minutes or so, I proceeded with the presentation.

"Gents, I would like to start by allowing the quartet to play free-form for a while in order to warm up and get used to you; I'd like for them simply to play a bit so you get to know them more personally than the previous venue could have allowed."

I turned the transformer's switch all the way to the right. The machines began their wonderful articulations. As the sounds washed over me, my turgidity was free to develop; I wondered how my brothers' restrictive clothing was serving them, and I hoped that any sense of claustrophobia their organs might be experiencing would later find mitigation.

I was about to explain how the 703 provided six key metaphors that connected, in a direct sense, the male G spot with an expertly manipulated frenulum when Johnny broke in:

"See? Do you hear it? That's the sound. If I could mic it and amp it, maybe distort the tubes, I think these machines would make the right sound. The problem's gonna be how to transfer the sound to other instruments. But there's gotta be a way."

Needless to say, I was furious, and if the smallest cue led me to believe he intended to continue this bellicose monologue, I would immediately retreat to the sewing room closet where I would rub up and down against the ironing board with such fiery intensity that it would only be a matter of seconds until I achieved vengeful rapture. In short, I would show them a side of me they would not like.

Johnny noticed the gathering storm however, and he placed the situation in a new light with unexpected delicacy:

"Damone, I'm very excited about this music you are working on. Understand? It's very good. So in this, um…demonstration, maybe we could open with any questions we might have, because I don't honestly think with hearing something this amazing up close like this that any of us are going to be able to hold back, right fellas? I said, *right fellas?*"

My brothers attempted a 'Right!' in military unison; they failed miserably. The failure was followed by jocular acknowledgment. Dee Dee suggested they try again with him counting off.

This was not the first time I heard that now infamous, guttural four-count that prepares dupes and suckers for the aural maraudings on their "records." No, I had heard it before: on the Coney Island pier under blazing sunsets before we jumped into the sea; on the beach near our house when we fired Roman candles into the night sky; in the green field when we'd race to the bus stop; in the depths of a toilet bowl during the apprehensive final seconds before a very nearly felonious swirlie.

This instance however was the first time that four-count lurked menacingly near my creations; I had no idea then that it would become the ubiquitous introduction to every single act of thievery they would ultimately commit. I had no idea, so like a pure white Helen Keller of lambs, I wandered sweetly into the lair of the wolves. To taste such innocence again…if only for a moment.

"What do you think, Dee Dee?" Johnny asked.

"Yeah. I hear it. But this is flat like a floor, ya know? If you want this to work it's got to be more like tables and chairs and shit."

"Whaddya mean?" Johnny asked.

"Like how you got all mad because I could play little songs on your guitar and I never touched a guitar in my life, but even now you can remember them, like *Lunatic Lunge?*

"And *Blowtorch Hustle*," said Tommy.

"Right, you don't forget but you have to think of the lines before you start," Dee Dee said.

"I don't get it, you mean like the words to the song?" asked Johnny.

"No, but that's part of it. Say we were on the boardwalk walking along the wall by the Aquarium, and I had a can of spraypaint—I'd paint this song by just holding the can and walking along painting one big straight line. Now, hey man, Damone, I think your music, you know, is really incredible, and this is one of the things that's great about it, you get that, right? It's like this long line. But for what *you* want to do John, you gotta do it like this."

Dee Dee drew in the air with his finger.

"You start with a little hill here…then you have the first line that's flat, then you go up a sharp slope here, now you're running flat again, repeat that, then do another line down here…that'd be an intro, a first verse, and the first chorus. Next you do the whole thing again, and then here…you raise it up even further, run flat on the top for a while, and you got your middle thing, see?"

"Bridge," said Tommy.

"Whatever, man. All you gotta know is that you always gotta have a middle thing, especially if the song's about chicks. Then you jump off the edge, and start back up flat, but you draw a second line right over this new line; there you got a third verse sorta amped up with a backing vocal, more drums, or louder guitar. It doesn't really matter as long as it gets thicker. See, because these songs, you know, you can't sit around strumming the guitar or learning other people's shit, because that's all, uh…"

"Secondary," Tommy said.

"Yeah man, it's all secondary. Good songs don't come from your hands, John, no matter how fast those fuckers move they can't replace the inner-baby, man, because that's how you write songs, know what I mean?"

"Nobody knows what you mean, Dee Dee," said Johnny.

I unfortunately could not make that claim. As I listened I realized this was an abstract yet accurate portrayal of sound coming from a Ramone brother whose greatest artistic achievements to date had been modern paintings on sidewalks done in the blood spraying from faces he punched, and here he was suddenly spouting his own artistic manifesto. I would have been more upset at his interruptive pontificating if I hadn't been so surprised.

"Like when a kid runs around singing, "La La La La," or whatever, those are the basis of real good songs. That's why we like the Stooges, man—it's little kid simple, but sexed up for teenagers. People that don't like it aren't any fun and they don't understand fucking. I mean sex, not fucking...I can't really say it right, but I mean they're outside of sex and they want to get in, but if you understand certain music right off, then you're in already. That's why I get more chicks than you guys, because as soon as I look in their eyes they hear songs. Not for real, but they feel feelings like songs because I get it. Get it?"

"No, but who cares. I just need you to do that shit you did before again. I don't need to know your life philosophy," said Johnny.

"I'll come to your band's next practice if you want and I'll show you what I mean," said Dee Dee.

"Yeah, that's great, a guy that can't play except for one string coming to teach us how to write songs. That's really great," said Johnny.

"You can show me, Dee Dee, that'd be really good," said Joey.

This never-ending gauntlet of horrific aspersions put me into dumbfounded catatonia; I didn't know, really, whether I should be angry at how they were running roughshod over my well-planned presentation, or at the fact that they had been secretly colluding on some type of musical endeavor. In any event, if they expected me to sit there quietly while they violated my primacy, they had another thing coming.

"Shut up! I demand silence this instant! What is this tripe you allude to, these songs and these marching bands? How dare you suggest the wanton transfer of my concepts to some primordial setting where neanderthals mindlessly stroke their instruments, spewing out ribald popular trash? I shan't allow it, I simply shan't! Now explain yourselves forthwith, or I shall pummel you with both blows and viscous issue!

"Now hang on a minute Damone, you got it all wrong—let me explain before you start breaking out the viscous issue, okay pal? See, you just said a minute ago about how your music should be played and conducted if we might consider performing or directing with other..."

"Orchestras," said Tommy. Johnny continued:

"Yeah, other orchestras. Now, we can't talk about this stuff like you can, Damone. See, we're just amateurs, you know? Idiots compared to you. Right guys?"

My brothers murmured assent.

"Yeah, so we're like idiots, but when we heard that concert, we thought how great it would be to make music, and since you're our brother and everything, and František and mom are good players too, well, we got excited and we wanted to make music too. You know. Like you. Well, not *like like* you, because you're a real composer and everything like, uh..."

"Mozart," said Tommy.

"Right, like him. We need to pick up on the terminology and shit, but you understand what I'm saying? You know, if you're willing, we'd like to spend some time with you and learn some of your songs."

"Well...perhaps I can accept this, perhaps even endorse and aid you, but what of this drivel of Dee Dee's about manipulating my concepts, these vile suggestions that they might somehow be reduced to cannon fodder in order to expand that contemptible little footnote to music known as rock and roll? What of that? Do you think me deaf, perhaps, or imbecilic?"

"Come on. Look, do you really think Dee Dee could actually do any part of what you do? Seriously? It's so out of the question, that I'm actually quite shocked, Damone. I'm very disappointed in you, actually. Very disappointed."

"Disappointed?"

"Disappointed. You're a Ramone, Damone, a part of this family, and with that comes a certain responsibility, a certain pride in being secure about whatever it is you do, you know? I mean come on, look at him...yeah, he gets all the chicks, that's what *he* does, but a musician? You know what, I'm not even going to waste my time explaining this, because if you don't get it, well...maybe Szilarda was shtupping the milk man."

I looked from Dee Dee to Johnny as I ruminated on these professedly sensible assertions. Nonetheless, even while I allowed their mellifluous logic to seduce me, I retained some doubt. In hindsight, I should have apportioned this doubt to an impregnable vault where I could have cultivated it until it blossomed into the sorely needed saving grace that never materialized. Instead, I surrendered to the lowest form of submission by attaching belief to flattery; because of Johnny's references to my kingly potency, I relented and embraced their lies. I not only placed my head in the guillotine, but I also provided the timber and labor to build it.

"Okay, now we've gone and wasted Damone's precious time," said Johnny. "That means we have to reschedule so he can get back to composing, right Damone? Damone has a very special brain, and it needs plenty of alone-time. Damone, we're going to sea shortly and you're not going to be composing for a long time, except what you can work on in your bunk. This is going to be a long voyage because we need to catch up. Every dealer in the city thinks we're out of the game for good this time, so we need to make an impact. I'm not supposed to say anything, but because I'm a nice guy, I'll tell you this—brush up on your Spanish. Yeah, we've got Montez, but with what he's been up to lately the only thing he'll be using that skill for is...you know. So it's mainly up to us to bring the blizzard back to New York, got it? Good. Now let's clear out so the artist here can work. Damone, I think it would be great if you composed a special thing in honor of the voyage, sort of an ocean thing, nothing long, but maybe another one of those...what is each song called?"

"Quartet," I said.

"Right. Write one, and before we set sail you'll perform it. Sound good?"

Woe unto me, but it did. His feigned interest drew me into a whirlwind of joyous artistic frenzy punctuated by the most numerous and delicately extracted odes to womanhood I had ever deigned to coax forth, and this buoyant mood is evident throughout *Sixteen Times, Twenty-Four Hours, Only a Little Blood.*

Of course this spritely tone poem that melded the lightness of my early quartets with the masterful execution of the middle quartets and the cerebral sprawl of the late quartets was not the sea-homage I thought it, but rather the requiem for my future's total death. In a certain respect it did represent my finest expression of musical irony, as its dancing, playful tones served as the Brandenburg Gate to the personal hell I continue to burn in to this day, the hell where I will likely perish barring a miraculous reversal that rides on the unlikely and absurdly ironic hope that the sewing machines might save me once again.

CHAPTER X.

WHAT I HEARD IN THE GARBAGE CAN.

In the days after the fateful meeting that doomed me, it was altogether evident that Johnny's words indeed portended an incredibly long voyage, likely the longest we had ever undertaken. The unfortunate journey to Bermuda had hitherto been our longest, but because that particular voyage was more of a spontaneous expression of insanity on Montez's part than an official excursion, I was loath to consider it an achievement; no, it was in fact a ridiculous accident characterized less by outstanding seamanship and more by the voyage's crowning moment when we all urinated in a bucket and Danny attempted to purify the contents by creating a still with bunson burners and a long tube of plastic bags held together with masking tape. Needless to say, when we finally managed to hail a passing yacht, we all had apparently reached silent agreement that we would use a different example to define our suffering to our rescuers, choosing to simply tell them we had run out of fresh water two days earlier.

This time our front room was filled with the resilient provisions of the sea: potted meat, multifarious jerkies, canned hams, bottles of lime juice, two milk crates full of pornographic magazines including rare under-the-counter editions, and so much fresh water that it seemed we might be attempting the first trip to Mars. Johnny even authorized a rum ration; however scantily apportioned this classic seafarer's luxury would be, it nonetheless indicated a wise loosening of discipline in order to keep our spirits up during the long voyage. This was especially important when none of us except the inner circle of Johnny, Montez, and Danny knew our final destination; the rest of us would have to take it on faith that our masters' course would be wisely executed and bounteously returned.

The *Havana Banana* was loaded nocturnally in a secret berth known only to the inner-circle. We loaded Danny's giant truck—no mean feat, considering its height—and he'd roar off down the beach toward Breezy Point with his headlights off.

After three nights of loading, Danny whispered into Montez's ear. Montez—wearing sunglasses under the night sky—nodded slowly to Johnny, and Johnny told the rest of us that it was done.

We sat on crates in the truck bed. As Danny eased the truck over the dunes, I experienced an overblown sentimental longing for home as I watched František, silhouetted by the porch light, waving between the stepladders we had used to load the truck, two to his left, two to his right.

His childish waving. He turned around and picked up all four ladders at once. His bobbing walk toward our house faded into the grays and blacks of night and distance. I allowed two tears, confident nobody would notice in the windy darkness.

We sped down the beach. A couple raindrops hit me in the back of the neck—under a cloudless, star-filled sky. I turned and looked at my brothers. They also were ensnared in the moment's eerie nostalgia for a past that didn't exist yet. We looked at each other, not embarrassed, but somehow baffled and unified. Johnny looked away and stared beyond the cab over the dark beach as if he was providing extra eyes for Danny so he wouldn't roll over some ancient wastrel sleeping off the bitterness of a lost life.

But then Johnny lifted his arm and drew it slowly across his face, just like the rest of us had. We all turned toward each other at once, for we had all been watching the back of Johnny's head and his long brown hair blowing behind him, searching for any old something to grab on to, even if it was a pure, reliably Johnny reprimand for our bizarre sissified fit. Seeing that gesture from

Johnny somehow made us all feel as if the Earth was not quite as solid beneath us as it had been only minutes before.

I looked at the pared-down crew: Tommy, Johnny, Joey, Marky, Mickey, Tommy. Danny Fields driving, Montez by his side. The truck roared, the black waves crashed. Danny drove on the water's edge because the wet sand was harder and the breaking waves would wash away our tracks. Salty spray from the tires blew over us, glazing our jackets with seawater. We wore the Ramones uniform: jeans, sneakers, t-shirts, biker jackets. Tommy and Joey wore sunglasses in the dark, just like Montez.

We developed our look in the early '60s, but with greaser hairdos. As the decade progressed we grew our hair. By the summer of 1970, if you had been sitting in the dunes and Danny's truck roared past, you'd have seen the Ramones as you know them. Yes, these were the strangers—my own brothers—that mercilessly thrashed my life until nothing was left but a contemptible anti-structure that made a crushed cockroach appear to have a bright future by comparison, but nonetheless: to have been one of them, walking with them, sailing the seas with them, marching through New York's streets with them—was an experience unrivalled.

It's impossible to explain the electricity, the manic power, that came over us during those rare moments when we were in accord, our fiery natures acting as a momentary bond rather than the source of constant instability. As a family, we were like a chaotic element that not even the most brilliant chemist could keep together for more than a moment, but when that moment was achieved, the element that emerged blazed with magical radiation. From that wellspring came the indefinable something—the magic it—that put us heads above the rest, whether at sea or on a common Saturday when we'd suit up, hit the city, and command every sidewalk, everyone instinctively stepping aside knowing instantly that we were not to be fucked with.

Although I had been paying attention to the night's mysterious qualities instead of our progress, I was fairly sure we had crossed the Rockaways and backtracked along the opposite shore, the one that faced New York instead of the Atlantic. Danny drove slowly now. This was the final, wary phase where we watched like hawks and said nothing.

Danny looped around to a filthy beach near the Marine Parkway Bridge. We had passed our own house on the opposite side of the long slender island. I knew this beach—known as Bottle Beach or Garbage Beach, it had been an old city dump. All of us had spent hours there with Joey, digging through the ancient bottles and cans searching for small, white medicine jars made by the Cleveland Company at the turn of the century; they were the only jars Joey would use to store pills or lubricant. He still used the original two he initially found, but he was worried about breaking them, so he was constantly trying to increase his supply—he now had over a hundred. Nonetheless, he continued to ask us to help him dig for more because no matter how many he had, he never felt it was enough.

The ship was moored in a nearby residential marina. I was concerned because the water there didn't seem deep enough for the *Banana*. When we got there, Danny drove his massive truck on to the wooden dock as if he was driving that herd of elephants across the Brooklyn Bridge to reassure a doubtful public. In this case, I was that doubtful public, and despite Danny's confident bluster, I still cringed as the absurd truck vibrated across the decrepit planks.

Danny stopped next to our boat. We hopped out and got to work. There were two people waiting on the dock that helped with logistics but never came to sea, Billy "The Dwarf" Lipsby and Big Japan. The Dwarf was not an official midget, but he was close—he was a stout little powerhouse with fire-hydrant legs and arms absurdly similar to Popeye's—nobody could load a ship faster than The Dwarf. Big Japan was a dumb grinning slob, a bronze giant with beady green eyes and a brown mullet. Danny said he got the name Big Japan in Haifa when he won a half-marathon in death-valley like conditions—the race was nearly called, but Big Japan said if he was willing to run, what was everyone else's excuse? More than half the runners collapsed, but Big Japan kept plowing along, going around a small 440-yard track over fifty times. What winning that race had to do with a conceptually large Japan, I can't explain.

We finished loading. Danny reversed the truck down the dock at a ridiculous speed. He parked sloppily and sauntered back to the boat. Johnny shouted orders. We prepared to cast off. When Montez turned over the *Havana Banana*'s massive old engine and I heard the gurgles and roars and felt the vibrations, I experienced that old familiar thrill: the Ramones were setting sail.

Montez eased the boat toward open water while Joey leaned over the bowsprit as a second line of defense against obstructions. The rest of us carried out Johnny's orders with military precision— no hesitations, no questions, no bumbling collisions. It wasn't long before we rounded Breezy Point Tip and sailed into the high seas. Once we were surrounded by the black raging sheet that led all the way to Great Britain, my earlier sentimentality was washed away, replaced with confident exuberance. The voyage would be raw and wild and the spoils would be replete: hills of coke in the *Banana*'s hold that would rival the Namibian dunes.

I could tell from the angle of the shore's retreat that we were heading directly west. I couldn't understand this, because I had assumed Johnny's hints about Spanish had referred to a Central or South American port of call, perhaps even a Cuban one. Barcelona, however, was not a possibility I would have considered, and I began to fret that Montez had again gone mad, and he was taking us on a doomed voyage to Davy Jones' Locker.

After several hours however, Montez cut the motor. The sea was black and choppy; the *Banana* tossed and rocked in cold misty darkness. The sea was just high enough to suggest that cutting the motor might not be such a great idea if we wanted to keep the bow facing the waves; nonetheless, the ancient *Banana* seemed to be handling itself better than expected in the slapping, tumultuous waters.

"Okay, we drift with the lights off until you hear otherwise. Anyone smokes on deck, fist to face. Damone, since you've been such a royal fuckstick, you get first watch. I want you on deck until just after sunrise, and if I catch you lying down or jerking off, you'll regret it. We heard your bullshit, now it's time to pay to the piper," Johnny said.

I was livid. Since I had been so long away from sea, they should have eased me back into a seafarer's labors by going easy on me, perhaps by allowing me to take a more modest first watch of half an hour or so, but remembering the ill-fated deal I had made with Johnny, I bit my lip. They retired below decks. Cold spray blasted into my face. I prayed that their bunks would collapse or that Joey or Mickey would vomit on those sleeping below them.

I tightened my slicker's hood and steadied myself on the foredeck as the seas raged around me. Considering the provisions we loaded, it seemed unlikely that we were already waiting to rendezvous, but I supposed it was possible. Perhaps our voyage would be long but local, a series of small purchases close to home. In any event, I was standing on deck, freezing, with the entire night ahead of me.

I degenerated into simmering fury. Of course Johnny knew full well that I never wore a timepiece, so to tell me I was on watch until just after dawn meant that I'd have no way of measuring the tedium. My ever-increasing boredom would surely make the miserable night go on for several hundred eternities, each one longer than the next. Such was the price of artistic expression in a dictatorship.

In order to calm my rage and perhaps because of it, I drifted into a fog of erotic visions, imagining the *Banana* being received by hoards of half-nude people on some tropical shore where brightly colored birds would stimulate my senses; there'd be endless jungles of giant-leaved plants that I could crouch beneath, and in their verdant shadows I would express union with the underbrush.

My arousal was becoming distracting. I grew concerned that what had begun as a way to kill time during a dull watch had taken precedence over the duty's required vigilance. But I had crossed the Rubicon; to return to the clear, rational thoughts of the post-orgasmic self whilst trapped in a barbaric pre-orgasmic condition was obviously impossible; my only options were to either jump into the freezing black sea, or to swiftly relieve myself of the pent up torrents.

But to be caught on watch removing the impediment would be ruinous; to have any one of my brothers be greeted by the sight of me on the foredeck writhing around on my back in throes of delight while my right hand illustrated a sassy independence of spirit would end with me being kicked to a pulp, admittedly a third avenue by which I could rid myself of the drive toward the self, but not one that particularly appealed to me.

I retreated to the poop deck. A trash drum stood just outside the cabin—this early in the voyage it contained little, leaving ample room for a flexible, desperate man. I eased one leg in and then the other on top of the banana peels and soda cans. I pulled down my pants and did my best Thurman Munson, disappearing neatly into the big drum. In this semi-privacy, lurching about at sea, I embarked on a swift employment with the hope getting it done and returning to my post before anyone noticed my absence.

Despite the circumstances however, it was impossible not to drift a little, to conjure luscious details and generally slow the pace. This was not an irresponsible, voluntary decision, mind you; the stroking caused waves of involuntary hypnotic thoughts that barricaded reason behind a wall of flesh and motion.

Such was the contrast between this ecstasy and the drudgery of watch that I suppose I lost track of time. The unfortunate spell was broken by a jolt to my hiding place and the sound of voices. Oh, loathsome dread! It was hopeless. I waited like a frozen maggot for a crushing rain of blows.

But it did not come. I heard Johnny's voice from below the can, and I realized with great relief that he had sat down on deck and had leaned back on the can. His words were clear, for the sea's turbulence was diminishing.

"I knew he wouldn't be out here."

"Want me to find him?" asked Dee Dee.

"Forget it. We'll deal with it tomorrow. Anyway, who cares now, ya know?"

"Right," replied Dee Dee.

"So when's it going down?" asked Marky.

"Sooner than you think, but don't worry about it. All in good time."

"I don't know, it's kinda mean," said Joey.

"Mean? What's mean is letting the rest of us bust our asses while he jacks off."

Considering my present endeavor, it was impossible not to allow that they were perhaps speaking of me—I nearly burst from the can in fury at the insinuation; to think, the very people for whom I had performed not only my Cycle, but also the sea-themed tone poem prior to our voyage were now speaking of me disparagingly, as if their efforts were somehow of a higher order than the incredibly difficult work I had been engaged in concurrently. What Johnny said next however both relieved and puzzled me.

"Robinson's in for it. That fuck is getting taught a lesson. Joey, you're a good guy and all, but trust me—you'll thank me for this in the long run. We gotta move on, and me and Danny have put a lot of thought into exactly how it's going down. You'll see the good sense over time, and you'll forget all about that madhouse."

I felt better knowing it was not me they had been speaking of, but I realized that while I was preoccupied with composing I had missed a great deal of street action and family life; my brothers had new acquaintances and dilemmas that I knew nothing about. Whoever this Robinson was for instance, he had clearly done something to piss off Johnny who was now calling on the full force of the Ramones to exact revenge. I swelled with pride in the depths of the can, deciding that I would earn some favor with Johnny tomorrow by volunteering to help dispense with this Robinson person, especially if I couldn't concoct an explanation for why I'd abandoned my post.

"Joey, can you throw this out since you're up?" asked John. I was horrified—Joey was not the type to throw out trash basketball-style. I prepared myself for discovery and brutality.

"Hey, what the fuck asshole? You know how I feel about that," Johnny said.

"Who cares, like one fucking can is gonna make a difference in the fucking ocean," Dee Dee replied. I relaxed.

The drum shook as Johnny stood up.

"Dee Dee, you gotta stay out here since Damone's gone and because you throw shit into my ocean. Mickey will relieve you in two hours."

I swiftly saw through my original purpose; I midwifed the conclusion by picturing myself at an erotic shine stand where a nude woman polished the underside of my pleasure with a snapping shine rag made of semi-fermented banana peels. After regaining my composure, I eased myself up until just my eyes were peaking over the drum's lip. Dee Dee was leaning over the stern watching the water. I exited the can with feline stealth, and then I stood astride the cabin as if I was just arriving from the foredeck.

"Dee Dee? What are you doing up, man?"

"Damone, where the fuck were you? Johnny's gonna kill you for leaving your watch."

"Who left? I was on the foredeck. Right, as if I'd abandon my post."

"Well, if you're out here then I'm gonna crash. You better not disappear again, man."

"Come on, just tell Johnny I was around the whole time, okay? Remember, technically Johnny ordered *you* to be on watch now, so you're welcome."

"Whatever, Damone. You better watch it—Johnny's down on you. See you in the morning."

I all but forgot the strange conversation from the previous night when I woke up and went to breakfast, which was lunch for my brothers and for Danny. Montez lunched alone in the bridge.

When I entered the small green kitchen, my brothers were already gathered around the table, stuffed into benches and chairs. Mickey stood over the stove, flipping sizzling pink slices of ham in a skillet.

"Hey, look who's here," said Johnny. "Damone has decided to grace us with his presence. Good timing—we were just about to enjoy some rum and ham. Have a seat, bro. Come on, you can fit next to me."

The smell of frying ham, coffee, and their jovial faces restored my cheer and vigor. Mickey put down a steaming mug in front of me. He turned around and dumped ham on a plate.

He brought it over. I tried to take the plate, but the handoff went awry, knocking my coffee to the floor. As the coffee spread beneath me, Danny said:

"Handsomely done, my lad! And handsome is as handsome did it, too!"

I smiled broadly while grabbing napkins to clean up the mess. Although this flattering ball-breaking was welcome, I wondered at Tommy's and Johnny's laughter; it seemed disproportionate, and it was directed at Danny's friendly mockery rather than the spill itself. Unsure of my standing, I decided against saying anything that might be perceived as an enraged demand for an explanation. I focused on wiping up the coffee and sexual thoughts rooted in the equine.

After breakfast I went on deck. I was surprised to see familiar land—we were anchored just off Silver Point. This made no sense; we were only a short cruise east from our starting point, and furthermore we were near the shore in a way that contradicted last night's seemingly committed foray into the open sea. Nonetheless, I didn't question it since I would get no answers.

Johnny called us to order twenty minutes later and told us to raise anchor and set sail. Unfortunately, the *Banana's* capstan motor no longer functioned, so when we raised anchor we had to manually slave at the capstan bars like the crew of an 18th century English frigate. Needless to say, this was not my favorite part of being at sea. We made it slightly better by singing as we pushed, favoring *Fifteen Men on the Dead Man's Chest* or a rousing version of *The Man From Nantucket* for which Dee Dee had composed a sea shanty melody. Manning the capstan bars gave birth to the "Gabba Gabba" chant, although we still were faithful to the original "Gooble Gobble" at that time.

As we gathered around the bars, Dee Dee said, "Hey Damone, you pick what we sing, okay? Whatever you want."

I was pleased; normally only Dee Dee or Johnny got to choose sea shanties. I chose *With My Little Stick of Blackpool Rock*, my overall favorite, although it was closely followed by *The Ying Tong Song*. In the case of the latter, Tommy had offhandedly mentioned it one time as a joke, the implicit suggestion being that we would never be able to properly do the song. Johnny's reaction was to hound us, berate us, and scream at us for weeks until we could do a shockingly accurate rendition. He made it his dictatorial mission; he wouldn't even allow us to have casual conversations with each other until we had mastered the song. He would turn on our bedroom lights in the middle of the night, throw buckets of cold water on us, and make us stand at attention and perform our parts over and over until they were pounded into our brains.

For Johnny, Tommy's suggestion of limits was an unacceptable degradation of the Ramone name; in his mind, it was a name that could only be associated with discipline and attention to detail. As a thank you from the rest of us for setting those events in motion, we stuffed socks with gravel and put on ski masks, and then we snuck into Tommy's room and beat him mercilessly. When he'd had enough, Dee Dee said, "No more song suggestions...ever!" and we retreated to our respective quarters. Admittedly, the ski masks were meant to lend a certain gravitas more than to effectively disguise our identities.

I must give credit where credit is due here, and acknowledge that it was Johnny's incredibly disciplined approach and uncanny ability to organize my brothers into a tight unit that made it possible for them to successfully steal my music. Although they didn't create it, getting human players to mimic the mechanized perfection of my Quartet Cycle was their own achievement. Without Johnny's leadership and without my brothers' ostensibly contradictory ability to close ranks along Apollonian lines, they would never have pulled off their crimes. I say *ostensibly*, because as a Ramone I innately understand the mysterious interplay between the Apollonian and Dionysian elements within the Ramones, the magic interplay that organized the family's collective creative urge and sent it spewing forth into the world.

We roared as we pushed the capstan. I gave it my all; normally I'd just pretend to push and let the others do the work. We got the anchor up and took five. Johnny addressed us:

"Good work, guys. Listen up, we're sailing into the islands for a special mission. We're a little top-heavy in certain respects, and we also want to create an emergency store of drugs and cash on one of the islands. Montez and Mickey will stay on board, the rest of us will take the skiff to shore."

We returned to our posts. Montez guided us into Jamaica Bay. I was pleased we were going ashore, although I had some concerns about how much digging would be involved in hiding the stash. Nonetheless, I was flattered I had been chosen to go.

Montez cut the motor just off the coast of Ruffle Bar Island. We dropped anchor. We loaded tools and a sea chest into the boat and lowered it into the water. Johnny took the oars, guiding us toward Ruffle Bar with swift, powerful strokes.

The boat scraped onto the sandy shore. Tommy leapt from the bow. Dee Dee tossed him the rope and then he jumped out to help. After unloading the skiff, we pulled it fully onto shore. Oddly, the murky coast was littered with coconuts as if Ruffle Bar was a tropical paradise instead of a marshy island near New York City.

Johnny led us into the island's interior. We marched single file through tall grass. We entered a forest. Johnny and Dee Dee hacked branches with machetes as we marched. Danny Fields followed last with the treasure chest on his back, having refused all offers of help.

We reached a small clearing. Johnny distributed shovels and ordered us to dig. Danny Fields was significantly better endowed for digging than the next best digger, which was certainly Johnny. But Johnny had to step aside as Danny essentially dug half the requisite hole by himself while the rest of us slaved away on the other half.

The digging was miserable toil and the woefully short breaks Johnny sparingly doled out were useless. I began to think of less and less until I was reduced to a reptilian state where the hole was the goal and the Earth was standing between me and it. An eternal condemnation later, the hole was dug. We leaned heavily on our shovels and gasped.

"Not bad, guys," said Johnny. "Let's take ten and have a drink before we bury the chest. You deserve it."

To my surprise Johnny removed several bottles of white wine from his pack and passed them to Danny who swiftly opened them one after the other with his Swiss Army knife's corkscrew.

"Damone, I'm impressed," said Johnny. "You don't dig for shit, but you put your heart into it. Drink up—that bottle is yours alone. Perseverance like that, well—it can come in handy. In any number of tough situations."

I drank deeply while the others laughed, I think rather impressed at the incredible rate of speed with which I demolished the bottle's contents. When it was gone my thirst was sated and reality's cold hard edges were gently pulled out of focus.

"Okay guys, all we gotta to do now is lower this thing in—here, use the ropes—fill it in, cover it up, and we're done. Then we drink and relax. We aren't sailing anywhere tonight. I'm thinking we camp out here and enjoy dry land when we can—we're going to be in the *Banana* for a long long time."

We buried the chest, carefully covering the spot with a thick layer of the rotting foliage that characterized the ground around it. It looked like we had never been there. We threw the tools over our shoulders and headed back to the shore.

When we emerged from a tall copse of reeds onto Ruffle Bar's sandy shoreline, I dropped my shovel and made unusual sounds: there was a strange tug anchored alongside the *Havana Banana*. I moved not.

"Damone, pick up the shovel. You worried about that boat? Don't be. We know them, goofball," Johnny said.

"How's that exactly?"

"Not your business, Damone. Just relax, everything is fine."

Thus reassured, I picked up my shovel and followed the others to the water's edge. We set down our things and dragged the skiff further onto land. Johnny told us to make a firepit while he and Danny prepped thick veal chops, pasta, and a light tricolore salad. The rest of us gathered kindling, birch bark, and driftwood. Soon we were sitting around a crackling fire enjoying more wine, shots of rum, and the prospect of roasting marshmallows and telling tales under the stars.

As the flames diminished and the embers grew thick, we eased our whittled sticks into hot red crevices until the fluffy white marshmallows impaled on their tips were brown and crispy. The stars emerged. The sea gently lapped the dark shore. We passed the rum and ate the marshmallows.

To my delight, Danny announced that he had yet another Mad Mathilda story. Mad Mathilda was Danny's first wife, a vulgar woman of poor disposition with whom he spent four years, years spent mainly in horrific domestic disputes—the police visited them nightly in their trailer park outside Mesa, Arizona. At the time, Danny was working as a tattoo artist and tire shop manager, and his wife—rumored to be a reformed lady of the night—spent her days drinking Southern Comfort and carrying on, and, according to Danny, occasionally falling into recidivism when she needed booze money.

I took a pull of rum and stretched out in front of the fire. I closed my eyes as Danny set up the story: him wandering into the desert one night with his shotgun to hunt wild coyotes, his wife alone in the trailer without anything to drink. The fire occasionally popped over its steady low crackle. Small waves whispered up and down the length of the shore. Danny's voice, my brothers' laughter. I surrendered to blissful oblivion.

Part III.

THE MAN OF THE ISLAND.

CHAPTER XI.

MAROONED.

I opened my eyes in the pre-dawn chill. The fire was long out, and the wind had kicked up: the waves were large and loud. My head was pounding. I sat up and rubbed my eyes. While I slept off the previous night's revelries, waves had been crashing over my prone form.

Danny and my brothers were gone. Their blankets and the cooking gear were still there. There were still a few marshmallows left in the bag; a nightmarish horseshoe crab was investigating the sugary blobs. A series of normal assumptions went through my mind: they had gone on an early morning constitutional in the interior, perhaps to hunt wild fowl; they had returned to the boat for more supplies and would pick me up shortly; they were playing a typical Ramones prank, yet again, on good old Damone.

But even as I half-heartedly entertained these soothing notions, the dark truth was already known to me on a visceral level, a level that was painfully aware of what Providence had in store for me before I had even reinstalled my identity on that fateful morning. But if there were any last vestiges of denial still gasping for life, the sight of the *Havana Banana* exterminated them with crude finality: the old ship had been scuttled.

It was near shore, sunk in shallow water. The gunwales were still well above sea level, but the waves exploding skyward as they broke against the ship foretold her fate: the *Havana* would never sail the high seas again. The battering waves and shifting sands would demolish and consume her aged remains. The new tug that had anchored next to the *Havana* was nowhere to be seen. There was nothing on the grey horizon except screaming gulls.

I attempted to convince myself that I had merely been overlooked in a hasty pre-dawn departure, and my brothers would soon notice my absence and would either retrieve me or send Big Japan to do it. On the other hand, I was just across the water from the Rockaways and Brooklyn was visible from Ruffle Bar's western coast; I could easily hail a passing vessel and request a ride back to the mainland. If my brothers had forgotten me, I would show them—when they returned to Ruffle Bar, I would be gone. If they had marooned me out of malice, I would return home and besmirch every utensil in every conceivable manner prior to their return. In fact, both scenarios recommended a replete besmirching.

I decided to hail a ship from the southern coast where the likely point of emanation would be either Broad Channel or the Rockaways themselves. In the case of the latter, I could be home in a matter of hours; less if I had enough change for the bus. I stripped naked and headed to the shore.

I stood near the water and waited. A motorboat approached from the direction of Broad Channel. I spun my jeans in one hand and my t-shirt in the other in a swift paddle-wheel motion while I leapt up and down and screamed. Indeed, the boat seemed to adjust its course in deference to my display. Nonetheless, I intensified my efforts to ensure my rescue.

The boat paralleled Ruffle Bar's coast. The driver decelerated. I could see the passengers now, an older couple and some kids. My rescue was imminent.

I threw myself backwards like a stuntman in a Western who has taken one firmly to the jaw, but unlike that unfortunate cowboy, my backfall was executed out of sheer exuberance. While on my back, I clapped my feet with joy as an homage to my rescuers, but only for a moment. When I felt the gesture had run its course, I stood up. I placed my palms a foot from each ear, and then I treated my torso as if it were a large, unwieldy lever, leaning right and left, all while maintaining the position of my hands as if they were supporting a dense metal bar that had been driven through my head via the ears.

The people on the boat reacted oddly, as if they understood not one bit of my gesture and could infer none of the obvious facts from the context. The man's expression illustrated pure dislike for a total stranger, which perhaps was all I needed to know, and his wife expressed open-mouthed awe, as if she had never seen an acrobatic feat before. The children on the other hand—a lad of 12 or so and two younger girls—laughed as if I was a clown. At any rate, none of their reactions remotely corresponded with empirical reality; apparently Broad Channel was finally getting its share of immigrants too. The boat's motor roared, and the vessel soared away from Ruffle Bar.

Although my second option didn't offer as direct a route, it would likely provide faster transit to the mainland. Ruffle Bar's western coast faces Floyd Bennett Field; we had always assiduously steered clear of that area because a police station that conducted sea and air patrols was based there. Now I hoped that the police presence would lead to swifter deliverance. I resumed my display on the western shore, hoping to attract attention and dry my clothing in the process.

No sooner had I raised my arms when I heard a boat, but it emanated from whence I came rather than from Floyd Bennett; however, it was indeed a police boat as the flashing blue lights clearly indicated. Perhaps I had misjudged the passing family after all, and they had merely been unequipped for a salvage operation of this scope. Granted, I was not infirm, but as they rightly presumed, my return to civilization would undoubtedly require a chaplain's council in addition to a dispassionate medical team to witness what was likely to be an especially dangerous session of purgative procedures; surely the NYPD were far better prepared to address such logistics.

The police boat cut its motor. Three smirking officers stared at me. None of them spoke. When I yelled, "Please help me!" they nearly laughed. A large, bluebearded officer responded:

"Yeah, we'll help you—by giving you our special *tip of the day*, courtesy of the New York Police Department: get the fuck off this island, pal—you're trespassing."

"But esteemed officer, I am not here of my own volition; I have been abandoned on these Godforsaken shores by my cretinous brothers. I am the victim of a childish prank!"

"You're going to be the victim of a childish nightstick if you don't put some clothes on—we already got a complaint, but you're welcome: we're gonna assume you're drying your clothes. Second, you're trespassing—get off the island immediately."

"By what conveyance? Granting the occasional moment of spiritual rapture, walking on water is not yet my forte. I implore you, take me to shore in your boat! I shall be a most humble and grateful stowaway."

"Does this boat look yellow to you? We're not a taxi service. We'll be back in an hour, and if you're still on this island you're getting a ticket. Get off the fucking island, you're trespassing. Swim if you have to, looks like you're already blowing up a flotation device. Christ, can't escape the fucking city, not even out here."

Indeed, with rage came turgidity, a turgidity I slapped viciously from right to left, a gesture which only extraordinarily cynical police officers would find amusing, for as it was, the officers laughed loudly at my rebellious demonstration.

"Oh, this provides delight? Then enjoy some more!"

I struck a Sumo pose while my wand thrashed to and fro between my merciless hands. But rather than enrage and humiliate the officers, they merely laughed and sped from the island. If that lot was representative of the state of the city's police, large scale reform was definitely in order, and the emergence of Frank Serpico a few years later was nothing if not belated.

Over the next forty minutes, no boat came close enough for me to hail. I took cover in the reeds to hide from the NYPD. Sure enough, about half an hour later the same police boat approached from Brooklyn. When it reached Ruffle Bar it cruised the island's perimeter while I simply waited it out. Although I could not see whither they went, it seemed to be toward the Rockaways.

I spent two more hours observing the sea and hailing close-at-hand boats. My attempts were fruitless except for one sailboat piloted by two young women that passed by the island; when they saw me leaping about on shore, they tacked toward open water rather than investigate further despite my cries for help. That Kew Gardens thing no longer struck me as such an aberration.

Although I dislike pandering to organized religion, I decided that the following day I would hail ships dressed. It was a calculated risk; I would lose my semaphore flags and the eye-catching characteristics seemingly inherent in nudity; I noticed the effects were especially pronounced on islands. Nonetheless, I also recognized that naturism was not to everyone's taste, even when demanded by survival.

I spent the rest of the day wandering the island's interior in search of a more suitable place to spend the night, as the shore was now out of the question with the police hovering about. I needed a hidden place where I could have a small fire in a crevasse deep enough to obscure it while I warmed myself. I also wanted to board the *Banana* to see if I could salvage anything to make my stay more comfortable. I needed to act: the *Banana's* carcass seemed none too sturdy, and the police might come around to investigate the wreck, although they'd likely assume our boat was an ancient shipwreck dredged up by shifting currents rather than a recently seaworthy craft.

I wandered among the reeds, trees, and clearings. Birds sang and beasts careened in the underbrush. The island's interior was devoid of the urban detritus that littered the coast; the underbrush was pristine and the air was fresh. As I wandered, my disposition improved greatly, and I began to revisualize this horrible event in a positive light: I was alone—my brothers could not brutalize me; it was quiet—I could hear the music in my head with greater clarity; I was isolated and naked—I could masturbate with impunity. Perhaps, I thought, Providence had forced this situation upon me so that I might discover utility within.

I certainly had time to ponder what could have motivated this tomfoolery if it was not in fact a typical Ramones prank. I believed that it was; nonetheless, I thought it prudent to consider alternatives. It never occurred to me that my abandonment had anything to do with my music; rather, my first suspicion was that they resented my absence from the *Banana* during the composing of *CWDSL*; I considered them too dense to distinguish between composing a great work or any other activity; they could only judge from the standpoint of their limited worldviews.

It did occur to me then that Danny Fields had shown an inordinate interest in certain experiments I had been conducting over the course of several voyages when time allowed; namely, attempting to isolate lecithin from soya beans. In particular, he seemed especially focused on my attempts to tinker with hydrolysis and fractionation; after a few days during which Danny took detailed notes which he claimed were merely the scratchings of a disinterested hobbyist, I stopped my work because Johnny cracked down on the experimentation, claiming that I was wasting alcohol. My objective was to prove a theory I had about giving man the ability to hold sway over his own semen volume, and as I wandered around Ruffle Bar I didn't discount the possibility that they—using Danny's notes—were planning on taking credit for the science. When their true aim was ultimately revealed, I completely forgot about this incident. By the time I saw lecithin readily available in any deli or drug store, and further was informed of its semen-inducing properties, I was so apathetic to treachery that I simply made a note of it. Seeing my findings repeated and further elucidated by a large food corporation that I can't name for legal reasons is immaterial; rather, I'd like the event to stand as yet another example of the duplicity I have suffered. Perhaps it will help those you who are seeking to blame the victim by discovering a "pattern" in the cruel escapades to which I have so often succumbed.

Night descended on Ruffle Bar. I could now wander the coast freely. I returned to the shore near the wreck of the *Banana* to consider a salvage strategy; perhaps useful stores had been left behind. I waded toward the half-sunk boat.

The sea bottom was mucky and alarmingly deep like movie quicksand; I worried that it might suck me under and I'd be forever lost along with the *Banana*'s remains. I needed to work quickly; if the *Banana* were on similar ground, the Earth itself would consume it in a matter of days or even hours.

I got on my belly and glided across the muck until the water became deep enough to doggy paddle. I boarded the *Banana* via a rope hanging from the bow. I walked across the deck and descended into the hold.

There was already substantial water in the ship; I had to hurry and retrieve what I could. The good news was that it looked as if my brothers had simply abandoned ship without taking any of the provisions we had loaded in anticipation of a long voyage. If anything, it looked like they had moved some of the stores from the hold to the kitchen and onto the deck, as if they had planned on taking it but then something happened that forced a hasty exit.

Transporting the provisions to shore presented a challenge, however Providence meant for me to acquire them: the skiff was back, neatly secured in its moorings. For a moment I considered leaving the stores and taking just a few days worth of water, as I could use the skiff to reach Brooklyn at my leisure. But the deprivations that had barbarized my youth had instilled a sensible frugality: it would be foolish to waste good provisions, particularly the rum and spicy jerky. I proceeded to unload the stores in a logical order and put them in the skiff: water, liquor, pornographic magazines, food, canvas, rope, tools, clothing.

The work was terrible, but I managed to take seven boatloads from the *Banana* that I hid among the reeds. My final inventory indicated that I had retrieved everything worth retrieving. Of particular note was the incredibly large amount of fresh water we had on board in anticipation of sailing anywhere from Miami to Tierra del Fuego—this otherwise would have been my greatest concern. I crouched among the reeds and awarded myself for an endeavor well done, and then I fell asleep among the boxes and the foliage that hid them.

CHAPTER XII.

BIRTH OF A SYNDROME.

Male voices woke me in the night. The sea had become so calm that not even the soft lapping of miniature waves was audible. The voices from shore echoed across the water and among the still reeds.

I thought my brothers had returned, but as the voices continued I realized I was mistaken. The conversation was ornamented with the same moronic laughter I heard when a posse of varsity-jacket numbskulls was jamming my head into a toilet at one of Queen's esteemed institutions of higher learning. Ah, boyish laughter! Could there be a more regal expression of *élan vital* than the compensatory merriment of the poorly endowed, especially when heard while being suffocated by the stench of cum-stained, sweat-soaked football pads? I peered hopefully through the reeds.

Four boys were pulling a rowboat onto shore. Two of them looked like Neanderthals and were grunting far in excess of what was necessary to represent their efforts. They surely made similar sounds when they were "coached." The other two flouted my expectations. One was tall and thin, the other fat and short. They seemed pleasant and approachable. Furthermore, their boat was large and far more seaworthy than my skiff; although buoyant, the skiff did not fair well on big seas; even the short journey to Brooklyn was not without some degree of peril.

Nonetheless, I remained in my hiding place. The whispering reeds behind me contrasted jarringly with these boisterous representatives of the metropolis across the water; if I revealed myself, I would be swiftly returned to my notably unimpressive place in a hierarchy of primates governed by brute force and the willingness to be the loudest and most forceful proponent of a narrow idiotic position, whereas I was part of a hierarchy that did not exist yet among my own kind, a hierarchy in evolution's future where brilliance and merit sit at the top and stupidity sits at the bottom, even when that stupidity is encased in a powerful, vigorous body. No, in my empire true order would be installed, and vigorous bodies would move large objects as ordered by the decrepit intelligent; there would be no "big bosses" ordering about the Dagwoods of the world simply because God blessed them generously with height, weight, and fuckface.

In my energetic mental reordering of the world's hierarchical systems, I failed to notice that my body had its own corresponding response, a jerky charade flashing off the excess energies of my pounding mind as it raced along toward a more righteous future. When I tipped over into the underbrush and the sound of my jangling belt buckle mingled with the cracking of twigs, I was just as surprised as the four young interlopers on shore.

They had just opened beers and were talking and laughing during some collectively related anecdote that I had blotted out in favor of my own mental narrative. When I fell over, it was the abrupt cessation of their discussion that alerted me to just how precarious a situation this truly was, or at least how truly precarious it had become, since in all likelihood my current state would be grossly misinterpreted. Their first response would likely be based on exactly the sort of unsavory conclusion one would expect from young men well suited to be models for the sand-kicking beach bully in Charles Atlas dynamic tension advertisements. I scrambled to yank my pants up as one of them shouted, "What the fuck was that?"

"In the bushes," another responded. They dashed into the reeds. I charged into the interior. Crashing and grunting followed, accompanied by: "Look! It's a fucking sicko." I had not managed to completely raise my pants.

They were fast, but I knew the terrain: I steered them into a thorny bramble that required foreknowledge if one hoped to avoid bloody entanglement. A roar of phlegm-choked oaths rang out behind me.

I sprinted toward the marshiest portion of the island. I fled into a bed of reeds and dowel-like plants growing from viscous muck that resembled something several thousand giraffes might produce after eating at a cut-rate oyster bar. The muck reached my sternum as I waded in, choking and gasping in the stench of churned, eutrophic filth. I doubted my pursuers had the will to follow me into this vulgar sea; nonetheless I forged on, certain that capture would lead to a sticky end.

I snapped one of the dowel stalks that surrounded me and put it in my mouth. I closed my eyes and eased myself beneath the surface of the muck, using the stalk as a breathing tube. I became a swamp tuber, moving not and breathing as smoothly as I could after my evasive sprinting.

Was there partial biological devolution? Yes. Was there a rekindling of primordial fires? Perhaps. In any event, the days after I resurfaced were a blur of tearing around the island on all fours, bellowing at celestial bodies, and uninhibited extruding whatever the source. It all happened after an unknowable number hours and days spent beneath the swamp when I emerged alone into yet another black Ruffle Bar night, my tormentors long back in their cozy world of frat house gang rapes offset by the occasional coed gathering.

I returned to my former level of consciousness one bright morning on the shore: I was on my knees, arms raised toward the rising sun, my nude torso golden in the early light. I unleashed a final primordial howl across the sea, and then I resumed being a modern man with a coalesced identity. My foray into primitive consciousness was not devoid of fruit however; I emerged into a new, comfortable state that was based on an entirely different way of viewing my situation on Ruffle Bar. This new orientation was felt at that point, but not understood or defined. The events of the following days clarified its nature.

I spent my first day of contemporary consciousness in blissful languor, roaming the island enjoying the flora and fauna. Ships passed, but I took no interest in them, overwhelmed as I was by a low-key yet powerful contentment. I sang a duet with a Savannah Sparrow; I allowed a fly to sit upon my arm and bite my flesh; I sat in the moist sand near the shore absorbing the spray of the crashing waves; I attempted to find the island's absolute center; when I located this place, I squatted in the underbrush and hummed Brahms. By twilight, I was feeling a healthy tiredness that I hadn't felt in many years, a tiredness that was pure and directed toward an absolute sleep rather than the impure sleep of the exhausted troubled. I lay down on shore and looked at the stars until I drifted off.

I was woken in the night by voices of every sex. I lifted my head. A party had landed roughly twenty yards from where I lay. They were a jovial lot; holding cans of ale, smoking cigarettes, and smiling broadly at each other as they frolicked about. There were eight or ten of them, all in their teens. They were lackadaisically unloading camping equipment from the boat, more intent on drinking ale and shoving each other playfully.

I sat in the sand in the darkness beyond basking in their joviality. The warmth among them seemed like an extension of the campfire they were now building from paper and kindling. I watched them with deep pleasure from the shadows. It was impossible not to consider this common vignette of youth against the backdrop of having grown up in the Ramone household, a household so profuse in both its flaws and singularity that it overwhelmed all of us with its arcane demands. Speaking for myself, I never experienced the loose meaningless pleasures of the youths I now observed, and I doubted my brothers had either; however, I did not view the party before me with envy, and I did not look back on my past with bitterness or regret. Contrarily, my life and its chasms had been mollified by my time on Ruffle Bar, and I felt purged of envy and hostility in an overarching way.

The pleasurable reveries which contrasted so starkly with my entire life up to that point had created a fissure whereby my mind assumed that the beach party was a television show, a mere fiction, an idealized product of network writers designed to trick a flawed America into chasing unattainable perfection. Consequently, when one of the figures stared in my direction, it didn't occur to me that I might have been spotted because I understood that although I can see figures behind the television's glass, the figures inside can not in turn see me; hence the hypnotic appeal of this voyeuristic device. Of course there were exceptions; for example, Montez took us on "vacation" to Detroit to meet with a possible connection one year, and I had the pleasure of several Sunday conversations with the Episcopal minister Sir Graves Ghastly; however, these exceptions were few, and my inclination on Ruffle Bar's shore to simply stare back at what I perceived to be a fictitious figure was statistically reasonable.

But the figure spoke to me. He said, "You okay, guy? You all alone out here? Bring this guy a beer and a sandwich, he looks like he could use it. You like chicken salad, guy?"

I assumed a kip position so I could skitter backwards on all fours like a crab.

"Don't be scared, guy. We're nice people. Cold? Join us by the fire. Eat, drink, tomorrow we can take you back to the city if you want. How long you been out here?"

I leapt up and sprinted toward the swamp. I bolted through forest and reeds, I feinted left and right, I dashed into darkness and shadow.

I dove into the underbrush and burrowed into scrub. I heard cracking sticks hither and thither. Someone yelled, "Don't be scared; we want to help you."

I wasn't so easily taken in. I lay still, opening my mouth as wide as possible as if I was demonstrating how a midget might perform fellatio upon a horse in order to quietly disperse my gasping. Breaking twigs and idiot voices faded. The last few shouts echoed faintly. Katydids, crickets, and a lone owl reclaimed the night.

Although confident I could outwit any renewed pursuit, I decided to err on the side of caution and remain where I was; I was well hidden in the foliage and somewhat comfortable. I drifted into a wary sleep.

CHAPTER XIII.

MY TIME ON THE ISLAND.

I woke in soft light to the day's first bird songs. I was well rested despite my harrowing night. I stretched in the undergrowth and writhed on my back to sooth the many insect bites I had accrued. I stared at the sky for ten minutes. I stood and proceeded to the coast.

All that remained of the revelers were discarded cans and an upright vodka bottle. The sand was grooved where their boat had been pulled ashore and then back into the sea.

The vodka was nearly full. I held it up against the pink and gray sky. I removed the cap and smelled it. I took a deep drink. I sat down. The sea was gray and green.

Why, I wondered, did I run from people that were friendly and concerned about my plight? Why did I recoil from what had undoubtedly been my best opportunity to return safely to the mainland?

Although I couldn't articulate the process or reasons, I knew it was related to the time I spent submerged in the swamp and my subsequent rebirth in a transient primordial state. In the days I spent on all fours defecating and howling, I had reconnected with a deep human freedom—predatory, omnivorous, sexual, and perennially unemployed. This was the true state, the absolute to which all men aspire but erroneously attempt to reach through years of hard work and planning, somehow not realizing or resisting the fact that all one really had to do was nothing and paradise would be instantly realized.

I decided I would remain on Ruffle Bar for the rest of my life. As soon as I articulated this thought, a deep serenity spilled forth; I forgave the cruelty that had brought me there; in fact, I blessed my brothers, for it was ultimately their actions that mattered, not the intentions or feelings they had when committing them. I saw how actions based on malice could manifest as acts of love, exactly like the deeply conflicting thoughts one has while petting a tiny dog.

I began work on a new shelter. I had been sleeping under a sheet of canvas stretched across boxes recovered from the *Havana*; now that I had decided to spend the rest of my life on the island, I got to work designing something permanent. In this respect my sewing expertise was invaluable: I created a masterpiece of intertwined branches, reeds, logs, living bushes, soil and stone that I submerged into the landscape; I needed sanctuary from rescuers, police, bullies, and naturists. I would not be caught out again.

I then set about creating a lifestyle. I was master of the Ruffle Bar night; the spate of visitors that had plagued me turned out to be anomalous; in the following weeks not a soul set foot on my island, and the only boat that passed regularly was the police whom I assiduously avoided—as soon as I heard the trademark drone of their motor, I took refuge in the tangled outback.

Darkness was freedom, so I became nocturnal; sunrise was my sunset. Each summer day's final ritual was an onanistic tribute to the bright sky, with delicate ass play sending additional shocks of pleasure through my writhing body. In the cold months, I virtually never left my shelter, instead creating an Art of Physical Silence underground; this was an entirely new form of quiet dance blended with a form of yoga hitherto practiced only beneath the Belurgi water tank; when spring arrived I would emerge supple and lean.

There was only one perturbation to my rhythm: I ran out of drinking water after one hundred days. Foreseeing this problem, I had tried to create a variety of caches for rainwater, all for naught. My attempts to capture and melt snow were effective to a point, but the endeavor was inefficient; had I not spent so many winter nights dragging snow-covered sheets back to my shelter for processing, who knows what level I might have attained in the Art of Physical Silence; as it was, I had to be content with the Yingzee Position—a position whereby the hand snakes below the thigh-back and grapples viciously with what it discovers anew, and the Vicknow position—a position whereby the buttocks is stretched contrarily toward sky and earth, each side in opposing directions.

I would have to visit the mainland to get water if I intended to stay. I could use the skiff, build a new craft, or repair one of several derelict boats that littered Ruffle Bar's coast. I chose all three options.

First I repaired a gutted motorboat. My work did not return the boat to its original integrity, but with ample calking, canvas, and wax, the battered hull was made seaworthy. Next I built a raft from driftwood; the end product was not beautiful, but it would be an effective platform to carry extra barrels and other freight. When I set sail, my vessels would form a sea-train with the rowboat first, then the raft, then the skiff trailing behind in case of a catastrophe and for extra shipping space for water or whatever else I picked up.

So on foggy summer nights when the sea was quiet, I'd row into the darkness. These nocturnal voyages filled me with terror and comfort simultaneously; on the one hand, seething anxiety spread beneath my flesh at the mere thought of being captured and forcibly returned to the mainland; on the other hand the shroud of fog and the whispering black sea reiterated my freedom and resplendent monasticism; I became the direct heir to those that had navigated the bay before me, the natives and early settlers who could row through the fog without fear of reproach.

I knew these islands well. I had been sailing among them with Montez and my brothers since I was a boy. Broad Channel had been a key port of call for the *Havana Banana*; the town's ramshackle houses on stilts, decrepit wooden walkways and piers, and marshy grasses were all familiar to me, as was the insular Irish fishing culture that made the community unique. For these secretive people, a bearded stinking misanthrope filling drums with fresh water at the pier might have been odd, but I was in no danger of being reported to the authorities; on the contrary, their aversion to outsiders and law enforcement was as powerful as my own, stretching back to Prohibition rum running and beyond, all the way back to the Emerald Isle's ancient code of silence.

The rest of my life consisted of an increasingly predictable bliss. The dark obsession that had seized my soul on the mainland was gradually diminished by birdsong, the crashing sea, the sound of my gasping lungs as I sprinted inland to avoid horrific sportsmen with their binoculars and canoes, and by the sounds of the Ruffle Bar night—the buzzing of insects, the roaring squalls, the wind in the reeds and trees: the music now came from without instead of within. Although the pilot light of genius continued to burn in my soul, the great white fires of creativity had been reduced to a gently hissing smolder.

I was glad of this. Although I was proud of my work, I paid a severe price for the creative process; my delicate body was driven beyond exhaustion, my chafed member begged for respite, and my mind was perennially tortured by the hopeless task of giving perfection corporeal form with tools that made its compromise inevitable, not to mention the gaping chasm that would open up during performances, not only because of the limitations of instruments and venues, but ultimately and to a much larger degree because of the subjective, small-minded little worms for whom the works were performed. No, I did not miss my duty to the muse.

In my lowest moments—when I am groveling for slops and offal; when past turgidities, so easily earned, are mere fragments and whispers overshadowed by today's downcast pliancy; when jade rage flares up in impotent righteousness—in these moments I long for the island, for those peaceful days in the steady circle of routine, the happiest days of my wretched life. Oh! Ruffle Bar, why did I forsake thee?

CHAPTER XIV.

PETER.

Island life became a craft consisting of several threads; over the years, I made subtle adjustments to each one in order to get better at what I did. My overall area of expertise was life itself, and my areas of specialization were the individual components that comprised it.

The island made this simple. On the mainland, modernity virtually guaranteed an extended shelf life, but the price was to be full of chemicals and impurities that made the longer experience a nauseating one: superficially glossy, but spiritually sick and empty of passion. My forced return to the primitive reduced me to a man brewed in strict accordance with a Reinheitsgebot far older than that of 1516; existence consisted of a few basic components, which contrary to urban expectations, dramatically increased my zest for life and the immediacy of moments; by not utilizing the cheap shortcuts, true meaning came of its own accord.

The combination of time and simplicity also allowed me to make judicious, incremental adjustments to the threads of my life—this method bore substantial fruit. For example, to be warm during the winter months, I built a second roof and a second set of walls approximately 6 inches from the originals; I stuffed the space between with reeds and dead grass. This adjustment made my subsequent winters cozy, but the satisfaction in creating utility exceeded the pleasures of comfort.

Likewise my voyages to the mainland: into these I infused a sophisticated aesthetic. In addition to adjusting the scheduling and the logistics, I also added the occasional variation as circumstance allowed. For instance, I introduced a route called The Flagrant; this route concluded in dawn's pink glimmer as opposed to the blackness that was my wont. The Flagrant included a mental performance of Tchaikovsky's *Souvenir de Florence* based not on the original, but on František's piano version; I would guide my craft through black choppy water while attempting to reconstruct the piece as I would perform it with my machines based on František's artful allusions.

I also improved the vessel itself. I initially had to row, and although this was invigorating it was quite taxing; by the time I reached Broad Channel I was exhausted; it was difficult to haul water from discreetly spigotted homes to the boat while maintaining vigilance. By the time I rowed back to Ruffle Bar, I was physically destroyed. In order to rectify this, I added a mast, boom, and rudder to the craft. I was extremely proud of the result; although the boat had originally been a motorboat, adjusting the structure to accommodate my additions was a feat, particularly in the case of the rudder. It was a challenge, but I viewed the task as redemption for Joey's scorned attempt to build a makeshift sail with broom handles and sheets only to have Johnny annihilate his well-intended efforts.

And so on. I was sitting in the bushes one late afternoon contemplating these things as I watched the sea, wondering how I might kill any complacence growing in tandem with my self-improvement when a craft appeared on the horizon that contained the answer to this very query.

The motorboat was coming directly toward my hiding place. The formerly calm bay began to roil with the ill-timed waves of an unnatural source. Several figures in baseball caps were in the boat. They were shouting above the motor's throb.

They cut the motor and allowed inertia to carry them toward shore. The bow hit the sandy bottom with a muffled scuff. One of the men leapt from the boat with a rope and gave it a strong pull. Two others followed and helped the first drag the bow ashore.

Two men remained in the stern. One was a powerfully built middle-aged man wearing a tank top and a Yankees cap. He was holding another man down, not allowing him to rise from his knees. The man on his knees was talking; the man standing above him said:

"Shut up!"

But the man on his knees continued in an unbroken stream of words. The others had dragged the boat further ashore and had paused to catch their breath.

"I tell you," said the man on his knees, "I know sophisticated, and you aren't it. Now on Long Beach? All *Ocean's Eleven* types, so handsome and with such great hair."

"Shut up."

"In the Bronx they aren't sophisticated and the black girls aren't as pretty as in Brooklyn. But the Spanish girls, oh—so beautiful. But they always have boyfriends."

"Can't you get him to stop?" said one of the men.

"I'm trying. How far you want to take it? I think this guy is soft, you want me to beat down a softhead?"

The men laughed. The man on his knees continued:

"The prettiest black girls are in Queens. Brooklyn has the prettiest Irish girls, but the boys aren't sophisticated and have awful hair. The Irish Riviera? Every boy on the boardwalk is an *Ocean's Eleven* type, always with a beautiful girl, but I think the girls must be from Brooklyn, not Breezy Point, and definitely not Gerritsen Beach. I understand you're from there. Nobody there is sophisticated."

"Help me get this idiot out."

Two of the men got back in. As they attempted to drag the man out, he went limp like a resistant child. He slipped from their grasp. He kept rambling:

"You don't even know what sophisticated is in Gerritsen Beach, I can see that. Really, I think you're savages."

"Say 'sophisticated' again, I'll drown you. In Gerritsen Beach we don't steal beer! Savage!"

I suppressed a laugh at the cretin's derivative retort. The odd prisoner was undeterred:

"Never been down on your luck? I steal beer every day, but today I didn't steal anything. But if you were down on your luck in Brighton Beach, I'd steal beer for you. But you'd stand out. In Brighton there's Jews, Russians. Even the Russian drunks are more sophisticated—"

"What did I tell you?"

"—are more sophisticated! Sophisticated! Sophisticated! Than you. Europeans all have such wonderful hair. Every Frenchman is an *Ocean's Eleven* type, most of the English too. And those sophisticated accents."

Despite his limp ragdoll defense, the men—who had become plagued with contagious laughter at their ludicrous charge—were successfully dragging him across the motorboat's prow. His legs flopped to the sand as they dragged him off the boat.

"Listen up," said the man in the Yankees cap, "You ever show your face in Gerritsen Beach again, we aren't gonna be so nice. Next time we break your legs, got it?"

"Come on guys, I don't have anything to drink, I'll die out here, take me back to Brooklyn. I'll get you beer. Please, pretty please, take me back to Brooklyn!"

"The idiot could die out here, Robby."

"Unlikely. Boats everywhere."

"But it's possible."

Robby—the man in the Yankees cap—put his hands on his hips and looked down at the man who was now covered in sand.

"You want to be carrying that around?" said the other man.

"I could die out here Robby. In your heart you're a kind man, you must be to have such regard for rules and regulations, you understand I did not commit a victimless crime."

"Shut up. Okay, we leave the beer. Happy, asshole? You get to keep what you worked for. But I swear, you ever..."

"Oh no, there's been a terrible misunderstanding. If you're in Brighton Beach you can find me in the library, I'll return the favor. Don't go, please! You can't leave me here, it's cruel. Please!"

The men shoved off. They pushed with oars and started the motor when it got deeper. They raced from the island.

The man stood up and watched the boat until it disappeared. He continued looking as if he expected them to come back.

He stared at the empty sea for ten minutes. He sat down on the garbage-ridden sand. He leaned back on his arms and continued scanning the grey horizon. Ten more minutes passed. He leaned forward and held his face in his hands. Five minutes passed. His shoulders shook. He sobbed. He actually looked toward the heavens and yelled, "Why?"

Although I sympathized with his plight, I have to say I felt a jab of pride at the fact that I hadn't done the same. Ramones do not cry like bitches.

The men that marooned him were right: if he sat there weeping long enough, a passing boat would spot him. If he got a grip on himself he could accelerate the process by signaling or crying out, granting I'm not the model for success in that particular endeavor. Anyhow, if he stayed on shore the NYPD out of Floyd Bennett would find him and, in their way, they'd serve and protect him.

I just couldn't allow that to happen to him, recalling my early days on the island before I had established processes and procedures. He had been abandoned with nothing but his wits and a case of recently stolen beer, in all likelihood still somewhat cold. Although I still had a substantial amount of hard liquor from the *Banana*, I hadn't had a beer since 1970; by my calculations[14] that was about four years. I was furious with myself for my excessive caution when I went to Broad Channel for water; surely I could have devised a way to get beer. I would punish myself with vicious pinching of the tip at its most sensitive and then I'd remember to get some beer of my own.

I emerged from the bushes.

"Excuse me sir, can I perhaps be of help?"

He turned around, exhibiting no surprise; rather, he seemed resigned to the inevitability of the next horrible encounter. It touched my heart.

---

[14] I counted the number of winters.

"I saw those men shoving you about; have they abandoned you here?"

"Afraid so. I wasn't stealing this beer."

"You don't need to explain."

"I was only walking out the front door because the aisle was narrow and I couldn't get to the end of the line."

"That's fine."

"I was going to walk around and go back in—"

"Really, it's fine."

"—through the back door."

"It's neither here nor there how you acquired it as long as you share it. May I?"

"Be my guest."

"Thank you."

He opened one too. I said:

"Cheers."

"Cheers. I'm Peter. Can you help me get back to Brooklyn?"

"Damone."

"Can you help me get back?"

"Possibly," I said, "but not at this instant. See how the sky is growing dark?"

"No."

"A terrible squall is brewing. I have a boat, but we would both drown if we set out now."

"It's a beautiful day."

"I'm a seafaring man, and I assure you a tempest is brewing. We shall drink this beer and consider our options. Follow me. Grab the case."

I led him into the interior. Gulls cried and the reeds rustled. Peter grunted with exertion; the sounds he made were disgusting beyond ken, but hearing them was better than carrying the beer. We reached my abode.

I reached into what appeared to be a dense thorny copse covering a low-lying mound. I never made concessions to comfort over discretion when I constructed my home, so my forearms were frequently mangled and bloody from opening my door, hidden as it was beneath a twisted mass of hostile thorns.

I opened a trapdoor. I lowered myself into the dark hole.

"Hand me the beer. Careful. Thanks. Come in."

I lit a candle embedded in the clay wall. My fortress was largely underground. Thick driftwood and lumber from abandoned vessels comprised the ceiling. The roof was covered with stones, clay, and topsoil. I planted thorn bushes and stinging nettles that I had carefully set aside and cultivated during the construction process. Even if an interloper was wearing tall protective boots and they stomped across my verdant bunker, they would feel no difference between it and the rest of the island's terrain. So proud was I of this sturdy clandestine dwelling, that during the winter months I would sometimes spend weeks inside, only emerging to empty the bucket beneath a silver winter moon.

I gestured toward the raised alcove I had carved into the clay where I slept. It housed four of the *Banana's* mattresses: two to create a quasi box-spring and two on top of those for maximum comfort.

"Wow, did you build this all yourself?"

"It's not such an accomplishment relative to the vast portions of life I spent on it, say, scraping a root out of a wall for five or six hours."

"Wow, look at this beautiful old box stove, it must be a hundred years old. And so ornate."

"Box stove?"

"Yeah, my aunt upstate has one. It works?"

"Of course. I dug it from below an old building foundation nearby. The chimney is hidden in a hollow dead tree. I had a hell of a time moving it across the island."

"I wish I could do this; I wouldn't have to live in the library bathroom. Where does that go?"

"Storage room, but the tunnel continues; it's an escape route in case I'm discovered."

"Can I look?"

"Of course," I said. I lit a second candle and handed it to him. He entered the arched doorway next to the bed. His voice came from the tunnel a moment later:

"Wow, it's huge."

I was proud—I entered the tunnel to observe Peter's face.

"What do you think?" I asked.

"I can't believe how sophisticated this is. What are those seats for carved in the walls? Visitors?"

"Never, you presumptuous miscreant! They're all for me."

"Why are you yelling at me? I'm only paying compliments."

"Pardon me. I've been told upon occasion that my reactions to the sweet are apropos to the bitter."

"You sound like you're trying to sound like the bible."

"Thank you."

"So this room?"

"As you see, it's rectangular with the exception of this curving wall; essentially it is half of an oval."

"What are those stairs?"

"They aren't stairs. It's an altar, albeit secular. As you see, the ascending terraces' peak is a pyramid of cans. Hormel chili. My supply is dwindling, unfortunately. Each can is a universe. Have you tried it?"

"Damone, are you a homosexual?"

"How dare you, sir! I don't even have sex with women, let alone men!"

"Then what's this...totem thing?"

"An homage to the organ is not an homage to the sex. Can not one eulogize a dog while disdaining its master? Do you not, sir, enjoy yours?"

"I like to take it out."

"As indeed you should."

"In restaurants. What are those boxes?"

"Supplies I recovered from the sunken vessel that brought me here."

"Can we go down the escape tunnel?"

"Later. I suggest we return to my living quarters and make short work of the ale. Grab that whisky from the shelf, the Seagrams. That's right. I shall supplement your generosity. Come."

"I never would have guessed you could do all this. I mean, with all due respect, you don't look like an architect. No offense."

"None taken; when I see my image in the mirror as of late I share your sentiments, although I must say I look quite the rogue boyar."

"So how did you end up here?"

I told my tale, substituting the true nature of the Ramone family business, telling him instead that we delivered fresh bread. After I said it I burned with regret, realizing I should have substituted a more costly commodity such as palm cockatoos or De Brazza's monkeys that would justify the noir secrecy of our voyages. But Peter didn't seem to make any inferences from the discrepancy. I ended my tale by reiterating what I had decided several years earlier: I would remain on Ruffle Bar for the rest of my life.

"But don't you miss New York, the *Ocean's Eleven* types and the beautiful black girls in the Bronx? The handsome Presbyterians in Riverdale?"

"The what? No, I don't. I've never been happier."

"You don't wonder what happened to your family?"

"Do they seem like they're wondering about me?"

"Apparently not."

"So there you have it. Why expend energy mourning an illusion? They're strangers to me now."

Peter retreated to a mattress I had placed on the floor.

I drank a beer in bed, took a dram of whisky, closed my eyes and wandered among savory imaginings. Peter, however, chose to interrupt my reflections by grunting in a suspect staccato and by breathing in a similarly dire manner.

I looked over in dreadful anticipation. Sure enough, he had surrendered to the rhythmic corollaries of some gruesome montage of *Ocean's Eleven* types and beautiful minorities in far-flung neighborhoods all over the five boroughs beneath his tightly closed eyes; he was baring his teeth in a morbid grimace; he looked as if he was engaged in his final writhing seconds before the guillotine drop. I was appalled. I said:

"Can you please not do that in front of me?"

"You're doing it too!"

"Yes, but I live here."

I wondered what sort of home Peter grew up in to have developed such a wanton disrespect for decorum; I sighed in exasperation as he rolled over on his stomach, a gratuitous gesture that did nothing to disguise the nature of his continued oscillations.

"At least let me blow the candle out," I said; "And I expect immaculate containment—use that filthy shirt of yours."

He didn't answer. I lay back down and tried to recall where I had left off, but it was no use—the spell had been broken. The sound of the familiar rhythm, recalling those long nights on the *Havana Banana* when the sea was a plain of glass and the only sound was the frenzied intersecting rhythms of my brothers in their bunks as they chopped away at their sailor's desperation. I soon drifted off.

CHAPTER XV.

THE PRODIGAL VIPER.

The next morning we breakfasted on bluefish and the few remaining beers. I had been restless the night before. Unable to feign the sleeping schedule of a normal man in deference to my guest, I surrendered to my nocturnal habits; I threw ten beers in a rucksack and spent the night roaming the island until the beer was gone, then I cast my line into the sea and was almost instantly rewarded with a monumental battle with a bluefish; I was grateful for the muscles I had built on the island as I battled the powerful fish.

Now the fish was sizzling in a cast iron pan. Peter sat on a log as I tended to the fish and drank beer. After breakfast I'd take a nap of ten to twelve hours; at sunset we'd sail to Brooklyn to return Peter. I'd also acquire more beer, perhaps with Peter's assistance; I had forgotten its hoppy charms, and now my taste for it had been reignited with a fury.

I was concerned however about an increasingly ominous sky. My prediction of a tempest the day before had been a seaman's tall tale, but now the sky looked truly foreboding. I didn't care when we departed, but Peter had already asked me at least ten times when we were going to leave. From the wisdom of my peaceful vantage point, I could no longer understand the appeal of the screeching, roaring, unforgiving monstrosity across the water, the nightmarish antithesis to my happy life on Ruffle Bar.

And from what I had gathered about Peter's life, his urge to return to Brooklyn also seemed extraordinary; so horrible were the tales he told that I could only assume he was an incredibly unique masochist who derived pleasure from vagrancy, homelessness, and frequent shoplifting arrests.

He resided, he explained, in the Brighton Beach Branch of the Brooklyn Public Library. Although his parents lived nearby in Seagate, he rarely saw them; it was unclear whether this was his choice or theirs. He spent his days on New York buses, trains, and subways. He was familiar with every neighborhood in the five boroughs, sharing highly detailed, precisely quantified information about which neighborhoods contained the most sophisticated young people—those with the best hair and the prettiest minorities. He was especially enamored of and always on the hunt for what he called *Ocean's Eleven* types; I had no idea what that meant.

In any case, he was eager to return: he was pacing about ringing his hands like a man desperately in need of surgical gloves, but unable to buy them because a female cashier was working.

"Peter, please. Why are you pacing? We must wait out this storm. We have liquor, food, a comfortable shelter when the rain comes…"

"I want to go back. I want to go back."

"In good time."

"Will you stay in Brighton for a few days? I'll show you girls and I'll steal beer."

"No. My place is here. It's starting to rain; if you're done with breakfast, let's go home."

We returned to my abode. I lit some candles and then I shut the trapdoor.

"How will we know when the storm stops?"

"The escape tunnel. It exits via a stump that, in addition to providing fresh air, acts as a conning tower."

"Wow, Damone, you thought of everything."

"I've tried to address every conceivable threat to my solitude."

"But you might be sorry you didn't reconcile with your family. Sometimes you have to swallow your pride for your own good."

"Shut up. I'm completely immune to such platitudes; they are products of television with no scientific relevance. People only miss their families when their families are missing; it's sentimentality born of guilt. No, I am an Arctic shrew amongst men; should I be forced to endure their "company," should I be exposed to their loathsome "brotherhood," I will swiftly perish. As Mother Theresa so wisely stated, "Hell is other people." Now if you'll excuse me, I must retire. If you require recreation, the pornography is in the other room in a yellow box, but I must insist you sit exclusively in throne number eight during your session."

"But do I start counting from this side or the escape tunnel side?"

"Very amusing, Peter, very amusing indeed."

I disrobed and went to bed.

I woke up in darkness. I lit a candle. Peter was sleeping. The dull sound of a muffled roar came from above; the tempest had arrived. I approached Peter and looked at his wristwatch; it was of unexpected quality considering the reprobate it was attached to; likely another item he had filched.

It was already ten. I wondered if perhaps my isolation had compromised my sense of time; I had felt quite sure it was four or five at the latest. I woke Peter with a brisk slap to the face.

"Ow, what was that, asshole?"

"You'll thank me shortly. Get up, I'm rather enjoying this unexpected conviviality."

"My teeth even hurt, you jerk. When are you going to take me home?"

"We can't set sail now, it would be suicide. Frankly, I was hoping you might continue with your challenging repartee."

"Got any coffee?"

"I don't drink coffee."

"But do you have any?"

"I have an enormous amount; didn't I just tell you I don't drink it?"

"Geez Damone, you're strange."

I told him where the coffee was. He mixed the raw grounds with cold water and choked down the dense grainy mess.

"Damone, you really like living like this? No hot coffee?"

"If I wanted it, I'd cook it over a fire, but I don't. Plus there's a squall on."

"I mean, okay, you don't want to see your family and you don't like people. But what about entertainment?"

"I have all I need."

"What about museums, opera, Broadway?"

"Complete hogwash. I refuse to engage in the collectively agreed upon farce that any of those tortures provide pleasure. The only reason people attend cultural events is to experience the sensation of something ending. They'd be just as well served visiting their proctologist as they would be by seeing the *Ring Cycle*. In any case, modern man simply doesn't have that sort of time."

"But didn't you say you made music yourself?"

"Silence! I refuse to speak of this! I'd rather concede hypocrisy than attempt to explain my logic to such a monumental imbecile."

"Fine. You got a sweater or something?"

"In my sea trunk. Over there, it's unlocked."

He opened the chest.

"Nice jacket. Nice jeans too. These tennis shoes—so white."

"My quintessence, Peter."

"What are these?"

"My finest Vinyl Vaginas."

"Vaginas?"

"I keep them for sentimental reasons, but you're welcome to try one."

"Thanks. What's in this leather thing?"

"Map. Some currency."

"Can I wear the black leather jacket?"

"Yes, but treat it nicely and return the contents of the chest in the exact order you found them, with particular care directed to that outfit. And you can't wear the shoes."

"It's hard for me to imagine you dressing cool, looking at you now in that awful coat."

"Do you like it? It's two raccoons, my brother Tommy's jeans, my father's fox fur, and several pieces of canvas; the lining is entirely composed of my father's women's underpants. I needed a warm, full length coat for winter; fortunately my family left everything when they absconded."

"It's a long way between that and this jacket."

"We all wore it: black leather, jeans, basic white sneakers. Our uniform."

"Your dad too?"

"No. By the time they marooned me it looked like Liberace was at the helm. You should have seen him during our down time. He had pants made from boa constrictors and he made shoes with their heads, can you imagine? He added eight-inch clear heels. He wore a giant gold medallion of a rhino face with a huge horn that made wearing a shirt impossible, so he didn't. He had a white fedora with a four-foot brim-span and an entire peacock's tail sticking from the hatband. Us brothers wore the uniform and my one sister, Ramona. I might have had more sisters; we had sibling twins Tyler and Terry, but we never knew if they were boys or girls. We tried to find out by walking in when Montez or Szilarda—my parents—were bathing them, but we never found out. I tried, and my father sprayed shampoo in my eyes and screamed, 'You must never know their genders!' Then he kicked me in the balls while I was blinded by the shampoo—it was dandruff shampoo, the blue stuff. Ever get it in your eyes? It hurts. My father rarely spoke, and he had yelled in English; normally he mumbled to himself in Spanish. Anyhow, we'd wear the family uniform, and when we'd walk down the boardwalk, people got out of our way. We all got our haircut at 46th and 3rd. I had this tall, weird brother named Joey. The barber once told Joey that that year—maybe 1967—marked twenty-two years at 46th and 3rd, and that he had worked on the same corner in Bucharest for exactly twenty-two years before that. Somehow for Joey that meant he could only get haircuts during that specific time period: when the barber had twenty-two years back to back, respectively in Bucharest and New York. For eight months Joey was constantly getting haircuts. He'd leave in the middle of movies to get his a cut. He got four in the same day once. We told the barber not to cut his hair, but he kept telling Joey that each haircut illustrated a new aspect of Joey's personality and he'd cut it again. My older brother Johnny was livid. Johnny would beat up anyone. One time he beat up an entire family including the children because they laughed at my brother František because František had inserted a lollipop into his anus—his own, not Johnny's—and had been pleasuring himself. But he was not the same as the rest of us, not like you and I. He was a genius; he was one of the greatest pianists in the world in both performance and breadth of repertoire. He'd play the same thing repeatedly, compulsively—but then he'd play an obscure Scriabin or Prokoviev out of the blue and completely by memory. One time he played the second movement of Ravel's String Quartet, and he used the piano strings themselves to do the pizzicato parts. Anyhow, Johnny was mad but he wouldn't beat up the barber because he was eighty-six. Johnny said you have to respect your elders, especially if they worked hard and came to live the American dream. Plus no other barber cut hair like the Romanian, and Johnny was very proud of his hair. It glimmered and swung like no other hairdo on a head, and the rest of us did everything we could to get ours like Johnny's. I wish you could see how we looked when we'd march down the street together. The hairdo was key—it was long but we weren't hippies, not by a stretch: Johnny always said when his construction worker buddies commented on his long hair that you can't get close enough to a hippie to punch him if you have a flattop—I liked that a lot. The hairdo was a bowl cut on top, then it hung in a mop-like way. My brother Dee Dee's looked more like a helmet, Johnny's like a mop—"

"Like the C.C.R. guy."

"The who?"

"Creedence Clearwater Revival. I always picture the C.C.R. guy chopping trees or frying bacon in a cabin."

"What?"

"But your brothers are more like a motorcycle gang. Your last name isn't Ramone, is it?"

"Surely Peter, I've mentioned it to you several times while you've been my lodger."

"No you haven't."

"I haven't?"

"No. Yeah, it's amazing, but I know your brothers. I mean, I don't *know* know them, but I know *of* them and their wonderful hair, so daring and handsome. And fierce."

"What is this tripe, this counterfeit reality you're going on about? Is this Brighton Beach humor? Really, what sort of pathetic knave would attempt a jest so statistically unlikely to succeed? "

"It was this spring. A place called Performance Studios. I can show you if you want, but I can't go in, that pretty much always happens to me. I can't ride the 67, 69, or 64B in Brooklyn either, unless there's a temporary driver."

"Shut up about the Metro Transit Authority and explain yourself this instant about where you think—quite wrongly I assure you—that you saw my brothers."

"My Uncle David took me out, he does it every two months to check up on me and to do something that costs money because I made him think I can't get money. He says he has some friend that knows this weird band playing their very first concert and we went. Four guys come on stage dressed exactly like this with hair just like what you said and this really tall skinny one with a big nose says they're the Ramones, then the most handsome one yells, 'One, two, three, four,' and on 'four' they get in a big argument and the tough looking one pushes the tall one, it was terrible, then they—"

"That's them! The scoundrels! Then what?"

"Well, normally I don't listen to rock music, I like Dean Martin, Bobby Darrin, the Barry Sisters."

"Relevance, sir? Go on about the pack of bastards called the Ramones; can't you see the delight your little tale is bringing me?"

"It's like a bomb goes off, this non-stop wall of sound like nothing I ever heard, so simple but so bold and sophisticated. It sounded like a machine."

"What did it sound like, you duplicitous dog?"

"A machine. Ow, my back! Get off me. Ow!"

"Sounded like a machine, did it? The ratio of the output to the applied force equals me annihilating you? You swine!"

"Ouch, Damone, stop! I didn't do anything, I'm just telling you what I saw. Don't take it out on me, take it out on your brothers!"

At that moment I hearkened back to an incident years earlier when I was under the surgeon's knife. My spirit rose above my body. I became part of everything while maintaining a ghostly imprint of my subjective self, enough so that portions of the great wisdom were transmitted into my earthly body, which thankfully survived. I rejoined the living henceforth enlightened by my visit to the other side. Although at that moment, on the floor of my fortress with my raised fist poised to deliver vengeance blindly, erroneously, regrettably...at that moment I did not soar overhead and view my imminent sin as I had before, but the lesson of that cathartic little death acted as a permanently suspended eye that watched me always: guardian angel; my apportioned share of God's attention; my stern warning of eternal culpability; my humanistic delusion. Whatever it was, it drained me of my satanic rage.

I got off Peter and unclenched my fist. And to think, an attractive idea had already formed about how I would go about performing taxidermy *alla rustica* on the very person to whom I had given food and shelter; I imagined his gaping idiocy forever preserved under a coat of glossy tree sap as he looked down from a piece of sanded driftwood right next to the police boat license plate I had boldly unscrewed one night when, full of bravado and pastis, I had rowed the skiff directly to Floyd Bennett with the exclusive purpose of just such mischief; and to think how that specific craft forever remained 'the police boat without a license plate', thereby making it just as much a rogue vessel as those that it pursued. Oh, Serpico! Oh! Dvořák's *New World* against the Queen's constant currents! Davie Jones, how doth thy contend with housing demand in the depths of thy dark domain? Oh!

I sat down on my bed to catch my breath. Peter remained on the floor. He said:

"Damone, you need to drink more. One minute you're fine, then you're all firestone."

"I believe the phrase is fire and brimstone, Peter."

"Oh no, now what's wrong?"

"Gaaaaaaah!"

"Damone! Oh my God!"

"Gaaaaaaah!"

Peter leapt from the floor, grabbed a bottle of rum and forced it into my mouth. Translucent brown fluid sprayed from my mouth, nose, and the corners of my eyes, but even more went down my throat and merged with my fiery blood, lending me a fragment of clarity. I gasped and wiped my face with my forearm. I stared at the floor for a moment. I looked in Peter's eyes. I said:

"Peter: we sail tonight. Pack your things."

"I don't have any things."

"Then pack whatever odds and sundries intrigue you, for who knows when I will next be on this island. But ex post haste, for we sail within the hour."

"Damone, hear the storm? When you were sleeping I looked out of the stump; it's bad. I saw a tree fall, and I could hear more breaking."

"Peter...we are Leif Erickson's children."

"Speak for yourself, I'm someone else's children, my parents live in Seagate."

"It stands: we sail tonight."

"You said it was suicide."

"I don't have to justify my choices to anyone, least of all to myself!"

"Calm down."

"Oh God, why hast thou created me? To think of how much planning must of went into creating entirely convincing human beings designed solely to torment me. This grand farce, this illusion of a planet, of a universe, of other people, of Asia; all of these fictitious trifles designed solely to torment the only soul in existence, that of Damone Ramone. Ah, how amusing it must have been for you as you created each ludicrous detail of your little prank; I picture you, for example, designing Yugoslavian cuisine: 'Yes, these people will eat a diverse selection of grilled meat, ha ha ha! They'll serve it on metal platters, ha ha ha! With some red shit on the side, I'll call it ajvar, it'll be made from some bullshit gourd

I'll call red peppers, ha ha ha! Raw onion on the side. And I'll serve it from two convenient Queens locations, including Bosnian Express in Long Island City, ha! ha! ha!'"

"Damone, get a grip on yourself."

"Are dark raging seas an expression of your will, your plan, your unlimited power? I defy you! I defy you with my rigging, the swing of my boom, the crack of my mainsail and the mizzen's victorious skyward spike! I am coming home! Peter, I'll drop you off first since it's on the way."

CHAPTER XVI.

THE DARK VOYAGE.

Rivers blasted from the sky and typhoon winds flattened the reeds. The rain felt like gravel fired from cannons. The island was lit by thunderbolts that reached unbroken from Jupiter's seething red spot to the Atlantic's boiling surface. These towers of deadly light were followed by explosions of thunder that tore our ribs asunder and demolished our ears and any clinging vestige we harbored that the universe might have any future whatsoever.

Peter clung to me as I marched toward my secret mooring place on the island's western coast. Peter—once so enthused about returning home—begged to go back to my bunker. It was out of the question. Years of suppressed fury had been unleashed, a fury magnified ten-thousand-fold by the confirmation of my brothers' treachery. Nothing would deprive me of my revenge; certainly not a mere squall whose force was miniscule compared to the consecrated furies and righteous fires that burned within me.

We reached my boat. The menacing wind had torn off the foliage I had camouflaged it with. I ordered Peter to help me push the craft into the raging sea. Giant waves broke on Ruffle Bar's coast, but I was not alarmed; once we achieved open waters, I would master the situation. Although the storm was fierce, I had certainly contended with worse on voyages in the *Banana* that took us far out into the Atlantic's dark expanse. Granted, the *Havana Banana* was a steel, motorized tug whereas my craft was an abandoned fiberglass sieve converted into a sailing vessel, but it was swift and light. In any case, we were protected from the worst of the storm by the enclave of Jamaica Bay.

When the ship entered the sea, we leapt over the gunwales; a bluefish the size of a man did the same. It whipped its silvery bulk back and forth across the craft's bottom, knocking us both flat. Peter screamed in agony as the mad fish slapped its spiky tail directly into his face. I jammed my arms wholly into the fiend's pumping gills, and the two of us wrestled from bow to stern while Peter screamed and undoubtedly urinated. Refusing to be cowed by God's capricious omen, I dealt the fish a vicious blow to the head and it slumped into the swiftly accruing bilge water, dazed and impotent.

Meanwhile the ship had gone awry; it was parallel to the shore and was being repeatedly broadsided by a relentless blitzkrieg of towering waves. The frothing white explosions of the breakers threatened to tear the ship apart; if she held, we'd soon take on too much water and we'd scuttle mere feet from shore.

I leapt into the sea and grabbed the vessel by the snout and battled it until the bow was facing the breaking waves.

"Get in," I shouted, "and bail as you never have before."

"But you just told me to get in!"

"You fool! Use the bucket to empty the ship of water! And toss me that rope."

I took the rope and marched directly into the wall of waves, my face locked in an expression designed to terrorize the very soul of each white-capped monster; indeed, as if wilting before the undeniable will concentrated in my blazing dark eyes and stern, crust-covered lips, the waves disintegrated into harmless mist as they slammed into my rigid torso.

When I could drag us out no further, I ordered Peter to put the oars in the oarlocks; this simple act turned out to be an absurd challenge for my landlubbing urban comrade; I nearly drowned as I shouted instructions.

"The little thing hanging down, see it?"

"Where?"

"In about the middle. It's round and straight."

"I see it."

"Put it in the hole."

"Got it, okay."

"Make sure it stays in."

I dragged myself up the landing rope and heaved myself into the rolling, listing craft. I shoved Peter out of my way and took the oars. Pumping and pulling, I guided us into open waters.

I was confident I could achieve a swift tack to the west once we rounded Ruffle Bar's southern coast. In the fierce winds I reckoned we'd sail the length of the Rockaways and pass Breezy Point in less than two hours.

But the sea was challenging to say the least; I ruminated on how *The Play of the Waves* from Debussy's *Le Mer* fell severely short in its representations when considered from the viewpoint of actually being surrounded on all sides by said waves; in fact, Peter's impressionistic rendition was markedly more accurate: his head was tilted skyward and he was screaming continually, sporadically invoking the name of Jesus Christ.

In these chaotic conditions I somehow managed to raise the jib and mainsail; the roaring wind filled them with a terrifying crack and the boat fired westward atop the waves. I took the rudder and guided the boom while Peter screamed and prayed. The ship fought its way through black glassy valleys and up snow covered peaks.

Despite the challenge, I swiftly mastered a rhythm and became confident of our success. I yelled to Peter over the roaring sea:

"Look to the lee for clusters of lights; we should be traversing the Rockaways. The straight narrows when we pass beneath the Marine Parkway Bridge. I will direct us toward Manhattan Beach when we sail between Rockaway Point and Plumb Beach. From there we'll hug the coast until we reach Brighton. It's critical you let me know if we are too close to Breezy Point; we don't want to lose the protection of the Rockaways and end up in open waters so far from shore, understand?"

"Understand. Hey, listen to this:

There once was a man from Far Rockaway
That could smell a piece of ass a block-away
One night he got a whiff
But she had the syph
And now it's eating his cock-away"

I must say, I did not expect Peter to be the vehicle that would illustrate the careworn missive to not judge books by their covers, but I suppose therein lay the platitude's timeless wisdom; this stunning burst of vivid elocution was wholly unexpected, especially in the circumstances. Peter—who hadn't stopped crying, howling, or praying since we set sail—was now exuding the poise of a masturbated Cicero as he repeated the wonderful psalm.

"Bravo Peter! Repeat it immediately—if you stop I shall cut your tongue out, for what greater good could it ever conceivably perform?"

He recited the masterpiece again. Never had a poem resonated so superbly as this; I was humiliated beyond reason that I was not familiar with the piece, but my self-hatred was far overshadowed by the exuberance each syllable brought forth from my heart. It was as if Peter's sole purpose in existing at all was to give this impeccable opus the superb rendering it deserved. Intoxicated by man's loftiest emotions, I demanded he repeat it, again and again, with compulsive abandon as we traversed the deadly waves.

As might be surmised, I forgot to check if Peter had noted our position; I must have made him recite the poem thirty times before I recollected we were facing potential doom.

"The lights! Where are we?"

"No problem Damone, I'm pretty sure that's Breezy Point still."

Indeed, the lights of Breezy Point and the end of the Rockaways lay to our lee.

"I've been watching Damone. Those lights have been there for twenty minutes at least."

"In that case I shall tack northwest. In the meantime continue your recitation."

He resumed the poem. After ten more wonderful versions, each more moving than the last, I looked to our lee.

The lights were in the same place; we hadn't moved at all. I adjusted the rudder; I gave play to the boom; I adjusted the jib— but it was all for naught: the sea was passing swiftly beneath us, but we remained fixed to the spot.

And we remained that way until dawn. I don't know how many hours actually passed, but the sun was high when the rain stopped and the clouds parted. Although the waves were still massive, the storm seemed to be abating, at least in the high heavens.

The wind shifted, allowing us to break our paralysis; Breezy Point receded as I successfully resumed our northwesterly course. I predicted we'd be arriving in Brighton Beach in approximately two hours, as the seas were still quite high and we had lost our jib during the night.

When we left the protective wall of the Rockaways, the waves again towered over us; Peter resumed his cowardly supplications, and I was forced to replay the beautiful poem in my mind. I had no fear; the sun was bright, the sea was green and glistening, and my rage nearly felt like euphoria, so intoxicating was it.

Brighton Beach lay ahead. Swaths of white blotches littered the beach: Brooklynites already staking claim to patches of sand on this hot summer day. As we neared the beach, I had increasing difficulty maintaining a tack; the ship's stern faced the oncoming waves directly; they slammed against the flat transom with an incredible force that propelled us toward shore in a series of jerking hops. Individual swimmers and sunbathers were now visible, particularly a certain brand of pelmeni-infused local: vast Russian women that proudly displayed their fleshy spillage as they sunbathed standing up. The sight of female flesh, even at that distance, inspired a geyser of lust; I would need to swiftly locate a private place on shore for my first voyeuristic expulsion since 1970. In fact, I feared that my developing turgidity would become so hard that it would become brittle, and in the required physicality of guiding the ship to shore, I would shatter it with the slightest tap upon an unrelenting surface.

But the problem was doused out of existence when a massive wave careened against our stern, breaking out the transom with a crack. We swiftly began to founder just outside the lifeguard's buoys: as if sinking my craft through obvious poor seamanship wasn't enough, I'd suffer the additional indignity of having some overly-bronzed ninny whistling at me to swim within the boundaries.

"Grab the bluefish, quickly!" I yelled.

"Please Damone, don't make me."

"Then take hold of my sea chest, you coward!"

I seized the bluefish by a gill as the ship sank beneath the waves. We were in the shallows, so the mainmast still protruded from the sea when the craft settled on the ocean floor. I clung to it as Peter took charge of my sea chest, using it as a flotation device and kicking along behind it. I hesitated a moment as I hung from the mast, observing the crowd of bathers that had gathered to ogle the ludicrous spectacle that, unfortunately, I had authored. I had half a mind to revive the bluefish with a brisk slap, hurl myself upon its back, and, using its gills for reigns, guide us both back to Ruffle Bar that instant.

At the same time I observed myself through the eyes of the gathered crowd: a wild-eyed bluebeard coming hither in a small, decrepit craft clearly inadequate for such a violent, frothing sea; a man now largely above the waves with his legs and one arm locked on the foundered vessel's mast, the other arm down at his side casually wielding a massive bluefish as if hazarding death and losing my vessel had all been expected, minor incidentals to ensure that the big one would indeed not get away; I saw my long black hair, slick and dripping, hanging down to my waist; my massive dark beard belligerently advertising my absolute disdain for "society," for "company," for "teamwork"; a beard that instead spoke of rugged individualism, freedom, and an absolute rejection of petty norms and flimsy human hierarchies.

I would not retreat. I would return to their tepid civilization in a blaze of white hot vengeance; I'd see my mission of justice through to completion; I would vanquish their nascent plagiarized dream; I would cut it down with my sword of righteous ownership and properly filed copyright forms or at the very least a self-addressed sealed envelope.

Peter meanwhile had reached shore. He had stripped to his underwear and had mounted my sea chest; I noted the prevalent grayness of his undergarments with a certain sympathetic camaraderie. He was waving and gyrating as he yelled to me across the sun-kissed waves:

"Damone, hurry! Svetlana has a great lunch special, David took me there! Svetlana has a great lunch special, David took me there!"

I smiled, relinquished the mast, and fell into the churning bright sea. I rolled onto my back, hugged the unconscious bluefish, and kicked toward shore.

Part IV.

AN EPOCH OF PURSUIT AND INJUSTICE.

CHAPTER XVII.

SVETLANA.

I joined Peter on shore. I held the bluefish in my arms as if it was my bride. An old man with an eagle tattooed across his chest approached me, pointed to the fish, and spoke Russian. A substantial clot of sunbathers surrounded us; the children took particular delight in the fish, a delight presumably magnified by our undignified manner of arrival. Nonetheless, I found myself enjoying the attention; I circled around and around showing off the fish whilst jerking my head toward the boardwalk, my goal being to keep my face in the same direction for the maximum length of time relative to my turning in circles, a method of stabilizing my mental processes that one occasionally sees in certain Olympic sports, albeit much more quickly performed thanks to skates and ice.

We headed toward the boardwalk. Peter hefted my sea trunk on his back.

"Hey Damone, do you have money?"

"A substantial amount."

"But why do you have money?"

"If you have any recommendations as to where I might have spent it on Ruffle Bar, I'd be pleased to receive them."

"But why do you have it in the first place?"

"I was part of a successful endeavor, as I explained. Where is this restaurant? We must eat quickly."

Peter pointed to a cluster of tables on the boardwalk. A man stood behind a podium in front of them.

"They have wonderful salads, Damone."

"Good. My roughage has consisted of seaweed since shortly after the Altamont festival. Good day sir, a table for two please."

After mere minutes on the mainland, I was already subject to waves of uncertainty emanating from the perennial other; I felt the clash of absurd subjectivities before I even swam to shore: people. People wallowing in their monstrous self-satisfaction, clinging to flimsy morals passed down from tribal generation to tribal generation, nonsensical morals forcibly superimposed on bodies that clearly have far more sensible agendas; I loathed the entire festering mess. I vowed that as soon as I vanquished my brothers, I'd return to Ruffle Bar.

In the meantime, I was staring right into the face of just such bias; predictable, dull, myopic—the maître d' at Svetlana. He said:

"You can not bring this fish to here, it is not possible."

"I assure you that it is, sir. Now please step aside, we haven't got all day."

"Please sir, don't make me get to my brother."

"Why not, you're already getting to me. Fetch him forthwith, see if I care. I'd enjoy meeting another apple from the same tree. You know Peter, everyone always talks about the effects the apple had on Newton, but nobody ever discusses the effects the impact had on the apple; don't you think a hard impact would damage an apple, possibly make education and career advancement more difficult?"

"Damone, these are Russians. I don't think it's a good idea to make them angry. Their women are extremely pretty but the men aren't so sophisticated."

"Peter, I have money. Commerce always overcomes conflict, particularly with boors like this. Ah, here they come now. Presenting the brother: I picture a sport involving logs, a river, perhaps a little ice…"

"What is problem?"

"We'd merely like lunch sir, but your brother is refusing entry to this bluefish."

"Are you wanting to sell fish? Lunch is free we take the fish."

"I knew from the second I laid eyes on you that you were an intelligent man. Take the fish. You should teach your brother how to run a restaurant."

We sat down at a table next to the bar that afforded a view of all the outdoor diners in addition to the boardwalk beyond. To save time I ordered six mugs of beer.

"Damone, you can't talk to people like that. You're lucky he wanted that fish. Are you always starting problems like that for no reason? Let's not make a scene."

"So Peter, you must contact this Uncle David of yours and find out when my brothers are "performing" next. This is priority one. In the meantime I'll confront them at home. If we spend an hour here, kill some time on the beach and I take the bus, I should be in Fort Tilden around six. Most of them should be home. Where can we touch base, say tomorrow?"

"The library here. I'm always there. Let's order Damone, I'm starving."

"Unless you're vigorously attempting to remove a wedding ring I didn't notice before, I'd suggest you halt or revise that particular motion you're making under the table."

"But look at that Russian girl over there. They're so big!"

"I'm familiar with that woman—very—but unlike yourself I'm discreetly addressing that familiarity through my pocket. I don't need to look under the table to see that you've opted for a more direct approach; would you mind putting that thing away? It's one thing if you're home, but this is a fine dining establishment— "

"Miss! Excuse me, miss?" yelled Peter.

"What in the name of God are you doing?"

"Over here! Over here!"

"Jesus Christ, Peter, sit down."

"I like you!"

"Great, here comes her date: the Caporegime."

A man in a black dress shirt and silver pants overturned our table. The six beer mugs shattered on the boardwalk. Peter stood up; his pants were down around his ankles. The angry man grabbed him and threw him into the case of smoked fish in front of the bar. I hurled a chair at the man's back.

"Run, Peter, grab my sea chest and run!"

The chair had merely dazed the man; he turned and charged. I raced across the boardwalk and leapt the fence to the beach. I sprinted toward the sea, leaping over sunbathing women and playing children. I wrenched a green dinosaur swim-ring from a little girl and ran into the frothing sea. The man pursued me no further.

I crashed through the waves and dove into the water. I looped beneath the green dinosaur, emerging with the ring around my chest. I kicked hard toward the open sea.

CHAPTER XVIII.

THE HOUSE.

I swam past the mast of my own foundered vessel, crossed the lifeguard buoys, and swam into big water. Back on shore the orange-shorted fool blew his whistle and the little girl from whom I had wrested the green dinosaur screamed. But the waves and increasing distance soon found me alone, surrounded by the sound of the sea.

The Rockaways were approximately two kilometers from Brighton; with the wavy conditions I predicted a two-hour swim. The waves, although still high, had mellowed. Fueled by the events at Svetlana, I swam with vigor, aided by the green dinosaur. It seemed like far less than two hours when I felt the sea bottom beneath my feet. I left the sea.

My multi-pelt overcoat was heavy with water and my long hair was dripping. To alleviate my shame as I forged inland, I continued to wear the green dinosaur around my waist; if any passerby were amused by my wetness, it would be apparent that I had simply been swimming.

Getting home was a simple matter of crossing the Rockaways and then turning left at the southern coast. As I got closer to home, particularly after reaching the southern coast's sandy expanse, my fury reignited; everything from their patronizing friendliness on the *Banana* before my abandonment to the recent discovery of what I was sure was some horrific, plagiarized mutation of my compositions was coming together to make me angrier and angrier. I exploded into a veritable strut on the wet tidal sands, imitating the march of ceremonial Greek soldiers while I simultaneously wrapped my hands around the green dinosaur's neck and simulated a variety of chokeholds and strangulations as I marched eastward. I was pleased that the import of my mission was so easily discernible in my rage and bearing; as I marched down the beach, respectful women lifted their children bodily from my path; those old enough to frolic without supervision removed themselves of their own accord.

I reached the narrow path between the dunes that led to the Ramones estate. As I ascended the dunes, I shouted Prokoviev's *Dance of the Knights*: marching in time, fists swinging in the air, a cruel piece of machinery, a stomping golem from some martial vision of Marinetti's. The few bathers on the isolated beach watched in awe. I imagined myself ten feet in front of me, crossing the dunes, descending to the house. I pictured myself knocking on the door, hearing my brothers scurrying to hide, the entire Ramones clan lying on the floor, giggling and smirking at my expense. But this was unlikely; at the slightest tap, František would invariably bellow and sprint from wherever he was in the house and hurl himself into the door in joyous, indiscriminate greeting— the memory added an undercurrent of nostalgic yearning beneath my rage. And Johnny and Ramona, for their part, would never indulge in any collective frivolity such as lying on a floor to deceive a visitor. No, I would not be the victim of such childish malfeasance.

I ascended the slope, moving to the rhythm of Prokoviev's thunder. I reached the peak.

The house lay in rubble, razed like a Gomorrah suburb. My gaze was paralyzed by the atrocity. I don't know if I was stupefied exactly; by that point I was somewhat steeled against horrific shocks; in fact, when postulating what would come next from the direction of my brethren Ramones, my visions were largely catastrophic. Nonetheless, seeing my childhood home in such a state offered its own unique emotional brutality irrespective of the heinous acts perpetrated against me by my family. Until the moment I saw my house in ruins, it was as if every birthday candle I had ever blown out still burned in a near and analogous universe designed to sustain only love; now however the candles truly went out and real darkness fell.

I descended the dune. The house was completely destroyed. There was no trace of foundation or wall hinting at its former grandeur. I climbed the pile of stone, cinder blocks, and splintered timbers, searching among the mess for any old furnishings or possessions, but there was nothing. The Ramones had abandoned ship. I looked around one last time. There, protruding from a narrow crevice was Joey's sacred spoon. I put it in my overcoat. I turned toward the sea.

I was exhausted. The sky was coloring with bands of pink and violet. I sat beneath some shrubs on the dunes. I dissolved into merciful slumber as the pearlescent expanse whispered its beautiful song of apathy, wave by crashing wave.

CHAPTER XIV.

THE PURSUIT BEGINS.

In the morning I called Peter from a payphone near the bus stop. The woman picked up before the first ring:

"Brooklyn Public Library, Brighton Beach Branch."

"May I speak to Peter please? This is his uncle David."

"Are you coming? He's doing it again."

"Doing what again?"

"Are you being flip, Mr. Ellsberg? He's "reading" National Geographic in the children's section."

"Tell him to stop."

"Unfortunately we can't. He's exercising free speech."

"That's excellent."

"Right, it's terrible. I'll go get him."

While I waited I heard sounds befitting an eighteenth-century madhouse: screams, reprimands, weeping. Apparently the power of the shush had waned during my years abroad.

"Hello?"

"Peter, It's Damone."

"I tore pages from that magazine with the naked girls and passed them out. I'm sorry."

"I heard, National Geographic."

"Hustler."

"What Hustler?"

"I needed it, Damone."

"From Ruffle Bar? You desecrated the Christmas Miracle?"

"My uncle says he'll come later, I'll find out about your brothers' thing. Are you coming?"

"I'm coming now."

I hung up. The old bus stop was the same, a dusty hot patch and a shack. A few partially dressed bathers waited for the Q35 that hauled the initiated back and forth to the empyrean fragment called Fort Tilden Beach. The invisible border divided the roaring city from a vast sunny world where young naked bodies frolicked and talc-white gulls screamed across an endless blue sky. The sea was clean, forgiving, fizzing at the edges like seltzer. The beach was embracing; it looked like the scent of sandalwood, it sounded like a Norse God bathing after battle. It was everyone's personal Eden, if they could find it.

The bus arrived. The mix of faces, scents, and attitudes was strangely comforting. I had expected an elevated revulsion after Ruffle Bar's sublime solitude; contrarily, I found that humanity ensconced in a Brooklyn-bound bus radiated a sedative comfort as if we were an intimate tribe gathered around a bonfire.

My reverie did not last long. Boredom follows higher thought like a tail follows a rat. I focused on the tan flesh of the homeward-bound female bathers instead of humanity in its entirety—there'd be plenty of other chances to contemplate the meaning of the multitudes.

Scrotal tingling always emerges victorious over science and the arts, let alone gainful employment. No wonder that with each rung one ascends on the cultural ladder there is an inverse effect vis-à-vis libido and a corollary effect vis-à-vis age: the elderly enjoy God and Wagner because they can; the young are slaves to swift, lubricated thrashing. Imagine the inventions, the revolutions, the symphonies and architectural triumphs young men would bring into the world if only they would cut off their own penises. Oh, humanity's cheap pain! The ever-widening chasm of lost potential that only gets wider as billions of ejaculations career toward the trillions on an insane journey not to Andromeda but to our collective demise, to the final scorching of all that is and all that could be! Oh, Cathars, Cathars, rise up from your graves!

But in the meantime I imagined myself crawling up the aisle on all fours, slithering out of my already unbuttoned jeans with an effeminately writhing pelvis motivated by an entirely masculine intent. The young ladies I was so rapturously ogling had special qualities far beyond flesh correctly apportioned and braised; they possessed a singular languor, a magnetic spiritual hue that one can only cultivate by spending several hours on a beach devoid of those orange-shorted vermin with their dollar-store whistles and metastasizing pectorals; what has gone wrong within them that they should demand attention like a house-sized orangutan's rump? To think of the distinguished virulence of insane Orangemen marching unarmed through County Armagh at midnight being so thoroughly degraded by those nightmarish orange shorts and the morons within; if you wish to save me, prevent a second date with the obese femme-fatale destiny has allotted me, fate and my own monumental shortcomings; the woman who will assuredly bring my final undoing, whether she brings it with bottle, knife, or rope. Will you be there with your whistle when she comes? Wonderful—I'll nap until we reach the Brooklyn College IRT.

Two bus rides, an elevated train across Brooklyn, including a ghostly stop at Neptune Avenue, which, arguably, represents the strongest architectural parallel to the critical fourth instrument in my Cycle. Although I have my own upwardly-thrusting spiritual energy, the sheer volume of spiritual matter rocketing heavenward from the Neptune Avenue Platform is unparalleled. No single person can ever generate the power inherent in certain key locations where intersecting spiritual Arcs, history, visual outlay, and ambience both empirical and intuitive all come together to create a veritable fission reactor of spiritual energy.

The Neptune Avenue Platform is certainly the most notable location like this in the United States, although remarkably, the Chrysler Building almost rivals Neptune Avenue's force; this incredible binary occurrence is surely the reason New York is overflowing with mystery and trillions of unnamable qualities. I've often hypothesized that the binary action of these locations might rely on an Arc between the two in addition to the far more obvious spiritual obelisks emanating directly from both locations, and the byproducts of this arrangement create magnetic qualities in the ratio of one to each New Yorker. I would guess that the magnetic component is generated first and subsequently draws the resident to New York like light to a black hole, whether they are drawn from other regions or from nonexistence itself.[15]

Needless to say, my walk from the Brighton Beach stop to the library was a stagger through blood and fire, so besieged was I with further conjecture on this matter. The sounds of Russian on Brighton Beach Avenue exacerbated my forward-thinking to degrees most extreme: I obsessed over images and emotions from the Great Spiritual East. These thoughts drove me too close to a violent maelstrom, and a large chunk of my aura was ripped asunder; it was found[16] eighteen years later trapped in an ethereal riptide cycling endlessly between the Kremlin and Prague's Vyšehrad Castle. Vyšehrad hosts the most powerful energy flow through the veneer that is our dimension into the massive latitudes of the Fourth through the Eighth dimensions. It is said that because of this, Prague's lovers perch along Vyšehrad's walls at dusk to smoke, drink, and bask in the connectivity provided by the geyser.

I entered the library. Children screaming, teenagers chatting, drunks sleeping, lunatics moaning. At the check-out, a Russian woman with a giant black beehive and a floor-length mink coat was screaming that she would not pay her twenty-cent late fee.

Peter was at a table with four similarly disheveled men. He was droning on about stealing beer for pretty Spanish girls or some other such drivel. I joined them.

"Damone! These are my friends. This is Damone. He saved my life."

"Which of you is his uncle?"

---

[15] All births in the five boroughs plus continuous residency beyond one hour. Also includes births occurring in motorized vehicles outside the five boroughs driving with good faith intent to return/arrive.

[16] But, of course, not returned.

"I don't think none of us."

"My uncle's not here yet, but only fifteen minutes Damone."

"Excellent. You gentleman wouldn't happen to know if any of these elderly women are from Bukovina?"

None of them seemed familiar with the region, let alone if anyone in the library could claim origins there. I have a terrible fear of elderly women from Bukovina vis-à-vis their willingness to tie young men to flaming tractors in motion.

I did my best to contribute to the pitiful small talk. I noticed that it was significantly more tedious to participate in lumbering repartee than, say, staring at one of my dirt walls on Ruffle Bar.

I was listening to a grey-headed dolt blathering some nonsense about John Mitchell depleting a hotel mini-bar and getting caught walking back into the lobby with replacement liquor purchased from an outside vendor when a well dressed young man with curly black hair greeted the table.

"Hey guys. Hey Peter. You must be Damone."

Were I Johannes Brahms, I'd have suggested this stranger prematurely assumed the "Du" form; as an English speaker I had no choice other than to accept his crudity. Peter's uncle indeed.

"Pleased I'm sure. Where are my brothers?"

"They're the Ramones? I caught their first show at Performance Studio in March. I know a guy who helps them carry equipment. They're different, man. They're playing at a club called CBGB in the Bowery a few days in a row. What's the date today?"

"Sixteenth," someone said.

"So they're playing tonight. Can you handle money, Damone? Or can you buy Peter's ticket and I'll pay you back? I'm good for it."

"I'll pay it."

We made our arrangements and said our goodbyes. My initial thought was to dispense with Peter, but then I thought having another body along might lend me more authority if he assumed the proper grimace.

Not that he was necessary: I felt like a Genghis Khan that had absorbed all his hoards. Woe unto my brothers for their foolish crime. A deal contingent on damnation would have indicated more prudence than deceiving Damone Ramone. They did not know the demon they had unleashed. There would be feasting, blood, mastication, defecation. But first I would enjoy their little "performance" so I could witness firsthand their pathetic, doomed attempt to generate some creatively underfunded musical half-breed so beneath contempt that any connection to the original masterpieces would be all but obliterated to everyone except, perhaps, Arturo Toscanini, Sir Georg Solti, and myself.[17] Challenge me, will you? I'll put you in a place that would make being trapped in a Bosch painting seem like a trip to the ice cream parlour on someone else's dime.

I admit, although my rage was largely self-generating as I moved toward consummation, I made some mental adjustments to further add to its brilliant fire and implacability. Specifically, I tried to work myself into a tongue-biting frenzy over having been marooned; yes, I was furious about it insofar as it pertained to the theft of my masterpieces, but I wanted it to be characterized by a rage *exclusive to it*; in other words, I wanted to isolate and magnify my indignation at the fact that my own brothers would maroon me, irrespective of the reasons.

But I was failing. A gnawing sensation—the schism of the self-aware hypocrite that induces nocturnal wriggling—occurred simultaneously whenever I attempted to blow the bellows on my righteous rage. For I was plagued by a fact undeniable: I had thoroughly enjoyed my years on Ruffle Bar. In fact, once I settled the score with the lesser Ramones, I would return to the placidity of the island's whispering reeds and pliant coastal sands, never to be heard from again. In other words, the world would have my musical legacy but the world would not have me. Or rather, I would not have it; this ludicrous spinning ball carpeted with prancing idiots of every stripe with their relentless chatter, and worst of all, their patronizing smiles. For in the end, aren't all smiles patronizing at the core, even that of the mother staring down at her blanketed newborn? No. Give me a hole, a generous

---

[17] Sviatoslav Richter might also recognize the derivative nature, at least viscerally.

harvest of fluke and blue crabs,[18] an agile right hand, and fuck all to the rest of it.

Peter interrupted my reveries by suggesting a stroll on the boardwalk:

"Let's walk a while, Damone. The librarian saw what you were doing to that table."

I had intended on a session of 256, and where better than a library to conduct it? A man opens a book of no less than 512 pages to page 256, place his penis within, and then closes the book with a crack. Once encased, the palms are used to exert vice-like pressure on the book as if one were making wine. Although this would have provided serenity, there were simply too many hours ahead to address them in this manner; a walk seemed a reasonable alternative.

We walked toward Coney Island. Brighton: strolling couples, grey headed, Russian. Laughing teens speaking a pidgin of deep Brooklynese and Russian peppered with Yiddish slang. For entertainment, I parodied a high-minded scientific tone and demonstrated the immense potential in self-spank propulsion and finger-flutter flying.

A scene in front of a café interrupted my demonstrations: a lone drunk Mexican was dancing to the wild pained exuberance of a Hasidic musician. Peter was highly amused, and I admit the odd juxtaposition was theoretically funny. But the unhinged Danubian scales, their indigo joy born of sorrow and Balkan slivovice—only served to remind me of the dark tower of sound from the other world that called me to be its sole corporeal interpreter, only to have the gift corrupted by my own brothers. The biblical proportions of my tragedy provided no respite; a eulogy a thousand years on does not reduce the agony of the martyr today.

So when Peter launched into never-ending descriptions of the brutalities and tragicomic melees that apparently characterized nearly every closing time at the Brooklyn Public Library, Brighton

---

[18] I confess to the consumption of the occasional roseate turn, peregrine falcon, piping plover, pie-billed grebe, and northern harrier. These victuals were only consumed however on Ruffle Bar feast days.

Beach Branch, I allowed it. I feigned interest with silence and grunts while I drifted among my own turbulent thoughts. Admittedly, I was intrigued by the creative methods Peter employed to hide in order to spend the night in the library: lying on top shelves; secreting himself behind the Encyclopedia Britannica; taping himself beneath tables, and so on.

We were crossing the no-man's land between Brighton and Coney, a desolate stretch of planks where sparsely scattered ambassadors from both ends of the boardwalk mixed like isolated stars in the outer edges of two galaxies slowly coming together. Peter's juvenile droning had dulled my senses; I realized we were walking too quickly, likely due to my bristling and seething. We still had ample distance to travel along the New York Aquarium wall, but the ampleness relied on the judicious allocation of every step; at the rate we were going I'd end up pacing the Bowery like a jilted husband in the maternity ward waiting room.

Luckily Peter's drivel collided with the residual fragments of my earlier ruminations on Vyšehrad Castle in Prague: Peter was describing how after the library was closed and dark and the sound of the security guard checking the doors from outside confirmed the all-clear, the vagrants would simultaneously emerge from bookshelves, under tables, above the ceiling tiles, and from beneath books in the donation bins and return carts. They'd rise as if from the dead to resume storytelling and drinking, whispering among the dusty stacks.

"Peter, are you familiar with the Golem?"

"He's the first Jewish robot."

"Well played, sir. You are exactly right."

"I'm not dumb, Damone."

"Rabbi Loew of Prague, arguably, created the first successful Golem—it is his role that you shall play. I will play the Golem. I shall lie here as if I were fragments of clay, and you will animate me."

"Why do you get to be the Golem?"

"Because. Now begin."

I closed my eyes and imagined myself as random veins of gray and brown hidden in the Earth's subcutaneous darkness. Peter scurried and leapt while imitating the sounds of medieval medical equipment. Although his interpretation relied a bit heavily on Johnny Sokko and Boris Karloff, he avoided being overly derivative by adding his own surprisingly original motifs which were, at times, almost erotic; at the same time they maintained a soulless mechanized quality that resembled having sex with a car or vice versa. I in turn came together and rose up as a giant man of stone with sternum thick and round, and with legs like Doric columns.

I plodded down the boardwalk. It took us nearly three hours to reach the West 8th Street train stop, a ten-minute trip had we maintained our earlier pace.

Getting on the train was difficult. My head alone was nearly three feet wide, and while attempting to get on all fours to crawl into the train—I wouldn't have fit any other way—I crashed my head into the door frame, and then the subway doors closed on my giant stone ankle with a loud clang that turned every head in the car.

Not wanting to break the seats, I lay down on the floor in the center of the car, stared at the ceiling and chanted, "I am the Golem, I am the Golem," while Peter walked up and down the car chanting back, "He is the Golem, he is the Golem." By the time we got off at Broadway-Lafayette Peter had collected over five dollars in change from impressed travelers.

We headed toward the Bowery. I instructed Peter not to return me to human form until we were almost touching the den of iniquity called CBGB. Passing pedestrians were either awe-struck or delighted at the sight of the massive Golem gravely stomping down Bleecker Street. It occurred to me that I was just as adept at being the Golem as I would be in any number of vocations, and it made me mourn life with its myriad choices that ultimately created only one thin line: it meant that real life consisted of wondering what would have happened on all of those other paths. Although my Muse largely disabused me of these concerns, my heart wept for the lesser masses continuously tortured by freewill.

CBGB, OMFUG, 315 Bowery. Three-Fifteen: To this day when those satanic runes radiate from a digital clock, I can't help but engage in violent self-abuse. It matters not if the cruel equation appears in green or red, *Ante Meridian* or *Post Meridian*—its results always verify that the half empty glass is a scientific fact rather than a pessimistic point-of-view.

The club was thirty feet ahead; I estimated we'd arrive there in about an hour. Filthy youths cavorted under the CBGB awning, smoking, laughing, leaning on parked cars. It was hard to believe they had willingly gathered to see my brothers play "music," but who was I to explain the palates of cretins. On the other hand I was going to sue them for every dollar they had handed over to my thieving brothers from their moist, stained pockets.

He emerged from the sea of hoodlums and tarts, brightly illuminated like the yellow guy in Rembrandt's *Nightwatch* by the scintillating fires of evil: Danny Fields.

Danny metamorphosized among the crowd like something imagined, like a coagulation of the cigarette smoke and apocryphal New York City mist that snaked from the sewers and floated in front of the club.

I screamed at Peter:

"Free me! Begin the incantations this instant."

"You are Damone again."

"You must do better!"

"You are now Damone again, Damone Ramone again."

"More, you tepid fool! Must you be so bloody noncommittal?"

"You are now Damone again, Damone Ramone again, a man come forth from the sea who blows his nose on all men, especially men named…named Glenn!"

"I am free, but oh! I am awry, I am not right. There was an imbalance, something incorrectly recorded in Loew's account. You must right the wrong with a proper psalm, a rhyme of rhymes like that which you recited when we were all but doomed in the black raging sea!"

"*There once was a man from Far Rockaway that could smell a piece of ass—*"

"Not the same one, you fool! Do you wish to destroy us both? Equal but different!"

"How about:

There once was a whore on the dock
From dusk until dawn she sucked cock
'til one day it's said
She gave so much head
She exploded and whitewashed the block"

Thunder within. I rushed across Bowery. Cars honked and obscenities flew. I lunged through the crowd and dove at Fields.

He knocked me to the ground with a single blow. I had forgotten the power of his pipes, honed by his years as a man before the mast. A woman said, "What's up with that guy?"

"Some nut, probably speeded up," said Danny.

I got up and brushed off.

"Some nut, eh Danny? Is that what I am? Or am I perhaps someone familiar to you?"

"You're not. Take a hike."

"I'll take a hike, right inside this club."

I walked to the doorwoman. I offered money.

"You jump Danny, now you think you're getting in? Sorry."

"I have the requisite amount. My problem with Fields isn't your concern. Now let me in."

"If you don't leave I'll call my husband."

"Just go, man," said some hoodlum behind me.

"Listen, nobody wants trouble," said the woman.

"You don't understand: I'm Damone Ramone—the Ramones are my brothers."

"Good one. Get the fuck out of here."

"Miss, I was marooned on a desert island for years, I only just got back and I'm sure my brothers will want to see me."

"If you didn't hit Danny, that just might have worked, but no. You gotta go."

"Come on, man, there's a line here," said the fool behind me.

"I shan't!"

I charged the door. The woman screamed. I entered the club, a filthy graffiti-covered cave. I didn't see my brothers. I screamed:

"Joey! Johnny! It's Damone. Dee Dee! Tommy! Are you here?"

I was hit. People grabbed me from behind. I couldn't break free. But they couldn't throw me out either: growing up in a house full of brothers prepares one to wriggle.

I pedaled my legs in the air. I thrashed about. Someone pulled my hair. Others came to the aid of my persecutors, surrounding me, grabbing my legs. I knew exactly how the corpse of Che Guevara felt as they stretched me full-length and carried me out the door.

On Bowery they swung me back and forth by my arms and legs while counting off:

"One...Two...Three!"

I flew into the gutter. I got up and charged the door again. I was summarily rebuffed by a Maginot Line of scumbags. As I tumbled back into the gutter, the stench of sweat and leather stuck in my nose. I could not mount another charge; I lay in the gutter gasping to the sound of laughter and mockery.

"Damone, are you okay?"

Peter helped me up. There was no sign of Danny Fields or my brothers, but the doorwoman and her goons were watching me. I shuffled across Bowery to Bleecker as if I had accepted defeat. Peter followed.

"After the performance begins I'll attempt another entry."

"Damone, I don't think it'll work."

"Peter, I don't surrender. I keep coming and coming until I get what I want. Can you believe this? Denied by my own brothers. They're hiding in there of course, the cowards."

We sat down and leaned against a building.

"In the meantime Peter, if you'd recite that poem about the exploding whore, I'd be most grateful. To think, such a wonderful sonnet heard for the first time in such circumstances. God is generous with irony, Peter, no one can deny that."

Peter began. I allowed myself to be swept away by the brilliance of each word and by Peter's admittedly sonorous rendition. The sound of the poem washing over my repose disengaged pain from my psyche; I was able to take inventory, rest, and ultimately nap.

Peter woke me with a yank. I didn't recognize my surroundings; I had been cocooned inside a convincing sense of my recent reality's falseness. I had in fact expected to open my eyes to the old familiar walls of the sewing room. When my head cleared, I was scorched by the source of my humiliating optimism: a familiar sound.

It was utterly mangled of course, like watching Wan Hu's attempt at flight next to an Apollo liftoff. Nonetheless, there was no mistaking it: *Pretend We Aren't Related*, Opus 38, from the *Chicks with Dicks Sleep Late* Quartet Cycle.

I ran down Bleecker toward the club. I ran across the street. "You again," yelled the doorwoman. I tried to push past, but the bearded man shoved me to the ground. I got up and charged him with my head down. He stepped aside and pulled me forcefully in the direction I was already going; I rammed the wall instead of the man. I blacked out.

A hard slap. Peter.

"Damone, let's go, they called the police."

"Like that's gonna happen," someone said. Laughter.

Then a siren. "Well holy shit," said the doubter. I stood up.

Peter walked me from the club.

"Peter...we're going back again. We'll wait for my brothers outside."

"Damone, no. You need rest. Remember, they play tomorrow. Do it tomorrow, okay? They'll be on the lookout tonight."

Peter's logic was sound. We trained back to Brighton. I wilted into the donation bin. I watched the dirty vagabond hands of Peter and his friends as they buried me with yellowed, musty paperbacks. As the last few covered my face, my world became dark, still, muffled. A few specks of light filtered through the books. I was out before the library was even closed.

CHAPTER XX.

THE PURSUIT BEGINS AGAIN.

Voices muted by ragged paperbacks woke me. I wasn't sure if the night had passed or if I had only dozed, so I lay still listening. I thought I heard Peter repeating his gold standard for beauty and class: sophisticated.

Or not: I pushed my head from beneath the donated books.

"Morning Damone, have some breakfast."

"Breakfast? How?"

"Doesn't open till one, and the guard today used to be one of us."

"One of you?"

"He was here all the time, so the library hired him. He's on medication now."

A red-faced old man brought me a coffee.

"How did you fry these eggs?"

"The coffee machine burner."

My challenges on Ruffle Bar had given me a keen respect for that type of survivalist ingenuity. I recalled a bad moment on Ruffle Bar when I chewed on the rotten underside of a horseshoe crab before I had implemented all of the improvements that, taken together, converted a desolate island into paradise.

When the library opened, the vagrants left and joined the other neighborhood bums under a boardwalk pavilion. They drank from paper bags and played chess. The beach vagrants arrived, backs covered in dirt. The homeless shelter group arrived in ludicrous Salvation Army clothes, faces nicked and bruised. The library vagrants were the aristocrats; some actually had their own apartments, or like Peter, they were the imbecilic black sheep of local families, the remote cousins that taught the strangest lessons all grown up.

I'd never realized just how much alcohol can help in challenging situations. I spent the day passing bag after bag of mint schnapps, sloe gin, and a variety of sweet wines. As the hours passed, I became increasingly confident all would turn out well.

After dark, Peter and I walked across the beach and climbed a lifeguard chair. The moonlit waves crashed softly as we passed a bottle of Blue Nun and discussed our plan. It seemed increasingly sensible to just wing it, so we went back to the avenue where Peter stole a bottle of vodka. We forced it down before catching the Manhattan-bound train.

But apparently I had miscalculated because I had to disembark at Avenue X so I could vomit into a trashcan. We boarded the next train, but its motion made me sick again, and we had to disembark at Kings Highway so I could vomit into a trashcan. We boarded the next train, but its motion made me sick again, and we had to disembark at Parkside so I could vomit into a trashcan. At Parkside the endeavor concluded somewhat optimistically: nothing emerged other than a few searing, sunflower-yellow specks.

Nevertheless, before DeKalb I was overcome with nausea, and when the door opened I attempted to leave so I could vomit again. Peter tackled me and pinned me to the subway floor. I tossed him off. He grabbed my legs. The doors shut. We wrestled up and down the train as it roared across the Manhattan Bridge while the passengers shrieked. Peter dragged me to the end of the train, opened the door, and held me by the hair while I dry-heaved between the cars.

When we got off I was reinvigorated and somewhat the soberer. I was forced to thank Peter for taking charge of the situation; if we had delayed much longer I might have missed my chance.

We sat between parked cars on Bleecker. I read the logo *Impala* as it morphed from one logo to two and back again. I exerted an effort befitting a Bulgarian dead-lifter to freeze the ever-splitting logo. Peter produced a pint of sloe gin, which on the one hand made the Impala challenge worse, but on the other hand my confidence skyrocketed in direct proportion to the increasing number of logos. I passed out.

Peter woke me with a poke and said, "Damone, people are coming out, I think it's over."

I watched the crowd streaming from CBGB. The majority of the crowd disappeared into the night, but a sizeable number remained in front of the club talking. No sign of a Ramone.

Until Tommy an hour later. This would be a pleasure, an easily digested *L'amuse-bouche* prior to the main course. Granting he was the least likely of my brothers to have devised the nefarious plot, he was the most likely to have cured its weaknesses.

I crossed Bleecker. Peter followed at a circumspect distance. When I was nearly under the club's awning, Joey and Dee Dee appeared. I grabbed Tommy by his jacket and I threw him to the ground.

"Attention, everyone! May I have your attention please? It is I, Damone Ramone, the composer of the music you have just enjoyed! Did you appreciate its blend of passion and minimalism? Antecedents, you ask? The eighth string quartet of Shostakovich comes to mind. Were you looking to these miscreants for answers? Or would you be better-served asking them, say, how to rob a homeless person at knifepoint? Perhaps this long-boned jellyfish has the answers, this squirming impostor. Tell us, Joey, please—we would all like to know—how did you resist the impulse to adopt certain atonal qualities of the Second Viennese School?"

"Come on, man."

"Come on *man*? How about, 'Come on *Damone*?' Tell me Joey, how much money did you make tonight with your performance of "original" music? Are you off to the Russian Tea Room to gorge on vodka and caviar, singing the old seafaring songs at the top of your lungs, confident they won't dare throw out such wealthy, gout-bound geniuses? Tell me, Joey, what *is* the going rate for highway robbery these days? Pray tell."

"Here man, take everything I got if you want more wine or whatever."

Joey reached into his pocket. A black leather lightning-bolt sent him spinning helplessly away.

"What did I tell you about giving money to bums, Joey? You need money, buddy? Get a job!"

"Oh, hello Johnny, glad you could join us. Are we buddies now? How're mom and dad?"

"Johnny, I got rights to twenty-five percent of what we made tonight so if I want to help this guy I'll do whatever I want because it's my eleven cents."

Johnny grabbed Joey by the shirt.

"You can do whatever you want as long as it's what I want you to want and I don't want you to want that. Now give me the money, I'm going to hold it for you in a trust!"

"What trust?"

"A trust called my pocket. Now stop talking to this bum and let's go."

"None of you are going anywhere until I get my just deserts," I said.

Johnny punched me in the face. I hit the pavement. I watched them jumping into a van through a bleary swath of eye-snot and shame. The van sped away.

Peter helped me up.

"I'm sorry Damone, that didn't look like it worked. But I can see you guys are brothers, that's for sure."

"Because of our looks?"

"Yeah, but more cuz of how you argue—in that brother way."

We descended into the subway. I demanded that Peter pretend the subway car was sixteenth-century Wittgenstein and to let the flagellation begin, but he failed to ken that I was Martin Luther so I chose to look the other way. I stared straight ahead and said nothing until we disembarked at West 8th Street.

I suggested we walk to the end of the platform to gaze at the Cyclone and the Wonder Wheel and the never-ending expanse of the midnight sea.

A powerful wind blew across the dark amusement park below. An ominous howl emanated from the AstroTower; in the night the truly mysterious nature of the faceless black spike was revealed beneath the iron sky, against the rolling sea. I communed with the purity of my own magic obelisk that also stabbed into an empty sky that seemed, at times, to smother us when we were abandoned by the sun.

But at other times, such as that fateful night I stood on the West 8th platform with Peter, spiritual action coalesced with spiritual geography to alter the meaning of the night; it was no longer the refuge of bogeymen, of things that go bump, of coffins and skulls; it became the night sky of dreams where one flew fearless through tungsten puffs bathed in yellow-tinted moonlight, soaring in the cleansing wind across the spiritual highways: the AstroTower, the Neptune Avenue Platform, north to the Chrysler Building. Above the dark streets, the chasms of possibility running north and south on the big island, and then the Arc across the sea to Vyšehrad, an earthly haven for souls that crossed the membrane while their despairing corporeal bodies still wandered wretchedly across the vulgar Earth.

The sound of urine spraying against the barrier accompanied by a warm mist ricocheting onto the top of my left hand broke the night's spell. I looked down at the pooling stream rolling toward my shoe.

"Sorry, I really had to go. Drank a forty when you were fighting with your brothers."

I slapped Peter on the back.

"No worries, my friend, no worries. I was in a place so good I just might have stayed, and I still have unfinished business among you. Can we still get in the library?"

"Yes."

"Let's go to the library and we'll regroup in the morning. The fight has just begun.

CHAPTER XXI.

INTERLUDE AMONG THE DUNES.

The next morning we were deprived of a leisurely breakfast because the library opened at eight. Peter woke me in the small hours and said we had to go; I felt as if I had just closed my eyes beneath *The Hardy Boys: The Mystery of the Chinese Junk.*

We broke our fast with three bottles of sweet wine guzzled behind the library dumpster. The fortified syrup bandaged my soul under a lightening sky. We dispersed, our optimism substantially reinforced. Although we each had our own story, I am sure every man came out ahead with each swig of nectar. Speaking for myself, by the time I sat on a bench to watch the sea and take stock of my situation, I approached everything with wisdom and tranquility.

My brothers weren't performing again until August 24th, so I had time to plan a new attack. In the meantime I required solitude. Although he'd been helpful, Peter could not stop spouting his delusional tripe, and I needed time to think. When I explained this to Peter, he understood. He presented me with four bottles of port and saw me off at the train.

I returned to the Rockaways, to the dunes near my childhood home where I had secreted my sea chest. I had no desire to see the rubble of the Ramone estate, but such was the beauty of the dunes and the nearby beach that no amount of personal tragedy could tarnish it; in fact, despite its proximity to the monument of cowardice the house had become, I still intended to partake in sea and wind, in sun and stars; I would not let a temporal tragedy deprive me of all that was light.

Despite my brothers' thus far successful defense of their vile travesty, I stepped off the Q35 feeling oddly light of heart, as if my mood had disengaged from both reason and recent events. As I walked across the green expanse toward the beach, I punctuated the journey with short bursts of skipping. I felt like a schoolboy as I smelled the grass and savored the heady mix of brandy and wine offered by the heavily discounted yet stolen nonetheless port—my second bottle of the day.

But my joviality was dealt a blow when I reached the crevasse where I had hidden my sea chest—it had been ransacked. The missing clothing was not of import; the missing money however was another matter. Although I still had a respectable amount on my person, the bulk had been in the chest. Fortunately I had carried the oilskin with me, so in addition to money I also had the map indicating where additional drugs and cash were hidden on Ruffle Bar.

In the days that followed I lead a dual life. Part of me never slept or partook of leisure, but ceaselessly devised vindictive capers of every hue, all designed to even the score with my brothers. The other part of me was immersed in soft contemplation, in a gentle tranquility of crashing waves, sunsets, and symbols of waning life seen in every depletion, from a dying bird on the path to the resigned consumption of the last few inches of port in my final bottle.

It was the latter situation rather than a desire for camaraderie that led me to visit Peter in Brighton Beach. He agreed to my request with enthusiasm, proud—as he should have been—that I recognized his prodigious liquor-stealing skills.[19] He brought me three gallons of gin.

I thanked him and was about to board the elevated train when he said, "Wait, hang on a minute."

"Yes?"

---

[19] Peter was a veritable artist of sleight-of-body and sleight-of-perception; it bordered on the paranormal. How, for example, did he conceal half-gallon and gallon bottles with no discernible change to his appearance? I witnessed it firsthand on several occasions, and can offer no logical explanation.

"I was thinking about what went wrong at CBGB's, and I think I figured it out."

"I was brutally beaten by family and friends, have you sniffed out some additional nuance?"

"They didn't know who you were."

"What in the name of God are you talking about? I grant you, I'm obviously not uppermost on their roster of concerns, but it's absurd to suggest they've forgotten me completely in four years."

"Your brothers all sorta look the same, and I thought you said something about how you all go to the same barber to look even more the same."

"Go on."

"And now you have that big beard and your hair's way longer and you're wearing that...that coat made with dead things and trash bags."

"With all due respect Peter, where exactly are you going with this?"

"Damone, I'm saying you don't look like you, you look like some street guy."

"Says you."

"Damone, you need to get cleaned up. The door people aren't going to let you in to CBGB or anywhere else. If you wear the same clothes as your brothers and get your hair cut, you might even get in free if you say you're one of them or that you're helping move their stuff."

"I understand that aspect, but I don't at all follow this other line of thought: my brothers don't know who I am because of my appearance?"

"Damone, let's go to that barber and you can go to the dunes after."

As we rode toward Manhattan I stewed in humiliation. I knew Peter was right somehow but I simply could not render any palatable cause-and-effect equation that would allow me to understand why. But since I intuitively understood that his concept was the product of some sort of consensus-based logic—something anthropologically sound and collectively understood to such an extent that even Peter could explain its dynamics with confidence, even with a certain swagger—I knew I had to make a leap of faith and surrender to his nebulous counsel. In sum, it was clear to me why recognition would be statistically more likely the more similar a group of individuals looked, but it wasn't at all clear how that effect could somehow be reversed by dissimilarity; it seemed hair-brained, like the Soviet plot to reverse the flow of rivers. At least I'd have a chance to interrogate our old barber—perhaps he knew where my brothers were now living.

But the old man was even more laconic than before. He claimed not to remember me even though he had been cutting my hair for most of my life; nonetheless, after hacking through my Rasputin beard and D'Artagnan locks, he shaped my hair into the traditional Ramones hairstyle. When he spun the barber's chair around and I saw myself in the mirror, my experiences of the last four years were reduced to dark clumps of hair on the barber's white tile floor: the exterior proof of my hardships and eventual reverence for solitude was gone. I was now just another face in the crowd harboring a story that nobody would ever postulate from my clean-shaven blandness.

Next we went to a secondhand store where I did my best to equate the Ramones uniform. Although the black leather jacket I purchased wasn't quite biker enough and the jeans I purchased were absurdly short, I walked out of the shop as a reasonable facsimile of my pre-desecrated self. I was pleased with my strutting reflection in the shop windows. I imagined I had a long forked tongue, and I flicked it at every person who dared meet my gaze on Third Avenue.

I spent the following days in a delirium of seaside sunsets and public transportation. I became a pair of eyes fixed at a central point while time and the world passed in a gliding montage, a collage stretched between two slowly spinning axles cranked by an even, steady hand. The gentle tides of gin were causing an ever-widening dilation, a total expansion of colors and perceptions with each ebb and flow of the juniper-infused perfume that made breathing so deep, slow, and easy.

I rode buses and trains. I wandered streets and parks. A new centrality emerged in the fields and paths of Prospect Park. I wandered through an overgrown enclave of dead fountains and cracked benches where I witnessed acts of love with which I did not empathize; however, I sympathized with their ardor and deviance. I asked a nude Negro wandering among the trees, "What is the name of this hidden place?" He replied, "This is the Veil of Cashmere." He then embarked on a series of pantomimes, and I swiftly left that hidden place.

I ascended a tall, forested hill. At the top I discovered a small, circular asphalt path going nowhere—I found its symbolic mockery oddly comforting and I walked around it 100 times. I removed my jacket and took off my t-shirt. I shoved a portion of the t-shirt into my mouth that roughly equated the width of my face. I dreamed of lemons and bitter herbs and tangy cherry taffy until my mouth gushed saliva, thus moistening the shirt, thus making it very nearly translucent, thus allowing me to stretch it across my eyes to create a hazy lens through which I viewed the park, the trees, and Brooklyn far below me; the moist, gossamer-thin t-shirt made Brooklyn look like Budapest seen from Gellert Hill, and as I gazed down I distinctly heard the dancing minor keys of millions of gypsy violins and I longed to fuck women. I put my clothes back on and wandered down the hill, joining the throngs of walkers and runners on the park's main path, staring at the beautiful faces, those that met my eyes and those that cast their eyes downward to my constrained homage.

As the sun faded into the honeydews of a Brooklyn afternoon, I found myself standing just beyond the ring of people encircling the park's ancient carousel. The backs of heads transfixed me as they moved slowly left to right as the music played, the children screamed, and the wooden horses flashed by. It was as if human heads were nothing more than sliding typeballs moving back and forth within clicking clacking Selectrics operated by frenzied secretaries.

This thought immersed me in the depths of a convulsive despair so tangible that it felt like demonic possession, a malaise imbued with cruel powers far in excess of the tortures of a fevered mind—no, this was a demon indeed, a messenger from the beast wrestling with me in order to implement an eternal reign of despair. Ropes of sunlight burst from my forehead, leaping in all directions like sunspots fired through flexible transparent tubes. I punched, kicked, and howled in protest.

Thus engaged, I did not notice that I had veered into the crowd. The carousel had spun to a stop. I was muttering and jabbing, flashing off jagged bolts of superfluous thought. When my pants slithered down revealing the fleshy valley designed to protect one's anal ring, I did not notice this trite indignity. I wasn't even capable of recognizing it let alone addressing it, so caught up was I in burning off excess brain waves while simultaneously organizing the history of the Selectric Dynasty.

I'll probably never know, and maybe it doesn't matter, whether it was the partial exposure of my dark fecal valley or my jerking contortions that so inflamed the crowd, but at some point they turned against me to a man. It was like some humorless authority figure had dragged the needle across the record to terminate a glorious party, except in this case the music and the colorful guests existed solely in my head, and although none of them outright liked me, they were at least apathetic enough to let me unobtrusively lurk at their margins.

The same could not be said for the crowd of hostile idiots now staring at me while I futilely attempted to hike up my pants. I never thought I'd miss watching Selectric II draw and quarter a ten-thousand strong herd of swine that had been found guilty of high treason, but that's why they call it irony. What is desperately rolling around in torrents of felonious livestock blood compared to staring into the eyes of an indignant Park Slope parent? They clearly wanted to beat me until I was a bag of pasty marrow and splinters, a chicken forgotten on the rotisserie for weeks on end. Even the children, those snot-besmirched apples of eyes, looked at me as if I was dung. I rolled over and formed a human X, and then I used my posterior muscles just as I had done one night on a putting green. I lifted my head, turtle-like. Our eyes met.

Children laughed. Men cursed. Women hissed. For reveries beyond my control, they wanted to hurt me. For deliriums that had punished me for all my years, they wanted to punish me further. For being perennially on the fringe they wanted to cast me out.

But not her. An invisible hand reached out to an invisible person. She disappeared behind the shouting commoners. I stood up, turned my back on them, and slowly walked away.

Part V.

A DIVERSION OF THE HEART FROM GOD ALMIGHTY.

CHAPTER XXII.

LADY.

I sat on a dune. Peter approached from the direction of Riis Park Beach. He was wearing swimming trunks and carrying a black briefcase. I had left him as a yammering child, but now he appeared saintly and regal. Although I knew when he paused over sunbathers he was dispensing lewd compliments, I imagined instead that he was distributing loaves to humble supplicants whose flurry of gestures expressed gratitude rather than threats to summon the police. As I watched him stagger blindly into the water after a woman threw sand in his eyes and declared he was a sick son-of-a-bitch, I felt such affection that I jogged down the dune rather than wait for him to come to me.

"Peter," I said, "What a pleasant surprise. Madam, he meant no harm. This way."

"She misinterpreted my meaning."

"You don't have to tell me, my friend. Come, up here. Please tell me you have something for us to drink."

He opened the briefcase. Five bottles of vodka. Sunlight danced through ascending bubbles as I poured one down.

"Hey Damone, you'd better go easy if you want to get anywhere at CBGB's tonight."

"Tonight? What's the date? It can't be the twenty-fourth already."

"It's the twenty-fifth. I couldn't find you yesterday."

Embarrassment hit me like a two-by-four to the chest. Shame's scarlet fires burned my cheeks. Rivulets of sweat spewed from my brow. To buy time, I feigned a neurological disorder where my arm and hand would not obey the orders of my mind. I lifted the vodka, but rather than insert the bottle into my mouth I jabbed it over my head, then over my shoulder, and then directly into my sternum. After jamming the bottle into my stomach with a little more force than was necessary, I pretended the mental episode was over and drank normally, pouring vodka down my throat as if it was water. After I drank, I exaggerated the burning in my throat by gagging, coughing, and throwing myself wholly into a fake seizure.

My ruse succeeded—Peter shook me by the shoulders. He asked me if I was okay, then he offered me a bottle of soda which I feigned great interest in, as if I had never seen this soda called *Sprite* before. Peter didn't mock my error regarding the date, but nonetheless the mere idea that he could have had I not embarked on my deception filled me with disgust and self-loathing. From then on I would have to live with the idea that perhaps he had only been playing along, pretending to believe my ruse, when in fact he was taking smug satisfaction in my mistake. I can't say I ever fully recovered my trust in Peter after the incident.

"Are you okay now?" he asked.

"Better. But still shaken. Shall we open another bottle?"

"Fine, but please don't throw it around, I risked my ass for this. If you're having problems drinking lay on your back and open your mouth and I'll pour it in."

"Yes. Yes, perhaps that's best. Thank you, Peter. I don't know what came over me."

"Damone, you're under stress. You're not really yourself. Just rejoining normal society is difficult, and then on top of that you have this problem with your brothers. It's a lot. You're doing okay considering."

"Thank you, Peter. Hand that over here."

"Maybe we should skip tonight's show and relax. Your brothers play again in a few days."

"We're going back tonight. A couple drinks will fortify our resolve. Come, be merry."

"Damone, sometimes you can have too much of a good thing."

"Too much of a good thing? And coming from you, no less. Perhaps you meant it ironically. Yes, perhaps you did. Give me the bottle."

"Jesus, Damone. You can't drink like that."

"I just did. By this evening I'll disprove your foolhardy little axiom. I was at this burlesque show, and after a striptease a guy behind me declared the woman's breasts were too big. Why don't you get in touch with him and you can form an association that blacklists women whose vaginas are too tight. Hand me that fucking bottle and open another."

"Whatever you say, Damone. Just don't say I didn't warn you."

"When I came up here the other day, Prokoviev's *Dance of the Knights* served as a psychological soundtrack. Are you familiar with it? No, of course not. Anyhow, it's composed in an entirely rational sequence. All the notes connect to form a complete sentence, a suspension bridge of sound. Furthermore, each member of the orchestra must perform specific acts in a clearly delineated progression—each downstroke, for example, is succeeded by an upstroke, or there are perhaps sequences of downstrokes, but absolutely nothing is random—everything is rational. Nonetheless, the piece acts as the whole of its parts: the final product is incendiary, and the main victim of the detonation is rationality itself. You're hogging the vodka. Thanks. I mean, these endless semantic arguments where God is pitted against science seem rather silly, don't they, when one has just heard *Dance of the Knights*. Do you concur?"

"Like you said, I don't know the song. Damone, I'm telling you, that is very strong liquor and if you keep drinking like that you're going to be sorry."

"Who is you to advise me? You're a drunk yourself, a liquor-thieving scoundrel."

"But I know how to drink, I'm from Brighton Beach, and I think you're overdoing it."

"Icarus had a goddamn good time getting there, pal. A damn good time. You better believe it. Yep. You'd better believe that, my friend."

A transparent, tremulous curtain descended from the heavens. Meandering legs of wine ran down the curtain from the sun into the glistening sea, as if all of creation spread out before us was a gigantic snifter and Peter and I were two extremely fortunate fruit flies.

Peter had introduced me to several ingenious Brighton Beach Russian delectables designed specifically to accompany vodka. I longed for these marvelous things: salty fats and fish, miniature pickles, onions and dark bread. I found myself having to consider how exactly to phrase the suggestion that we should go to Brighton Beach and enjoy some of these specialties, when the scene before me not only crumbled and rose again into an entirely new tableau, but all recollection of what had been transpiring before was eradicated. A second narrative of reality had been running alongside of my existence like a demonic wolf running swiftly in the underbrush beside a desolate road, trailing a horse-drawn cart it intended to attack.

I sat on my white mare looking over the parapets. I was clad in armor. Red and yellow pennants adorned with two-headed falcons whipped in the wind. My knights stared from the battlements. The sky was green and gray like aged copper. A broad yellow band shone between the firmament and the dark skies. Below us the enemy knights waited in dense formations.

A chalice wrapped in golden rings of light floated in the sky. I dismounted. I walked off the rampart's edge. My knights followed. They screamed and fell to their deaths, whereas I walked on air toward the chalice. I took it in my hands and drank. My horse joined me. I mounted her and we galloped across the clouds.

As we soared along the curvature of the Earth toward the roaring sea, a dragon attacked us. Its neck was twice the length of my steed and its head was that of a reptilian dog's: a gigantic forked tongue leapt across crocodile teeth. Its wings seemed too small to be carrying it at such speeds, and its tail was ten times the length of its body. I ran my javelin into the dragon's neck. It flew screaming into the freezing altitudes. My horse sped toward earth.

The beach was racing toward us, but I feared not. My horse galloped smoothly, reducing our altitude in steady increments. We joined a group of fifty knights whose pennants were in tatters. Nonetheless, they held them aloft proudly. They had ridden into the sea to cool their horses' hooves. They seemed baffled, as if they had expected to find an unexplored continent after crossing mountains but had instead found the sea.

There were also some miserable peasants washing their heads. Some even drank the sea's salty waters. I wondered what tragedies had befallen this gruesome bunch. Fortunately none of them recognized their Overlord. I was not in the mood for embarrassing displays of exaggerated humility.

My horse had donned a blue shirt embroidered with golden lions. I was complimenting both the shirt and the miraculous way that my horse had somehow donned it when a knight wearing oddly similar colors attacked. I drew my sword. There were clangs of steel followed by his death scream.

Onward to repast and homage. I rode my horse through a gigantic arch into a crowd of naked maidens. I was clad in golden armor and a red cape. Women sang and tossed rose petals. I struck poses most regal and puffed my massive chest beneath my golden breast-plates.

Then a familiar voice enjoined me to make haste toward a dark lake. I placed a silver winged helmet on my head. I wore a modest chain-mail and I carried a long gray shield. Urgent whispers insisted I board a small craft, a boat of brilliant gold covered with intricate carvings of flora and fauna. A white swan pulled us into the black lake. I stood in quiet solemnity among swirling gray mists. I felt a surge of gratitude toward this solitary swan, for I heard hostile voices behind us.

We arrived on the other side. The mist faded. The swan walked onto the shore, secured the boat, and helped me alight. A bridge, the dark trees, and a large stone building across the water all seemed familiar. As we disappeared into the darkness, the swan assumed human features, but only for a moment. I struck my head on a branch and fell to the ground.

I was alone among trees. There were cans and milk cartons on the forest floor. The moon was high. The mists had dispersed. I stared across the water at the Prospect Park Boathouse. This was inconceivable. Although I had indeed travelled through a different reality, I was certain I had headed south. No matter. I was still insulated from hard focus by the massive amount of spirits within me.

I walked around the lake. Why, in the middle of the night, would she be there? It was impossible. Nonetheless, the fact that she *had* been there was enough for a man smitten such as I. Oh! Our bodies matter not unless we desire to fuck. And fuck we shall!

I walked toward the building. I tried the door and every window. I hurled myself at the door. I bounced off and fell to the ground. I climbed the ticket office. I pulled myself to the roof. I crawled to the observation tower. I broke a window. I eased myself on to the mechanical wheel, descended a rod, and slid down a pole. My heart raced, as what I had perceived as the unlikely yearnings of a man in love now appeared to be postulations of distinct possibility. I slithered among them until I reached the outer ring.

I caressed each one as I passed, practicing a Braille of Love as I searched for the contours of her face, her throat, her Roman nose, her thick lashes and hair. I regretted the false promise imparted to the others by my touch, but it was a necessary cruelty.

My hands found her. I placed them on either side of her face and ran them slowly down her long neck. We looked into each other's eyes in the shadowy light where true objects and phantom images were indistinguishable, but the reality they created was true, a world of dreamscapes and disembodiment.

Our lips brushed, then again, then again, but again. My hands caressed her long supple limbs. We threw feints aside and fell to, mouth to mouth, soul to soul, pounding heart to pounding heart, no longer two, but one. I had found my Lady.

CHAPTER XXIII.

THE GREAT ESCAPE IS A DREAM.

I was woken by the poke of a groundskeeper's stick. I had passed the remainder of the night on the long wooden porch of a farmhouse. As my mind cleared, I saw that I was still in Prospect Park and had taken refuge on the antique porch of the Lefferts House. Alas, to have woken to such an idyll: to have drank myself back to the 18th century and the quaint responsibilities of your average rural Kapellmeister, perhaps organizing the local musicians for a harvest concert in the nearby chapel.

But no, as the groundskeeper clarified in a solidly contemporary briefing wherein he described a variety of penalties he would execute with his stick if I did not vacate the premises forthwith. I sat up and rubbed my head. He moved off and resumed picking up trash from the yard.

I was torn between returning to the carousel or heading to Brighton Beach to plan the next attack on my brothers. What a strange intoxicant is love: what had been my sole occupation only days ago now seemed like a questionable pursuit compared to the dictates of my loins.

But these thoughts were the misleading impulses of a fevered mind as the spirits receded and the malaise took hold. Fortunately I recognized them for the chimeras that they were. After a little hair of the dog that bit me, my priorities would once again be sensible.

I shuffled from Lefferts House, head pounding. Although I had been hungover before, the flow of booze in and out of my psyche in such large volumes had no precedent. This steady, dance-like rhythm was building a corollary melody on top of my tortured psyche, a melody that was particularly sharp and sonorous in the morning. The sharpness was characterized by an anxiety-based dissonance—I was filled with a strange apprehension without object, a distressing sense of impending deadlines when no deadline loomed.

Based on that, it might seem odd that I also described the melody as sonorous, but therein lay the brilliance of the new spiritual condition grafted onto my soul by booze. In addition to tormenting me with the screeching anxieties of a Shostakovich quartet, it simultaneously soothed me with the divine grace of a Bach cantata. Practically speaking, it meant that my morning mood was infused with a sly sensuality: a flirtatious, insinuating charm that not only aroused me, but others as well. It was as if the stress of withdrawal, which should have induced shame and a longing for solitude, acted paradoxically by inducing a seductive gregariousness fueled by skyrocketing lust. Again, it does not take a genius to see the irony there, since the solitude required to sate sexual desire was set aside in favor of an enjoyable yet ultimately counter-productive immersion in social situations.

I decided that I would indeed visit Lady, but only to gaze at her from afar. I realized that I would be more effective during the next sortie against my brothers if I was fueled by unconsummated love.

I didn't understand that roiled passion might overwhelm all other spiritual and corporeal concerns. On the other hand, allowing passion to displace all else might have been a better way to spend time than embarking on a vengeful and ultimately fruitless crusade; but what did I know of these things in the summer of 1974 when I was so fervently committed to my vindicating mission?

These turbulent thoughts plagued me as I approached the carousel. A mob surrounded it, laughing and pointing at the miserable steeds. As if being lashed to a post and spun around all day wasn't enough, most of the stallions also carried howling children. I cursed the imbeciles who bred those beastly lights of lives.

So when I witnessed some emasculated Park Slope "father" lowering his prince onto Lady's back, to say I glowered or scowled would severely understate my expression; no, these mild descriptions don't even come close to the flesh-distorting mask I terrorized them with: the gaping maw, the iron-smelting eyes, the brow furrowed by every glacial landform of every ice age, tendons like bridge cables exploding from my taught neck. I dedicated every contorted feature, every cutting line, every sweating pore—to their immolation.

I maintained a laser-like focus on Lady and the malignancy in her saddle. My work paid off: a woman approached the man who had placed his child on Lady. She informed him of my presence, and, one would think, the obvious reason for my fury. But I overestimated these people; I should have known that such shameless abusers would not understand someone sympathizing with the horses, let alone loving one of them.

Events unfolded swiftly thereafter. The carousel spun to a halt. The carnival organ fell silent. A cordon of people surrounded me. I stared through them to where my beloved was fixed to the dreadful wheel. I thought of the terrible vertigo she must be enduring as she tried to readjust to stillness, only to be spun around again as soon as she recovered.

The crowd hissed. I had planned on simply ignoring them, but their growing numbers and escalating malice forced me to pay them mind. A self-elected spokesman stepped forward, a petty, vain man who started each day by saying, "I'm a leader," into his shaving mirror. I pictured him putzing around the house on a Saturday afternoon, marshalling the family in their household duties: "Son, I'm putting you in charge of weeds. Did I happen to mention I'm a type A personality? I once read the attributes and decided that's the kind of guy I am, or rather want to be, because in reality I'm intimidated by everyone and I perceive social leveraging in every benign encounter even though it isn't there. And I'm notably uncomfortable with ejaculating, I always remain completely still and never make a sound when I do it."

So caught up was I in imagining the self-deceptive twaddle this boor would require to prop up his little man's ego, that I had to say, "What?" when he addressed me in reality.

"I said, you've been asked to stay away from here before. I want you to leave here and never come back, or you'll face serious consequences."

"Really. And will I be facing these consequences before or after *The Adjustment?*"

"Adjustment?"

"Of course. The Fecal Adjustment: when you lick your mother's feces from my sated phallus. The Fecal Adjustment—do you need it illustrated? Here, like this."

I dropped to my haunches and commenced the demonstration. After several seconds of spirited display, I stood up to continue our exchange.

"What are you waiting for, my good man? Hop hop! I don't have all day to tutor you on simple commands; if you aren't going to drop and engage, I shall be forced to entreat the others to do your work for you...Miss, I'm putting you in charge of Fecal Adjustments, you and that pathetic excuse of a man next to you, the one in the blouse."

"The police are on the way."

"Oooooo! Oh no, what will I do? The *police?* Oooooooooooo!"

"I ought to punch you in the mouth."

"But you won't, will you? Hence someone scurrying off to summon the law. How do you live with yourself, eunuch? The NYPD has more important things to do, I assure you, and they'll be thoroughly displeased that you've called them for nothing. No, you need something with substantial meat on the bones that they can really sink their teeth into, something like...like this!"

Women screamed and men made faces like they were at their first autopsy. I pointed it hither and thither at the crowd as if we were in an outdoor amphitheatre and I was the main event. I felt like I was manhandling a powerful firehouse to break up a crowd of hopeless protestors, and for a moment I envisioned myself as a sadistic Hungarian policeman in 1956 just because such an inflammatory charade would surely irritate Tommy to no end, and

I laughed heartily. I augmented the vision by picturing fat, undulating blobs of smothering blue goo shooting from my hose at the crowd, wrapping themselves around their struggling forms like cold, wet shower curtains in a drafty locker room.

I pulled my pants up before the vision could truly be described as replete, for I did not doubt the police were on their way, and I wanted them to find nothing but cruel hearsay and my ironclad denial when they arrived.

The crowd seemed unsure of itself. I understood, for modernity had stripped the mob of its natural crescendo: apprehending me, parading me through the streets, and then crucifying me outside the city gates. When the climactic moment arrived only to discover it had no object or purpose, it fizzled impotently and disappeared. I stuck my face out in a near-parody of monumental smugness, grinning so hard my eyes became slits. I locked my hands behind my back and strode about, pushing my face toward the crowd, occasionally butting it toward them aggressively so I could watch them leap back.

The police arrived, two standard-issue officers, young, devoid of swagger.

"What seems to be the problem, sir?"

"Officer, absolutely nothing. I was minding my own business, not speaking a word, perhaps moving slightly in time with the carousel music but certainly not dancing, when this gentleman picked a fight with me."

"I did no such thing, I…"

"Sir, back away. Let us do our job. Now, we were called because…"

"He exposed himself after we called you."

"Did you expose yourself?"

"How dare you! If there's some loitering law I was unaware of then educate me, but I won't answer to false accusations!"

"He was here the other day, he stands around staring at the children."

"How dare you, you libelous swine!"

I leapt toward the man who was casting aspersions upon my good name. The officers tackled me, pummeled me with their nightsticks, and handcuffed me. They picked me up beneath the arms and led me away.

"Calm down, asshole. We don't have time for this bullshit, but they claim you exposed yourself."

"Those people are liars, officer! Where do they expect a man in my position to spend the day other than a park? I lost my job, I lost everything. My own family left me, they took all my money, they destroyed my house, they stole my livelihood. Now these people want to kick a man when he's down? The shelters kick you out in the morning, now I can't go to the park either."

"Shut up. Don't go there anymore. Park's big, go somewhere else. You a New Yorker?"

"Born and raised."

"Okay, so you know these new Park Slope people—awful. Treat us like servants. Look at it this way, you got a place to stay tonight."

They drove me to the 78th Precinct and locked me up. I introduced myself to the other gentlemen in the cell, shaking each one of their hands with both of mine with a diplomat's largesse. They seemed amused by this, particularly an older black gentleman who responded to my handshake with a deep bow. When he said, 'Pleased, I'm sure,' with a distinct upper-class English accent, I made note that one could fall further than I had. I was ashamed at finding solace in another's misfortunes, but I must say that my humble Queens roots insulated me from the stellar self-loathing that aristocrat must have felt at being locked up in the same Brooklyn jail as the rest of us. Little did I suspect that a string of ever-greater failures would make the distance between a larva and a sexless worker ant assigned to cleaning up the queen's waste a more appropriate social distance to measure myself against.

I sat down in the corner. I longed to masturbate, as one might imagine considering the unpleasant circumstances, but people kept passing outside the bars. I was forced to discreetly use my elbow to stimulate my loins by pretending to massage my inner knee as if I had injured it during an athletic competition; for example, during a running race one might expect to garner such an injury, particularly if their training regimen had been overly rigorous.

I assumed a severe expression and stated loudly to each of my cellmates: 'My knee hurts!' I shouted as if it were an oath or a threat while looking each one of them directly in their eyes. I continued the false knee-rubbing until the hardness of my elbow found a rival in the hardness of my member. I adjusted my expression and bearing until I resembled the anonymously painted 17th century Dutch masterpiece *Portrait of an Elderly Lady*. I imagined I was wearing the same austere black clothing, and I assumed that mimicking her facial expression would dissuade the others in the cell from looking at me and possibly discovering the true nature of my movements.

But even as the physical pleasure emanating from my genitals began to escalate in accord with my discreet ministrations, I grew sorrowful; I recalled an incident many years earlier when I had first seen the painting in an art history book of Ramona's. She had been sitting on her bed with Johnny paging through the book while he ridiculed the paintings. With respect to *Portrait of an Elderly Lady*, Johnny said the woman appeared to be wearing an air filter from a Ford F350 around her neck. They both were highly amused, and enjoined me to come and look. Although Johnny's facetious comparison was not at all unfounded, it amused me only for a moment; instead, I found myself distracted by a different aspect of the picture: the woman appeared to be masturbating a thin, tendril-like penis in her right hand. Outside the irony of her gender—transexuality was not common in 17th century Holland, to the best of my knowledge—I found her suggestive, masturbatory gesture to be extremely arousing, and I was overcome with a need to execute this gesture upon myself. I pretended to be offended by Johnny's mockery of the painting; I told them they were both unconscionable philistines whose company I could not bear. I bade swift retreat to my quarters where I viciously manipulated my genitalia with my right hand while I pretended my left was resting on a cane or armrest in the exact manner of the portrait, which, if I correctly recall, was thought to have been painted around 1630. Recollecting the happiness and gentle absurdities that had once characterized our family house, it was difficult not to slip into a maudlin mood despite being near orgasm on the floor of the jail cell.

I was thus engaged when an officer banged his nightstick back and forth between the bars. "You," he shouted, "you on the floor jerking off. Get up, you made bail."

"Can I stay for a few more minutes?"

"Let's go, guy. Up and out. Get dinner at the soup kitchen."

"Who paid my bail?"

"If I have to ask you to get up again, we're going to have some problems."

I offered no retort, but when I left the cell I accented my frown by pulling the corners of my mouth down with my forefingers. When the officer laughed, I realized the empty vanity of my display—he had all the power, and I had none. I vowed to be more judicious in the future when forced into the dissident's role.

I headed for the subway. The police had sternly warned me to stay away from the carousel. That was a mandate I simply could not obey. I would return as soon as I procured some type of disguise—I would not be kept from Lady. I imagined us sitting on the dunes watching the sunset, drinking port, sharing the careless laughter of freshly minted love. So caught up was I in love's vertical emanations, I nearly forgot our relationship would inevitably lead to love's horizontal emanations. This thought was so incendiary that I struggled not to think it—I could feel the flames of passion burning along my inner thighs and throughout the sub-tropical underbrush of my dark, wiry Mons pubis. The condition was made all the worse by not having completed what I started in my jail cell.

I was on a bench waiting for the Coney Island train. I slipped my hand into my pocket. As I pinched and rolled my frenulum of prepuce of penis, my erotic focus was broken by a moment of clarity—this fondling of the self in order to depressurize my longings was the salve of cowards; a true man would not behave like this after finding his great love. A true man would take action. I recalled the vision that had guided me to Lady. Was the man now sitting on a bench massaging his sexual organs through his pocket the same man who drank from the golden chalice in the sky, that dispensed with dragons, that drove his steed through the clouds, javelin aloft?

Nonetheless, since I had initiated the act prior to this illuminating moment, I considered the impending orgasm to be grandfathered in as it were. I finished what I had started, and then I boarded the train. I fell asleep almost immediately.

After arriving at Coney, I rushed to the Brighton Beach Public Library. I walked in and sat down with the vagrants.

"Damone, where have you been? I was worried after I lost you in Prospect Park. Geez, were you drunk. I'm surprised you didn't end up in jail. Remember when you tried to ride my back and I wouldn't let you, so you got on some other guy's back who was sunbathing with his girlfriend? And then you poked their dog with a stick and everyone came to watch him kick your ass and then you ran into the water and I had to apologize? Luckily the dog was okay, but then you did it again to that little orange dog; thankfully it belonged to an old lady so she couldn't do anything. Then we rode to Brooklyn and I had to steal that boat because people were coming. I thought it was the police so when we got to the other side I ran. I thought you were behind me but then you disappeared. What happened?"

"What in the hell are you talking about? Don't answer, it's not important. I need some tools. Can you get your hands on a saw, maybe a crowbar? How about a hammer?"

"Are you making some furniture?"

"No, I'm asking you a question—can you get tools?"

"Probably. When do you need them?"

"Tomorrow. Meet me at the Prospect Park carousel just before dark. Don't look for me or call out my name. I'll appear at the right moment."

"What about the next Ramones show, your brothers…"

"All in good time. So you'll meet me as I said, at the carousel before dark?"

"Yeah, sure. No problem. Geez, Damone, you always have some crazy thing happening."

I left the library, intending on spending the night in the dunes. Then I realized the distance would only irritate my nerves, which were already frayed down their lengths. Come what may, I decided to pass the night in Prospect Park near Lady.

I had to laugh as I watched myself behaving in this way, so mad with passion that I was playing the cliché fool in love, but I supposed every man had his day. But I was not entirely bereft of reason; my money was running dangerously low; I needed more immediately if I hoped to fund both revenge and romance.

I attempted one of Peter's tricks: I told passerby that I had just been released from Riker's and I needed train fare to get to Queens to see my brother who owned a construction company. After paying my debt to society, I wanted to lead an honest, simple life. I executed the con without reservation, so fueled by passion that what might have been humiliating felt noble and empowering.

It was remarkable how well this flimsy ruse worked; I collected money so quickly that I continued the scam long after I had accrued enough. After a point it was no longer the profit motive that drove me. The addiction was picturing the unimaginative décor inside the heads of those that chose to support my "cause." Imagining each donor's version of "an honest, simple life" was particularly riotous. I imagined them placing me in an absurdly banal home life based on petit bourgeois aspirations that were always out of reach because I refused to waver from the righteous path, even though I could easily have gotten ahead by holding up a couple liquor stores. Nonetheless, this life would provide some "blessings," perhaps an overweight wife of Norwegian descent, adept with the rolling pin and mischievous after baking with kirsch. There would be the requisite collection of horrific figurines and a tintype of some gaunt imbecile whose arrival in America we'd backdate each time our apartment got bigger.

These visions became so increasingly ridiculous that I began to revel in my falsehood; I finished the day by telling my final donor that thanks to him, I could now purchase *How to Win Friends and Influence People*; I wanted to be the very best carpet salesman I could be, because I had no intention of...and here I exploded into laughter because I just couldn't formulate the rest, something about improving my children's chances for a better future which I would not be able to do on a bricklayer's pay. I dashed up the steps just as the sky roared with the sound of an incoming train. I leapt inside the closing doors.

When I got to Prospect Park, I steered clear of pedestrian paths. When I was forced into the open, I leaned forward as if I was a bent old man, but far in excess of any osteoporotic degeneration I had ever seen; more like my disease was abject terror at the prospect of resembling anything other than a walking paperclip. This mode of travel allowed me to look behind me from between my own knees, providing me with veritable "eyes in the back of my head" as I crossed fields where I was particularly vulnerable. The park was no longer an idyllic place of picnics, fresh air, and soothing greenery; it was a hostile demilitarized zone designed to prevent Lady's escape.

I situated myself in a wooded area with a clear view of the carousel. I stood in the bushes breathing heavily, trying to gain composure as day moved toward night. I gasped and gently caressed my thighs and pelvis. My spiraling thoughts settled. I would stand in the bushes thus, and then lay down in the underbrush at nightfall. I would rise at dawn and stand guard just in case some other misfortune was unleashed upon me; for example, the demolition of the carousel or the replacement of the horses with giant raccoons or God knows what. Who knew?

At this point my relationship with God was indeed a personal one, perhaps too personal—I was beginning to see Job's experiences were not so taxing after all. Indeed, it seemed that God had singled me out for suffering, and if he intended me to derive some wisdom from it, I couldn't begin to discern what it might be. That misery was miserable? It was ironic, I thought, that God chose to reveal himself to me not by wondrous works or divine revelation, but by a clichéd path of humiliation and injustice when he would have been just as well-served sending me an altar boy that could fry eggs in his hands or a woman with nineteen vaginas.

An unfortunate irony revealed itself—I was, in a sense, indeed a man recently freed from Riker's Island. Neither my incarceration nor my departure was voluntary in any real sense; both situations were enforced by life's bullying winds. I supposed that the absurd situations I conjured up beneath the elevated train were fragments of a shattered carnival mirror: tiny grotesqueries that were, at best, once part of a perverted whole. No, my prospects were not in fact much better than my imagined penitent. How, I wondered, would I sustain myself until I was properly credited and remunerated for my compositions?

I assumed that my brothers, as purveyors of a revolutionary sound, albeit stolen and adulterated, would be paid in accord with the music's global impact. Guessing conservatively, I estimated that each performance at CBGB represented gross income of anywhere from 1 to 1.5 million dollars. The premier was held at a different venue; although I was not familiar with its capacity, it was safe to assume it had been chosen for good reasons and my brothers were compensated accordingly, say in the area of 3 million dollars. All in, my compositions had already grossed millions of dollars. I had lost count of the number of shows my brothers had already played at CBGB—in fact, I was unsure of the day or date by this point—as you might have noticed, men who drink from the Bailey Fountain in Grand Army Plaza don't start flipping through their day planners after slaking their thirst—but even without an exact tally, it was a certainty that millions of dollars had already been stolen from me.

In the meantime, I was in no position to take on gainful employment; although I could have worked in a tailor's shop, what good would the paltry wage do? Surely my brothers would tour the world. What then? Stuck in a common job, I would be limited to confronting them at New York City performances, performances attended by their staunchest supporters and overseen by a security detail composed entirely of former Employees-of-the-Month from Ceausescu's Securitate.

I supposed I could be a house musician in a restaurant, but my quartets would, in a pinnacle of gross injustice, be received as a local musician's hackneyed portrayal of someone else's brilliant works, a quaint little homage shoved between *Those Were the Days* and *Strangers in the Night*, the performance of all three suffering from the difficulty of playing music while one is drooling over the steaks being devoured by the bourgeois pigs who are all ignoring you anyway. No, never would I expose myself to such humiliation. Better the nomadic freedoms of street hustling, each day a primordial struggle initiated by the jackal's fearsome bark instead of the rooster's homey cackle.

The sky was growing dark. From my place in the bushes, Lady was nothing more than an occasionally glimpsed pink blur; I often mistook some other object or person clad in pink for her, and I would panic that someone was taking her away or I would be thrilled that she had escaped on her own and was bounding toward my hiding place. These were the mirages of love of course, and when darkness obscured my view of the carousel, I lay down to sleep, for I needed to be sharp of wit and limber of body.

CHAPTER XXIV.

THE GREAT ESCAPE IS A REALITY.

Light filtering through branches. Arms and legs spread as if I'd fallen asleep making a snow angel. A good omen; a surrender to the sky that I hoped, to some extent, would absolve me of the previous day's blasphemies. For although I had my quarrels with God and his non-existence was all but certain, I clearly needed all the help I could get. I said prayers from several religions, approximating the ones I knew little of based on clichés and what I learned at meat shops. I concluded with a prayer to Odin, thinking a war-friendly God might be more helpful in the circumstances. If I did much more cheek-turning, my head would soon be spinning faster than the carousel that was my obsession.

I resumed my vigil. The carousel was still closed and the only people in the park were vagrants, martial artists, and total idiots. That being said, I did my best not to judge the sparse passerby, trying to remember that each of them had their own shitty story or however that particular bit of philosophical nonsense went. I also paid mind to the fact that God helps those who help themselves, i.e. he doesn't exist. And so I passed the morning under the protective rainbow of a polymorphous religion; the cacophony achieved order as religions sang in harmony or clashed painfully. At their center was the black hole of atheism. This dreadful yet powerfully attractive nothing was orbited by the rest: Mansonism was a comet, whereas Masonism was Jupiter-like. Christianity was a grey planet that smelled like a coatroom. Hinduism was covered with green leaves and purple trees. The Norse religion was two huge polar caps separated by a tundra equator; one river wrapped itself around the planet like a herring-filled belt. Judaism was a planet with no outdoors, just endless rooms filled with dusty volumes and arguing scholars, but if one could somehow get through all the rooms and arrive at the planet's core, they'd find a giant globe of ice-cold slivovice.

This latter thought reminded me of how shitty sobriety felt, an abstinence meant to facilitate Lady's rescue. It hadn't occurred to me that not drinking might diminish my coordination and cunning more than drinking. Although I had always enjoyed booze, I was just beginning to appreciate how it provided a tranquilizing equilibrium, an escape from the fevered thoughts of a great mind. At the same time, when the magical fluids departed, the brain accelerated into an interstellar overdrive like the "warp speed" of science fiction. In this accelerated state, there were explosions of truth and seething anxieties that could bring one to their knees; however, these episodes more often resembled illumination than paranoia.

But in the meantime I was beginning to quiver, and I felt exposed as if I was a blotch under a microscope. At the same time I was overcome with a teeth-gnashing sexual frenzy, an erotic heat that made me feel as if lightning bolts were shooting in circles within the tight confines of my brimming prostate. If I did not get a drink soon, I'd be screaming at the top of my lungs for help right in the middle of a freakishly voluminous ejaculation—I did not care to think how confused onlookers might react to such a paradox-rich vignette.

But leaving the bushes would be sheer idiocy. If I saw another weaving vagrant, paper bag in hand, I would dart out in a stunning daylight attack, seize the liquor, and return to the woods. Or I'd target a family man who'd be less likely to pursue a filth-covered maniac brazen enough to snatch his chardonnay.

But neither opportunity developed, and the park was getting busy. I leapt about and stared through the bushes at couples strolling, families arguing, the Hasidim meandering. I made a desperate plea to the latter, sticking my face from the bushes and hissing:

"Excuse me sir, I'm a Jew, and I'll take a mitzvah and a pint of sloe gin."

"We're not those Jews. And it's not that time."

"Kind sir, have mercy, I'm a brother in need."

They didn't stop. I realized I'd have to fall back on the standard ointment: I slid down my pants. Instantly feeling better, I disrobed completely. Seeking stable growth while insulating against volatility, I embarked on a slow, short-stroke technique that would provide subtle comfort, but would avoid the unpredictability of rapture. I simultaneously scanned the perimeter, particularly the area facing the boathouse and carousel where the greatest numbers of pedestrians were passing.

By adhering to this strict approach I managed to peel off the hours, accidently ejaculating only once when an obese woman leaned forward after dropping a coin. But I found the post-orgasmic chasm to be oddly navigable; I swiftly crossed the dark prolactin sea and achieved another erection.

But masturbation can only take you so far. I was shaking and cold, yet the backs of my knees were sweating profusely. Two anxieties overwhelmed me—a terrible fear of being discovered in the bushes, and an incredible sense of shame for every wrong word and deed I had ever committed in my entire life. And I was only one large glass of vodka away from leaving it all behind.

But the sun was high, the park was full, and no crimes of opportunity presented themselves. I was forced to pass the day in a special hell, staring furtively through the bushes while keeping myself perpetually on the edge of orgasm.

Beneath a fading sun, I entered madness. Tears ran down my face and my body convulsed. My penis was screaming for release, never having been kept in a state of turgidity and denial for such an extended length of time. Nonetheless, I drove it on like an exhausted horse in the desert as I unsuccessfully tried to ignore the ants crawling all over my back.

I was beleaguered by a vision of my brothers sitting on a giant couch in a gilded hotel suite. They were laughing as porters brought in four massive, custom-made brandy snifters, each one so large that it was riding in its own cart; brandy snifters so large they could effectively be worn as diving helmets. Each snifter contained an undulating sea of golden-brown cognac. When the four carts stopped in front them, they simultaneously picked up the snifters with both hands and drank deeply as if engaging in some orgiastic, self-referential communion.

I had no choice but to take a calculated risk and let fly with the orgasm; even a fleeting moment of exaltation, a near parody of respite, would be worth the special hell of the post-orgasmic self suffering under two brutal regimes: alcohol withdrawal and the self-loathing that always followed escapist release. I hoped Peter would arrive soon, bearing alcohol. I dropped to my knees. I tossed my head back. I squealed in nightmarish delight.

When it was over I hung my head and gasped. My racing heart was skipping beats, creating an uninvited suspense. The leaden curtain of guilt and futility came crashing down. The bugs crawled and bit. A telepathic beam of mockery shot into my brain from a hidden moon. I had had enough: I log-rolled on the forest floor, back and forth as swiftly as possible, until the physicality and absurdity of the act shook off a tiny amount of torment.

I stopped and sat up. I was covered in dirt and leaves. My filthy clothes were scattered around me. I let the agony wash over me like a waterfall, permitting it do whatever it wished, impossible to stop, futile to try, nothing to do but surrender, surrender and suffer immeasurably, possibly until death, and in all likelihood, for eternity after that.

Peter appeared. Even in my tortured state, I noticed he had a strange bopping way that not only described his walk, but also his perennial otherness, his sense of himself as an outsider always on the lookout for an ass to ogle or a wallet to steal. He was a man, I realized, that would never be able to blend into the woodwork or disappear in the crowd.

I suppose it was euphoria that allowed me to think of something other than my malaise, for indeed, I was thrilled to see him as he walked among the park-goers who instinctively moved away. I put on my underwear and stepped from the bushes. I waved my arms wildly and screamed:

"I'm right the fuck over here you fucking motherfucker!"

I wanted my calling card to stand out against the mumbled conversations of parents and the playful shouts of their filthy broods. I leapt back into the bushes. As I had hoped, he was the only person walking toward me at all, let alone walking as if he was a man at a baseball game who'd spotted a colleague. I crossed my arms and leapt about. He crossed the concrete, spread the bushes, and entered my lair.

"In the name of God, please tell me that black case has what I need."

He rolled the four-number combination into place, popped the latches, and opened the case. He opened a bottle of ouzo and handed it to me.

I handed it back. I got on my knees. I raised my face to the heavens and shut my eyes. I opened my mouth wide. Peter understood: a never-ending stream of tranquilizing liquorice poured down my open throat.

The ratio of fulfillment to deprivation is wonderfully appointed in the realm. It's a cosmic duality: a black hole that sucks up thought, light, and hope; but upon fulfillment, it becomes a bloated red star, hot and swollen. I muttered, "God that's good. I can't believe it," as relief blossomed throughout. I stood up.

I stared at nothing as if it were the first sunrise after years of fog. Peter opened a second bottle and handed it to me. He opened another for himself. We drank quietly for ten minutes.

I said, "Peter, you're probably wondering what this is about."

"A heist."

"Of a sort. But in this case we are not stealing an object, we are freeing a sentient being."

"Oh."

"Yes. We are freeing someone held against their will, who also, incidentally, is the woman I love."

"Oh. I didn't know you met a girl."

"She's quite close, actually. Over there."

"Where?"

"The carousel. Over there."

"The ticket lady?"

"No, of course not. Seriously, do you think I'd allow myself to be seen flitting about the Village hand-in-hand with that? Thanks."

"Sorry. Then who?"

"The pink one. Hang on, wait until it stops. Hang on. No, unfortunately she stopped on the other side."

"Why don't we just walk over there?"

"Impossible."

"So get dressed, then we'll go."

"Why do you think the two are connected? But yes, perhaps getting dressed is a good idea. Nonetheless, we're staying in the bushes. When the park is empty, in the dead of night, we'll set her free."

"From what? Crazy boyfriend?"

"Of course not, you fool, unless the boyfriend were some type of mechanical man who needed disassembling. What do you think these tools are for?"

"I don't know."

"But don't you have a guess, haven't you perhaps ruminated on the possibilities while traveling here?"

"No."

"Well, what does one generally do with tools?"

"Build stuff. Fix stuff."

"What else?"

"Sell them."

"I see I have no choice but to tell you outright. We're going to break into a building with them."

"You mean like the first fucking thing I said? A *heist*? Like I already said, so I had to think of different stuff since you already said it wasn't that? You can really be an asshole, Damone. I bring you booze, I come up here from Brighton with a bunch of tools I had to steal from a garage, didn't ask any questions, and you act like a jerk. Seriously, maybe that island was the best place for you. Here, take another drink of free liquor. Asshole."

"Um. I'm not quite sure how to respond to that."

"How about saying sorry, even if you don't mean it, at least while you're drinking my ouzo?"

"Peter, I was only trying to help you, to teach you how to critically think…"

"Well don't. I do my thing my way, you do your thing your way. I mean, yeah, I can learn something but so can you, and neither of us has to act like a dick, you know, when we're learning stuff. Was I a fuckface when I told you to get a haircut? No."

"I apologize. And not just because I'm drinking this ouzo that you so generously provided."

"No problem. Apology accepted."

"I'll try and phrase things with more consideration."

"Okay, enough about it. What exactly are we doing here tonight?"

I must say, after Peter's outburst, I thought it prudent to strike him. But if I responded rashly, there'd be no more ouzo and no setting Lady free. I thought of Johnny, ever the dictator, and I realized those traits were not his alone. I got back to the task at hand.

"My beloved will be locked in the carousel house when they close for the night. When the coast is clear, we break her out."

"I don't get it. They'll see her sitting on the horse and ask her to leave before they lock up."

"You don't understand. I mean, perhaps I haven't explained myself well. She is always there. Look, look right now! That's her, the pink one!"

"Are you talking about one of the horses?"

"Of course, what did you think I meant?"

"Oh, I get it. Those are antiques, they must be worth a lot of money. That's a pretty good idea, Damone. I wish I had thought of that. I was confused because you were calling it your beloved and stuff like that, like it was your girlfriend. But wait, didn't you say…oh. I get it."

"And she feels the same for me."

"Oh. Okay. Okay, that's fine. Tell me what you need me to do."

"For now, nothing. We must wait."

I got dressed. We sat down in the underbrush. As I drank, I realized a good portion of my anxiety regarding someone stealing Lady was a chimera, an illusion created by an over-stimulated mind. I still watched the carousel, but I was no longer trying to scratch bugs out from underneath my skin.

The crowds thinned. It got dark. The carousel spun to a stop. The organ went silent. The workers began cleaning up and rolling down the steel blinds. They locked up and departed.

Nonetheless, we still had several hours to kill. Night's arrival did not mean I could walk about freely; there were still the police to consider, and someone might steal the tools while we roved about like idiots. I told Peter that he should take a nap. I decided I would dart about among my own thoughts like a vigorous little tadpole, newly born, wide-eyed, and full of curiosity.

And it was a strange fugue indeed that had constructed itself in those impassioned hours. There was an essential motoric rhythm underlying the construction, and a persistent repetition of the chromatic motif in my pants; this was the drone upon which everything else was constructed. But the individual voices, developing on the wings of my burgeoning alcoholism, raved like a million sexually aroused madmen mingling with several thousand humorless mathematicians at some absurd convention.

Nonetheless, a portrait was being painted with a bizarre potpourri of brushstrokes; some in violent conflict, others in such immaculate accord that surely black was being painted directly on top of black, delivered by the same hand with the same brush from the same batch of paint. In other words, the structure was one of chaos and order operating symbiotically in the same space. One's initial impression was disorder, but with the development of a deeper visceral response, one would begin to sense that the structure was in fact guided by order; in fact, if it were possible to see the architecture underlying the project, the order revealed would be stringent to the point of psycho-proto-fascistic, a structure without hope of variation: rigid, relentless, implacable. Perhaps even dull.

My concern was that analysis that deep would be a zero-sum game. Although there would be a certain release of intellectual tension achieved by illuminating the mechanics of the thing, the relief would be counterpointed by futility rooted in determinism proved; in many respects, the proverbial "leap of faith" relied on an illusion of chaos, and to finally create notations so accurate as to reveal something thought out in the same banal way as the *Art of Fugue* or the *Hammerklavier* would be distressing indeed, for despite the most optimistic way to digest determinism—Calvinistically, for example—it nonetheless is a letdown to any realist, because at the end of the day, most people either know or feel that the idea of freedom and determinism being compatible is a laughable pipe-dream, at least for anyone with the analytical skills of a fresh-water perch or better. Because really, who wants to step forward and confess that they're dumb enough not to see determinism's infinite minutiae at work, and therefore are free?

So for me to move forward, granting that such a crude description borders on a crime against humanity, I had to retain faith in chaos, in a disorder that rendered determinism silly, the dainty little product of minds better suited to choosing garden gnomes and floral wallpaper. A few concrete examples are possible here, granting that to truly convey a proper impression would likely require at least ten or twelve million such examples[20], and any one of these examples would have to be considered exactly that—something devised strictly for illustration purposes with absolutely no reliable connection to reality whatsoever. I have enough legal problems already. Now, with that agreed upon:

For example, when many years later I saw the painting *Pillars of Creation* by the Native-American artist Eagle Nebula, its threadbare familiarity hit me like the grill of a truck taken from behind. For roughly an hour I was in a stupor: catatonic yet somehow erect. Fortunately the museum was a little out-of-the-way place where the staff was thrilled to have anyone there at all, let alone someone who actually appeared to be contemplating the art, so they paid me no mind. When I emerged from the stupor and my eyes registered the painting once more, I left in a mad rush, resulting in a slight abrasion to my fingers from getting them stuck in the donation can while running out the front door of said community center.

---

[20] *Damone Ramone: Twelve Million Examples* and/or *Volume II.*

I rushed home[21] and put on Bach's Brandenburg Concerto No.5 just prior to the first movement's harpsichord solo. I disrobed and rushed to a comfortable armchair, managing to arrive and splay my limbs with a particularly open languor involving the armrests before the solo commenced. I embarked on a journey into self-abuse that's rhythms and upward trajectory precisely mirrored the harpsichord solo, and as the solo rushed toward its wild crescendo, my flaying motions followed suit, and I reddened in time with Karl Richter's mad yet aggressively precise rendering.

When the solo reached the crescendo, I filled the eternity between the solo's conclusion and the orchestra's resumption with a white explosion; I felt as if I was at the helm of a spacecraft that had lost all control, doomed by a mechanical failure that oscillated wildly between interstellar overdrive and the landing mode. I gripped the wheel as tightly as I could, but the ship was simply too far-gone; it jerked, careened, spun around. I lurched back in the pilot's seat and pulled my face into itself, just as one might on Earth at the wheel of a car veering through a hazardous situation. My eyes made advanced Grave's Disease seem like a virtually unnoticeable condition, so bulbous and engorged were they. My pelvis battled the will of my arm, hand, and kicking legs, leaping and straining forward like a large, willful dog on its first walk of Spring. Oddly, in the midst of chaos—the blinding flashes, the insane descent—there was a sensation of triumphalism not unlike how one might feel upon hearing an orderly row of uniformed buglers codifying a favorable edict with resplendent blowing.

As I emerged from my reverie in the underbrush of Prospect Park, an image of a small submarine shooting high into the air from beneath the ocean's surface flashed through my mind, but the submarine was in fact a space vessel, and its flight from the sea was preceded by a flight into the sea from the exosphere. Needless to say, this vision and all the bells and whistles accompanying it resulted in some thrashing and ruckus as I convulsed among the

---

[21] *Home*, in this case, is somewhat removed from the original meaning. Let's just say it was a furnished architectural structure, largely functional, and occasionally private.

twigs and garbage, which probably was not the wake-up call Peter had hoped for.

He sat up. He looked over at me and I stared back: wild-eyed, sweating, gasping, the vision's corollary still firmly in hand, although noticeably depressurizing with each restorative gasp and hygienic shake of my curled fist. "Sorry," I said. "Jesus Christ," he said.

I had mirrored Bach's use of horizontality and verticality to recreate the Cross; the horizontality was provided by the motoric rhythm and recurring motifs, and the verticality was provided by the voices, and by the construction of a series of giant towers in my mind that were exactly rendered by Eagle Nebula all those years later. Nebula had been inspired by a spiritual episode on a remote island in Lake Superior. This episode was not inspired by an atypical agent; it was inspired by the ingestion of spring water that poured forth from layers of limestone that characterize the island beneath sporadic patches of glacial till and fine white sand. Nebula and I are two of many molecular arbitrators representing the *Pillars*, two tiny specks of a massive spray. The actual *Pillars* have corporeal form in deep space, far beyond the reach of any telescope, only revealing themselves via spiritual avenues between them and their chosen mediums.

In any case, within that framework we clearly see the features of a life poetically led yet pragmatically constrained.

Peter was still looking at me.

"Peter," I said, not without a certain playfulness, "looking a bit peaked over there; but at least you had more balls than Marchand."

"What?"

"Than Marchand. He chose, quite wisely, to flee Dresden prior to a competition against Bach. The mere idea of confronting such a virtuoso on stage where Marchand would in all likelihood be humiliated before the whole of Europe was simply too much, and he fled Dresden like a yellow-bellied worm. What do you think of that?"

"I'm not sure."

"What I appreciate about the incident is the power of music to terrorize, to insist on supplication, respect—to humiliate. Think of it, that hubristic fool traveled all the way from France to take on Bach, and then, thinking better of this foolhardy proposition at the final moment, he scurried about gathering up his things, and then he raced down the stairs of the inn making little squealing sounds as he effeminately demanded that his servants prepare the horses. I imagine some ridiculous falsetto as he screamed at the coachman: 'Faster, faster!' And then the whole cowardly entourage raced into the setting sun, back to France where he could safely wallow in mediocrity. I'm quite certain Bach was not surprised, in fact I'm sure he knew exactly what had happened while the crowd whispered conjecture among themselves regarding Marchand's absence. Yet even though Bach surely predicted this outcome, he nonetheless prepared a piece, Brandenburg concerto number five, that would have destroyed Marchand beyond repair—what Bach wouldn't have paid—or me for that matter—to have seen Marchand's face during the harpsichord solo. And played by Bach himself! Can you imagine being alive to witness such things?"

"When are we going to break into the thing? It's pretty late now I think."

"Indeed, pay me no mind, me and my flights of fancy. Yes, I believe it is time to proceed."

A single lamppost lit the carousel house. Although nobody had passed for nearly an hour, I was concerned about police on horseback riding up just as we were liberating Lady. In addition to the officers arresting me, the police horses would surely behave like the Red Army entering Berlin should they be granted access unfettered to the carousel house. I turned to Peter.

"We need to both walk like this."

I illustrated the paperclip posture that allowed one to see behind them as they moved forward.

"This way we can move toward the carousel while still seeing behind us in case anyone is coming, although, on second thought, you'd best do it facing the other way so one of us can see forward."

"Why doesn't one of us just walk forward normally?"

"Yes, that would be another way to do it. Granting you that, I have to tell you I have an incredibly low tolerance for asymmetry. I don't want to get into the details here. Let's just say that if we're out of order I'll be…distracted. It might reach such a degree that it could have disastrous results."

"No, I understand that. There's this guy who lives in my uncle's building, and sometimes when we leave he's standing right outside the door. My uncle says, 'Watch this.' We walk out, my uncle holds the door for the guy. But the guy just stands there looking mad. We walk a little further and my uncle says, 'Okay, now turn around.' We turn around, and the guy is slowly walking backwards; ever see *Kung Fu*? They walk on the rice paper? You have to see it, it's a great show. Anyway, the guy walks backwards, then sideways, then forwards, until he forms a perfect square. He ends up at the door again. A lady walks up and unlocks the door and holds it open for him. He gets that same angry expression, and he freezes. When the lady goes inside he starts all over again making the square. I swear Damone, it took four times because people kept going in and out and they'd hold the door. He jumped off the roof one day and killed himself. The bushes were all flat. The sound woke up the Chinese lady, the one with the blind dog. She said he was still alive for a while, but he died in the ambulance."

"Right. Sort of like that. Grab the crowbar."

We assumed paperclip positions as we crossed the concrete.

"Over here, at the booth. I'll go then I'll help you."

I had no difficulty mounting the ticket booth, but even with my help it took Peter several attempts before we were both standing on its roof. He continued having problems when we climbed to the roof proper.

We belly-crawled up the slope of the roof. I slid through the same window as before. Peter followed.

I led the way across the mechanical mess above the carousel. I eased myself over the edge and slid down a pole onto the saddle of one of the unfortunate horses. I shushed it and caressed its ear. Peter's head peaked over the edge of the machinery above me.

"Just do the same thing," I said. "I'll dismount and help you as you descend."

Peter slid into the saddle.

"Get off that thing and help me find Lady."

"It's better if you do it on your own, like the knight in shining armor arriving. She doesn't even know me."

"Perhaps."

"So I'll just sit here and call me when you need me."

I walked toward the horses, preferring to recognize Lady by her face rather than reveal I could also recognize her from the other end. This meant I had to pass the others and meet their eyes, some supplicating, others accusatory. But I was only one man.

Lady. I was a sailor trudging up a hill toward his wife after a long voyage, a careworn sight made extraordinary by the knowledge of brevity and fate.

We locked mouths. Our tongues danced. I ran my hands down her neck. Fires burned.

A loud cough. I ignored it. A louder cough.

"Peter, what the hell is the matter with you? Close your eyes if you can't be mature about this."

"Damone, it's not going to be easy getting her off this carousel, I promise. Afterwards you two will have all the time in the world to do whatever. It'd be too bad if we got all this way and then we didn't set her free, I think."

I looked at Lady.

"He is right, my dear. The first order of business is freeing you from this dreadful pole. Peter, bring the tools."

As Peter predicted, the task was arduous. Many passages of this tome pay tribute to the glories of stiff verticality; this is not one of them. Removing Lady from that fucking brass pole was a torture for all three of us. Removing it from the sweep above was particularly difficult, although wresting it from the platform below also elicited disgusting grunts. It was several hours of yanking and jerking before the pole was finally relinquished and Lady was free.

To a point. To take Lady out the way we'd come in was impossible. We'd cause substantial damage and make a lot of noise—I did not need a reunion with the Park Slope police.

There was only one option: when the morning staff slid the steel shades up we'd run for the woods. We detailed the plan, and then we spent the rest of the night speaking in low tones, with

Peter honoring my sporadic requests for privacy for intimate moments with Lady.

During one of these moments I heard banging outside. They were opening up, and I was engaged in the love act. But what I thought would be my undoing turned out to be a blessing: I was not only nude, but gloriously turgid. All eyes would be fixed upon me. The steel shutter opened, revealing morning light and Parks Department pants. We waited until enough shutters had been rolled up for us to run in opposite directions.

I leapt from my hiding place. I screamed and glowered as I brutally yanked my own brass support rod, intermittently stopping to point it threateningly at the young, heavyset man who was staggering backwards in a blend of sprint and fall that was quite notable. Indeed, it was a not a sustainable feat: he fell on his ass. He yelled for help as I wagged in Loki's mad dance, shape-shifting from a writhing salmon into a crippled old woman with an extremely unique cane and then into a barking seal.

The tormenting serpent began dripping venom into Sigyn's bowl, and I'm quite sure she briefly appeared in a translucent flash, so transfixed were the park workers. The final gush and filling of the bowl was accompanied by the sight of Peter staggering toward the woods with Lady in his arms. He disappeared into the trees as I squeezed out the last few drops.

I dashed away. The workers did not follow. Mindful of other pursuers, I took a circuitous route. I leapt into the trees and darted among them. It was still quite dark beneath the canopy. I joined Peter and Lady. I felt like I could conquer the world.

CHAPTER XXV.

I DIDN'T.

In the days following Lady's liberation, one David Ellsberg—Peter's Uncle Dave—was very helpful.[22] His suggestion that we coat Lady in papier-mâché to disguise her as a large piñata earned him my lifelong gratitude, but he was helpful in other ways. Regarding the former, it was no mean feat getting Lady to Uncle Dave's Coney Island apartment. We carried her down Ocean Parkway rather than risk calamity in the subway. Any number of bandits might've kidnapped Lady to auction her off or reduce her once again to a concubine in some spinning harem. Indeed, we received a great deal of attention on the Parkway; it was mainly children admiring Lady's beauty, but one old man followed us for a block, all the while insisting that Lady was of Russian lineage; another young man, looking quite pleased with himself, asked if we were a ménage à trois.

Uncle Dave pointed out that the population of free carousel horses was relatively low, and that the rogue city-state New York had laws on the books that legalized ownership of Lady and her ilk. Per his recommendation, Peter and I were now sitting on the kitchen floor of his apartment cutting newspaper into strips while

---

[22] Lest you think Mr. Ramone blames everyone around him for his misfortunes out of misguided hostility, this passage speaks otherwise. Mr. Ramone hopes those of you that still doubted his impartiality now see that this is a thoroughly objective account devoid of hyperbole or the rearrangement of facts in order to support an extreme or untenable position.

Lady looked on. Uncle Dave entertained us with lively banter while we worked.

"So what's your next move, Damone? Your brothers play all the time now at CBs. You manage to get in touch with any of them?"

"I haven't, which I believe you know, hence your rhetorical question is not appreciated."

"Sorry, Damone. No offense meant. But what're you going to do now?"

"I'll spend a few days with Lady in the Fort Tilden dunes, a honeymoon of sorts if this rain lets up. What month is it, by the way?"

"September. September, 1974."

"Are you insinuating I might not know what year it is? I doubt you know Sir Edward Elgar was born in 1857, but did I walk in and start quizzing you?"

"Of course you know the year, I was saying it more for myself. So you'll track down your brothers after the honeymoon?"

"Yes. I'll clarify my thoughts among the sands of my youth, and then I will again attempt to get into the so-called club. As your nephew pointed out, a change in my appearance was long overdue. Now I look like my brothers again. This time I shall succeed. Good God, imagine having to work this hard to get inside that ludicrous roach bordello."

"You better take a shower and shave. You know, to maintain the look. It might be a good idea."

"Indeed. Yes, perhaps you're right. Thank you for your offer."

"You know, you sound pretty contemptuous of modern music, of rock and roll. Have you taken the time to give it a fair shot?"

"I've invested the requisite three to four minutes, yes. And I have a sister who's rather a fan. Her bedroom was adjacent to the sewing room where I worked, much to my grave misfortune, so I had the "pleasure" of hearing a number of popular tunes, granting my sister tended to fixate on a few favorites."

"But you were what, literally on a desert island for a few years? Let me play you some records."

What followed was a tutorial on the latest aural atrocities, celebrated mainly by young people, but increasingly by a broader audience. Uncle Dave played several works by artists that were under the impression they offered some sort of self-styled complexity, a certain artistic expansiveness and bleak vision. It was these musicians, Dave stated, that my brothers claimed to be rebelling against by offering brevity, clarity, and accessibility.

I was baffled. I wondered if Dave had perhaps misunderstood their explanation, for although my brothers had desecrated my work, both the antecedents to which it paid homage and the contemporary antagonists that it challenged were highly self-evident. I couldn't remotely understand how something like my quartet, *Really? Smell It Again* could be positioned as an antithesis to Pinchas Floyd's *The Dark Moon Cometh*, one of the recordings Uncle Dave seemed especially enamored of. My work as an antithesis to the 2nd Viennese School, obviously, but to *Brain Damage*? Granting the latter was, at the very least, appropriately named, the precept simply did not hold.

To be fair, Uncle Dave did play some works of note; a few were positively transcendent. I liked, for example, *Mighty Fine Time* by Bill Wyman, which Uncle Dave found highly amusing for some reason, especially after he was unable to convince me that the Rolling Stones project to which Wyman was also attached produced far better work, playing me several examples: *Tribute to the Devil, Great Expectations, Build a Shelter*. Granting the wisdom of the latter based on firsthand experience, I still held that Wyman's *Monkey Grip* cycle far exceeded the creative scope of the Rolling Stones despite their prominent position. Granted, there was a degree of bias at work, because I simply could not get my head around this concept of "joint songwriting credit." To me this was a complete absurdity, yet Uncle Dave insisted it was standard practice among rock and roll "composers." I mean, it's clear that Nikolay Myaskovsky could write a symphony[23] honoring the collectivization of agriculture, but it's not so clear how collectivized agriculture would go about writing a symphony honoring Myaskovsky. But despite the obvious logical fallacy, Uncle Dave held it to be true, so we let the matter rest.

---

[23] The 12th, in case you didn't know.

I also liked some of Queen Freddie Mercury's work—he seemed to be trying at least, although Uncle Dave's assertion that his work might serve as a "bridge" between my tastes and rock and roll, thus easing me into an appreciation of the latter, was more than a little annoying. About twelve years later, in fact, I became retroactively enraged about the idea and wished I could go back in time and punch Uncle Dave in the face when some fool critic of mine was claiming the titles of my quartets were derivative, comparing them to two works entitled *Becoming a Man/Freud Was Wrong* and *Orgy of One* respectively, two horrific numbers by some fools calling themselves The Meatmen; I went into a complete rage, during which Uncle Dave and his complacence came to mind, and I thought, 'Sure, let's see you make one of your little "bridges" to one of those little ditties, say, from Scriabin's *The Poem of Ecstasy* to *Orgy of One.*' So intense was my rage that I foamed at the mouth, bit my antagonist's dog, and had to spend a short time in a place, if you'll allow me the dignity of referring to those weeks with a certain discretion.

Which leads to the one artist that, I must say, impressed me greatly. I hated all of his work, but such was the impact of the one piece of his I did enjoy[24] that he earned my unwavering respect: Alice Cooper. The piece I'm referring to, for those of you who haven't read my *Letters from Hamburg*, is the positively wonderful work called *Years Ago/Steven*. From the opening notes of this veritable operetta, I was transfixed. It was as if I listening to a transcription of the very darkest corners of my soul. I vaguely remember Uncle Dave becoming alarmed as I slipped into a transcendent state, granting a certain crudity to using a term that implies rising above one's self, as if music or any other intoxicant can convert one's divine soul into a shoddy hot-air balloon ride. The type of transcendence I experienced was inward looking, and did not include trumpets or light; my *descendence*, as it were, was dark, a psychic implosion into a slightly moist place. I had a vision of being in Ramona's bedroom, alone, my family gone forever. I

---

[24] Here I use "enjoy" loosely; calling turning white with terror, perspiring, and entering a catatonic state "enjoyment" is arguable, but in interpreting music I'm wont to liken "enjoyment" to "impact."

was staring out the window, sweat pouring down my pallid brow. A single candle burned at her bedside. A bedside to which she would never return. I stared out the window, not at the seascapes and dunes of Fort Tilden, but at an empty playground, as implied in Cooper's work. So deft were Cooper's allusions, that I thought I saw translucent glimpses of faces once known, of the howling children that I could only ever watch and to whom I could never connect, and I felt such intense self-pity that it was beauty, and I recused myself from many ancient stains. I also absolved myself of a mild interest in putting on a woman's baby blue see-through nightgown and then staring at myself in the full-length mirrors of strangers.

The overwhelming impact of *Years Ago* was of course colored by recent events—the astute among you may have noticed the parallels between *Years Ago* and carnival music, carnival music of the type one might hear, for example, being played on a carousel organ. Its insistent knocking forced opened my door, and I relived the sense of staring at the world through impenetrable glass, pressing my palms, my face, and my organ directly against it, knowing since birth that I would never penetrate it. Watching that dreadful wheel spinning, hearing the music, longing for Lady, a love I would ultimately never possess. I sweated even more. I was back in the dark bushes.

This incident did far more than Freddie Mercury to create a begrudging respect for certain rock 'n' roll efforts; if not for the works themselves, than at least for the composer's intent, so often complex and unique, but so ham-handedly executed in the pop milieu, and accompanied by such ridiculous outfits and outlandish grimaces.

I was also impressed with Bowie's *Sweet Thing/Candidate*. I simply couldn't understand how the same man who'd composed *Sweet Thing* could also be the host of that horrible yet hypnotic television show of which Johnny was so enamored where Bowie would "debate" a variety of liberal guests. One time Johnny forced the entire family to watch Bowie debate Noam Chomsky, and I remember thinking that although Chomsky sounded right, Bowie *looked* right, and that counted for so much more. Pitted against the charming, cruel glitter in Bowie's eye and his repose, confident to the point of languorous, Chomsky never had a chance. That confidence is obvious in the mastery illustrated by *Sweet Thing/Candidate*. It therefore made no sense to me when Bowie performed debates with a disturbing lack of dissonance; for example, when he performed with Thomas Sowell, the piece was a monochromatic offering at best, even during its finest moments, of which there were few.

Regarding Bowie's harpsichord recordings, there were also few—few to none. This was disappointing. A record of his harpsichord work certainly would have established him as a renaissance man, granting that the howling cross-dressers that attended his concerts wouldn't necessarily share the tastes of the right-wing Scotch connoisseurs that followed his television work. Whether either group contained harpsichord devotees is an unknown. What is clear is the vision of futurist dictatorship to which Bowie clearly leaned; in *Diamond Dogs*, it is painted both literally and musically. This is further supported by his television efforts, although it is arguable. It can be said that those efforts at least served to hasten Republicanism's rightward drift, even if this was not what Bowie had intended.

I was sitting on Dave's kitchen floor hearing *Years Ago* for the first time. I was vaguely aware of Dave's distress, particularly during the latter portions of the piece. Thankfully Peter prevented him from intervening in my reverie. But when the piece ended and I emerged from my trance I immediately noticed the little incident.

"Don't worry Damone," Dave said, "It happens to the best of us. I'll get some paper towels."

Dave was highly amused by the unfortunate little incident; others might not have greeted it so affably, for example others that hadn't smoked an enormous amount of marijuana. Don't forget, that was our family business—I know when someone's high. But his mirth was infectious nonetheless—Peter pointed to the floor and laughed. I also laughed, proud of the relinquishment since it was the byproduct of an overwhelmingly fruitful delirium.

Enlightenment and levity set the tone for another foray against the Ramones—my brothers were performing the following evening. I was optimistic thanks to Alice Cooper and my bladder's élan. As usual, this spark of optimism was immediately deluged with dreadful news as soon as it was noticed by the fates that guarantee my perennial misery.

I showered and borrowed some clothes. I adjourned to the kitchen where Uncle Dave and Peter were admiring the now incognito Lady. She was mummified in newsprint. The plan was to paint her pink once she was dry.

There was a pile of magazines on the table that hadn't been there earlier. I had a premonition that they were a continuation of Uncle Dave's "lesson" on pop music circa 1974. Indeed, he began forthwith:

"Welcome back. If you're wondering what we're listening to now—"

"I'm not."

"—It's Iggy and the Stooges."

"I thought this was a lesson on today's music, not on torture methods of the East German Stasi."

"You haven't even heard it yet."

"Of course, you're absolutely right, the caterwauling plastered on top of a musical gang rape is clearly a segue, a judiciously placed segue to provide counterpoint to when the quintet's pianist takes over and moves me to tears with his lyrical renderings."

"Quintet?"

"You'd have heard me the first time if it wasn't so loud. Not "too loud" mind you, because that would imply this music would be acceptable, theoretically, at some volume, whereas the root problem is that it exists at all."

"But how could you tell there's five guys playing? That's pretty amazing."

"Thanks Dave, thanks for the jeans, the aftershave, and the stellar insult to my *Raison d'être*."

"Sorry, man."

"I'm assuming you've assembled these periodicals to further enlighten me, so let's "get it on" as you serious rock and rollers like to say."

"Here, this is an article on Iggy and the Stooges. That's Iggy, the lead singer."

"He should start asking for extra mayo and triple cream in his...give me that goddamn magazine immediately, you butt-chinned miscreant!"

"Christ, here. What's gotten into you now?"

"What's gotten into me? I'll tell you what's gotten into me: 'Danny Fields of Elektra Records discovered The Stooges in Ann Arbor, Michigan.' For the love of God, is that really what it says?"

"That's what it says."

"It can't!"

"It does."

"I can assure you, Danny Fields was never in Detroit in 1967...no, wait...what the hell? I spent the afternoon confessing to Sir Graves Ghastly...but how could they have had the foresight? Perhaps the photograph's been manipulated."

"What are you talking about?"

"I know this lickerish ruffian, I've known him my whole life, and I can assure you he doesn't travel the country searching for the latest pop talent. And that's not his real hair. He has a flattop that matches his redneck personality to a T."

"Are you sure it's the same guy?"

"Well, let's see: he's named Danny Fields. The person I'm talking about is named Danny Fields. And the guy in the picture *is* Danny Fields. Does that answer your question?"

"What the hell, Damone? That guy in the picture is a big-time record exec. He had something to do with Jim Morrison."

"No he didn't."

"Do you even know who Jim Morrison is?"

"One of Ramona's phases. He performs *Light Me On Fire* or *Cum On My Baby, Light Her On Fire*, some crappy thing, on television, her and Johnny ridicule the guy, as they should have, but then Ramona's hatred becomes strange, obsessive; she's constantly muttering, 'I hate that Jim Morrison, I hate him,' like a psychotic, then one day she bursts into tears and declares her love, but after the declaration she's still carrying on with the, 'I hate you, you bastard, hate you!' But it passed."

"He died. And it's called *Light My Fire*."

"Let me guess, self-immolation *on stage*? Hung himself *on stage*? Had himself drawn and quartered *on stage*?"

"Not exactly."

"Tell me more about Fields, please. *Your* Fields."

"That's about it, really. He signed Iggy and the Stooges, the MC5. Writes articles."

"And this long hair, it's not an anomaly?"

"No, I'm pretty sure that's his real hair. Or if it's a wig like you say, he wears it all the time."

"This is beyond incredible. I'm sure this all fits together somehow, but at this point I'm flummoxed."

"Flummoxed?"

"That's right, flummoxed. What of it? Anyhow, tomorrow night I'll get to the bottom of this. You'll see. This farce is coming to an end."

"Damone?"

"Yes?"

"What's a liquorice ruffian?"

The Ellsbergs burst into laughter, and since I had no idea why the question was amusing, I was not offended or aroused. Go ahead, laugh. Why not? The entire planet Earth was, not to mention the Gods in heaven, so why not? Laugh, gentlemen, laugh and be merry while we're under the sun, for is not a living dog better off than a dead lion? I haven't always been sure.

Part VI.

BACK TO THE FRONT.

CHAPTER XXVI.

PRESS ON! A SHITTY FATE AWAITS THEE.

Peter patrolled Bleecker, I patrolled Bowery. I was freshly shaved and showered and the uniform was on: I looked every inch a Ramone. Likewise Peter—Dave had lent him a black leather jacket.

It had been raining for over a week. I postponed my honeymoon. I accepted Dave's offer to house Lady until the weather improved. Having to withhold my passions while they were at their flaming zenith made me a bit irritable, as one might imagine. But I found utility in it by channeling my rage into the conflict against my brothers. Even Johnny would meet his match.

I would have taken Lady along if it hadn't been raining, as I explained to her before I left. I couldn't risk the rain destroying her disguise: we had to lie low. David reassured me that 1974 was keeping the NYPD busy—they wouldn't be allocating many resources to tracking down Lady. He said more people were getting killed every year since the decade began. I couldn't help but wonder if my brothers' crimes in 1970 hadn't been part of the cause of this expanding malaise of violence, if not the sole cause: the Gods had roiled at their thievery and hubris, and were now wreaking punishment on the wicked city. It certainly was something to consider.

That morning I did receive some good news—Uncle Dave said Peter and I could stay at his place for the rest of the month as long as we promised to be out by the first of October. After carefully weighing the pros and cons, we accepted his offer. I think it was a wise choice. We celebrated with Fruity Pebbles, five or six drinks, and four joints.

We watched the premier of a TV show called *Land of the Lost*. They watched it, I should say—it had little value for me. Dad saw three moons last night; hence they conclude they are in another world? If I see *one* moon, it's cause for concern. My views on the show amused Uncle Dave, although I attributed this largely to marijuana. I explained that the lost family's experience was banal relative to even the most average breakdown of Jovian probability distribution. Because of the father's repressed neglect-urge, the family experienced a small chink in the cumulant-generating function that in normal circumstances would have moderated the neglect-urge; in other words, the father would have arrived at a Bernoulli number expressive of the Riemann zeta function in the form of peep show visits, homosexual liaisons at highway rest stops, molestation of underage interns, etc. The mode is immaterial, but the result is predictable: he misjudged his repression, or the mode of it rather, hence he drags everyone down into that so-called *other world*, which in fact was a simple distortion in electromagnetic radiation on its way through a wormhole.

Dave seemed to think the provincial nature of the family's experience, especially as I explained it to him, was somehow very funny indeed. I began to get offended. He said, "So Damone, you're saying that if you were there, you could have got back to Colorado right away, and not had to deal with Grumpy?" I said, "Yes, of course Dave." He said, "Are you sure about that?" I said, "Yes, I'm sure about that." Dave laughed so hard he turned red.

As I walked back and forth on Bleecker, my mind started to grind over the episode. It became increasingly clear that Dave needed a good dressing down. I was furious that a "set" for a respectable television show was actually a front for the perversion of transversable wormhole stabilizers, stabilizers that I had a direct stake in, and as such, always kept a certain amount on my person. To show Uncle Dave what's what, I'd stabilize a wormhole, and then I'd concoct some pretext to get Dave on the BMT, oh I don't know, maybe to go shopping downtown, but on the way I'd say, 'Dave, why don't we get out here at Neptune Avenue for a minute. I'd like to show you something.' He'd agree, we'd disembark, and there on the bench right in front of his face would be that fucking family—the Marshalls, if I recall correctly.

There they'd be, your run-of-the-mill bear, punk, and bitch sitting right fucking there. I don't care if I ever set foot in Prague; I can still, to this day, tap into the energy Arcs of which the Neptune Avenue Platform is an integral part. Everyone talks forever about whether it can be stabilized, but nobody bothers to look at what's right in front of their face. But why should I care? While they're standing around talking, having meetings behind closed doors, ruminating, pouring themselves a little water, I'm actually out there in the streets getting it done. By the time they're finished with their territorial pissing match, their cunt-ass "brainstorming," I've already closed the deal—transversable wormhole? Stabilized, motherfuckers.

I was fuming at this point, swearing and stamping my feet, pointing my finger right in Dave's theoretical cowering face as I sputtered and cursed. Oh! Such oaths have never been heard!

But then it hit me: Béla Bartók's apartment was less than three minutes away at 350 Bowery. I could teach Dave a lesson and confront my brothers without missing a beat. I headed to Bartók's.

Someone grabbed my arm. I spun around. "Keep your hands off me, you lousy son-of-a-bitch!" I screamed.

It was Peter.

"Damone, calm down, Jesus. Where are you going? You should stay close to the club."

"Go back to the club immediately, I have an urgent matter to attend to. I'll be right back."

"Okay Damone, whatever you say, but don't blame me if we have to wait until the next show."

I walked on. Through Bartók, I'd prove my point to Dave, but I also had a score to settle with Bartók. I always credited him with recognizing that messing around with atonalism was a transgression, whereas just skirting its border could be fun, sexy even, without breaking any vows. But I realized that what I had always perceived as knowing when enough is enough was actually naked flirtation. In other words, I'd been giving him the benefit of the doubt when I should have been interrogating him on what he thought about while he was "writing" the allegro vivace from his string quartet number 1. Nothing good, I assure you.

I didn't know which apartment was his, so I rang every bell in the building. Voices choked and crackled, battling for the foreground as they zipped from the box.

"I want to see Bartók!"

"Who?"

"Bartók!"

"Wait down there."

A heavyset woman in her fifties appeared. She inspected me through the glass. She opened the door.

"Every two years or so someone does this. I'm not letting you look at my apartment, you have to understand. Anyway, there's nothing to see."

I turned my back on her with the utmost disdain and left. I had come close, which in this case was more than sufficient because the distortions were favorable. In fact, being slightly off would only reinforce the stabilization I had just enacted. To wit, Bartók's funeral took place[25] inside the radius of the energy field located at the site of the Chrysler Building, but at the extreme edge where some distortion would reasonably occur: at the Universal Chapel at Lexington and 52nd Street. The Chrysler Building is located at Lexington and 42nd Street. His dissemination along the energy Arc following his corporeal exit was imperfect—it was close enough to function, but distortions were inevitable. There was nothing he could have done to avoid this: his point of emanation was not aligned. His distorted exit was preordained. His obsession with hoarding and distorting Hungarian folk music was an attempt to

---

[25] Did you think I expected Bartók to answer the door? Fools.

transmogrify what he intuitively sensed but could not name—that he was lost in a parallel energy field. By contrast, a particle right on the mark would be Mahler; his Moravian point of emanation all but guaranteed him immersion in strong energy; that is why his relationship with Bohemian-Moravian folk music lacked the obsessive quality that characterized Bartók's relationship with Hungarian folk music.

When Bartók's sons and the Hungarian government pursued Bartók's reinterment, they naturally thought their motivations were subjective, but they were actually ordered to do it by the electromagnetic Arcs. This maintained the integrity of the distortion because the distance between the Chrysler Building and the Universal Chapel is mirrored planetarily by the distance between Prague and Budapest: the geographical distance between perfection and distortion. Hence, examine the Chrysler Building's analogue at Vyšehrad—the Basilica of St. Peter and St. Paul—and you will clearly see the emanation and reception points for the true Arc, whereas the Arc emanating from the Universal Chapel lands in a wormhole that is probably located in a Budapest bordello or bathhouse.

That is why at the moment I turned my back on the woman at 350 Bowery, the reanimated Béla Bartók that materialized on the Neptune Avenue Platform was undoubtedly Béla Bartók, but the reanimation contained distortions which are visible when you compare photographs of the reanimated Bartók with photographs of the original Bartók. Reanimated Bartók assumed the identity Ralph Lauren, and Lauren's choice to create a false history rooted in Eastern Europe was a reflection of his intuitive understanding of how he came to be and which spiritual expressways took him there.

The tragedy of Bartók: the Magyar homeland and its lamenting violins expressing the never-ending loop of time and the eternal sorrow of being so close yet so far from the Chrysler-Vyšehrad highway. The other tragedy is that I never had the chance to bring Uncle Dave to Ralph Lauren because I was soon consumed by my own malignant obsessions, one of whom was walking down Bowery carrying a gigantic amplifier: Mickey Ramone.

Peter jogged up. "That guy looks like you," he said.

"My brother Mickey," I said. "Just look at that rapacious weasel. That's probably a gigantic box of money on his back."

"He looks like he's having a real hard time. Why aren't your brothers helping him?"

"They're probably at a suite in the St. Regis giving a press conference. Wait here. If I start getting beaten by a mob as usual, help me. Otherwise I'll signal."

I ran to Mickey.

"Hey. Hey!"

"Get away from me."

"Drop it Mickey, and tell me what the fuck is going on!"

"Get away, I don't know you!"

"Spare me, Mickey. Want me to go downtown and get our birth certificates, you untoward vermin? Because I will."

"Never saw you before in my life…"

"Or I'll hire a private dick, but one way or another I'll make it worse for you, I swear I will. I'll immolate your soul!"

"Okay, fine. I'll talk to you this once, but make it fast. Jesus, Damone, you still all fucked up with that drama club talk?"

"Wonderful. Maroon me for four years, see me again, insult me. You, who's living off my musical legacy. If it wasn't for me, you wouldn't be carrying that amplifier right now."

"Thanks."

"How much are they paying you?"

"Not enough."

"Bullshit. At least ten thousand dollars a week, plus expenses. Liar."

"Damone, they aren't paying me shit, they…what do you think the expenses might be related to this work? Just curious."

"How much are they paying you? And what did you do to the house?"

"Damone, I don't know what you're on, but I'm just scraping by, okay? And I'm telling you, you better fly, because if Johnny finds out I talked to you, we're both dead. He's completely out of his mind over what happened with President Nixon, you know, the usual bullshit."

"Oh, I'm sorry to hear that. Poor little Johnny's upset because he and the President exchanged some unpleasantries at a soiree for multi-millionaires? Heartbreaking."

"The hell you talking about? Watergate? Nixon? He resigned last month?"

"The President quit his job? Shows spirit."

"Damone, look. I'm your brother, you sorry fuck. I want to help you, okay? But can you, for once in your life, listen to someone? Can you?"

"I'm listening."

"You gotta talk to Johnny. Not me. You know that. But you gotta let him cool down over this Nixon thing. It's all he talks about, how the liberals are shaming the country by humiliating an American President who resigned when he didn't even do anything wrong, blah blah blah. I swear Damone, he was even talking about breaking him out of jail if he goes. I mean, he's crazy. You know how he gets."

I took pause.

"So what are you suggesting?" I asked.

"I'm suggesting you let sleeping dogs lie for a while. Watch TV, and you'll know exactly how his mood is going to be. But definitely not a snowball's chance in hell will you get anywhere with him today other than the emergency room. Joey's about to puke he's so stressed, and Tommy too, you know, those guys are political."

"I won't wait forever, Mickey. You guys really screwed me. You should call your band The Judases."

"Damone, I'm not in the band. You're a piece of work. Get outta here before Johnny comes around. Good to see you're okay, man, seriously."

"I've never been better, Mickey, why would you think otherwise? I've lived on rotten fish and seaweed for four years, like the Japanese."

"Hey, I think that's them. Go!"

I hesitated, wondering if his soothing words were mere rascalism; but his reasoning was solid and his demeanor forthright so I gave him the benefit of the doubt. The thing that didn't make any sense was the cornerstone of his story: the President of the United States had told America to take this job and shove it.

I had been swindled yet again of course, but to turn around and go back would be too humiliating. I was consumed by a momentous rage; as I crossed the Bowery I made helicopter blades with my arms and spun like a whirling dervish through the screeching, honking cars. When I reached the other side, I got down on all fours and stuck my ass out. I made a pathetic, supplicating face. I looked up at the passerby and tried to make eye contact while I said, "Hey everyone, I'm a bitch boy, a pathetic little bitch boy," over and over in a grotesque nasal whine. It was an effective emollient: the extreme humiliation drained my anger, and after twenty minutes of the purgative, I was able to stand up and brush off my pants. Peter joined me.

"I figured you knew what you were doing so I just watched."

"A prudent approach, Peter. Please excuse me."

"That's fine. As long as you're okay now. What'd he say?"

"Did the President of the United States resign?"

"Yeah."

"Why?"

"Him and some Mexicans and this moustache guy who can light his own hands on fire without getting hurt broke into a motel, and at first they got away with it, but then, I don't know, I guess some of them were bragging about getting away with it and Nixon had a tape recorder in his office and somehow Bernstein and Bernstein got the tapes, and they persecuted. A helicopter came and picked him up from the White House and took him home. But nobody would tell where they hid the stuff."

"Bizarre. Who's President now?"

"The Vice President."

"Okay. Good. Thank you for the information. Let's go back to your Uncle's."

"What'd he say?"

"He said to come back after Johnny calms down about Nixon."

"Well, can you imagine such a thing? The President of the United States breaking into a motel. Imagine waking up and seeing President Nixon going through your wallet. Hundreds of millions of Americans are very, very, very angry. And the Chinese too since we built the tent. Everyone."

"But not like Johnny. Come on, let's go home and watch your Uncle's TV."

"Kennedy was so sophisticated."

"An *Ocean's Eleven* type."

"Yeah, exactly Damone. That's exactly what he was."

CHAPTER XXVII.

A SWORD HANGING OVER HIS HEAD IS THREATENING HIS HEALTH.

I began my vigil as soon as we got back to Uncle Dave's. Fortunately he was watching television. He invited us to sit down and offered us a joint.

"And grab some drinks. Live it up, guys. And grab the *Pledge*, that dust on the TV is bugging me."

"What are you watching?" asked Peter.

"In a few minutes Evel Knievel is on. Not him, movie about him. Saw it before. Not bad."

"You know him, Damone?" asked Peter.

"I do not, but his name is intriguing."

"He's a motorcycle stuntman," said Peter, "and he's jumping over a giant Canyon full of snakes tomorrow in a rocket-powered cycle or a rocket, I'm not sure, but it's a rocket."

"My brothers' sort of thing. Sure, I'll watch it."

I had decided before the film started that I would loathe it, not because I had anything against Mr. Knievel; I was simply in the mood to loathe a film. Fortunately I kept my prefatory hatred to myself, avoiding having to stammer through some half-baked explanation if I appeared to like it, which, much to my chagrin, I did very much.

From the opening shots of a Soviet-style arena, I was hooked. I blotted out my life and luxuriated in visions of what might have been, picturing myself strolling across the amphitheatre's expanse, forever alone like the Genius of the Carpathians. Optimistic

Socialist Realist music reinforced my vision. I saw myself crossing the field and mounting the stage. Once I was on stage with my hands reaching toward the kingdom of heaven, the gates would open and the masses would flood in: stampeding, screaming, sacrificing beasts and offering me their naked flesh.

When the music shifted into a threatening minor key and the lone hero entered the arena, I was in awe—it was my vision precisely realized. The ominous music and isolating long shots presented a hero challenged, but destined to emerge victorious. He would tear himself from the confines of self-criticism and formalism, and, if necessary, he'd punch his fist through the television screen and cross over.

Peter and Dave were high and making remarks befitting the condition: Knievel rolled his cycle into the middle of a racetrack, and when he leaned forward, Dave suggested he was chewing his own cock. After he rested the bike on the kickstand and walked out of the frame, Peter said that he had forgotten his vibrating anal butt plug. I shushed them with a threatening hiss.

Well, it turned out the lone man was just some menial flunky, a loser and a hack whose lot in life was to raise and lower kickstands: a few minutes later, the real Knievel came rolling up in a limousine with a military escort. He emerged from the limousine with a scepter and a sob story. What followed was a horrifically dumbed-down version of the 1931 film *Road to Life*. After taking a shit on hope, I joined Peter and Uncle Dave as they developed a perverse narrative.

Thus: a midget sucks Knievel's dick in a crowded bar. Breaking into a bank to steal the Chamber of Masturbation. A bull fucks Knievel and an elderly carnival barker, then they all suck each other's dicks, then the bull sucks the barker's dick, they pass around a flask of horse cum, an alcoholic fucks a bronze bell, a horse performs autoerotic asphyxiation, the alcoholic dies after being thrown from a bull, all the cowboys run out to fuck the corpse. The cowboys take the body away to fuck it in private, then Knievel has a red handkerchief in his back right pocket, which means he drinks dog urine at the source while fucking crowds of Guatemalan men, and then a guy in a porkpie hat fucks the roof of a pickup truck. They put the drunk corpse into a station wagon and Dave said, "Nice Woody," and Peter laughed and I didn't understand why.

Then Knievel naked with bloody knee pads on from sucking off the bull, the horse, the midget, the old barker, the corpse, the blond girl who could turn into a transvestite at will, and several random cowboys, then the blond girl and him took turns beating each other with a fly swatter, then Knievel said, "It isn't infected or anything is it?" and the doctor said, "Get your hand away," then there were handjobs, blowjobs, and venereal diseases that burned Knievel's dick off in front of his girlfriend, then Knievel came and the doctor was surprised that all he had to do was pull off a bandage to make Knievel come.

Knievel came again, he masturbated through his towel and the doctor drank heavily, then he poured whiskey over Knievel's penis, it hurt, so the doctor said, "Would you like a bullet to bite on?" Knievel said, "What does it look like, is it infected, why is it aching like that?" and the doctor replied, "Because it's broken and full of metal, you damn fool." Then the doctor said he'd break it again, and "Probably the other one too."

We discussed Knievel's two penises, but I started having an eerie suspicion the movie makers had intended just that. Knievel started masturbating again. He fell during a jump so we had a moment of silence until he was in the hospital with a nurse rolling him under the giant dick-sucking machine. She said, "This won't take but one minute,' but Knievel got too excited and before the nurse could lower the dick-sucking machine Knievel yelled, "Give me your hand," and the nurse screamed, and then the doctors gave him a sex change.

But then a pimp brought two tall, striking women into Knievel's hospital room, which definitely threw us off balance. The movie seemed to be pandering to our interpretation, and I think I speak for all of us when I say we felt a little used. But he was admittedly in top-form, attempting to run over a high school girl after lurking outside her school. After trying to kill her he seduced her, and we were humbled once more.

Then, in the final minutes, there he was again: the flunky, the fluffer, the loser, the clown. His kickstand responsibilities had been supplemented with the responsibility of holding Knievel's scepter while he jumped twenty trucks. Slow motion, cheers, heroism, gleaming silver rings and anthems. Even the flunky jumped for joy and grinned like an idiot, the cunt-ass in his red shirt and black hat, a simpering, lisping, slime-ball. He even rubbed Knievel's chrome with his hankie, and I think he may have zipped Knievel's fly prior to the jump.

Knievel lifted onto shoulders, followed by a voiced-over soliloquy on how millions and millions look to him for divine inspiration in their meaningless lives, and he provides their meaning. Then he claimed to be the last gladiator in the new Rome, and that he competes against destruction and wins. He concludes by stating that the only choice is our death, and his will be glorious. More Socialist Realist music, but of course, no sign of the human garbage, the scepter holder, who, in Knievel's words, "Doesn't get paid to think." To be fair in my portrayal of that miserable worm, hired only as a reminder to Knievel of the enormous distance he traveled from his humble beginnings: *that* miserable worm was at least recognized and paid for his work.

Next we watched a beauty pageant. I found the pageant rather dull except for a delightful flute solo from Miss Wisconsin.

"I got a flute she can blow," said Dave. Dave intoxicated was not the Dave I initially met at the library, who seemed like a young career man.

When Miss Wisconsin appeared during the swimsuit segment, I said, "That's the sort of woman I could settle down with."

"Ha ha, that's great Damone. You could settle down with her, huh?"

"I don't know what's so funny. Someone can't sit around and talk exclusively about their bodies, although it's critical. With her, we could talk about music, about her flute playing."

"Yeah? What'd she play?"

"What do you mean?"

"Earlier. What'd she play on the flute?"

I was ashamed despite my inebriation because I could not answer Dave's question, so I said:

"Do you know her measurements?"

"You don't know what she played."

"What are her measurements? Don't know? I'll tell you: thirty-seven, twenty-five, thirty-six."

"Fuck off, how we going to check it?"

"You wear a thirty-one waist, thirty-four length. You wear a fourteen and a half neck, thirty-three sleeve, sometimes thirty-four, shirt."

"You went through my clothes, you crazy fucker."

I gave up. We drank and smoked. I don't remember falling asleep.

The high-pitched tone of an off-the-air TV station woke me. Colored pillars filled the screen: grey, yellow, light blue, green, pink, red, dark blue. Black pillars bookended the colored pillars. Colors could be corrupted or purified, separated or mixed. Although the off-the-air screen image pointed to the end of music and art by coming very close to infallible expression in both mediums, it fell just short; not because of its own shortcomings, but because of mine, and, by extension, humanity's. We were not prepared for that final, unchanging tone or the massive black canvas. I wondered if my work—even as expressed through my brothers' mutated compositions—had propelled us too far too fast, almost as if we had created our own wormhole that moved the Third Dimension closer to the final black screen than it should have been by the late 20th Century. Would the collective soul thank me or condemn me when we entered the Fourth Dimension? And so hung the question. For it was me, not my brothers, that would ultimately be held responsible for unleashing such force. I got up and turned on the stereo.

Dawn returned my comfortable illusions. I ground a knuckle into an eye. Dave appeared.

"I gave some of your records a spin last night," I said.

"Thoughts?"

"Paper Lace, *The Night That Chicago Died*? A fucking war crime. On the other hand, Sweet's *Fox On the Run*? Quite good."

"You mean you liked it?"

"Sure. I'm not a dogmatist. I don't think, 'I'm a man who dislikes rock,' and then behave as if it's a dictum. If it's good it's good. *Fox* is a modern *Ode to Joy*, but the joy comes via hips rather than head. But what of this separate pile, all horrible: Hues Corporation, John Denver's *Annie's Song*, *Billy Don't Be a Hero*?"

"Ladies, Damone. The ladies like that pile."

"I see that's working out well for you, Dave. Perhaps some of your ladies would have enjoyed our analysis of the Evel Knievel film in addition to these records."

"Touché, Damone. Talking shit, getting high—you seem to be cooling out over here. Why you watching TV with the sound down? Sunday morning's all crap, and I found out you gotta go somewhere and pay to watch Knievel's jump."

"News on Nixon."

"You missed the big stuff."

"Perhaps. But a galactic shift is rippling the Illuminati. They behave radically during these periods."

"Who's an Illuminati?"

"The President."

"I don't think so."

"He's Henry Ford's son, correct?"

"Not related."

"But he's someone. Skull and Bones?"

"Never heard that."

"Where did he attend school?"

"I don't know."

"Well, he's something. A Freemason, perhaps. You don't get that job any other way."

"I don't think so. I think he's just some dolt from Ohio or Michigan. I know he played football. Anyway, what in the hell are you talking about?"

"Nothing. Let's just keep the television on, if you don't mind."

Of course the galactic shift resulted from the contraction of the wormhole that I had stabilized for petty reasons. Looking back, I had no idea why I had been so enraged with Dave. He had been nothing but kind, barring a few gaffes. I was distressed about my brothers, but I would have been even more distressed had I not spent the last few days at Dave's enjoying camaraderie, drugs, alcohol, and television. I had overreacted, and now I had one very confused Béla Bartók wandering around Brooklyn. I couldn't have known then that the wormhole jump had imbued him with contemporary versatility that allowed him to create a false history and a career in fashion design. It was possible that his new history had also been a graft, a bit of spray from the wake of the electromagnetic energy that I slipped through the wormhole. If this was the case, his history would still be false, but would be more durable as a result of its actually having happened, not in real time or naturally, but laid down backwards like a film shown from finish to start at great speed.

"Damone," Dave said, "you here or what?"

"Pardon, Dave. I was thinking about an injustice I committed against...against a friend."

"Mind if I play some music since the sound's down?"

"Of course not, but let's avoid your Iggy Poop."

"It's *Pop*."

"This time it was intended, Dave. I'm not entirely devoid of wit."

"Funny guy, Damone."

Dave put an album. Something like a slow, underwater version of the Andante con moto from Schubert's Piano Trio No. 2 in E-flat major came from the hi-fi, performed for a rude, shouting crowd. A man called out to the kids to do something, but it wasn't clear what—something to do with changing the weather. Then they were invited to an animal sacrifice.

Something official was happening on the television—suits, lights, special announcement.

The man singing threatened the crowd with an electric wall of sound—overkill in the circumstances.

On television a wooden toothpick-holder man sat at a desk between two Turkish water pipes. The camera moved closer as the wooden man spoke.

The singer, fearing the belligerent crowd, stuttered badly—or extremely well depending on your view—as he attempted to sing "Benny." I leapt to the television and turned it up. I yelled:

"Stop that music immediately!"

"It's been on five seconds! What the hell's wrong with you, you said you didn't mind."

"On the television, President behind a desk!"

"No way."

"Is that your President Ford?"

"Holy shit."

Ford was saying:

"It could go on and on and on….Someone must write the end to it…I have concluded that only I can do that…and if I can…I must…There are no historic or legal precedents…"

"No!" I screamed.

"What's wrong?" said Dave.

"He's going to execute Nixon himself, and immediately! Oh God, why do you refuse to gaze upon me?"

"Damone, I don't think he's going to do that."

"But he's right, once he's on death row, it *could* go on and on. He has to sate the mob's bloodlust or Detroit will burn again. I'm sunk, sunk! A vermin's tale with a predicable ending. Oh! When the sperm struck the egg it was my death knell!"

"Damone, if you'd shut up for a minute we'd be able to hear what he's…the details of the execution."

"Why are you laughing?" said Peter. "Damone's right, Uncle Dave. They'll hang Nixon on the networks. If they don't everyone's going to riot."

"Jesus, what is wrong with you two? I can't believe I'm letting you stay here, I must have been baked out of my mind. One: he isn't going to execute Nixon. Two: let's shut up and listen, k?"

Ford talked about the nation, ugly arousal, mercy, friendship, difficulty, bad dreams, and then he exhorted ten angels.

"Oh, no," said Dave.

"What's the matter?"

"He's going to let him off the hook. I can't believe this."

"You think so?" I asked.

"Quiet, here's the big moment. No way. Oh, shit. You must be kidding…are you kidding? It's a fucking travesty. This can't be happening. Justice is dead. The country is dead."

"Well," said Peter, "what did you expect, Uncle Dave? Nixon probably gave Ford a cut of the stuff."

"What stuff?"

"The stuff from the motel."

"Is that how it worked, Peter? Ford sold out the country for some towels?"

"It doesn't matter," said Peter, "Nixon could've done a hundred porno movies and strangled fifty hookers in every one, and Ford still would have let him off. What's robbing a motel compared to that?"

"You're probably right, Peter. I got the ideals, but you got the street smarts. What did I expect?"

"This is absolutely fantastic," I said.

"Don't tell me you're one of those," said Dave.

"No," said Peter, "he's happy because his brother is going to be happy, so he's probably going to get his money."

"Happy for you, Damone, whatever that's about. Let's smoke."

He shut off the TV and played the stuttering singer. We shared a joint. We drank a bottle of Benedictine and listened to more records. Dave went into the kitchen to find some wine.

I was elated about the pardon, which made me sorrier for Dave. I felt filthy, like some parasite that lives in human refuse. Even though Dave would never know about the vindictive games I'd played with the cosmos, I felt like a duplicitous wretch as I finished his Benedictine and waited eagerly for him to return with the wine. I hadn't had Benedictine since Montez's ill-fated attempt to maintain a well-stocked bar. Why he'd even think such a thing, I'll never understand. Dee Dee and I nicked the Benedictine the day he bought it and poured it into a lobster pot full of ice, orange soda, and Hennessy. We destroyed it with František. We didn't care because we felt like our profligate father owed us, but in Dave's case that didn't hold. I had already noticed a snow shovel outside the building that I'd discreetly bring upstairs later for a little absolution action in the bathroom—there'd be no snow for several months.

Dave returned with wine. "Hey," he said, "Want to go to a bar and watch the Knievel jump?"

"When? I have to go to CBGB tonight."

"Five-thirty or six, I think. Your brothers play when, like eight or nine? Go directly to CB's after the jump, you'll have plenty of time."

"Thanks, Dave. I believe that today's my lucky day, or in other words Knievel's not making that jump, so yes, I'd like that. Watching that megalomaniac fail spectacularly will be a lovely overture."

"That's not very nice Damone. Knievel's all right."

"Just like Enver Hoxha."

"Who? Forget it, just be ready to roll around four-thirty."

We left at four-thirty. Peter helped me carry Lady.

Knievel failed to jump the canyon. The "motorcycle" was in fact a one-man rocket ship and not a bike at all. I didn't understand this. It would be like someone proclaiming they would long-jump from New York to London, then they go first-class via British Air while everyone watches the "long jump" on television with bated breath. In this respect, I had to give kudos to Knievel—it was a brilliant caper that turned the Emperor's new clothes concept against the mouth-breathing masses. It was the sort of mass-hypnosis I longed to impart.

That's not to say I wasn't impressed by the jump so-called, no; on the contrary, I thought his vertical course toward meteor storms, eternity, and certain death illustrated more panache than a horizontal course across some run-of-the-mill terrestrial canyon. But Knievel's dramatic elevation in hubris immediately prior to the jump—or perhaps even in the rocket itself after take-off—could not be matched by the rocket ship's performance, a phenomena I increasingly sympathized with as I matured.

The flaming rocket fired into the sky. It reached its zenith. It plummeted toward Earth. The almighty Evel Knievel bailed out and parachuted to the bottom of the canyon like the inebriated

Francis Gary Powers over Sverdlovsk. I realized that although I lacked the aforementioned talent of bending the masses to my will, I was definitely headed in the right direction, or depending on one's interpretation, I was headed toward an even more powerful mastery—the ability to sway fate in my favor, for surely these cosmic signs portended the annihilation of my enemies. Once they were swept into the dustbin of history, I'd return to my righteous place and be credited accordingly, and with my ascension I'd assume my birthright as Lord of Mobs.

After Knievel's inadequacy, we drank until it was time for Peter and I to head to CBGB. We put Lady over our heads—me in the rear—and left.

On the train we dealt with the usual taunts. I put my arm around Lady's neck. I caressed her. I whispered reassurances. The commuters became even more provocative. Of course there were many families and children that looked favorably on Lady and commented on her beauty: even in her piñata disguise, Lady's sleek lines were evident, and her inner-vibrancy was reflected in her athletic bearing. But it only takes one bad apple to spoil the mood, and the one young man who suggested that Lady and I "get a room" was just such an apple. The entire train christened the upstart a modern-day Voltaire with their uncontrollable laughter at our expense. But I had bigger concerns, so I reminded myself that the only thing that really matters is how we feel between the sheets, and I forged on.

At least Peter and I were getting better at carrying Lady—we exited the train, ascended the stairs, and headed toward CBGB bearing Lady over our heads as if we were duplicate Protopopovs bearing our Belousova. People smiled and laughed as we walked the streets of the Lower East Side. I was on an express train to victory; of this there was no doubt.

We crossed Bleecker. We stood near CBGB. Lady stood between us. The gathering crowd assumed that we were part of some groovy escapade inspired by the tone of the times. Most people thought Lady was a piñata, which pleased me. They asked questions about where we'd be breaking her to bits later, which did not please me.

We were early. I asked the doorwoman—the same one that had ejected me when I was hirsute—if the Ramones had arrived. She said they'd set up, and were now eating in a restaurant nearby. She said, "When I saw you over there, I thought *you* were a Ramone!" I merely smiled.

I was resting my hand on Lady's back and talking to a rather attractive young woman, lending credibility to the theory that beautiful women gravitate toward men associated with beautiful women, when I saw Dee Dee, Johnny, and Tommy approaching on Bowery. I said, "You'll have to excuse me miss, three brothers with whom I have a blood feud approacheth."

Now there'd be no pretending not to know me—we looked like we had fired out of Szilarda in quick succession like bullets from a Gatlin gun. I raised my hand and said, "Halt! I command you to halt. Present your papers, please."

"Get a load of this guy," said Johnny.

"What's *he* doing here?" said Dee Dee.

"Shut your fucking mouth, okay?" said Johnny.

"Good going, Dee Dee," said Tommy.

"Slip of the tongue, Dee Dee?" I said. "Drop the act, Johnny: you're owned. Where's Joey? I want you all here for the moment of reckoning."

"Get out of our way, asshole," said Johnny.

"I won't. I'm not afraid of you. Nice way to talk to your *brother*! Attention everyone, I'm their *brother*! That wrote all their *music*!"

I hammered down on the condemning final word of each sentence like I was banging the gavel on Judgment Day. Their eyes darted between me and the kids in front of the club.

"Hey, you're nothing but a weirdo!" said Dee Dee, and he slapped Lady. I leapt to Lady's side and rubbed where Dee Dee had hit her while reassuring her that everything would be all right.

"Hey," said Johnny, "what the hell is *this* about? You talking to that horse?"

I didn't answer.

"I asked you a question. You think that horse hears things and feels things? Let me show you something."

Johnny shoved Lady. She fell to the sidewalk. I charged Johnny like a rabid panther. Dee Dee dove for my legs and tackled me. In other words, my normal CBGB routine.

"Hold him down," Tommy said. "Look here, we don't want trouble. We got a show to play, but if they need to kick your ass, they will. I'm strongly advising you to go back to where you came from."

"I tried Tommy, but it doesn't exist anymore! When are you fools going to end this farce?"

"I don't know what you're talking about."

"How do you live with yourselves? I'm a lone Abel surrounded by a barbaric hoard of Cains!"

"You're a lone asshole surrounded by a barbaric hoard of fists," Johnny said, "and I don't want to see you here again. Now, you got a choice. You get this…"

He kicked me in the balls.

"And this…"

He kicked Lady in the stomach. She slid across the concrete.

"Or take a walk and never come back, understand? And if I ever see you talking to this horse or rubbing it or fucking it or jerking it off, I'll do something you won't like. You fuck pussies, not pink piñatas, got it?"

I did get it, but I was unable to express it at that juncture, occupied as I was with the excruciating pain of my public emasculation. I wheezed and squirmed in the fetal position on the Bowery sidewalk, the street having been home to such notables as Mark Rothko the Expressionist painter.

"John, I think we should go now. I think that's enough," said Tommy.

"I'm not sure it will ever be enough with this guy, the stubborn blockhead. Let's go."

Peter knelt beside me.

"I'm sorry Damone, I was running and that other one tripped me and threw me by my shirt, the one that slapped Lady first? Man, is he strong! When he threw me I must have flown fifteen feet before I fell on the ground. Gosh, he's really strong, and he obviously uses a blow dryer."

"Help me up, I'm not feeling well. Help me stand Lady up. Thank you."

"I know you, we're going to try again right now, aren't we Damone? Damone?"

"Peter…yes, we will try again, of this there is no doubt. But not today. I was weakened by that blow. And what they did to Lady. I'm not sure I can forgive myself. I don't regret bringing her, but perhaps I should revise the strategy if she's to accompany me on the next foray."

"So what are we going to do?"

"Let's go back to your uncle's. Have a drink. Or two. Watch some television."

"Damone, I think that's sometimes smart. You shouldn't feel bad. I have a cousin, and he has this problem where he can't walk past stuffed animals. You know how people leave them on stoops? He takes every single one home because he says they have souls. Their owners put them out in the street and the dolls feel lost and betrayed. People do that so other kids can play with them, but he's too worried that no kid will adopt them or someone might pick them up for their dog to chew on, and they'll feel pain when some poodle or German shepherd or schnauzer or Chihuahua or bulldog or pinsch—"

"I get it, Christ. Move on."

"—or spaniel or mastiff rips them apart. I never thought about stuffed animals in the street until I heard about my cousin, then I started seeing them all the time. I see tons, but I never tell my cousin because his apartment is full of them. He had to throw out his furniture to make room for the animals. At first it was okay, but now he has five or six thousand. It's not good. The weird thing is he told Uncle Dave that he doesn't actually want to take them home, but he has to because it's his duty as a human being. He even said he was going to move upstate and live in a field so he wouldn't always be running into stuffed animals. In the city he's always worried about how many thousands must be sitting on stoops wishing someone would come along and give them a good home. He sometimes cries himself to sleep. And my cousin is forty, so he can't get married unless he moves upstate.

"But he's not weird at all, he's totally normal except for that. He had a good job in some tax office in Brighton Beach, I think on Neptune. I know he wears a tie to work and his office has big windows. Across the street there's a closed gas station, and they put a really tall fence around it with barbed wire on top to keep out copper thieves and heroin addicts. One day he's working at his desk. He gets bored and stares out the window, maybe at the clouds or at a pretty Dominican or Russian girl. But all of a sudden he sees there's a stuffed animal stuck in the fence, but way up high where he can't reach it. Plus he's at work and they have big windows and they don't all go to lunch at the same time, so if he goes and tries to get it everyone at work will see him. Usually when he picks one up and he's with strangers he says it's for a dog or a friend or a friend's kid or a kid in the neighborhood, or he says he's going to donate it to an orphanage—"

"I understand. Please move on."

"He car-pools so he can't work late to save it, so he stares out the window all day. He can't work or tell jokes because all he can think about is that stuffed animal—it was Raggedy Ann—stuck in the fence. She could fall or get ripped apart by birds or removed by maintenance men, but he can't do anything. So he goes home in the car pool and tries to forget about it. But he can't sleep, so he decides to take public transit to work really early. He'll climb the fence and save Raggedy Ann. So that's what he does.

"He gets there in the morning and he starts climbing the fence, but he's all dressed for work in his tie and dress pants. It's a hard climb, so he's going slow—he forgot how much climbing cyclone fences hurts your hands so he didn't have gloves on. I could have told him that. But what he doesn't know is that all his bosses and the secretaries got to work even earlier than he did for a meeting, and they are watching him climb the fence across the street, and then they're watching him have a hard time getting Raggedy Ann out of the barbed wire. He's up there for nearly fifteen minutes, which isn't a long time to watch a show or drink a six-pack, but it's a really really long time to stay on top of a barbed wire fence saving a doll, especially when it's across the street from your work.

"Eventually he saves the doll and climbs down, but now he's all sweaty and his work clothes are messed up. He figures he can fix everything in the bathroom. He walks in and everyone is staring at him and laughing. He's surprised and can't come up with any of his normal lies so he doesn't say anything at all, and they don't either. After a few seconds he remembers to lie and he says his niece collects Raggedy Anns. That was actually a very good lie—I think when he added the part about her collecting Raggedy Anns instead of just wanting *one* doll *one* time, I think that was the most important part of the lie to make sure it worked right.

"But it didn't. Maybe for one secretary, but bosses always see through that sort of lie and they always thought he was a total weirdo and a pervert after that, so all the years he spent as a normal person wearing a tie and doing a good job and talking about baseball were all wiped out in the fifteen minutes he spent at the top of that fence. He became maybe ninety percent weirdo and ten percent normal to his bosses, and that's the last people you want with those sorts of odds. So now he works at C-Town as a cashier and bagger. He doesn't wear a tie to work anymore."

"Peter, I can't tell you how happy it makes me that I remind you of that story. A perfect way to end a perfect day. Come on, let's go home."

CHAPTER XXVIII.

RECUPERATION.

In the morning Peter and I drank two bottles of caraway liquor mixed with Tang. Peter was adamant that we respect Uncle Dave's liquor cabinet, which meant that our booze was subject to the wild-card unpredictability of Peter's shoplifting. Granting some exotic cocktails, he always came through with something. By noon we were balanced.

My brothers' next show was on the 15th, giving me five days to recover from my last failed attempt so I'd be energized and pain-free for my next failed attempt. All my strategies, however clever, would ultimately lead to a confrontation with Johnny—there was no way out. He was the muscle propping up their dictatorship of lies, and I was certain to be defeated in one hundred out of every one hundred direct battles with him. If I hoped to sabotage the powerful machine behind the fists and black leather, I'd need a stealthier approach.

But I had no ideas. At least I had time, housing, and allies. Uncle Dave told me to eat whatever I wanted while he was at work. When the caraway liquor was gone, Peter gave me a pint of vodka as a stopgap before leaving to acquire more liquor. I was alone in the apartment which was ideal, because one of the people in the television had delivered an unambiguous message for me to take a certain action, namely the woman advertising *Cachet* perfume which was code for my standard product, and I was more than willing to oblige the strikingly beautiful woman's request to put some on her. She even pointed out the precise targets, and I was lucky enough to be able to answer the call twice before Peter returned. When he did we shared a moment of levity when he noticed the life lava oozing down the television screen.

That night we watched a debut called *Rhoda*. Rhoda had fled something awful in Minnesota. I couldn't concentrate because I kept theorizing about her dark past. Her constant joking struck me as compensatory and evasive. I did however sympathize with Steven Schlossberg, the never-seen stood-up date that spirals into dark obscurity as soon as Rhoda sees Joe, your typical strutting blowhard. Also worthy of mention was Rhoda's mother's hair; I pictured how different my life would be if I found a stylist that could duplicate it on me.

But the show ended in depression because of the never-seen doorman Carlton. Throughout the show I kept thinking that he had a very good job, perhaps the perfect job for me—he was constantly drunk, performed no heavy lifting, and nobody had anything but the lowest expectations of him. After the show I realized I was surrendering to defeatism.

I grew sad, and wished that I could somehow remake the show completely. I would dispense with all of the characters except for Rhoda's younger sister Brenda, who I preferred to the point of a nascent crush. My version would be called *Evenings with Brenda*, and Brenda and I would stay home eating cake and consoling each other for our physical and social failures, which in her case were entirely unwarranted; she was extremely cozy and cute. I did not share these adulterous thoughts with Lady, but I felt that the extreme guilt I experienced for not experiencing any guilt absolved me.

At least I had her, booze, and the wherewithal to try again, which was an increasingly suspect use of wherewithal. I was beginning to see hope as a self-destructive delusion, inspiration as a seductive trap. It seemed to me that reality, intuition, and the alignment of the stars were all assuming favorable positions for the exclusive purpose of tricking me into trying again so the entire universe could resonate from end to end with laughter when I failed, a fate decided on the first day of creation, likely over breakfast.

So I drank. Intoxication narrowed my concerns, allowing me to focus on the most important issue: figuring out how to discern the true signs. Although fate's deception seemed monolithic, I knew better—despite losing every battle, my belief that destiny's seemingly deterministic engines had hairline fractures had not been fully obliterated, and it was up to me to figure out how to exploit these almost invisible fault lines.

But I didn't have much time. On the 9th, I narrowed my concerns a little too much: I got so drunk that I forgot to deliver a birthday toast to the Democratic People's Republic of Korea. The last thing I remembered was Uncle Dave coming home in the early evening. He asked me if I had heard about the New York Dolls breaking up. After teaching me a little about rock and roll, he had assumed a new tone, talking to me about all those musical zeros as if I had been baptized wholly into the faith and we were now comrades for the cause. He said, "Yeah, they broke up, I'm sorry to tell you," as if Imelda Marcos had abdicated. He then put on some noise that was indistinguishable from any of the other noise he found so delightful. He handed me a record cover with the most miserable bunch of transvestites I'd ever seen in my life on it, five dark-bearded ninnies garishly mimicking feminine postures on a couch. I lost my patience. I said, "Dave, why does your life revolve around the escapades of these third-rate braying long hairs? Don't you have something better to think about?"

He looked at Peter, and then he cackled. Peter looked at the floor. A mushroom cloud of shame and rage blossomed within me. I upended a plastic half-gallon of gin until the bitter liquor vanquished my humiliation. I set the bottle down and floated toward the darkness at the end of the tunnel.

The next day Peter updated me on how our night had gone, explaining we'd had a low-key good time. We went to a movie called *Turkish Delight*, which I had no recollection of whatsoever other than a hazy image of a man spanking a naked woman with a red flower sticking out of her ass. I was curious about the context, but on the other hand oblivion had successfully destroyed many hours that I otherwise would have wasted perfectly good consciousness on.

Peter showed me where Dave kept the Playboys, Penthouses, and Hustlers, so we spent the rest of the day masturbating, drinking, and napping—the trifecta that makes bad days better and good days great. In the late afternoon I prepared a salad.

When Dave got home we smoked marijuana and resumed our rock and roll polemic. Full of beer and empty of longing, I was up for some verbal sparring; between orgasms I'd carefully considered the pop landscape, and I was ready to present its gross limitations.

Dave began by putting on an album by a band called Yes. I was delighted; the record was so far removed from rock and roll in the original sense that it was something else altogether, a patchwork of trickery, famous classical references, gratuitous vocal harmonies, and thematic ambiguity that, taken together, amounted to a bloated, purposeless monster. I laughed in Dave's face as each track further eroded his argument.

"Dave, I appreciate you introducing this exhibit—it means we can terminate our discussion now. Do you really need anything more than this record to verify that your rock and roll is dead beyond dead? Just listen to the absurd extremes those phonies are going to in order to seem innovative and cultivated—it's nothing but slops and offal! They've perhaps heard twenty prominent classical pieces, and now they think they're modern day Bachs and Mozarts. This is the Pinchas Floyd concept taken to its grotesque extreme—this silly idea that "genius" consists of grafting musical fragments that in the classical context would be used to introduce a five-year-old violinist to scales; that grafting random snippets of conversations into the songs or nonsensical sounds somehow provides philosophical depth…pah! It's not even worth shitting on these albums, let alone defending them. Particularly these latest messes you've played: Floyd, Yes, that Emerson, Lake, and Powell. Don't forget I'm not totally unversed in this drivel; my sister was a disciple of this crap, which gave me an unsolicited introduction to the mindless thumping and yelping called rock and roll, and these Frankensteinian contraptions you call "songs" were done by the Beatles last decade. How can these people live with themselves, pedaling such shamelessly imitative crap?"

"Did you like the Beatles?"

"Everything they did was horrible except for *I Am the Walrus*, which must have been a lucky accident. But don't change the subject, sir; I'm not finished yet."

"Sorry. Carry on."

"Last night…when was that, last night? You showed me that record by your now defunct New York Dolls—the entire city must be wearing black—and other than slapping on their mother's make-up and clothing, those people are vulgar, mutilated carbon-copies of your almighty Rolling Stones, are they not?"

"Okay, you have a point. Sort of."

"*Sort of*? How, 'Sort of?' Not only do they feature the same interplay between dark and light, the same ying and yang as your Mick Jagger and Keith Richards…"

"You know the guys' names in the Stones?"

"I recognized the duplication of the paradigm as soon as you handed me that New York Dolls disaster. And furthermore, this Johansen character not only looks like Mr. Jagger, he mimics his timbre, his tone, his syllabic organization."

"It's camp, Damone; he's more of a trope on a trope—"

"Did you just use the word *trope*? Surely you jest. And applied to such derivative nincompoops."

"But they're doing something raw, stripped down. The shows were very exciting."

"Have you seen these Rolling Stones perform?"

"Yeah."

"Where?"

"Twice, once in Newark Symphony Hall—"

"Revolting."

"—in '65. In '72, at Madison Square Garden."

"And where did you see your New York Dolls?"

"Mercer Arts Center."

"There you have it. You put your Rolling Stones in the Mercer Arts Center and your New York Dolls in Madison Square Garden, you watch who's "raw" and "exciting." You're an easily misled fool."

"You got a point about the venue, but I don't think that makes me an *easily misled fool*."

"I regret to inform you that it does. May I continue, sir?"

"You may."

"Hang on, I need to present the next exhibit."

I went through Dave's albums until I found it.

"Voila! I'm very curious what sort of justification you're going to concoct on behalf of this quintet of nitwits as they float through the clouds. Well, sir?"

"Okay, okay, but just because they look like that doesn't mean they don't have something new to contribute or to say."

"To *say*? Oh yes, I'm sure this *Walkin' the Dig* number is rife with redeeming social purpose."

"Damone, people enjoy the music, doesn't that matter?"

"It means nothing. People once enjoyed watching prisoners being drawn and quartered, does that indicate quality?"

"You're exaggerating."

"Dave, you own both these records; in other words, you paid for them. You're being taken advantage of, sir; by New York Dolls, by this Aerosmith, and by the wealthy industrialists that are pimping them. Dave: it's only 1974. That means this rock and roll, granting its antecedents, is less than twenty years old, and your Rolling Stones are maybe what? Twelve or thirteen years old?"

"Around there."

"And already there's New York Dolls and Aerosmiths, and nobody questions it? The machine has churned out not one, but *two* bands performing pitch-perfect parody of your Rolling Stones. Your rock and roll has already come and gone."

"Then please explain to me how your brothers, clearly a rock and roll band, somehow have based their work on yours to a point where you intend on suing them? How does that work exactly? Wouldn't that mean your music was somehow part of this whole scene that you despise so much?"

"I'm pleased you challenge me thus. My music was never meant to descend from the classical genre to the shoddy world of pop. This is a personal tragedy for me, of course. It's a tragedy for my family, of course. But what my miscreant brothers have also inadvertently done is put the final nail in rock and roll's coffin. They've dealt the coup de grâce."

"How's that?"

"My compositions are radical. They take music to an extreme. They take *physics* to an extreme, but inside the classical genre there's still space for that. There isn't in rock and roll. By taking my concepts and warping them into what they have, they have taken rock and roll as far as it can go—they have presented it in its purest essence. They identified its degeneration, and essentially said, "Let's stop this tomfoolery and finish this off: here's high-grade, pure rock and roll in its cleanest, most powerful form." It's like uranium relative to cement. Your Floyd and your Yes noted that something was awry, but their research went in the entirely wrong direction. They chose to pile on more and more diffuse genres and random noises and dark existential concepts and surrealistic cut-up, and it turns out it's all a road to nowhere. Does that make any sense?"

"Sort of."

"My brothers have done something extreme. They jumped ahead of the entire hoard of rock and roll numskulls, so now there's no place to go, nothing to add, no feelings to translate. It's done. That puts my brothers in a precarious spot. It can go one of two ways: they could become the biggest rock group the world has ever known, and when their career is over, there will never be another rock album made ever again—so at least they did that for the world. Or the rock and roll industry will discover that four guys from Queens are jeopardizing their monopoly, because nobody will care about any other group once they've heard rock based on my compositions. The music industry will collude to keep "Ramones" records out of stores and off the radio. The press will ridicule them but never praise them, and most people—sheep—will obey whatever instructions they are issued by the press and corporations. But ultimately the power of my brilliance is inherent in the works, which makes them invincible in the long run. Even in their perverted form, my works will declare empire. They'll dominate the world. You'll see."

"You were making sense up to a point, Damone."

"I'm making nothing but sense, Dave. But fortunately for those satisfied with regurgitated fare, it's also possible that some pale imitation of the industry will rise again, and people, in their never-ending willingness to believe they're precious, will flagrantly duplicate my works whilst believing that they are original artists deserving of blowjobs and paychecks. They'll form groups called the Shimones, the Simones, even, God forbid, the Damones. And they will hopelessly attempt, over and over, to reproduce the perfection of my quartets. They will fail. But it won't matter, because in the gigantic dolt-churn that humanity resides in, hack imitation is the standard currency. The deepest human yearning is to hide in the safety of that which already is. Sure, they'll dress it up slightly with false newness or feigned rebellion, whip up some sanitized version of the original with just enough difference in shading to make the average social coward feel risky, while in reality they only dare to subscribe to an "individualism" that has been collectively agreed upon. Aerosmith and the New York Dolls and nobody questions it? It's the same dynamic that leads these hippy morons to believe their trite movement is countercultural or shocking. They are only shocking to the most provincial and undereducated members of society, but to anyone with an original bone in their body they are just another hoard of useless conformists. And my works will breed even more of them. In fact I guarantee you the chemical reaction has already started. I'm sure any number of ignoramuses have seen my brothers perform and have said to themselves, 'That sounds amazing, but at the same time simple enough where I could do it,' and then they go do some fool thing like buy a guitar and form a band, when the correct reaction to the Ramones is to realize there is no point whatsoever to buying a guitar or to listening to any other rock group ever again, because it's done. Do you understand?"

"I understand your opinion."

"This isn't opinion, Dave. When these upstarts attempt to play my music by imitating the Ramones' version of it, what they don't understand is the only place they can go is *back*—that any changes they make are limited to taking pieces of things that were already done on the road to the Ramones, because all roads lead to the Ramones, and they don't go any further. So for instance, one of these kids outside CBGB forms a group and attempts to play—I mean, how ridiculous—an imitation of four guys imitating my quartets, but he wants to add something…what can he add? A guitar solo like your Almond Brothers? Some hack rip-off of a classical "riff" like your Protocol Harem? See? Once my quartets have been unleashed on the pop world, everything else becomes a regression. It's basic arithmetic, Dave. It's an unambiguous science. The Ramones have ended rock and roll. Thanks to me."

"You make some good points Damone, but a lot of them are based on the huge assumption that your music, as played by your brothers, is going to get the response you say it will."

"It will. It's simple math."

"And overall the whole thing sounds, you know, with this talk of finality and the end and you did it all, it sounds a little…"

"Messianic?"

"Yeah. Sorry, but that's the right word: Messianic."

"Why are you apologizing? The word is precise. I'm telling you, Dave—you don't understand the power of my quartets."

CHAPTER XXIX.

THE DAMONEFORD FILES.

Hours and days of alcohol and self-abuse. I hadn't devised a strategy for the next CBGB assault, but I kept slavishly returning to Dave's nightstand and the naked ladies within. The cover of the March 1974 Playboy alone was an insurmountable distraction.

On Wednesday we ordered pizza and Peter contributed five gallons of red wine. We watched the debut of a program called *The Little House on the Prairie*. There were horses, wagons, handshakes, and good old-fashioned hard work. It wasn't looking good. On top of that, the hair-sprayed star was a relative of an acquaintance, but I kept this to myself. But the outstanding feature of the show was its unmitigated wretchedness. The father threw together a shack, i.e. "The Little House" and it went downhill from there.

When one of the girls opened a hatch and said, "We have our window...we can see the stars!" I couldn't take it anymore and said, "Jesus Christ, this is absolutely fucking awful." Uncle Dave spit out his wine and laughed. We were exceptionally high and moderately drunk, but having more sail than ballast can only take you so far in the face of such sentimental schlock. When the little fool girl said, "Home is the nicest word there is," we all laughed so hard I almost pissed again on Dave's floor.

The father in the show, Ingalls, was clearly a freeloader and a bum, and no amount of mawkish soundtrack could avail him of that. After he strutted into the general store demanding to be fronted without collateral and was refused, we all knew it was just a matter of time before he started prostituting his entire family. I knew he'd end up like that, I just knew it. Any relative of Jonathan Cummings was surely just like Jonathan.

Jonathan Cummings was a kid that lived in the same building as some friends in the Forest Hills section of Queens, and he was the dandy supreme. He wasn't especially handsome, and he never took part in so much as a school play, but nonetheless he was always going on about how he was going to be a gigantic movie star because he possessed the magic combination: beauty and a connection. In order to correct his worldview and to improve his chances of integrating with the unordained masses, Johnny beat up Cummings every time he saw him, always making sure to rip his pretty-boy clothing and ruin his neatly pomaded hair. Apparently Cumming's grandfather or uncle was a guy named Eugene Orowitz who supposedly was Ingall's father, and Ingalls was supposedly Little Joe from yet another television nightmare called *Bonanza*. Little Joe disappeared after *Bonanza*. He reappeared in 1974 as Ingalls the supreme deadbeat—I hope there are no fools among you who believed his "broken ribs" story as he struggled with those bags of wheat. His pseudo-attempt to climb the wheat only to come tumbling down just short of the top was some of the most spurious buffoonery ever filmed.

Many years later, Little Joe/Ingalls made another incidental appearance in my life. In the 1980s, Black Flag—one of the many bands I supposedly spawned—composed a number called *Slip It In*, and it was such a radical departure from my vision that I took the utmost offense when the group's de facto leader Henry Rolo stated that the Ramones, i.e., me, were a tremendous influence on him. I initiated a letter writing campaign whereby I pointed out that *Slip It In* owed everything to *Gimme a Little Kiss* by Little Joe, and owed nothing to *Chicks With Dicks Sleep Late*. No matter my condition, I wrote a letter to Mr. Rolo every day in 1987 demanding he recant the statement, but received no response. Granted, some of the letters were below my usual standard of elocution. The eighty-six I sent where I attempted to "put the Black Spot" on Mr. Rolo in the manner of Old Blind Pew vis-à-vis Billy Bones were particularly subpar, and I must confess that the majority were motivated less by a belief in the diabolical powers of the Black Spot and more by the fact that a black smudge was often about as literate as I could be after a couple gallons of Blue Nun.

Getting back to 1974, things improved on Friday when we watched a debut called *The Rockford Files*. The opening scene featured an elderly derelict, alone on a bus drinking from a brown paper bag. He attempted to remain on the bus after it reached the end of the line, and the driver had to throw him off. The vagrant sought refuge underneath a boardwalk. He descended into the filth, leaned against a pillar, and drank deeply.

He was then strangled to death by one of the most terrifying and brutal individuals I had ever seen, a ferocious muscular murderer that added an uncomfortably sexual flair to his killing. That, I thought to myself, is exactly how I'm going to end up—in reference to the strangled vagrant, not the muscular murderer.

Rather than dispose me against the show, this prophecy had the opposite effect—I felt like my entire future was bound to the show's result. If the murder was not redeemed, it would guarantee my own ugly demise. If the murder was redeemed, it would guarantee that the opening scene to my winter years would be entirely different; for example, the bus driver would say, "Sure, sleep in the bus for as long as you wish," or I would retreat under the boardwalk, lean against a pillar, and drink in peace until I was delightfully annihilated.

But the main event was the man himself: James Rockford, aka "Jim." Rockford had a surly independence that was a unique version of my own: whereas my individualism was protected by a moat of rage, Rockford's individualism was engaging. He used his coarseness and his blunt rejection of those around him to somehow insinuate those very people into his life. The more he shoved them away, insulted them, informed them of their inadequacies—the more they longed for his company, even going so far as to pay him for it.

I was impressed. Throw in his golden car, sport coats, and seaside trailer, you ended up with a marvel to aspire to. But there was more: his manner and look earned him the company of an extraordinary young woman who he seduced with ease, and he devised endless clever ways to defeat and humiliate his enemy.

This was no small task—his terrifying adversary made all my brothers put together seem like a first-grader brandishing a crayon. Cornflower, for instance.

On Saturday I went to the city for supplies. My brothers were performing Sunday. This time, no regress—by Monday, the Ramones would be reduced to four howling castrati, I would regain my crown as the creator, and I would be remunerated for my trouble, granting that the latter is only a measuring stick for the artist.

I made the majority of my arrangements on West 36th, and put the finishing touches on my masterpiece on East 46th. By two o'clock, I felt like Richard the Lionheart, so confident was I. When I boarded the Brooklyn-bound train I felt like an air conditioner or a Dunhill cigarette.

When I arrived at the apartment, Dave and Peter were on the couch looking studiously grim. When they registered my new look however, they dropped their somber posturing.

"What the hell?" said Dave.

"Damone, you look great, so sophisticated," said Peter.

"Thank you, Peter."

"You've duplicated that Rockford guy's look down to your shoelaces? Look Peter, he even got the sideburns right. You've outdone yourself, Damone," Dave said.

"His hair is a little bushier than Rockford's," said Peter, "and the sideburns are a little long. The coat's a little dark, but that's no big deal."

I had opted for the sport coat and dress pants that he had worn during the second half of the show. I thought the ensemble was the most quintessentially "Rockford." The Rockford Files ad from the TV Guide featured three Rockfords seen from different angles, making it easy for the old Romanian barber to emulate the style. He was delighted to hack off my Ramones locks, which he erroneously assumed were those of a hippy.

"Damone, I'm guessing that's what happened to my picture," Dave said.

"How do you mean, Dave?" I asked.

"Come on, don't be ridiculous. Peter, is he being serious?"

"I told him not to do it."

"Yeah, but is he serious? Damone, I want to kick you out but I don't want to kick you out, understand? Where's my lithograph?"

"What lithograph?"

"The one that was in that frame that's been replaced with a torn out page from an art book featuring the original. It's a Calder, by the way."

"I don't notice any difference."

"I don't either, except my lithograph was three feet tall and the picture from the book is three inches tall. And you used the whole page with the text."

"Sorry."

"Taken all together, it's so fucking insane I'm not even mad."

"I'll have the money to get it back in a matter of days."

"What, you pawned it? Give me the ticket, I have to go get it."

"But why? I'll have the money shortly. It's a veritable certainty."

"Right, extremely 'veritable'. Something tells me I have the highest probability of getting it back if I go right away."

"Based on what?"

"Not that it matters, but I'm an actuary."

"He's an actuary."

"He's an actuary?"

"I'm an actuary. I'll pick it up tomorrow. And if you do get some money, I expect to be paid back. And buy me a new book. You're lucky because I'm high, you're Peter's friend, and what you did is such a weird story that you can still stay. But one more stunt like this and you're out."

"I'm sorry, Dave. I didn't mean for you to get tangled in the web of Ramone feuding. But I hope you can see the practical necessity of this."

"The scary thing Damone, is that I actually think I understand your logic, and even worse, I think it makes sense in a bizarre way. Peter, grab some beers."

CHAPTER XXX.

THE GYRATOR.

Back at CBGB. Another Sunday with hoodwinked idolaters. I recognized several faces. Despite my new image and the fresh hope it imparted, I was pushing away an impending sense of this becoming drudgery, the grind. This feeling did not deflate me however; on the contrary, it crystallized my will toward a lifelong commitment. The outcome of any one skirmish would never dissuade me from waging eternal war.

Peter convinced me to leave Lady with him while I went in the club. My overwhelming anxiety regarding this brief separation was disproportionate—I'd be right back and I trusted Peter to resist temptation. Nonetheless, the stress was so intense that I began to falter. Peter had to resort to insulting my manhood before I would turn my back on Lady and cross the street.

The doorwoman didn't recognize me. She observed my formal attire and apparently surmised I was a person to be reckoned with—perhaps a Deutsche Grammophon executive prowling the city for fresh talent. I played the part by assuming the exaggerated expressions of a scrutinizer, a contemplator, a judge; a man impervious to the opinions of those around him; a man capable of ruthless assessments, a kingmaker or the grim reaper of dreams depending on my whimsy.

However, steeling oneself against an imagined onslaught does nothing when cruel reality unfurls. It is one thing to picture one's lover in the arms of another; quite another to watch the entire love act through a peephole in the shower curtain—you can't predict how you'll actually react.

A whiny longhair in a checkered jacket introduced them. They counted off and began. This was the clearest representation yet of my music, but it was a hybrid, as if they had chaotically blended several of my quartets and then condensed the result, although oddly the recurring motif derived largely from *Petroleum's Folly*, one of my most obscure works. In terms of its transcription to a rock format, it was uncanny—it was indeed the end of the line. My brothers were playing a vast music of ideas within the confines of a severely limited form. The result, as I had argued to Dave, was direct, giant, and clear—a regiment of rocket-propelled soldiers blasting from the massive amplifiers. But worst of all, inside the sound, above the sound, below it—I could hear the sad mysterious pipes, the indigo violins, the funereal accordions—all of the dark sounds of the black tower of the east. They had pulled it through the hole.

I was paralyzed. I felt a deep sorrow, a sense of loss without precedent, a feeling of being more alone than I had ever been before, even on the murkiest Ruffle Bar night before my shelter was complete and I had not yet reconciled with my abandonment. At the same time a perverse undercurrent of pride flowed beneath my outrage and despair.

My brothers meanwhile were arguing on stage. Joey yelled, "I don't want to go down in a basin," which set off the others. They couldn't agree on what to play. Johnny restored order. He chose the number, the defecation entitled *I Don't Want To Go Down In A Basin* that Joey had mentioned. They began.

This was far worse than the first number. Joey gesticulated, twirled, dropped to his knees. He attempted a kip and failed. He massaged his lower back. It was a grotesque parody of my conducting style during *CWDSL*, my movements feminized and stretched along Joey's length until they were hypnotically perverse, like the dance of children mimicking lascivious adults. I was swooning with fury, but I could not move or cry out. I entered a Dissociative Fugue, but unfortunately was banished immediately after entry, thus maintaining a dreary consistence. My post-fugue self surrendered wholly, and I longed for a ceremony of traumatic bonding.

Joey's microphone stand fell. I approached the stage in a servile stupor. I picked up the microphone stand and set it neatly before Joey. I turned around and walked away. I left the club.

Peter greeted me outside.

"Damone? Are you okay?"

I said nothing. I lifted Lady and walked off. Peter followed. He offered assistance and I refused it. I turned down 2nd Street.

"Damone, what happened in there?"

"To the park."

We turned down Avenue A. We sat on a bench in Tompkins Square Park.

"Peter, I don't think I can bear it."

"How do you mean, Damone? What'd they say?"

"I didn't talk to them. I couldn't. They were playing and it appeared as an event beyond any attainable reality."

"What are you talking about?"

"A process beyond my mortal power to stop."

"What are you talking about? Their scheme?"

"They've opened a Pandora's Box, Peter. Unleashed a living force. Combining my quartets with modern amplification has spawned an orgasmic intoxicant, an impossible perpetual motion that contravenes the first *and* the second law of thermodynamics. I'm telling you, this epistemic impossibility crap is a fucking joke, a fucking farce akin to the world being flat."

"I don't follow you."

"It's already too late. You could sink CBGB to the bottom of the Mariana Trench with my brothers inside, and it would do nothing. Maxwell's Demon has opened the door, and the rest of time is the favored side."

"I don't really understand that poetry stuff, but this isn't you, Damone. You have to get up, get back there, and get those guys."

"I cannot."

"You have to. I didn't help you drag this horse—Lady—all the way from Brooklyn so we can turn around and go right back. Can you get back in?"

"Not tonight. I just can't."

"Then we wait outside for them no matter how long it takes. Let's go back right now."

"No."

"Yes. What happened to the Damone that sailed from Ruffle Bar in a huge storm to go and fight your brothers? All you have to do now is walk back to Bowery."

"Okay, we can go back and watch them emerge. If I don't have the wherewithal to confront them tonight, I give you my word I will rally after I am rested."

We walked back. I accepted Peter's help with Lady. We lurked in the shadows.

They came out sooner than I had expected. Either something had gone wrong or their performances were incredibly short. The latter seemed likely relative to the rarified energy produced by my quartets pumping through those gigantic amplifiers. It was not a force that could be sustained for long. Peter and I retreated into the urine-soaked depths of a doorway. They approached.

"I'm telling you, it was him," said Johnny.

"I thought so too," said Tommy.

"I didn't see anything," said Dee Dee.

"I don't think it was him," said Joey.

"You listen to me, I got a good look at him, it was him. Tommy says so too, that's two against one because Dee Dee didn't see him," Johnny said.

"And you guys messed up right there and didn't go into the verse. You must have been scared," said Joey.

"Shut up. I'm not afraid of him. And Joey, what did I tell you about doing that spastic fag bullshit like he did? I'm telling you, from now on stand still up there. Just sing. Don't do any of that mincing around, it's one more thing that could connect us to…you know."

"It was scary, the way he walked right up. He wasn't scared, he was cool. Something was definitely different. I don't know, man. I'm worried about this," said Tommy.

"Go," whispered Peter.

"No, wait," I said.

I let them walk out of earshot. I turned to Peter.

"Peter, I think we have an edge. Did you hear them?"

"They were talking about you?"

"Of course. To think *I* intimidated *them*. Ha! Ha Ha! If you could only have paid a visit to the universe of cowardice and surrender that was flourishing within me, you'd relish the irony as much as I! When I approached the stage, I was a sweaty-lipped husband rolling a fishnet stocking up his wife's leg so that she might be more attractive to better-endowed men. They had me exactly where they wanted me, but yet again, Damone riseth!"

"But they just walked away and you didn't do anything."

"Because we must think. How can we wage psychological warfare, how can we take full advantage of the moment?"

"Let's go to the Turkish guy on A for those really good French fries."

"Okay, let's."

CHAPTER XXXI.

THE ADDICTIVE PLUSHNESS OF SLIPPERY SLOPES.

The Ramones were playing again a couple days later, but it was too soon to orchestrate another attack. I was exhausted, and I hadn't decided how to best use my new advantage. I wanted to broadside them from the quiet darkness, burst from within their sense of safety so they'd never again trust their own senses or their images of themselves.

And I wasn't ready. I couldn't come up with anything on my own, although I thought standing directly in front of the stage staring at them would be a good starting point. But I knew this would eventually grate on Johnny, he would assault me, and my advantage would be lost via public feminization.

I decided I'd wait until the gig after next. In the meantime, I made the most of my time at Uncle Dave's: drinking, loving Lady, watching television, arguing with Dave. The latter pursuit usually occurred on weekends when Dave could get as drunk as Peter and I did every single day. Alcohol raised the stakes of our arguments; although good-natured, it felt like we had been ordained to decide the fate of rock and roll: if Dave came out on top, rock would be allowed to live for another week. If I got the better of Dave, rock and roll would be cast from the universe forever. I don't know if Dave fully understood the reality of the latter possibility; although I lacked the means at that time so to do, I could have developed those means had I given it my full attention.

Which was impossible in the company of television. It seemed like the more I watched, the more I needed to watch the next day, not unlike the exponential growth of my liquor habit. TV had a calming effect, a seductive quality that I could not resist. Furthermore, reciprocal communication improved daily; isolated past incidents, for example the Sir Graves Ghastly confessions, were becoming more frequent: more and more people inside the glass box were communicating directly to me. I can't take full credit for that; their efforts were also critical. That being said, I realized if I continued to recalibrate my cosmic orientation while contemplating how television fit in with the electromagnetic Arcs, I would eventually eradicate the fourth wall. Communication and travel would be free in both directions.

And so I watched until I saw the rainbow and heard the tone. And then I watched that, for therein lay the final destination: the 24-hour cycle of each network encapsulated the total cycle of time and the universe. Gazing at the nocturnal dead space following the national anthem afforded one a glimpse into destiny, of which the end of music was merely a constituent part. I was certain that past greats had shared this vision. I was very curious regarding the medium employed prior to television's invention. In other words, Shostakovich probably also used television, granting I did not know what happened to Soviet television in the wee hours. But what of those before? Beethoven presented a remarkably clear case: the tinnitus erroneously ascribed to his deafness was obviously a prophetic vision of the final music, the never-ending elongated tone which had no analogous component in the corporeal world at that time other than the incorrectly diagnosed "ringing in his ears." As for Bach, perhaps the structural ramifications of the baroque rendered the problem moot; if the end was the same vision-wise, did it matter if it was the *Double Concerto* or New York One going off the air?

Oh! Benedictine and Brandy! Beethoven, Bach, and Brahms! To drink the two French Bs while contemplating the three German Bs, Oh! What an ecstasy doth prevail!

What an ecstasy indeed. Peter kept us well supplied with drinks, and Dave with marijuana. His weed was getting better; I wondered if my father, who I hadn't seen in the Ramones' entourage, was piloting a ship alone in dark New York waters, continuing to feed the city with illicit substances.

I was in a capital mood one evening thanks largely to the combo outlined above when Dave came running through the door as if he'd eaten bad vindaloo, but he ran to the stereo rather than the bathroom. Sure enough, I looked over and he was brandishing yet another ominous cardboard square from which he extracted a black disc. I respected his fervor; he was a zealous missionary of his passions, vacuous though they were.

I, on the other had, was not in the mood for this. I had been watching two shaven-headed Chinese monks engaged in a slow motion kung fu showdown with the volume down. The lights were off, and I had been playing Ligeti's *Requiem* in my head to the best of my ability. It was a tightrope walk, and an injection of Dave's troglodytic slop would not help maintain the balance.

Unfortunately, the piece he played was intriguing, a rollicking blend of primordial rhythm and wild Middle Eastern melodies. The vocals were spoken word and Gregorian chant infused with the sorrowful East. I liked it, which put me in a bad position: I would have to continue to argue against rock and roll using this piece as an example when in fact I was enjoying it. We listened for a couple minutes. I said, "What is this called, Dave?"

"You like it, don't you? It's Türkü by Erkin Koray. He's Turkish."

I had found my out. I said, "Yes, it's quite nice, Dave."

"You like it? I picked it up today. Guy at work turned me on to it. So you like it?"

"Of course. I enjoy traditional Turkish music."

"But it's rock, Turkish rock."

"Pah! Rock? Whatever do you mean? This has nothing in common with your inharmonious imbeciles."

"Remember I played *2000 Light Years From Home* by the Stones? Remember?"

"I remember. Indeed, how could one forget such cleverness as Mr. Jagger steadily reducing the number of light years—I believe the final tally was one hundred—leading one to believe that the loneliness of the protagonist would soon end. One never forgets something like that."

"Was that Turkish music?"

"No, it was the Rolling Stones recording in a studio with thin walls while a Turkish group recorded in the next room, thus giving your 'joint-songwriters' the chance to pretend it was a purposeful addition rather than a fortuitous accident."

"Spare me, Damone. Come on, this is clearly rock. Listen to the beat, the rhythm."

"Sorry Dave, but you can't throw Turkish folk on top of drums and say it's rock and roll. It breaks the rules. Can you throw a drummer into Beethoven's String Quartet 14, Opus 131 and call it the new David Essex single? I think not."

"Rock doesn't have any rules. That's the beauty of it."

"It has very strict rules; it's the most dogmatic form of music I've ever encountered. To say otherwise allows for *War and Peace* to be considered a haiku. It isn't. That's why your Yes and your Electric Light Orchestra are so horrible."

"I don't follow."

"It's a strict, rigid format, the boring soundtrack for a strict, rigid culture. It's provincial drivel cranked out en masse for the most instantaneous conformists under the sun."

"What's an 'instantaneous conformist' as opposed to a regular conformist?"

"Some people take a little chipping away at before they become conformists. For example, look at you—at night you smoke marijuana and spin your montage of disasters on the turntable, but by day you're an actuary—the most *'square'* of jobs, by my reckoning. Your sense of otherness is increasingly a false construct, something that exists solely in your mind. In your mind and on your *'far out'* hi-fi system. But when you were in high school, I bet you never saw yourself as the actuary of tomorrow, indeed you did not. No, you likely saw yourself as a counter-cultural phenomenon, a beat poet, a bongo-thumping denizen of the Village."

"I know you enjoy insulting your host, but you're straying from the point. Rock doesn't have rules, man. It's open to complexity and simplicity."

"The underlying problem is you see rules as social restriction, as extensions of your father's mandates to cut the lawn and work hard at math and return the car by ten. That's true of some rules, but not artistic rules. For example, different types of poetry have different rules of meter, iambic rhythms and so on, and the artistry is shaving the language into the specifications of the mold, are you '*digging me*' Dave?"

"You've elevated being an asshole to an art form, I'll give you that. You're so good at it, I actually enjoy it. Go on."

"And the artistry is brilliantly filling those limits or subverting them in self-referential or coded ways; but if one overextends the latter endeavors, the work ceases to be attached to the rules it subverts. For example, subversive literature that is allowed in Eastern Europe by the censors yet still contains a dissident message: a children's book might contain a coded message about social rebellion or hypocrisy inherent to the socialist system, you follow? But when that same author emigrates to Canada and continues to write on the same themes, encoding them in the same way, the effort is meaningless because he's no longer writing inside the paradigm of socialist dictatorship."

"What's that have to do with rock?"

"Because rock's rules and the methods available to subvert those rules are severely limited. It's the most limited art form, the strictest; therefore bands are increasingly seeking renewal *outside* those rules—but it can't be done. You're drawn to my brothers' music because it's *my music*—original, revolutionary music governed by unprecedented rules—miraculously compressed into the rock format. Its creation was my miracle, but their thievery is their miracle because I must say, sliding my music into the rock and roll dimension is akin to transversing the most eccentric wormhole; it'd be like taking a chaotic galaxy and swiftly compressing it into an orderly, golf-ball sized black hole. When I composed my quartets, they were the ultimate expression of mathematical precision, continuity, and brevity compared to everything that came before, yet they simultaneously energize with subliminal chaos. So my brothers—and you have to hand it to them here—they recognize this revolutionary clarity. This clarity completely contrasts your swiftly degenerating rock and roll where "musicians" are adding layer upon layer of extraneous bullshit, crap that can't exist in rock songs—in endless attempts to resuscitate the corpse. My brothers, thanks to the divine material they perverted, have shaved rock down to the essence it's been seeking since Bill Haley, but never would have found without my music's intervention. My sister loved Phil Spector—closer, but still far, far away. The Beatles started closer, but moved far away. Then the really overblown garbage comes around, your Floyd and Yes, and everyone starts to feel nauseas because they are so far off course that the paradigm bursts and begins excreting sewage. Then, in one devastating thunderbolt, my music arrives and destroys everything, replacing it with an absolutist order that nonetheless inspires chaos. In short, the Ramones is the only rock and roll, the diamond paradigm. Everything that follows will be lifeless rock layered with other genres or "minimalist" rock imitative of the Ramones, but in both cases the trend is a gravitation toward the center, toward the black hole, toward the one true manifestation, which is my music as interpreted by the Ramones. Understand? Before my brothers codified it, rock was a bunch of loose asteroids floating hither and thither without any clearly defined star to orbit. The Ramones are that star. The center of the universe. Future bands copycatting them will never get it right, they'll always be derivative, but they will at least be playing variations on the one true theme. And the groups that trim the fat will be getting closer to the same, understand?"

"Damone, I like the Ramones, so I guess I must like your music too, although I've never heard it except the versions, as you say, that your brothers stole from you. I like them very much. But to say their existence means rock is finished and all bands in existence can only evolve by choosing one of two paths—flagrantly imitating your brothers or subtly imitating your brothers—that sounds like some sort of God paradigm or something."

"Yes, exactly. It sounds like you understand now."

"I should have known that's where this was headed. Let's get high. You want to hear more of this record or something else? Or watch the rest of *Kung Fu?* What would the Lord Almighty like to do tonight?"

I believed, despite his thick-fingered facetiousness, that Dave was recognizing my argument if not embracing it. This gave me pause. Removed from the white-hot rage that characterized direct conflict with my brothers, I noticed that my arguments were occasionally laced with a certain pride in their achievements, even though they owed them entirely to me. It occurred to me that they were Ramones despite their crimes, and I suppose if one is going to have his life's reason raped, pillaged, and burned to a crisp, who better than one's family to carry it out? It lent a certain intimacy to the whole thing, it kept costs down, and it put one in historical alignment with such company as Atreus and Thyestes or Fred Sanford and Aunt Esther, two feuding relatives to whom I'd been recently been introduced.

Ah, such are the mixed fruits of contemplation—one so desperately seeks leisure, Dionysian pleasure without end, but upon achieving it, one discovers its false promise. An overabundance of idleness leads one to think too much, and no amount of vodka-laced Mogen David can change that. Contemplation even tainted my relationship with Lady. For example, one day we were lying together after the love act in Dave's front room. I was delighting in her pink color, taking special pleasure in the fact that her disguise was pink, and beneath it lay an even more resplendent pink ornamented with rococo flourishes, gems, and intricate carvings. At that beautiful moment, an awful thought intruded and made the very pink color I adored suspect thereafter; namely, it occurred to me that my instant attraction for Lady, the fact that I immediately chose her over all the other carousel horses, was because she was pink—I realized that the color's magnetism might be due to a masochistic association with the pain delivered by the pink bat, the weapon of discipline in the Ramones household; that the hundreds of crushing blows I experienced at Johnny's hand might have caused a stress disorder akin to that experienced by war veterans, and the ointment I was applying was masochistic reenactment through my relationship with Lady, particularly the physical love acts I committed several times a day.

Or perhaps these thoughts were simply love's maturation, the accruement of depth and complexity. How could one know?

What I did know is that September was a time of softening. Despite frequent spells of purposelessness, I nonetheless was gaining more than I was losing via leisure, alcohol, and passion. I decided I wouldn't confront my brothers until October; by then I'd be fully rejuvenated and my strategy would be refined. I'd also be on the streets, which I tried to view positively—the challenges of a vagabond could only increase my cunning and resolve.

CHAPTER XXXII.

I SHOULD HAVE VIEWED IT NEGATIVELY: PESSIMISM AND DEATH AS THE OLD WORLD FADES.

And October came quickly. Tuesday the First was a mild day and I had little to carry. I was light of heart, as if I was embarking on a camping trip rather than on a major step toward my personal obliteration; I felt like spending the morning on the boardwalk watching people, talking to Peter, and putting my problems off until the perennial tomorrow.

Lest I be thought foolhardy, it should be understood that my nonchalance was based on reason; unfortunately, it was this very reason that led to a disagreement with Dave that, in hindsight, might have been why fate took such an unfortunate turn on that October morning long ago in 1974. To wit:

When Dave asked me where I planned on going that morning, I said my first stop would be 332 E. 84th Street to pay a visit to Brenda Morgenstern. When Dave laughed, I initially thought it was in reference to my rakishness relative to my commitment to Lady; when he then asked me if I believed Brenda Morgenstern was a real person, I realized the discussion had taken a different tack. I remained silent.

"Damone, seriously. I'm not asking to put you down, I'm asking because I want to understand where you're coming from. You've made plenty of interesting observations. On rock for instance—I don't dislike any music I liked before because of your arguments, but I admit I see it in a different way. Like when you ridiculed all those sounds that singers make apart from the lyrics and melody, those grunts and so forth? Now whenever I hear those sounds I can't help but hear their theatricality, their phoniness. Thanks, by the way, for degrading my listening experience."

"Yes, how exactly do they decide what constitutes a well-placed *wooo* of enthusiasm, or a *yeah, huh!* Because you know they listened to the playbacks with a certain pride, hence those grunts remaining on the recording. I've been forced to listen to many white performers with great embarrassment, for example, as they attempt to "Africanize" their plagiarized ditties with what they believe are the yelps and affirmations of one reared in the Southern gospel tradition. It's really quite shameless, such thievery."

"I didn't mean to set you off, I'm just saying that I'm interested in your points of view. So…in the case of Brenda Morgenstern, I'm asking if you believe that particular address is correct, and I'm asking how you distinguish the Morgensterns from, say, President Ford; how would I know, for example, who is fictitious and who is a real person?"

"Dave, Brenda Morgenstern is a real person, and so is President Ford. All of the people on the television are real people, no?"

"Well, the *actors* are real people. But the characters they play aren't all real."

"Do you think President Ford speaks and carries himself the same way he did when he pardoned Nixon when he's alone with a hair brush and a rubber glove? Or when he's just forced down an entire bottle of Wild Irish Rose at one go, but he hasn't eaten in three days?"

"Point taken, he's an actor too, as is everyone in their daily lives. But everything's by degrees, and I have doubts as to whether the Morgensterns actually live at that address."

"Yes, perhaps someone mentioned 64th Street while ordering a pizza, but my reconnaissance indicates 84th. So thanks for your concern, but I'm on top of the situation. Mind you, I'm seeking a platonic relationship."

"I just don't get it, Damone. I'm sorry, but you're going to have to report back on this. Shit, I might even go up there with you just to see what happens. I don't get it. You've made some remarkably cogent arguments regarding music, you clearly understood that

Knievel thing was a biopic, I mean I think. We made fun of plenty of shows together just like I would with anyone else."

"Uncle Dave, maybe let's talk about this next time we see you, okay?" Peter said.

"But I don't understand it, the guy's here one minute then off on a tangent the next."

"If you force my hand, I'll put you in your place with polygamy, you fool! You don't know me!"

"Damone, he didn't mean anything by it, he likes you and stuff. Come on, let's go to the boardwalk and drink some wine, it's a nice morning."

"Sorry, Damone. I'm not questioning you, I'm really not. And Peter's right, man. You're a very cool guy and I'll invite you guys back over, okay? Come on, please. We've had a good time, let's not part angry."

I did him a good turn by not pointing out that he was responsible for starting the whole thing in the first place. And to think how during our final week he had been so generous and engaging, even taking us out for a farewell party on a night when I was particularly upset over yet another program about immigrants making their way in frontier America, *The New Land*. As if making the immigrants Scandinavians somehow absolved it from being a shadow of the horrific *Little House on the Prairie*. The physics of contemporaneous unoriginality, perfectly mirrored rip-offs, was mind boggling enough, not to mention the scathing commentary therein regarding a human race willing to bend over and take anything offered up the ass as long it's familiar.

But worst of all, the opening number was sung by that crook John Denver, which catapulted me into a maelstrom of fury. To think of him being awarded the theme song, even for that piece of cinematic excrement, based on his rip-off *Annie's Song* was untenable. At my tantrum's peak, I insisted that we immediately purchase or acquire Tchaikovsky's Fifth Symphony to prove that Denver was yet another filthy, unoriginal, morally bereft monster, when Dave interrupted with his offer of a night on the town.

"Hey," he said, "Instead of worrying about how John Denver makes his money, let's go out for food, drinks and a flick. On me. I suggest *Flesh Gordon* or *The Night Porter*, what say?"

"*Flesh Gordon*'s not real porn, so let's see the other one," said Peter.

"How do you know?" asked Dave.

"Cuz I saw it, okay? So let's see the other one."

And we did. At the time I enjoyed the film, which, combined with free drinks, set up the good mood that he proceeded to ruin on the morning of October 1st, 1974. But ultimately, if you'll pardon a digression, I think that particular film was responsible for several missed opportunities and periods of melancholy that more or less destroyed the years 1988 through 1995. Suffice it to say that the female character's flagrant disregard for the integrity of the tailoring ensured that it was just a matter of time before I bore the brunt of the avalanche that she set up. Thanks, once again.

But at the time, it just seemed like an eccentric film insulated with seven martinis: well-gin, rocks, lime, extra dry. And two fifths of peach schnapps in the theatre.

So Dave's unexpected attack stung all the more. I couldn't help but wonder if our "farewell party" had been a set-up, if Dave hadn't arranged it precisely to elevate my mood so I would fall further when he shot it down. Needless to say, I was in no condition to attempt a foray at CBGB where my brothers were performing that night. Fortunately they were playing several shows throughout the month, so I had time to address these issues.

The next day however I was reading the paper in the Brighton Beach Library where we had slept the night before, and I read that the Greek archaeologist Spyridon Marinatos had died the previous day. This devastating news made me useless beyond performing basic bodily functions. Peter was rather baffled by why Marinatos's death should upset me so. I explained that certain things are personal. He pressed the point, so I invented some gibberish about how Marinatos personified Cypriot suffering. Needless to say, this tragedy made something as farcical as attending a Ramones show a veritable sacrilege, and I did not go to CBGB for their next two performances.

On the morning of the 12th I was ready for another sortie; in fact, missing two shows amplified my will to succeed at the next. But that morning I learned that the composer Joseph Wagner had passed while watching the World Series on television. This was not, of course, the Wagner of German opera, but a close friend of the family that Montez had met in the late 1940s, and with whom he caroused in Costa Rica in the early 1950s. In later years, one of us always had to prepare a special box to send to Mr. Wagner who had moved to Los Angeles. My brothers and I found Mr. Wagner's taste in drugs to be rather pedestrian, focused as it was on prescription drugs; we could not have known how universally popular his particular addiction would later become—yet another little known accomplishment of this severely underrated composer. Although I did not know him personally, I felt as if I did, and therefore cancelled that evening's CBGB assault.

When Chembai Vaidyanatha Bhagavatar passed on the 16th, I forgot about the next Ramones show and I didn't particularly care. This was yet another personal blow: the Carnatic voice was a key component of the tower, and Chembai had been the voice's chief medium in our solar system. I was devastated. Of course there were many voices, but they were all intertwined; the loss of such a crucial one was a tragedy for all.

Two was positively eviscerating: on the 24th, the great Russian violinist David Oistrakh passed. Oistrakh—who had played *Serenade Melancolique* in the Hall of Columns for Beria, Molotov, and Khrushchev while Stalin lay in state—had been cursed with a faulty heart.

A year after Shostakovich premiered his Violin Concerto Nr.2 with Oistrakh on violin, Oistrakh's house was burglarized. The thieves, masquerading as movers, took everything, explaining to neighbors that Oistrakh was moving to his summerhouse. The identity of these thieves is a question—were they common ruffians or henchmen of the state? In any case, two weeks later everything was mysteriously returned. The only inconsistency was Oistrakh's claim that a letter from Einstein was among the returned items; what he failed to mention was that there had originally been *two* letters from Einstein. Of course only he and I knew this.

Stealing everything was a feint; the thieves had come solely for the second letter. If it were the Soviet authorities, then critical information on chaotic dynamical systems would have been included in Parcel 24. Parcel 24 emanated from the Kremlin via the top-secret Metro-2 line, the shadow subway system built for Stalin and his closest functionaries. It was ostensibly built by the KGB, but obviously the system was a gateway to the multiverse, and its true architects were segments of the energy Arcs briefly personified. If everything went according to plan, Parcel 24 would have ended up in the secret underground city Ramenki-43. The world would have turned out quite differently, I can assure you.

But this was only one interpretation. Oistrakh himself fiercely contested it when he and Sviatsoslov Richter sent me a coded message via Bartók's Sonata Nr.1 for Violin and Piano. This is a unique case, because it's the only instance where one need not take my word for it; the most cursory listen will reveal the message as clearly as if it were a giant newspaper headline: *Damone, come hence and fetch the second letter. Use it to change humanity.*

Now humanity would never be changed. Not a very good October, to my way of thinking.

In November, my descent became palpable. I felt like a weak-legged ant with abilities that were useless to the colony—I couldn't carry a fruit fly's wing, I was worthless in battle, I had nightmares about *Raid*. I couldn't even clean up the Queen's excrement due to allergies. While treading the path of the ostracized, i.e. the one that leads away, I wandered over the lip of an ant lion's conical den of sand, and now my skinny legs were whirling uselessly as I attempted to slow my inevitable descent toward the beast's powerful jaws.

At least the city of New York was there to help. The security guards at the Brighton Beach Library weren't—they had tightened discipline, and were conducting thorough searches for stowaways before locking up. Peter assured me this was merely a phase, an inconvenience occasionally inspired by some regional director's grandstanding, and when said director turned their attention elsewhere, life would be good again.

In the meantime there were hyperbole-laden screening forms and sycophantic post-discharge reviews. My unwavering integrity didn't help; I was having problems completing the forms even though my very survival was at stake. Was I, for example, able to manage bowel and/or bladder regimen, independently, without the use of diapers? The little incident at Uncle Dave's cast a long shadow; was it an amusing anomaly or the opening salvo of a lifestyle?

Was I known to have a history of recent fire-setting? Definitely no worries there. Cranial halo device, worn continuously? Not while dodging the criteria for dementia, delirium, or major cognitive defects, if Dave's idiotic opinions were to be taken into account, that laughable Coney Island ninny, him and his Frank Zappa Live meets *Smoking on the Water* bullshit. The fool.

What I was definitely able to verify was the ability to manage, independently, care of indwelling catheters of any sort, just as long as I wasn't restricted to the meager, threadlike examples presented therein. No, I needed no help with my catheter, none at all—was the Druzhba Pipeline of Failure snugly lodged in my unmanly meatus, pumping millions of barrels of top-grade nonperformance into every aspect of my existence twenty-fours a day? Check.

Perhaps you're wondering why this non-chronic street-homeless individual was so hell-bent on acquiring the confident swagger of a Department of Homeless Services Returnee, HA Number rolling off the tongue, when in fact an alternative option *had* been identified? No. I swore before God that I would not return to Ruffle Bar a failure, and although I seemed to be passing through a brief ineffectual phase, Ruffle Bar still served as my Eastern Star—better, I thought, to be martyred on the New York streets than to concede by returning to the island besmirched. Just thinking this immediately relieved the pressure to leap into action—I had time, plenty of it, and trees that are slow to grow bear the best vengeance.

Next of kin? Pah! N/A. Emergency contact? Peter Ellsberg, three beds down. He's got a notarized copy of the will, a duplicate key to the safety deposit box, and I've tested him on the Swiss bank account numbers a thousand times. All set there.

But once you get through the red tape,[26] life in the shelters isn't so bad. In certain respects, working the system in order to get the most from it while occasionally switching shelters purely for aesthetic reasons can be a welcome challenge; people have no idea how hard you have to work to have no place to go. The effort distracted me from my problems.

And one learns new things. For instance, one time I went to Catholic Charities of Queens and Brooklyn to complete forms for subsidized housing,[27] the upscale endgame to homelessness for the aristocratic few—showboaters that illustrate that the individual's total needs are such that his or her needs can be met in the appropriate community setting—when I was accosted by a sweaty, obese man whose revolting belly was hanging out from a golf shirt that was small to the point of being a halter top. This walking vulgarity, between heavy breaths, informed me that he had been looking for me. I asked him how this could be, as I had never seen him before in my life. He said that was of no account because *he* had seen *me*, specifically at the temporary shelter set up by Our Lady of Refuge last Tuesday.

You can imagine my alarm when I realized that's exactly where I'd been last Tuesday. The man then pantomimed his intentions while describing his unshakeable determination in pursuing their consummation: he declared that he would follow me from borough to borough, shelter to shelter, until I gave him what he wanted. I ran out the door.

I looked over my shoulder. He was in hot pursuit. I thought, 'What an odd turn of events; New York is truly the gift that keeps on giving; just when I thought it can't get worse, alas, here we are with a refreshing new catastrophe.' It occurred to me that this beast might well make the original French hyena seem like a soft-handed pastor by comparison. At that moment I almost felt

---

[26] If you want a little alone time you must complete and sign a Discharge Form; be prepared to leave your dignity at the door.

[27] I was told by an old hand at the shelters to get on every list, no matter what the fucking list was, to get the fuck on that list and start praying to sweet Jesus.

sentimental regarding the subhuman crucifier to whom I ultimately owed thanks for crawling out of some Parisian bowel, thus inducing the transformation that created Damone Ramone the Great Conductor. As I ran, I thought I might derive similar utility from this brutish pig, assuming I escaped unscathed or reasonably scathed; although I didn't have firsthand experience, I assumed that expected utility would likely peak at the point on the curve where sodomy at knife-point was positively indicated. I kept running.

I lost him eventually, but I must say, I never underestimated the endurance of the fat again. Nonetheless, I was terrified to return to any shelter in the city, because the man did seem to have a supernatural divining rod that could determine my whereabouts, or so I believed. I decided to try my hand at cross-dressing in order to gain access to the Sisters of St. Dominic Transitional Housing Intake Center in the Bronx; with such an apropos name, I was sure the endeavor would be crowned with success.

It was, but so what. I got a notion in my head that compounded exponentially on the train to the Bronx that the women's shelter would be a different world; free of the fights, stealing, and vomit that characterized the men's shelters. Well, apparently chivalry ends where weeping wounds begin: the Bronx female screening form seemed strikingly similar to the Brooklyn male screening form, as did the horror-laden shelter once I—Lily Ramone—was processed. I don't know what I expected exactly; perhaps a Chekhovian spa with hot mineral baths, parasols, hoop skirts, and clever innuendos from charming bearded gentlemen. It wasn't like that.

At the same time, the bodies kept piling up. The old world was fading, the new world was rising—the world of Uncle Dave and his beloved *Fingerprint File*. Egon Joseph Wellesz went, a kinsman from the Hungarian Jewish Protestant Catholic tribe. At the time, his *Eklogen Opus 11* precisely represented my inner world and my premonitions of the future. Little did I suspect that a day would come when the dark ruminations of the *Eklogen* would seem like the *Rocky Theme* relative to my descent.

Alfonso Leng went next, composer and working dentist, on a day when I was suffering from an agonizing toothache. Leng's lyricism worked because he meant it. It wasn't mawkish or cinematic, it was divine music to masturbate to in floral settings. I lay in bed later in the squalor of The Bowery Mission, picturing Leng in the same situation. He would have surely come up with a better way to ease the pain. But it didn't matter anymore: Leng would never see nitrous oxide, plaque lights, or grape-flavored fluoride treatments. On the other hand he'd never hear *Rock and Roll Crazy Nights* by Loudness, so there was that.

The German physicist Walther Meissner was next. He visited me shortly after his death in a bilateral vortex. He said:

'Can you breathe in a vacuum and do you own a good winter coat?'

'Yes on the breathing. I'll borrow the coat.'

'Then come to the mountaintop.'

We stood on the peak. The white slope contrasted the endless blackness.

'The slope is steep: seventy-eight point six-nine degrees. And the temperature is low: negative three hundred Celsius. Now do as I do,' he said.

He leapt from the pinnacle. I followed. We soared downward just inches above the slope's surface. The slope was lit from within its chemistry, a soft white light. A fold in time allowed us to race down the slope for one hundred thousand hours without interrupting time in the dimension to which I would return and which Meissner had forever exited. He said, 'Now I must go.' There was no end to the ride. It will always go on, but I'm alone now. Meissner is elsewhere.

The Icelandic composer Páll Ísólfsson departed. I sat alone in an imaginary gothic cathedral and listened to the *Prelude in C Minor* directly followed by the *Postlude in A Minor*, ruefully noting the short nothing in between that I had apparently composed to kill a few minutes. There would be no preludes or postludes bookending my unremarkable little composition.

To be fair, Uncle Dave's world was not without casualty: one rocking and rolling Nick Drake evaporated, gut full of psychotropic desperation. Late in the month Dave had Peter and me over for tuna sandwiches and whiskey. He told me of Drake, and I so empathized with the rock musician's escalating isolation, wretchedness, and general weirdness that when Uncle Dave attempted to play his music, I yanked the record from his hands and broke it to bits against my knee. Would I, for example, be sympathetic regarding a bus containing Dexys Midnight Runners driving off a cliff after having heard *Cum On Eileen*? How about The Offspring[28] in a freak helicopter accident: they've been injured in a tour bus crash in Montana, and the rural hospital lacks the facilities to get them healthy enough to perform *Come Out and Play*, therefore they must be airlifted to a big city hospital. They ascend the stairs to the country hospital's roof. The helicopter, returning from another airlift, loses control and the entire band is beheaded, thus depriving the world of their *Conspiracy of One* album since I placed the theoretical accident prior to its release. Autumn was a time of sympathy. I did not wish to spoil it.

Nick Drake overdosed the same day the former Secretary General of the United Nations U Thant died from lung cancer. I had no interest or regard for Thant; in fact, I wholeheartedly supported General Ne Win's decision not to bestow accolades or a state funeral upon Thant when his body was returned to Burma from New York City: I believed Thant's positions were anathema to The Burmese Way To Socialism. I didn't believe Thant's claims that he had no foreknowledge when the former Prime Minister U Nu stood before the UN and recommended overthrowing General Ne Win. Thant claimed to be away on a business trip and had no idea U Nu was planning such a speech. Yeah, sure. Imagine how'd you feel if you were General Ne Win—here you are trying to do something great for Burma, and the entire planet worships U Thant and portrays you as a barbarian and economic moron, a weed to be plucked and thrown away in favor of economic liberalism, globalization, and smiling.

---

[28] At least they had the integrity to give me a nod when they chose their name.

Nick Drake and U Thant expired on November 25th. That night I heard a new voice that said: *NeMay Bellow Call Delay*. I tried to decipher its orders, but I wasn't sure if the message was literal. I heard it only in the evening, and generally it would repeat the nonsensical statement four or five times. I found the voice upsetting, so the next time I heard it I attempted to blot it out by shouting, 'Damone Ramone, fuck fuck fuck!' It seemed to sate the voice only to a point—I still was haunted by the strange incantation.

I began to suspect the strange words had something to do with Burma, combined as they were with obsessive thoughts regarding the deaths of Drake and Thant. Of course there are some of you that already recognize the words as a crude transliteration of *What is your name?* I did not realize this until 1978 when I learned some basic Burmese phrases prior to performing at the university in Rangoon, so you can imagine how I was plagued for the next five years.

There were some other unpleasant shocks relating to the Burma situation at its outset in 1974. I suspected that Uncle Dave might know something about it, but was hiding the information from me. I decided to ambush him. I visited his apartment one morning when I knew he'd be rushing to get to work. He buzzed me in. When he opened the door I said, "Dave, what was that you were saying about Nick Drake's connection to Burma? I was trying to recall."

"Oh, he was born there."

"What! What did you just say?"

"Geez, Damone. He was born in Burma. I think it was part of England back then. Family moved back to England when Drake was two or something."

"Why were you hiding that from me?"

"What're you talking about? You mean why didn't I mention it?"

"Phrase it as you wish."

"It just didn't come up, Damone. Good to see you too.

That was the beginning of my cosmic and ultimately corporeal relationship with Burma that culminated in the Burmese Anabasis. The tower's peak: my performance at Rangoon University in 1979.

But that was still five years away. In the meantime there were several million semis full of degradation to be unloaded, and I knew just the man for the job.

November was a wrap. That's how you keep all shifts working in the Slaughterhouse of Months, folks. December was dead other than the normal daily routine of shelters punctuated by occasional showers at Uncle Dave's or the Y. The Brighton Beach Library crew had identified a weak link in the chain, a new security guard who claimed to have twelve mistresses and reeked of liquor just as badly as any of the patrons he was there to contain. When he was working it was relatively easy to hide before closing time.

Little of note happened for the rest of the year. My brothers only had two shows scheduled and I wasn't going to either. On the 10th I was in a makeshift shelter in a church basement when I saw the already discussed masterpiece portraying the feud between the Miser Brothers, Heat and Snow. My sympathies lied wholly with Heat, the perennial victim of both circumstances overwhelmingly favoring Snow Miser and Snow Miser's own malicious willingness to pile on additional obstacles and insults into Heat's already miserable life.

On the 12th it was Uncle Dave again, rushing into the library with the pseudo-tragedy of one Mick Taylor voluntarily resigning from the Rolling Stones. For Dave, this was an inconceivable outrage. For me, who would stick two sharpened screwdrivers into my ears were I sentenced to join that blob of cultural deadweight, it was an obvious and sensible choice for Mr. Taylor. Dave on the other hand spoke of it as if Marcus Aurelius had died and it was the end of the Pax Romana, and all that was left was the swift descent from a kingdom of gold to one of iron and rust. My thought was, 'Who cares?'

But it got us over to Dave's and off the streets for a few days. I admit, I was oddly flattered by Dave's continuing to commiserate with me about rock and roll as if I, who loathed it with my every fiber, was one of its chief proponents and connoisseurs. Oddly, the dynamic morphed into actual low-grade interest, if only to surprise Dave or to concoct arguments in advance that largely relied on reduction to the absurd. Not too hard in the circumstances. What I didn't know then was that this foundation of knowledge would be useful later when I was forced to contend with the out of control growth of my imitators during and after the reign of the Ramones. But more on that later.

Uncle Dave kicked us out the day Andre Jolivet died. He asked Peter and me to see *Young Frankenstein* that evening as a send off. In terms of strategic living, I remain undecided regarding how much time should be dedicated annually to contemplating a moment in late 1974 defined by the death of Jolivet and *Young Frankenstein's* first week of release. Fortunately, only a select few are privy to the dynamic, and most of us do not know each other. That being said, I don't think anyone outside our exclusive group understands Jolivet's *Concerto pour Ondes Martenot et Orchestra* in the way that we do.

After the movie was over, I said goodbye to Dave and Peter and lay down on the theatre floor with Lady based on a tip from Peter. Sure enough, when the cleaning man came to sweep, he acted as if he could not even see us, sweeping over Lady and me just as lackadaisically as he did the floor. Peter assured me this particular crew of ushers and sweepers would always look for a reason to say yes, and as long as I was quiet and below the projectionist's line of sight between films there would be no problems. Voiding was restricted to showtime, but this was neither here nor there to me after the fourth viewing of *Young Frankenstein*.

Peter said it was ultimately my decision of course, but he highly recommended I vacate the theatre no later than Christmas Eve, as greater demand would invariably lead to greater enforcement. As it was, *Young Frankenstein* was turning out to be immensely popular, and my movements had to be precise when switching from hiding to taking on the appearance of a legitimate theatre-goer, albeit one accompanied by a large wooden horse.

It was the latter that led to my ejection before the midnight show on the 21st. The show was sold out, and although Lady took up only one seat when vertical, her height led to complaints from those seated behind her, and once again I found myself on the streets. I was reduced to my wits and a sport coat pocket full of salvaged popcorn.

Christmas in a shelter and a cruel revelation: Uncle Dave's "generosity" in taking us to *Young Frankenstein* was yet another not so subtle jab. I was furious that I hadn't recognized that he'd been ridiculing my creativity and the intensity of the creative act by taking me to that movie. I was sure that had I looked over during the film, he would have been casting me sidelong glances and smirking.

The day after Christmas Knudåge Riisager died, notable for his work's extreme contrast to Jolivet's, like prom dresses and flowers to asphyxiation and elderly men masturbating successfully.

But the worst was Farid al-Atrash. In all of his films there's a woman of unparalleled excellence gazing at him like you haven't been gazed at lately, but all of his film work is irrelevant: one is better off ripping one's eyes out than spoiling al-Atrash's music with the distractions of film, no matter how expressive these films were. At best, one should listen to the films with the sound down or listen to the music outside the films, but never the two together. And with that, we can fuck off on 1974 because I can assure you, New Year's wasn't even worth the mention Christmas got above.

Part VII.

THE END OF THE SEVENTIES.

CHAPTER XXXIII.

1975.

As a ship in a storm must jettison its cargo, I was forced to lighten my load to avoid sinking beneath the black waves. I knew my brothers were continuing to play and their reputations were growing; nonetheless, it was all I could do to provide myself with the basics—a warm place to sleep in the winter, a safe place to sleep in the summer. It's a difficult state to explain, because I had my wits about me and I was whole, yet I could not do more than was absolutely necessary to survive each day. At the same time, I developed a repulsion for my fellow man; I began avoiding Peter, and by extension, Uncle Dave. As 1975 dawned, I wanted nothing more than solitude, but unlike Ruffle Bar, which required constant industry, I wanted a solitude from both people and effort.

The city was merciful in this regard. I noticed a distinct loosening of mores since 1970. It was quieter and more relaxed. There was more graffiti, the trains were dirtier, and there were more porno theatres. There were more drug dealers about, or the ones that existed were making far less effort to disguise the nature of their work. Perhaps it was both, but either way trade was brisk, and for a moment I couldn't help but fantasize about the way things might have been had my brothers not betrayed me and we were still among the elite of the seafaring drug runners.

My brothers. They had no shows scheduled for January. They were probably taking an extended New Year's holiday; I imagined them sprawled on a white sand beach while Geisha girls waved giant fans and servants clad in white suits brought them brightly colored tropical drinks on silver trays. The tray I was employing at the time was plastic, and I longed to swing it directly into each of their smug faces. As it was, I had to satisfy myself with sliding it along the chrome slats of the soup kitchen counter as I waited for some smiling bourgeois do-gooder from Oyster Bay or Babylon to plop a starchy blob into my filthy bowl.

When February was largely over and I still hadn't seen anything regarding my brothers, I began to suspect that it was too late. They had either disappeared with their illicit earnings or they had retreated to an offshore location, perhaps Europe, where they would likely be greeted with even greater respect than in the United States.

But in February I saw a posting outside CBGB announcing three March performances over three days: the sixth through the eighth. I had to confront them again if I hoped to pull myself out of my morass. It seemed like idleness and drunkenness, two ostensibly desirable conditions, were colluding to create a third state, an inert condition that plagued my days and prioritized any petty task ahead of battling my brothers for justice and financial award.

On the sixth, I grabbed Lady and boarded the train to the East Village. Luck was on my side: Dee Dee was leaning against CBGB talking to a statuesque woman. They were arguing. I called out. They turned toward me. Dee Dee said something to the girl, and then he darted into the bar. I yelled, "Coward!" and rushed toward the door as quickly as I could with Lady in my arms.

The girl Dee Dee had been talking with charged me, knocked Lady from my arms, and punched me in the face. I dropped to the cement. She kicked me in the face. She slapped me in the face. She spit in my face. She said, "Get the fuck out of here and don't come back."

And there went March, 1975.

There were no "last straws" or defining moments that year. I required no further reminders or symbolic events to understand the borders of a condition I had already long been in. Even as I headed to CBGB that last time, I knew the attempt was doomed. It was only a shard of my subconscious located in the place where delusions reside that drove my every futile gesture, from buying the token to wiping the blood from my face, thus extracted by a feminine hand. No, surrender was preordained. Any gestures to the contrary were just the final extrusions of my convulsing viscera, the final stinking chunks of a disgusting poison called hope. If my story teaches you to disdain it with only a thousandth of my fervor, I shall consider these scribblings to have not been in vain.

When King Faisal was murdered by his nephew on March 25, my new understanding of the world permitted me a sympathy I otherwise would not have had. No, I knew exactly how the King had felt. Opening up his own home to his people so that they might gaze upon his regal visage, that they might supplicate before him, that they might return to their common lives with a bit of his wisdom and counsel, only to have his generosity turned against him, and not by some anonymous disgruntled taxi driver angry over the King's decision to allow television sets, but by his own flesh and blood, who, from what could be discerned, did it simply to do it, because who better than a family member to assassinate? In terms of access, trust, and a convenient affectionate gesture that ideally positions the body to receive a bullet or a knife, a close relative is indeed a wise choice.

What I could not sympathize with even remotely was the subsequent execution of Faisal's killer that summer. Justice? No, there my sympathy came to an end to put it mildly. Faisal may as well have gotten vindooramabingbong or dipthamoraschlongasoff as far as my understanding went. There was no contradiction to physics taking place on any asteroid or star that I understood any less than justice. When Pakistan renamed cities, mosques, rivers, and roads after the slain Faisal a few years later, I realized his "assassination" had occurred only after a shared wink as his nephew sent him on his hilarious little mission to serve as yet another gargantuan contrast for me to go splat against, especially following as it did my trip to Rangoon, my last hope in this universe of finding a place to hang my hat for a few deluded little moments until I got back to the business of sticking my ass out simply to verify that there were extraterrestrial bodies other than black holes that could also attract every single object in existence—even light took a detour to have a few quick pokes.

So when I felt a tap on my shoulder one afternoon as I was digging through a boardwalk trashcan, I forewent my usual grandiose bristling and simply turned around, thinking to myself how the enraged indignation of a great mind interrupted is reserved for, well, for great minds interrupted, and of course I was not one of those, of course not, ha ha ha! Could there be a more ridiculous supposition? I think not, nor do you, nor do all the babies in Buenos Aires, nor does anyone! What a great day, for the brotherhood of man has finally been achieved! We can link arms and sing at long last, for we are in monolithic accord! Shall I begin? No, I don't mind at all. I consider it an honor:

O Freunde, nicht diese Töne!
Sondern lasst uns angenehmere anstimmen,
und freudenvollere.
Freude!
Freude!

"Damone? Do you recognize me? It's me, Dave. Damone? Stop singing for a sec, will ya?"

"Stop singing? If that will bring you pleasure, Master Three Billion Nine Million Three Hundred Twenty Six Thousand Seventy Two. How is Master Three Billion Nine Million Three Hundred Twenty Six Thousand Seventy One, by the way? I've been meaning to drop by the library and grovel before him. I've just been so busy lately, you understand, servicing the needs of all sentient beings. If either of you misses me, you can always find me at the 53rd and Third of the interstellar highways of the universe. I'm the one on the corner wearing the red vinyl shorts."

"You're hilarious. Come on, drop that shit and have some lunch. Man, you need to clean up. It looks like Jim Rockford hasn't taken a case in a while."

"Just let me finish giving this rim job to Mr. E. Coli and then we can go."

"Seriously, put that shit down, you'll get sick. I've got chicken salad at home, maybe not the best, but probably better than that. Here, I'll help with Lady."

"Lead on."

"Where you been? Peter says he hasn't seen you in a long time."

"I've been working for the government."

"I should have known."

"I'm kidding. I've been working on some speeches."

"Okay. Oh hey, you remember Miss Wisconsin?"

"The pageant we watched."

"Yeah. Well get this—those measurements you said? They were right. I read them somewhere and I swear to God it's the ones you said. I ran it by Peter, he agreed. That's fucking wild, Damone. You didn't go through my clothes, did you? You actually can tell people's sizes just by looking at them."

"Well get this—that name you go by, "Dave"? It's your name. I ran it by Peter and he agreed. That's fucking wild, Dave. You said your name was Dave, and as it turns out, your name is Dave. You actually can tell your name is Dave by having been named Dave your entire life. Asshole."

"What's the matter with you? I'm telling you it's amazing and I'm impressed. That's a huge ability. And I hear you sew extremely well and make clothes. That's a huge talent. You should do something with it."

"It pertaineth not to my purpose, fuckface. There's far better things to be a savant at. Do I tell you how to live your life, David Ellsberg, *actuary*? Why don't we put our heads together and see if we can come up with a couple more exciting career choices, shall we? *Actuary*. Wow. You're really *leaping to the wild side* or however that monotonal mumbler of yours put it, one of those virtuoso poets of yours that you crammed down my throat. Why not? My throat is here for the world to cram."

"Weird you mentioned that, I got this crazy Lou Reed thing I gotta play for you. I'm curious to get your take."

Granting that past performance does not guarantee future results, I didn't hold my breath for Dave's "crazy Lou Reed thing."

I should have. After I shaved and showered I joined Dave in his living room. Dave had thrown my clothes into the wash, including my suit, but I held my tongue. Admittedly, having an article of clothing dry-cleaned that had been damaged by porcupine quills in addition to the usual soils and excrements was a bit absurd.

"Jesus, Damone, you can borrow a bathrobe if you want."

"Pass. Do you have any beer?"

"Christ, what's wrong with me? Yeah, hang on. And check this out."

Metal Machine Music, ladies and gentleman, is as good as anything I ever composed. It's not better, but it is equal while being different. The most shocking and terrifying aspect of the work is that it is culled from the exact same source as my Quartet Cycle. The biggest challenge facing any corporeal medium with access to this source is how to render the raw material into a transmutable form without damaging it. The material is volatile. It is devoid of contradiction in its perfect maintenance of chaos and order—they are one and the same in the source material, governed as it is by different physical laws. Even transmitting a shadow of this reality requires an unparalleled mastery over indescribably unstable substances. Well guess what? Mastery paralleled.

Dave, who had dragged me over to listen to *Metal Machine* to get "my take" seemed to want nothing other than to interrupt my listening to *Metal Machine*, as his "take" seemed to be that it was an unbearable joke. I ordered him to remain seated, allowing him to get up only to change records or get me more beer. Fortunately Mr. Reed gave us four entire album sides of *Machine*, knowing that you cannot, in fact, have too much of a good thing.

That being said, the quality of the work didn't diminish the fact that it portended disaster. Its quality just made it portend better. As if to underline the fact, I got into an argument with Dave after we drank some more about whether I had urinated on his floor in 1974 while listening to Alice Cooper's *Years Ago/Steven*, as I clearly recalled, or *The Ballad of Dwight Fry* as Dave insisted. Dave said that *Years Ago* hadn't been "released" yet, as if that could somehow reduce my ability to hear it. Whatever. I picked up Lady and left in a huff.

Of course these little conflicts were just ways to maintain rhythm and flexibility for the truly marathon disasters. And sure enough, on August 9th, the inconceivable: Shostakovich. I didn't find out until the following day. I was underneath a bench on the boardwalk. Four teenage boys sat at the next bench. One of them was reading the headlines in a parody of interest, peppering his monologue with shocked utterances in the *I can't believe it, have you heard* tradition. His colleagues found this very amusing, and I must say it had a certain charm, outlining as it did the utter unimportance of even the most biblical geopolitical events relative to our individual lives. But then he said, "Oh my God, I have terrible news: Shysterkovaks died."

"What?" I yelled.

"Shysterkovaks died."

"Let me see that immediately," I said. I bumped my head on the bottom of the bench as I attempted to reconcile my hangover with movement.

"Here," he said. "Right here. He died."

"Give me that."

He had indeed left us. The Shostakovich Peninsula, the Bach Ice Shelf, Berlioz Point, Rossini Point—literal cathedrals of ice named in their honor, cathedrals that will melt away along with any miniscule transient shadows of memory installed by this tome.

I checked into a shelter.

CHAPTER XXXIV.

1976.

I had looked forward to New Year's Day, 1976 since I first recognized the injustices of our dimension, especially relative to its fluidity—existence in the Third Dimension means chaos: time severely unaligned. It's such a disorderly machine that its function resembles an insane squall more than the orderly movement of a cause-and-effect equation. Twelve months? Seven days? Four seasons? One would almost think it a parody.

1976 certainly didn't offer any solutions. It would still be riddled with 60 minute hours and conflicting codifications of pints and pounds. However, the clean lines of 100 folded over to create 200 offered major symbolic relief. The arbitrary genesis of dating systems based on contradictory religions and scientific falsehoods formed the backdrop, and then the whole mess was slapped onto a geopolitical false construct, but nonetheless 200 is 200, so I decided to join the party.

But the Bicentennial's dawn was joyless, and that declaration doesn't even factor in spending New Year's Eve in a homeless shelter. Contemplate that for a moment, if you will. Every New Year's party you've ever been to was perversely aped in soup kitchens and Christian Missions the world over, and the celebrants, I'm sorry to tell you, were just as happy as you were about a New Year coming round the bend.

But what you really want to know is how I reacted to the record.

It was spring. I was sitting on the boardwalk with Lady watching the sea. The beach was empty so early in the year except for some lone walkers. A voice behind me.

"Damone!"

"Hi Dave. Peter."

"We thought you disappeared, man. What's up?"

"Peter, do you have anything on you? Something to take the edge off?"

"Sorry, Damone, no," said Peter.

"What, you want a drink? Come over, I'll give you a drink, and I have to show you something," said Dave.

I was sure that Dave's "something" would be a small price to pay relative to getting some elixir in me. Of course it would be some new program of change, yet another way to reshape my tastes and values, an introduction to a new way of thinking. At what point, I wondered, would this imbecilic practice cease? What, I wondered, inspires these perennial meddlers? It occurred to me that the "good intentions" that they truly believed in were but a cloak; in fact, as usual, their constant badgering was driven by rage and jealousy over facing someone with implacable convictions and absolute self-knowledge. Their attempts at "help" were, of course, attempts to immerse me in their sea of unknowing, that I might join them as they flailed about in the waves, pretending toward a self-actualization that would never come, mainly because the distance between their reality and their vision was paved with falsehoods, with wannabe little man wishes that would never be realized. I, on the other hand, for all of my miseries, did not share this malaise.

We arrived at Dave's.

"How you been, Damone?" asked Peter. Dave went to the kitchen for drinks.

"Not commendable, Peter. You?"

"Everything is exactly the same. I do the same things. I go to the same places. I see the same people."

"What about your travels?"

"The same. Yeah, I see different people, but I mean people that I know, the ones down at the library. But where've you been?"

"Blend. New York's social safety net. A blue plastic boat cover. A vent in Tribeca. The dunes. I was thinking of writing a book, actually, one with pencil drawings in the nineteenth-century fashion where I'd forever being seeking respite by riding around on one of those bikes with the giant front wheels, but no matter—almighty fuck! What the fucking fuck?"

Dave had appeared, holding out the record as if it were a painting. There they were, my four brothers under our family name: RAMONES. The photo was black and white, the four of them leaning against a wall—Johnny, Tommy, Joey, and Dee Dee. Johnny looked especially smug, proud of his little caper, and Dee Dee was wearing one of my old pairs of tennis shoes. Tommy, the pathetic weakling, was standing on his tiptoes in a vain attempt not to be the shortest.

"Why'd you have to show it to him like that?" said Peter.

"I'm sorry, but he'd find out one way or the other."

"Maybe not, Uncle Dave. You don't know," said Peter.

"Better here with us than in a record store window, right?"

"I don't know. I mean, the way you did it wasn't exactly...I don't know," said Peter.

"And how should I have done it?"

"You could have said, 'Hey, Damone, sit down.' You know. You could have—"

"Shut up the both of you, you fools! If *you're* irrelevant, how can your actions be relevant? Give me that filthy piece of musical pornography! Give it to me now!"

Dave handed me the excrement. I stared at the four thieving bastards. I turned it over. There was a photo of one of Montez's belts running across the bottom. The song titles were in the upper left, basically my quartets renamed with a variety of moronic titles.

"Here Dave, let me help you here. First, here—put the record on."

"Are you sure that's a good idea Damone?" asked Peter.

"I'm sure that it *isn't* a good idea, which is a remarkable leap forward for me when it comes to having ideas while simultaneously existing in reality. Put it on forthwith. And here—"

"Damone, stop! I paid for that!" said Dave. It was too late: I had already ripped the top-right corner off with my teeth, the so-called "credits." I held the record in front of my face and peaked over the torn portion.

"Oh, *you* paid for it. I see. *You* paid for it. Me, on the other hand, I've gotten a free ride, I haven't contributed a thing. One-hundred percent of the music, one-hundred percent of the concept, the full force of my genius, a brilliance that only comes along once every several hundred years—those don't count for anything, not a red fucking cent. Who would disagree? I certainly don't. In fact, I march at the head of the procession of those that don't disagree! Do you see me marching? Waving my banner, upon which is printed: *I don't disagree?* That's me! The emperor of non-contributors! The unchallenged overlord of creative parasites. Ah, here we are, the sound of something totally original, something totally new, entirely created by my four illustrious brothers."

The precisely dictated roar of *The Cuckold's Inspired Vesicle* filled Dave's apartment with my brothers yelling over the top of it. What can one say about such a tragedy, about such a perverse conflict between idiocy and prodigy? I could have listened to it all day, over and over; such was its pornographic appeal. I knew that my brothers had inadvertently stumbled into a genius of their own. As the man behind the mess, it was easy for me to hear how the contraption failed to gel on a quantum level, but the average listener would absolutely never notice this. I got into a heated debate many years later with Leon Botstein, the president of Bard College, on the corner of 100th and Amsterdam when I attempted to explain the quantum failure at the heart of all of my brothers' records, to which he responded, "Get the fuck away from me." In short, to the common listener it would appear that RAMONES manages to reconcile the vast spaces of relativity with the tiny spinning worlds of the quantum to such a point that any number of physicists—if they gave it the time—would have found the road map to the God particle, if not the particle itself.

But I knew otherwise. As the unwitting wellspring for the entire massacre, I could see the conflicting formulas in my mind as clearly as Mozart saw his symphonies. I heard the violent dissonance on the micro-level and it made me sick, yet I could not stop listening. I furthermore knew that only I would hear this dissonance, and thus would convince nobody of my authorship. It filled me with rage and surrender when I heard that undetectable conflict rendered: the untenable juxtaposition created a sound that I instantly knew would change the face of music forever. My brothers were destined for greatness.

I was destined for the gutter. Granted, I might get lucky on my way and pass a vomitorium where I could immerse myself in its overflowing tanks for a few moments, but why make the road to destiny unnecessarily circuitous? No. The fastest way from one point to another is a straight line, and I certainly wasn't going to test the dictum.

I spent the rest of the day listening to the record. I planned on listening to it 100 times, unsure if the formula indicated pure pain or a road to sweet masochism. Either way, I wasn't one to shy away from experimentation in the pursuit of progress. As I explained, the noise consisted of an essential clash: my brothers' hackneyed plagiarism twisted to fit the rock and roll format conflicting with the perfection of my original vision. The result was a compact enigma, a seemingly simple drawing in the air that revealed myriad complexities after prolonged contemplation. On the one hand, the purity of my quartets was utterly mangled by their transcriptions to rock and roll—it was the musical equivalent of watching Camille Saint-Saëns's *Swan* getting shoved live into a woodchipper. On the other hand, the revolting belching mess known as rock and roll got an overdue spring-cleaning thanks to its forcible superimposition over my Quartet Cycle. RAMONES essentially put an end to all the desperate, ill-informed flailings of the stinking long-haired idiots that called themselves musicians as they dug around among each other's crab-infested pubic mounds in their futile search for the next big thing.

The result was a brain-rape as far as the destruction wreaked on me and my art went, but that desecration and my personal misery would be overshadowed by a positive corollary effect: the creation of perfect rock and roll. RAMONES was the long overdue silver bullet that put rock and roll in the grave. And thank God for that, because even knowing that such a thing as *Prog Rock* existed was enough to inspire wistful daydreams about having one's skull split with an axe.

As time bore out, rock and roll didn't die without a fight. In fact, if you open your front door right now you can still see it in its vulgar death throes: skin blue and rigid; gangrenous extremities; penis grotesquely erect and twitching as it towers over the ossified landscape; eyes gone white; face twisted in abject horror at the realization there is no oblivion but rather despair's eternal continuation; thrashing and squealing and praying for forgiveness. This bizarre Rasputin seems to go on and on, the irony being that premature attempts to desecrate the corpse are the very things that keep the monster on life support.

In a perfectly functioning universe, the release of RAMONES would have silenced rock and roll. The natural ebbs and flows would have moved on unimpeded. Instead, we were almost instantly tortured with "bands they inspired," tortured with the nightmarish fact that at every concert, kids in the audience indeed went out and bought guitars, somehow completely missing the true meaning of the situation. It was a baffling phenomena—it was as if a horde of desperate gold miners had finally discovered the biggest vein of gold the world had ever known, and then they proceeded to bore into it searching for gold, or as if the announcement that a renowned doctor had finally cured cancer resulted in millions of people around the world enrolling in medical school with the objective of curing cancer. The cancer was cured, folks. Rock died on April 23, 1976 because my brothers finally brought it to life, and therein manifests the contradiction at the matter's core—my quartets and rock and roll are so diametrically opposed that they reached around time and touched each other, finally uniting relativity and quantum.

How could I have known in the spring of '76 that this reality would be condemned to wander the wilderness for more than thirty years before anyone would turn to face it? There I was, sitting in Dave's apartment taking the bitter with the sweet: yes, I'd been screwed up the ass with a galactic chainsaw on the one hand, but on the other hand I could unequivocally depend on a future devoid of *The Spin Doctors*. It should have been like traveling back in time and killing every single dictator-to-be at the point of birth, thus sparing the world centuries of atrocities, but somewhere along the line the formula had derailed, some drunken dyslexic fuck-up swapped an operator for a variable, and now somebody somewhere is not only listening to *Bittersweet Symphony*, but attributing its creation to the jerkoff pretending he's a hard guy in the creatively provincial video. And if you think that means I'm letting you two Englishmen off the hook, you've go another thing coming, lest we forget the "punk influenced" *Respectable* or *When the Whip Comes Down*: you're welcome. Anyhow, the point is that what should have been wasn't, and instead of putting an end to all misery, RAMONES pointed the way toward endless musical genocides too numerous to mention.

About sixteen hours later Dave nudged me and told me he had things to do. I could have begged—I estimated I had about eighteen or nineteen hours of listening left before I reached 100— but I thought, 'Why bother?' By about the fortieth listen of *I Don't Wanna Walk Around With You*, I got it—they didn't want to walk around with me. And by the fortieth listen of *Today Your Love, Tomorrow the World*, it sank in—tomorrow was already here.

I was in such a state of despair that it almost felt good, like some type of last-stop opiate at oblivion's dark threshold. Kicked out of Dave's, I turned to Peter on the boardwalk bench to which we had adjourned.

"Peter, I don't think I can go on. I'm very nearly suicidal."

"I went to high school with someone who was suicidal. Well, he wasn't suicidal then, but he planned on becoming suicidal later. He said it was better to die than end up like his grandparents who sat at the table not talking, and he'd know exactly when to do the suicide. He said he was going to climb the parachute jump and then jump without a parachute, but that's not important. He said his grandparents could drink boiling hot coffee and eat boiling hot soup, and it never bothered them. He said he tried his grandpa's coffee once, and his tongue got burned so bad that it swelled up to maybe four tongues, and he had to sleep with his tongue in a glass of ice water, but he kept knocking the glass over so he put ice water into one of those trays you put the paint roller in? But his grandpa had been drinking that same coffee for maybe five minutes already and nothing happened to him. His grandma was the same. He said he couldn't even put his finger in their coffee, let alone drink it, so he said that was the line."

"I don't follow you."

"He said, 'The day I can drink stuff that's so hot that I can't put my finger in it is the day I jump off the parachute jump.' His point being that when you can drink boiling water it's all over because you can't feel anything anymore, unless maybe you lit yourself on fire or got cut in half."

"Thanks, Peter. Thanks for that uplifting little yarn. Did he jump yet?"

"No. He works at a shoe store in Sheepshead Bay."

"Well, keep me in the loop."

CHAPTER XXXV.

1977.

Although I'm sure the process had been going on for many years, since before I was marooned or longer, '77 was the year I became aware of the escalating noise and silence. On the one hand there was fog pouring from manholes, apocalyptic streets, burnt out buildings. On the other hand there was color. Every train car and building was splashed with madness and life: proclamations, eulogies, tributes to beauty, love, rebellion, sex. Bright scrawls even celebrated the city's abandonment and death.

I knew that these changes signaled a twist in time, a cosmic distortion that I had ignored, immersed as I was in my own affairs. But as I walked across time's icy landscape into the next fuckhole, I had time to think—no amount of potion could kill one hundred percent of the electricity. It occurred to me that several long-traveling dynamics were converging like rural doctors at a convention in the capital, and the events associated with my family were a major and integral part of this convergence. Events later in the year further confirmed this, but even on January 1, the pieces were lining up: creation, treachery, exile, return.

Clearly some type of Velikovskian whirlpool had been set in motion around 1960, and its spinning had reached maximum velocity by 1977. Next, it would change forms and we'd turn a cosmic page under the auspices of this new mysterious structure. On a quantum level, my life was a miniature rendering or timeline where each event was predicted and described—I felt an absolute unity with the cosmos that year, which helped me to accept my total desecration. Perhaps this cosmic ship-in-the-bottle which I carry in my genetic code to this day was placed there so that I might be the standard bearer of truth, the white-robed bearer of stone tablets vindicating Velikovsky, because my story, while it seeks my own vindication, also proves catastrophism, as each of my hopes can be looked at as a civilization stomped out swiftly rather than by gentle Darwinian breezes blowing across the eons. Surely beneath each battering one can find the corollary cosmic event, and directly between the two lay the Earthly manifestation, or point of conflict. For example, one might begin their analysis with just such a chain: the ejaculation evaporating from my belly in the sea breeze—hearing *Summer Song* from upstairs for the first time—the Kennedy assassinations. And so on.

How, for example, was I in just the right place at just the right time on January 10, 1977? Standing in front of a Lower East Side record store watching them change the window display? A record store dedicated to promoting local talent? A store managed by an individual with no eye for talent?

That was the recipe that led to my seeing *Leave Home* for the first time, yet another despicable cardboard square featuring my four artfully doltish brothers plastered in front of some horrific modern architecture. The feeling that hit me resembled the way one feels when a diarrhea tsunami slams into one's wholly unprepared sphincter during a dinner-theatre date. It wasn't anger or shock, but a casting open of the doors, a relinquishment of the last particles of self-esteem. I watched them as they flew in every conceivable direction that one could travel away from me, and I felt for a moment like the swiftly abandoned epicenter from whence all matter jettisoned.

I marched into the store.

"I demand to hear that Ramones record in the window. I am extraordinarily pleased to see it, I fully intend to buy it, you have the ability to play it, so avast."

"If you fully intend to buy it, why should I?"

"Well played, young man. Now put the fucking record on or I'll jack off in your front window until the police come."

"Come too, feel free—why should the police have all the fun? Go for it. Do you see me stopping you? Go ahead."

Permission doused my libido like an ocean a match. I waited for him to hand me a script so I'd know what to say.

"What are you waiting for? That will attract more customers than our display. Come on. I'm bored."

"Look, those guys are my brothers. I'm Damone Ramone."

"Ha ha ha! What?"

"I see my reputation precedes me. Yes, it's indeed me, in the flesh."

"You said you're *Damone Ramone?*"

"My victimhood bringing you so much pleasure is grounds for a quid pro quo, no? Could you please put my brothers' record on?"

"Absolutely. Hey Tim, guess who this is? *Damone* Ramone, brother of the Ramones."

"Pleased to meet you Damone. What instrument do you play?"

"He was about to play the skin flute in our window. I told him go ahead, but he wussed out."

Their pedestrian banter was crushed by the armored legion of sound otherwise known as *Pipe Cleaner* from my Quartet Cycle. But *Pipe Cleaner* was peppered with interruptive swaths of *Trope, Masturbate, Pretend*...somehow though, these immeasurably huge chasms in the quantum order were easily jumped, as if the whole mess was united by some type of invisible matter akin to the ether, but composed of an entirely illusive shadow matter that somehow made the most violent fragmentations and oppositions appear as a precisely organized rendering. Somehow predictably was being harnessed to create huge amounts of energy so disproportionate to the relatively limited source mass, that I began to fear the three of us were in grave danger. But the fear being produced promised that there would be no bad end in the manner of a roller coaster, the Cyclone excepted.

After side one, the clerk flipped the album and we listened to side two. Nobody said a word.

When it was over, we sat quietly for a moment.

"So what do you think?" asked the clerk.

"I deeply regret that your introduction to my work was through such a perverted medium, but I appreciate your solemnity during the airing."

"Your work? How so?"

"Please. Do you think those four short-bussers came up with that? I wrote absolutely everything you just heard. The only thing those ignorant butchers did was mangle my brilliance near some traumatized microphones while they shouted inanities."

"Okay. Hang on, I want to show you something."

He went in the back. He returned with some magazines. He leafed through one, found a page and handed it to me.

"Read that. *Damone.*"

There were some photographs of my brothers performing on stage and standing in the street. I skimmed the article.

"What is this? Who publishes this libelous toilet paper? Now they're rescinding the family name? I assure you gentleman, we are very much brothers, all named Ramone. This is the most yellow piece of journalism I've ever seen, the most gangrenous tripe ever to vomit forth from a printing press. And this false-persona mongering, it's surely a joke—these are all real people. You can call them on the phone right now. This John Cummings for instance, he was a guy in Forrest Hills, he's related to the dad from *Little House on the Prairie.*"

"Oh yeah?"

"Yes. The irony is that Johnny used to beat him to a pulp on a regular basis. And Thomas *Erdelyi?* Livia Erdelyi was a woman my mother met once a month, she was from the same neighborhood in Budapest. They'd meet for lunch when we were little, and one time Mrs. Erdelyi blew a huge fart right in the restaurant. I have no idea who this Colvin is. But the Hymans I knew, they owned a corner store over there too, in Forest Hills. I'd fake seizures while Dee Dee stole candy."

"Tim, do we still have that other one, the one with the parents?"

"Yeah, I'll get it."

"I want you to take a look at this other thing. So if you say you guys are really brothers, why would they tell the magazine the names were pseudonyms?"

"Why do you think? To cut me out of the picture. To take credit for my music and to reap the financial rewards. This is just the tip of the iceberg—they did far more than just change their names."

"You're serious, aren't you? Here, look at this. Your parents."

"Let me see. Okay, that's not my mother at all. That's this woman Charlotte who owned an art gallery over there called the Art Garden. She bought a lot of weed from us. This has Danny Fields written all over it, so well thought out. They picked Forest Hills as their so-called "old neighborhood" because they know it so well. We grew up on Fort Tilden beach, but we spent a lot of time in Forest Hills because somehow Montez got us into that school district. Montez was our father."

"Actually, turn the page: you can take a look at your father."

"Wonderful. Fantastic. That's a Bowery bum named Peepshow Charlie. I bet they put him up to this because he was the cheapest deal. Johnny I bet. His real name is Frank Denardo. *"Noel Hyman,"* my ass."

"So where's this Montez?"

"No idea. I can't get hold of my brothers, let alone the rest of the family. Really, I've had it with this. Had it. Let's talk about something else."

"Okay. You watch the Superbowl yesterday?"

"In fact, I'll go. Thank you for playing me the record."

"Did I say you could take that magazine?"

"Can I take this magazine?"

"Sure, go ahead."

I walked out into a street that looked exactly the same. I headed to Tompkins Square Park to read the article again.

Further evidence of my brothers' increasingly airtight plot did not surprise me. In fact, it barely distressed me, ensconced as I was in surrender's merciful arms. What baffled me was the magazine's scathing reviews, not only of *Leave Home*, but also for their first album and for them in general. They were considered a bad joke, and the music was described as unlistenable and idiotic. Pure noise. I couldn't understand it—despite all my animosity toward them, it was impossible for anyone to deny that both records were works of groundbreaking vision. For better or worse, they were composed of a winning formula: 90% my genius, 10% their ability to reshape that genius into dumbed-down slop customized to the mass-produced palates of rock and roll numbskulls.

My bafflement swiftly turned to rage since the critic's words were only minutely directed at my bargain-basement straw men and almost entirely directed at me; it was irrelevant that the critic actually thought that the four empty-heads on the covers were responsible for the music when I knew the true state of affairs.

I read the critic's name over and over, a name I cannot disclose under the advice of my publisher. As I contemplated the coward's name, I recognized what was actually motivating the worm's position: fear, self-hatred, weakness. For of course, the world was not remotely ready for this—something so revolutionary that it jumped decades, perhaps centuries, to the actual end of music. The cozy world of 1977 was looking forward to a seemingly endless supply of borrowing and revising, of slowly moving the derivative ball forward, only to have their safe, insular world of circular mediocrity destroyed in twenty minutes flat by my brothers. Twice. No, of course they would attempt to stop it, malign it, criticize it, laugh at it, stomp it into oblivion.

The critics were the equal and opposite reaction to my genius. Just as my genius spawned legions of imitators, their ranks grew exponentially during those initial dark decades. They wrote their pathetic "reviews" with their smug little grins, each and every one a graduate of the Khrennikov school. Tikhon Khrennikov was the General Secretary of the Union of Soviet Composers from 1948 until the Soviet Union disappeared in 1991, but even after that he continued his appointment in his mind, criticizing his musical betters until he finally evaporated in 2007. He was art's greatest nightmare: a vindictive, jealous little man of limited talent. He called the shots on what was music and what was not, allowing him to reshape the rules so they coddled his mediocrity and punished genius. Shostakovich was his victim time and time again.

He helped convict Sergei Prokoviev's wife for spying in an attempt to destroy Sergei's sanity. In short, Khrennikov was a zero propped up by a consortium of mediocrity supported by force.

But the rabid ideologist in a position to stamp out the threat of genius is not unique to the Soviet dictatorship. The Khrennikovs of free market capitalism attack genius and innovation with just as much virulence as he did. There is no better example of this in the history of Western music than the Ramones.

This was the beginning of the proxy injustice that haunted me for decades—first I spent 15 years watching my music being either shit on or ignored, and then I spent another 20+ years watching multitudes of other "musicians" making millions from my ideas. Finally, I got some too-little, too-late recognition for my work via Joey Ramone Place and the Rock and Roll Hall of Fame. Either way, I was of two minds regarding my brothers—I was glad to see them suffering beneath the cruel pens of critics, but I felt the sting right along with them, not just as the creator of their music, but as a brother; however hard I tried to ignore that bond, sharing blood kept me locked in the familial dungeon. So I wanted them to suffer, needed them to suffer, but for this meager justice I paid a high price. When they were successful and being praised, I also paid a high price. That's being Damone Ramone.

During the following weeks, the record store clerks let me drop in and read magazines. In turn, I shared more details regarding my family's crimes. They took great delight in my story, mainly seeing it as a comic tall-tale, but at the same time the increasing number of hard facts and my absolute conviction made them partially sympathetic to my story—it was beginning to cast the shadow of truth. It occurred to me that even a handful of converts would make me feel slightly better; millions of converts, or the conversion of everyone on Earth, would make me feel a whole hell of a lot better. Hence, it was around that time I started having ideas about going to the press, or, if I could marshal my personal resources, writing a book. Of course having the idea is one thing, but then actually doing the work beneath the gigantic anvil of shame and shame's distilled antidotes is an entirely different thing.

But in the spring of 1977, I couldn't have predicted how things would go. At the time, I had to deduce based on the material at hand: two albums, ridiculed by most critics, hailed as brilliant by a few. The public was largely apathetic.

I searched the cosmos for a sign. The cosmos: a mathematical system, a machine of facts. If I could discern the formula, I'd get the answers.

Indeed: on May 30th, Paul Desmond leapt into the phlogiston. It was Desmond that blew the smoky sax over Brubeck's piano in *Summer Song*, his cool reed-work so magically transcribed by František's brilliant fingers. But what of it? I had my fact, but I didn't know how to interpret it. I couldn't even proffer a theory.

The lack of a theory, I believe, was largely because of the compromised agility of my mind at that time, or if not compromised, redirected. My life was becoming an inwardly focused affair—something of little consequence such as grooming an unkempt hemorrhoid was of paramount importance, whereas vengeance and money-lust seemed increasingly vain. It was summer. The liquor fell like rain. The spaces under the boardwalk were dry, the library felt like a second home, the security guards were jocular and worthless. The dunes offered sweet respite on warm nights, of which there were many that year.

Upon waking after one of them I wandered into a city that proved the Velikovskian cycle was complete: forces had converged, energy had been exchanged and transmuted, structures had imploded. Everything had been reborn as something entirely different. On that day, the new world had not yet revealed its face, but the world we had known had ended.

The sidewalks were covered with broken glass and garbage. Burnt out cars lined the streets. Buildings smoldered and smoked. People carried televisions and stereos in their arms. Everyone was smiling except for me. Perhaps for them, it was a new beginning. For me it was the long-predicted bottom.

Need I go into detail about the papers and rags, the vents, the shrubs, the nightsticks, the Wild Irish Rose, the intake forms, the bedbugs, the fights, the layers of dried urine? It was all just background noise as far as I was concerned. And small price to pay to be gazing at the giant blue skies, listening to the crashing waves, soaring on the sweet wings of booze. Without contradiction, I was happy to be miserable. Something was making it work.

Of course, events were waiting in the wings to fuck it all up. They didn't wait long. Four successive calamities occurred, and it was not long after the fourth that I found myself at sea again, rolling from my berth into the freezing, filthy bilge water.

Event One: It happened in that God-forsaken record store. I should have known better than to continue visiting, but morbid curiosity got the better of me. I already knew that the crowds at CBGB had grown exponentially, that the sparse cadre of weirdos had been replaced with teeming, worshipful throngs. I knew that, and I was massaging the wound nightly with an upwardly adjusted dose of defensive drinking.

And it was working just fine. I hadn't abandoned my search for justice, I had merely postponed it. I viewed my time outside the ring as necessary recuperation. It wasn't my brothers that jabbed me with the first cattle prod of '77, but the terrifying realization that their actions had produced a ripple effect. If I had known just how massive that effect was, I'm not sure I would have lived out the year.

It started with: "Check this out, Damone Ramone."

It was the clerk known as Tim. He handed me the cover and went to put the album on: Rhys Chatham, *Guitar Trio*. Like Dave, the clerks were amused by my insights, and despite my loathing of rock, my knowledge was increasing, particularly of the off-the-beaten-path variety that was increasingly prevalent that year.

When the music started, I was horrified. It was a significantly more precise rendition of my Quartet *Pretend We Aren't Related* than my brothers could ever of hoped to pull off. It was so precise, in fact, that I was sure this Mr. Chatham had somehow attended my performance all those years ago in Fort Tilden. I wondered if one of Montez's so-called "boyfriends" had in fact been the larcenous wretch Chatham.

"What do you think?" Tim asked. "In an interview he said he was inspired to write it after seeing the Ramones. What? What's with you? Earth to Damone, Earth to Damone...are you reading me?"

Event Two: It happened ten minutes later. In order to cheer me up without having the slightest idea what was wrong with me, Tim brought me some magazines to leaf through, not knowing there'd be more Ramones information, for as he stated, "They're rarely written up."

They were written up.

"What the fuck is this, then?" I yelled.

"What?"

"This is a picture of my uncle! How in the name of God is he involved?"

"Who's your uncle?"

"Tony Montez. He's my dad's younger brother. He did some west coast thing for my dad's business."

"What's it say?"

"That he's *Arturo Vega*? Art director? You've got to be fucking kidding me. Uncle Tony, an artist? Really, you should meet him sometime. Talk to him for five minutes and you let me know—is he more likely to work with tempera on wood or stick a pencil into an informant's kidney while doing three to five? Go ahead, you just give him a ring and tell me all about your impressions, I'd be delighted to lend an ear. And while you call him why not throw on that *Guitar Trio* again. In fact, put it on repeat."

Event Three: One should constantly think bad things to steel one's self against bad things. If you constantly think of shit and you step in shit, well of course. If you think only of brushing roses across the velum peach fuzz of nubile inner-thighs and you step in shit—motherfucker! You just stepped in shit.

I learned this lesson on St. Mark's one day when I was feeling unexpectedly chipper because I had hatched a new plan that was steadily moving from fantasy to reality. I was recollecting Evel Knievel's unsuccessful jump over the canyon and what a shame it was. But I knew Knievel was a prideful and ambitious man and would not take that failure lying down. Specifically, he had surely reengineered the rocket in order to improve handling and flight duration. I hadn't kept up with his career, but I thought it reasonable to assume that by now he'd redeemed the failed jump in grand style.

It occurred to me to approach Knievel and purchase the blueprints for his rocket once I had settled the score with my brothers. As a final flourish to drive home my total victory over them, I would depart the wicked city in the most ostentatious manner I could conceive, and what better than flying from the dismal shores of Brighton Beach back to my fortress of solitude in Knievel's rocket? All of New York would witness the event, forever equating my brothers' names with catastrophic humiliation and criminal ineptitude.

I was savoring these delightful thoughts as I meandered down St. Mark's. The sun was bright, smiles abounded, the scent of delicious food filled the air. I had a half-gallon of merlot in my bloodstream and two pints of vodka in my sack.

I wasn't paying attention, and I ran headlong into someone likewise lost in thought. I fell to the sidewalk. So did the person I'd hit.

"Sorry," I said, "I should have been paying attention—"

"Sorry man, I—"

"Well well well."

It was Dee Dee.

"Damone, are you following me?"

"How precisely does a person traveling…why, yes. Yes, I was following you. You can't escape me, Dee Dee."

"Well you better stop that! You know what I'll do."

"You can't escape me, Dee Dee."

"Shut up! You want to get punched?"

"You can't escape me, Dee Dee."

"Then I'll tell Johnny. And he'll punch you too!"

"You can't escape me, Dee Dee."

"You better run right now."

"You can't escape me, Dee Dee."

"Damone, Damone, head of bone!"

"You can't escape—what'd you just say, vermin?"

"Damone, Damone, head of bone!"

"How dare you, sir? Say that again, I'll show you an outcome that—"

"Damone, Damone, head of bone!"

"Are you sure it was me with the head of bone, Dee Dee? Remember that time you came home from school crying because you failed that math test—"

"You better not!"

"—in third grade, and you said you were the only one in class that didn't—"

"I'm warning you, Damone, you better not!"

"—that didn't pass, so everyone in the class got the ribbon that said 'I'm a Mathemagician' except you?"

"Shut up!"

"Remember? Every one of them went to the front of the class and got their Mathemagician ribbon...except you? And everyone looked at you and laughed?"

"Shut up!"

"And you cried like a little pussy girl? Do you remember that time, Dee Dee? Remember? Remember? Remember—ouch! You fucking fucker!"

"I told you, Damone! Don't say I didn't."

"The balls are off limits, asshole!"

"The Mathemagician thing is off limits, asshole!"

"My life's work thing is off limits, asshole!"

"What the fuck is that supposed to mean?"

"Fuck you, dick! You know goddamn good what that means, you and the other three fuckfaces!"

"Go back to your hole, weirdo!"

"Yeah, I'll go back. As soon as I even the score with you three dummies! You seriously think you're smart enough to pull it off, you that can't add three plus five?"

"Shut up!"

"I'll take all your money and *then* I'll go back to my hole. You'll see—I'm going to take a rocket to Ruffle Bar so everyone in New York sees and always remembers that I was the one that created all the beautiful music and that you were the one that was never a Mathemagician!"

"We'll see about that, head of bone."

"Yeah, okay. We *will* see about that."

I briskly backtracked down St. Mark's. The hot clarity of rage swept aside my false sense of inner-peace. In order to restore even an empty facsimile of my earlier mood I had to force down both pints of vodka at one go, pints I had intended on stretching out across a leisurely two or three hours. Now I would have to figure out where the next dose would be coming from. Touch a Ramone, and there it was: another giant chunk of life ripped right out. No. I couldn't allow it to stand. The time for action was approaching.

Event Four: When I walked past the record store a few months later, there was my Rocket to Ruffle Bar being flown directly up my ass by a Dee Dee whose delicate psychological fencing was far more sophisticated than I had given him credit for. Of course, although the imbecile seated on the rocket was an amalgamation of Tyler and Terry, the subtle implications of the lines and the blunt implications of the entire image were clear: there I was, the dolt, the ass-cheek spreader, the perennial doormat of the inadequate.

That was early November. Before I could actually listen to the album, I committed myself to a monumental three-week bender. I hadn't intended on doing so—the white-hot fury the incident generated was swirling inside my internal fission-reactor; I merely had to aim myself at vengeance and ignite the fuel. I made a terrible mistake in the shelter's rec room the next afternoon however, and the result was three weeks down the toilet: I sat down in front of the television. Had I not watched *Me and Dad's New Wife* the previous year, I wouldn't have been interested in following Kristy McNichol's career; however, a regular client of the Mission's named Bee-Lou had insisted we watch *Me and Dad's New Wife* in 1976 and I found it unexpectedly engrossing.

So without further ado, I watched the After School Special *Pinballs* starring Kristy McNichol, I drank too much, I cried profusely, it started getting colder, Thanksgiving was horrible, and three weeks disappeared in a puff of smoke. Now, I'm not speaking badly of the bender, lest anyone get smug that I was "learning the error of my ways" or what have you, no, not at all. The bender is always medicinal except when constructed on a poor foundation.

Not only was my bender built on a poor foundation, its negative cast was intensified a hundred fold by the emotional demolition job done me by the two films—the first scraped away my immunity, the second ripped my exposed heart to shreds. But these are the wily ways of alcoholic respite; it can steel one against nearly all of life's challenges, but when irresponsibly applied it can leave one vulnerable to ludicrous, overblown bouts of crippling guilt and sentimentality so overwhelming that a single ping from a wind chime or the slightest peripheral glance at an advertisement involving puppies and the elderly can leave one hospitalized for weeks.

Fortunately I couldn't afford a hospital, so midway through December I was wandering the icy boardwalk picking up newspapers to reinforce the ones I had masking-taped around my body, creating an outfit not entirely unlike Lady's. I was leaning over to pick up an abandoned *Post* when Peter called out to me.

"Damone, hey. I've been looking for you. Why haven't you been at the library?"

"I've been elsewhere, Peter. Elsewhere."

"Dave said we can crash at his place until New Year's. Isn't that great? That's almost two weeks, Damone. He felt bad because of last time and because of all those records your brothers keep making."

"Has he seen *Rocket to Russia*?"

"Yeah, he bought it, Damone. I'm Sorry. You heard it yet?"

"I've been preparing myself. Fuck it, let's listen to it. Got beer?"

"Lots, don't worry. You're talking all normal."

"Shut up."

We walked to Dave's. He opened the door.

"Jesus Christ, Damone; that's too much, man. Take that shit off. Peter, help me bring Lady in. I'm sorry, but you both look like total shit. You look like the mummy. Lady's not looking too great either."

Dave suggested I clean up and replace Lady's pink outer layer before we did anything else. When that was done, we sat down on the couch and Dave took out the black disc.

Unlike the shock I felt upon hearing *Leave Home*, I greeted *Rocket to Russia* with placid resignation even though its plagiarism was even more replete than the previous two albums. My brothers were getting better at the game, and the result was the most poignant manifestation of my quartets available on a recorded medium to this day. I had expected them to run out of gas after RAMONES—even with me as their guiding light, one can only go so far with severely limited means.

But I had to drop 'severely' after *Leave Home*, and 'limited' upon hearing *Rocket to Russia*. No, it appeared my brothers would not stop until every last note of my Cycle had been mined and reprocessed into aural junk food. I had to begrudgingly grant credit to the nuance of their rape, for I had been erroneously confident the farce would end after RAMONES.

Thankfully, they had pushed me to the limit. I reduced my drinking to sanity-maintenance levels, which largely consisted of low-volume morning drinking sessions. I was thus engaged on a Saturday morning when Dave joined me.

"Damone, you seem more clear-headed the last few days but here you are drinking at ten o'clock. How's that work exactly?"

"That's how you do it when you hit my levels, Dave. This is it, by the way. I'm going to have to ask you to come with me to CBGB. You, Peter, Lady, me, and anyone else we can muster at the library. This is going to be like the final push of the North Vietnamese. CBGB is going to look just like that embassy. My brothers are finished."

"I hate to say this Damone, but you may as well drink up. Your brothers are gone for the rest of the year at least. They left for England a few days ago. They played all over America this year and in England once already. You heard any of the British stuff, like the Sex Pistols yet? Damone?"

"We're going to England. Pack your bags."

"Damone, I'm not going to England and neither are you. How do you propose we get there? Anyway, I have a job; I can't just take off for England."

"Peter won't let me down. Nor will Lady. The humiliations keep coming and their nature grows increasingly nefarious."

"You have the money to fund this, Damone? Peter sure doesn't. Damone?"

The astute among you will have already noted that my destitution reflected frugality rather than the penchants of a wastrel, for indeed, treasure remained on Ruffle Bar: the hidden drugs and money that were the original pretext for my abandonment. Although I had taken the cash, I had left behind the drugs, including but not limited to three cases of a smokable version of Mandrax tablet illegally produced in Swaziland that, when combined with even the shoddiest grade of marijuana, reduced the knees to useless ornaments good for nothing other than facilitating a swift descent to a blob-state. Additionally, there was a respectable amount of American methedrine produced in a licensed, legal facility in the 1960s—a delicacy almost impossible to find in 1977.

The most difficult aspect of calling on my emergency reserves was returning to the island not as a victor, but as a desperate, sniveling maggot. A separate book could be written on the invective I barbarized myself with as I rowed across a dark, moonless sea. Nonetheless, when I set foot on the island for the first time since my ill-fated return to New York City, I felt a swelling rejuvenation that no factual circumstances could keep down. As soon as I stepped on shore, I was blanketed by the seductive notion of simply not returning. Indeed, my fortress was intact and relatively uninfested, my survivalist skills were reflex, and my revulsion for my fellow man had never been greater.

But I knew this indulgence would be a Pyrrhic victory; no sooner would I be settled into my old routine when the magnitude of my failure would start to haunt me like a telltale heart. I did not need the material fruits that a legal victory would bring; it would be quite enough to simply hoard the cash in a giant, moldy pit on the island, not to spend it, but merely to create a giant green ball full of vermin as a trophy of my coronation. The true prize was the moral victory, the setting straight of the record—the money meant nothing in the face of artistic justice. In that respect, I was impervious to financial enticements to simply shrivel up and disappear; no, this would not be a minor skirmish "settled out of court." Under truth's spotlight the cockroaches would scurry, and no day at the spa followed up with a couple hookers would disabuse them of that.

This thought tossed freezing water on my passing fancy—I made swiftly to the hiding place and dug the dirt from the treasure in a mad frenzy, grinding my teeth and laughing into the Ruffle Bar night that I had had the foresight to move the treasure from its original location to a place that only I would know. Although I couldn't confirm it, I imagined it was possible that Johnny and the others had returned to seize the original cache, perhaps to finance yet another ignominious project or to simply deprive me of a potential funding source.

And that is how Peter and I ended up on the pier near the Fulton Fish Market having a discussion with a longshoreman named Ice at 3:37 A.M. As to how the fundraising in Washington Square Park went, "swimmingly" comes to mind. Even though my original Rockford suit was a textile horror show by that point, wearing it distinguished me from the more obvious drug dealers of 1977, plus I'm not really sure I could have been arrested even if I'd wanted to be. The lack of police interest was astounding—it again occurred to me that had my brothers not embarked on their criminal path, we could have had a booming decade running the family business. At least I could fancy that my father was still in the trade in some sort of mythic, ghostly, homosexual manner even though I had a very convincing sense that he was far far away.

Ice remembered me as if not a day had passed since the summer of '69. He had been a critical contact of ours on pier-related issues: comings and goings of freighters, police, mobsters, other drug dealers, and so on. As such, he was perfectly positioned to give the low-down on any number of freighters where two tourists might hitch a ride for a reasonable fee. I was hoping that one of the freighters we'd rendezvoused with regularly would be in port so we could make the voyage among familiar faces. Flying was out of the question because I only sold half the drugs in order to have portable wealth available in England, and neither of us had a passport or the means to get one.

Ice said that there were no freighters I was familiar with in port. He said passage could easily be arranged, but I'd have to trust him to find the ship and make the arrangements. Everything he described was familiar to the point of dull—many were the times I had made such arrangements, the only difference being that instead of several kilos of cocaine or heroin, the contraband hidden in a vat of wheat would be me and Peter.

We met Ice again two days later. He told us we'd be setting sail for England in three days time in a freighter named the *Paralus* that sailed under the Greek flag but was crewed largely by Dutchmen. We settled the details and parted. Peter set off to pack, or so he said. I was free of such burdens; my sole responsibility was eradicating thirty-six hours.

I stocked up on liquor and headed to Greenwood Cemetery. My disposition had been morbid as of late. Paradoxically, I had found that spending time in a cemetery often mitigated a black descent, or in some cases, turned it around all together. All the indicators were favorable—rage well-directed, a voyage to England imminent, positive cosmic alignment. I did not need any vestiges of self-defeating morbidity dragging me down.

I dismissed Peter's suggestion that we spend the next few days at Dave's, and I forbade him from informing Dave of our departure. I would not allow that practically minded fool to shave my manpower by fifty-percent out of some misguided idea that he was "protecting" Peter by keeping him out of the United Kingdom and on the streets of New York City. As a result, I was forced to put Lady up in a horse hotel where I suffered the usual taunts, even as a paying customer—but it was better than blowing our cover by leaving her at Dave's.

Plus I was furious with Dave over his reaction to *Rocket to Russia*, in particular to *We're a Happy Family*—I would never forgive the outpouring of contrition and awe that followed the song's mocking fade-out. First, we had already listened to it several times and somehow the meaning didn't sink in, or Mr. Rock and Roll wasn't quite as finely tuned as he supposed himself to be, because he offered no reaction up to that point; however, after the particular airing in question, he said:

"Oh my God, Damone, I can't fucking believe it. I am so, so sorry I doubted you, man."

It's interesting to be consumed by a scorching white fire of lividity while simultaneously being completely unsurprised that the intellectually underfurnished primate sitting nearby would make such an incalculably idiotic remark.

"Man, I'm so, so sorry. It's like everything you fucking said, sort of, is condensed into that song."

"Please, Dave—tell me more."

"I mean, it's all there—your father, the family business—"

"Wait, how the family business? What do you know of that?"

"The drug thing, man, you told me all about it."

"I did no such thing."

"You did, man. You were super drunk, and you did."

"Let's not get caught up in the minutiae here, Dave. Go on with what you were saying."

"I'm just sorry man, clearly everything you said was true, because I highly doubt the Ramones would just happen to write a song that more or less matches what you told us."

"Uncle Dave, come on, we aren't surprised, why shouldn't it have matched?" Peter said.

But it was too late—the cat was out of the bag. That curly-headed fool had overdrawn the account, and there was no getting out of it now. I told him to fuck himself and then I went to the kitchen for a glass of juice.

So it was off to Greenwood. I would meditate among its green and grey shadows, set aside the cultivation of my rage, and connect my spirit to a gentle appreciation for birdsong, floral arrangements, and the whispering winds of death.

I arrived in the afternoon. I secreted myself among the shrubs surrounding a neglected mausoleum. I intermittently napped until I flicked my eyes open to blackness. Now it would be a simple matter of avoiding the one security guard who slowly drove around the cemetery with his brights on, effectively making him a deterrent to nothing.

As was my ritual, I headed to the grave of Elias Howe, credited on Greenwood's map as being the inventor of the sewing machine.

Since discovering this fact, I initiated each visit to Greenwood by visiting his grave and urinating everywhere. Howe's grave consisted of a megalomaniacal tower with a bust of the pompous, self-satisfied swine on top. Not content with lording over the other graves from on high, Howe surrounded his tombstone with a grassy area encircled by a low stone embankment—one had to ascend four stairs and walk between two lesser pillars that would have been ostentatious gravemarkers in and of themselves. If that wasn't enough, the glutton for pretention even had a large marker in the circular yard noting the burial place of his dog.

My M.O. was to ascend the stairs and free my organ once I was inside the circle directly in front of Howe. I then proceeded to share my opinion in a leisurely, studied way that followed a geographical logic. I wanted Howe to understand that I was carefully filling each quadrant of his little circle with my spray, that any one visit would definitely not be the last, and although I had not yet filled every quadrant, I intended simply to start over again once the task was done, lest Howe think that a day would come when I'd say, "My work here is done," and he'd never be seeing me again. No, I intended to remind him as often as I could through the duration of my life that his egotism needed to leave our dimension along with his bearded, swollen self.

After urinating, I'd retreat to the base of a large tree behind Howe where I'd pass the night drinking. I'd luxuriate in being out of Howe's sight-line, thus illustrating the imprudence in leaving a bust of oneself forever gazing in one direction, not considering at the time of commission that someone might seat themselves behind you for the exclusive purpose of instilling unease.

Which I was now doing. I had urinated on the tombstone itself and among the grass to Howe's right, and now I was sitting against the tree behind him sipping from a plastic gallon of gin and chewing on dandelion leaves and flowers as a chaser. When the urge to urinate rekindled, I would reenter Howe's circle of arrogance and spray accordingly.

Between the gin and the ritual, I was filled with a very specific pride relative to vindicating, partially, the noble death of another Greenwood resident named Stephen Fogg. Fogg had owned an upholstery company that specialized in furniture for ships. One day he asked his wife where he had set his vest. She told him it was on the chair. He immediately ran and leapt right through the glass bedroom window, dragging the curtains outside as he plummeted to his death. I had dedicated my last piss to him.

My next piss would be dedicated to all the sad dogs immortalized in stone in Greenwood, waiting eternally for a master that would never return. Unlike the wheeler and dealer Howe, their masters were not allowed to bury their dog along with them—Howe was the only one in the cemetery allowed this privilege; therefore, each time I urinated on his dog I apologized, for my fight was not with him—it was exclusively with Mr. Influence Peddler towering above.

But I never got to that round of righteous pissing—after a particularly big swig of gin, I drifted into the soft dark waves of ether.

As I raced toward the surface after a segment of time I had not yet attempted to sound, the only guidance I had was that my eyelids remained unassailed by light. In order to introduce a gentle ambassador, I reached for the gin, planning on a few lubricating sips while I rested my head on the ruffled bark of the tree and prepared to open my eyes.

But my hand remained empty as it floated about searching for the bottleneck. Nonetheless, I stubbornly refused to open my eyes and increased my hand's exploratory arc, until:

"Looking for this?"

I opened my eyes. Howe was sitting crossed-legged in front of me, holding out my gallon of gin.

"You'd better not be guzzling that, my good man. Give me that immediately!"

"Someone dead since 1867 is sitting here talking and that's your first concern?"

"We'll get to your chicanery in a minute, just hand me the goddamn gin. Please. Thank you."

"I confess to a few sips."

"I don't mind sharing, just don't overdo it. This has to last me two days."

"I understand."

"Let's be perfectly fucking clear, *Elias*. If you think I'm the sort that gets spooked by a sophomoric parlor trick, you've got another thing coming. I've slithered in and out of wormholes so far ahead of yours that my real age makes you an infant in urine-soaked swaddling clothes. Second, if you think your dime-store theatrics are going to make me recant a single ounce of piss, think again. I'm not afraid of you, Mr. Fucking Success. Fuck yourself."

"What do you know of me, sir? Do you even know who I am?"

"Of course, you invented the sewing machine. Then you started some factory employing dirty sick children, cranked out a few million, and then sat back counting your money while your child workers went home to die of tuberculosis on Christmas Day."

"It wasn't like that, Mr. Ramone."

"You didn't let them go home, they died right there on your factory floor? What have you ever *sewn*, by the way? Do you even know how, or do you fancy yourself one of those "big picture" guys?"

"Let me tell my tale. If, after a fair listen, you are still impelled to besmirch my resting place, then by all means carry on. But you strike me as a man who can appreciate having a story to tell that nobody wants to hear. You may find me disagreeable and perhaps the feeling will be mutual; that being said, you are my most loyal visitor and I am compelled to speak with you since: *He is as angry as a pissemyre, Though he pat haue al that he kan desire...*"

"Are they offering Swedish courses in the great sweatshop in the sky?"

"You don't recognize it? It's of no matter. Will you hear me out?"

"I'll hear you out, but if you make one more insinuating remark I'll send you back to 1867 with a bloody nose."

"I was one of eight children."

"I was one of nine."

"I grew up in a big farmhouse. We had to work hard to make ends meet. I disliked the hard labour. Fortunately, I was of delicate constitution and frequently ill. I sometimes feigned illness, a sin I forgave myself for because I understood that what my family perceived as idleness was in fact time spent in vital contemplation. I was sure that it was my destiny to create something so brilliant that it would redeem my frequent states of repose. That being said, I was weaker than my siblings, and although sometimes illness was feigned, I was indeed frequently and legitimately ill."

"I understand."

"I thought you might. I had several inventive relatives. My uncle William invented a unique type of wooden bridge, and my uncle Tyler invented the bedspring. My father was also clever. To supplement our income, he taught me to sew cotton-combs from leather and metal teeth, combs used to separate cotton after the harvest. My combs were so effective that this endeavor became a key supplement to our family income."

"I can sympathize—I also sewed a special device to supplement our income."

"What was the device?"

"Not important. What happened next?"

"I went to work for a master craftsman in Boston. I repaired every kind of machine. I traveled and worked constantly because I was paid by the piece—if I didn't work, I didn't get paid. Because I was frequently bed-ridden, I had to work as much as possible when I was healthy. My boss specialized in nautical instruments, which trained me in miniature, delicate engineering. At the time, many inventors were attempting to make sewing machines, and I often had to repair their shoddy work. The feature that all these machines had in common was that they didn't work. Their creators understood that the ideal machine *could* exist, but they lacked the means to turn their vision into reality."

"I understand."

"Even as you urinated on my grave, I intuited a kindred spirit. So around then I got married to a beautiful English girl of fourteen…"

"Elias, you old rake."

"What? I don't follow you."

"Nothing. Go on."

"We had our first child shortly thereafter. I was still living with my father. My work was often interrupted by long periods of bedridden convalescence where my dreams coalesced around my vision of a sewing machine: a machine that could do more in ten minutes than ten seamstresses could in a whole hour. I watched my wife sew while I convalesced—she was an excellent seamstress in her own right, granting that my skills are unrivalled."

"I'll take you on. I'm no slouch."

"I don't doubt that, Damone."

"Did I introduce myself?"

"Do I need to explain to a fellow traveler, a mapper of the multiverse?"

"Right. Carry on."

"I wrote down my thoughts when I woke from dreams. But no matter how often I communicated with the muse, I could not translate the concepts into a practical form. Attempt after attempt failed. My father continued to have faith in me, but he didn't have the money to continue to invest in my ideas. I found a patron in a family friend who took us in. He did his best to fund and supply me. The more years that passed, the more I was viewed as a layabout or a madman entertaining a ridiculous dream. Nobody believed machines could duplicate sewing's intricacy. Everyone told me to give up and focus on my health and my job repairing machines for others. But I refused."

"Well done."

"Nonetheless, time was passing, my patron's money and patience were fading, and I had not succeeded in making a functioning machine. He told me to leave, which meant I'd have to move back in with my father. I was overcome with anxiety, which made me ill and unable to work. I retreated to my quarters a madman, seething with visions but unable to give them form. My own wife began to look at me as one possessed. I felt as though I were burning in fire. This was the state I was in one evening in late 1844 when I fell exhausted into bed. But rather than being greeted by dreams, I traveled beyond myself, through a dark passage, into a separate and distinct place that you, for example, could travel to if you had the coordinates. Do you believe me?"

"Of course."

"I entered a freezing place commanded by a brutal dictator, an ugly enthroned brute with a bent, decrepit body and nightmarish grimace. His flesh was white, his hair a sweep of ice. His nose was morbidly long, his eyes bulbous, his brow deeply furrowed. He was clad in a flat white hat with a blue band, and his vestments were also blue. He pranced around in white tights and pointed blue shoes."

"I know him."

"You know him?"

"I know *of* him. He has a brother. He's the opposite of the one you met. I understand what you were facing. You transversed a wormhole."

"I appreciate your validation."

"Not at all. Continue."

"The king told me that my time had run out. He said he would give me a final twenty-four hours to make a sewing machine, or he would boil me alive. I realized this was no dream. To make things worse, I was given no peace: jeering savages surrounded me and poked spears at me. Concentration was impossible. The overlord observed my agonies from a massive ice throne that towered over the scene. Twenty-four hours passed. I had not built a working machine. They tossed blocks of ice into a smoking vat of seething fluid. They poked me with spears and forced me into the vat. The fluid paralyzed me. I was unable to thrash about to slow my descent into the poison that was both freezing and scalding. It was over. I was dying."

"You got kicked over to the Third Dimension at that point."

"I woke up. I was screaming, howling in foreign tongues. I was fevered yet freezing. I ripped the sheets from the bed, I overturned my worktable, I threw a chair through the plate glass window. I fell to the floor and howled, I rolled about, I got up and ran headlong into the wall. Finally I collapsed to the floor. My wife ran to me and caressed me. She helped me sit on the bed. I sat with my face in my hands, attempting to put my soul back together again. The vision seemed more real than the walls of my quarters. The demon king seemed more real than my wife who was now brushing my tortured brow. I told her of my vision. The images were fresh in my mind, particularly the savages' spears. I recalled how just after their sharpened points, they'd opened up into an eye. There it was! The solution struck me like a blow. For my invention to work, I needed to place the eye of the needle right after the point, and not at the back end of the needle. The tradition of hand sewing had led me and all the other failed inventors to place the eye in the wrong place. My mad vision rearranged my thinking beyond the prejudices of tradition, and I became the one to finally make the breakthrough."

"Amazing."

"I got to work. I locked my wife out of our quarters and dragged the bureau up against the door. I covered the window in bed linens to mask the constraining cycles of day and night—I would not be impeded by any provincial human habit. I worked for months without ceasing. My wife slid food under the door, and I attended to my bodily needs both great and small wherever I saw fit, ignoring the act as it commenced while I continued working. One time I even drank my own issue in order to save valuable minutes."

"No big deal."

"When I emerged, it was ready: a functioning sewing machine."

"Let me guess: that's when your troubles really started."

"Precisely. I made another machine, and one of the first things I made was a suit. Little did I know that I'd be wearing that suit until the cloth wore through, so miserable and poor were the ensuing years. But the stitches never faltered, not even after my undergarments were visible and my naked elbows poked from the sleeves."

"I don't doubt it."

"But I did one thing right: in 1846, I carefully diagrammed my invention and filed it at the United States patent office. At the time, I doubted I'd ever need to use the patent; in my youthful idealism I didn't understand that genius is one percent lab time, ninety-nine percent litigation. After that, my benefactor and I traveled to the Washington Fair, and I exhibited my machine. I had a regiment of seamstresses working behind me, but they could not even remotely match my speed. But I was shocked to discover that I could not sell even one."

"What were you charging?"

"Three hundred dollars."

"Seems reasonable."

"It seemed reasonable to me as well. It was only a year or two of wages at most."

"Um, I'm not the best with money to put it mildly, but that might have been the problem."

"My benefactor ran out of patience and turned us out. We had to move back in with my father. I had invented the sewing machine, patented it, produced it...and I failed nonetheless. I put on successful public demonstrations where I won all bets and beat scores of seamstresses with my machine, but I could not sell *one*, let alone convince a manufacturer to mass produce them. It seemed like no matter what I did, failure was my destiny."

"I understand."

"Part of the problem was that nobody besides me could work the machine."

"That might have been part of it. How do you mean?"

"I had a special touch with the machine; for me it was easy. But whenever anyone else tried to operate it, they failed. I was doomed. I was living at home again. I fell into a torpor."

"Then what?"

"It was a pathetic time. In an act of impotent defiance, I continued to wear the suit I had originally made with my machine when I thought I was at the brink of success. I even slept in it, much to my wife's chagrin. I became a virtual non-entity in my childhood home and in my marriage. Then one day my older brother Amasa rallied by my side. He had been reading about the industrial boom in England, how new factories were being built every day, and new machines and ideas were evolving at a rapid pace. Despite my pitiable state, my father and brother had not lost faith. My father bought Amasa a ticket, and he set sail for England with one of my two machines. I was too ill to go along."

"Unbelievable."

"He demonstrated my machine to English industrialists. A Mr. William Thomas immediately recognized its merit. He agreed to patent the device in England and he purchased it. He suggested

Amasa go back to America and fetch me, and he would give me a job in one of his factories. He was a producer of umbrellas and corsets."

"Interesting business model. What did he pay you for all this?"

"The price of a ticket for Amasa to return home, and the price of two tickets for both of us to return to England."

"Come on, Elias. You must have known that was a shit deal. You got fucked."

"I suppose I did 'get fucked,' as you so picturesquely phrase it. But I'd been humbled. I was prepared to do anything to improve my situation. I had been beaten down to nothing, to living back at home with my entire family. I was drowning in a black sea."

"I can see that. What happened next?"

"I had a decent period after that. I modified my machine for the production of umbrellas and corsets. Mr. Thomas arranged for my family to join me in London. He paid me a good wage relative to his other employees, and I made him a great deal of money. I suppose however that I did resent the arrangement deep inside."

"I hope."

"One day I had a tantrum over some trifling incident, some comment of Mr. Thomas's. I shoved him, knocked over several cabinets, and punched a hole in a window. He terminated my employment. He refused to give me back my machine and he evicted me. I was penniless, in a foreign city, and responsible for a young family."

"Wow. What did you do?"

"I got a job at a coach maker's, a very decent person. I saved some money, and he leant me a little more so I could send my family back to my father's house in America. They departed on a cold, rainy night. My wife had fallen ill, and was too weak to walk. I had to carry her to the carriage. The night she departed, I sat alone in my room eating a can of beans. I was too depressed to even go downstairs to get a fork, so I ate them with my hands. It was the lowest point of my life. My employer, Mr. Inglis, even had to lend me a few coins for the beans."

"I'm sorry. So what'd you do?"

"The only thing I knew how to do: I started work on a third sewing machine. It was more difficult this time, because Mr. Inglis was poor himself: it took longer to get the tools and materials, and I also had to work with him in his coach business to make ends meet, so I didn't have the time. I eventually made a third machine which I sold so I could return to America."

"What did you sell it for?"

"Five pounds."

"What, like five dollars?"

"The pound is worth a little more than the dollar, actually."

"Okay, so like five fifty? Whatever. You got fucked again."

"When I arrived in America, I had one English pence to my name, and no bank would exchange it. My wife was on her deathbed. I arrived in time to hold her hand as she passed away. I had three children to feed and one foreign coin nobody would exchange. I had to borrow a suit from my older brother to wear to my wife's funeral, and it was too big so I looked like a fool. They had refused to let me wear the one suit I had first sewn with my first machine. I didn't know which option was more humiliating, so I acquiesced."

"I don't know what to say."

"It gets worse. We moved in with my sister. And then I discovered the real nightmare: while I was in England hand-sewing coach seats and mending saddles, a slew of sewing machine manufacturers had appeared in America, and they were all flagrantly using my patented model."

"No fucking way."

"It was indeed the fucking way, my friend. Singer, Blodgett and Lerow, Yankee—all making fortunes by stealing my ideas."

"Amazing. What'd you do?"

"My father remortgaged his farm to pay attorneys to serve papers to all the companies. I went back to work as a so-called "machinist" again. There I was fixing anything from coffee pots to old shoes to keep my father off the streets; meanwhile slews of people are making millions off my ideas. They were even putting on shows in circuses and fairs to exhibit "their" inventions. Fortunately a few of the smaller companies paid up so we could continue litigating against the larger companies, who simply ignored us. See that asshole over there?"

"Who? I don't see anyone."

"The gravestone. Hunt? The one just a few feet over there."

"Sure. A million times."

"Well, someone had quite a sense of humor putting our graves next to each other. He'd begun claiming that *he* was the inventor of the sewing machine. He had no documentation, no patents, and no actual machine. He claims—if you can believe it—that he didn't patent the machine because he was worried it'd put seamstresses out of a job. Can you believe such nonsense?"

"Why is he right there?"

"I have no idea, my friend. I had even paid my attorney to sail back to England where he bought back my third machine, which he used in America as further proof of my ownership. In court, I always wore that first suit I had made with my first machine, and I'd demonstrate on the third machine right in the courtroom. By the way, that original thief in England? His people couldn't work my machine, so at least I had that. But in America I still had nothing. I was reduced to reading the papers to find out when Singer was doing demonstrations. I'd show up and disrupt them. That ended badly of course. As I said, I wasn't physically blessed whereas Singer was a large, athletic man. One time we fell to blows in front of a large crowd, and after knocking me to the floor he singlehandedly lifted me up and threw me out onto Broadway. I fell on my rear while all the passerby laughed. Another time he threw me down a flight of stairs."

"You must be kidding me."

"It's true, unfortunately. Go look it up. Meanwhile, Singer and Blodgett and the rest, they're pouring money into that asshole Hunt over there, trying to construct a false history whereby he is credited with inventing the sewing machine. He's a failure and in their pay of course, so what's it to Hunt? He's making money simply by providing false testimony. But in the end Damone, truth always prevails. In 1854, it went all the way to the Supreme Court, and they ruled in my favor. Ha! I got the last laugh. Not only did they owe me royalties on every single machine they sold in the world, they owed me back-royalties for every machine sold up to that point. I was a millionaire overnight."

"Wow, what a fantastic story. Even though I knew you'd persevere, I somehow was starting to feel like you wouldn't."

"Well, the story doesn't end there. My victory initiated The Sewing Machine Wars—I opened factories, Singer sued me, I sued Singer, Singer sued Blodgett...on and on. I spent more time in court than in my mansion or at the racetrack. We lost years of life until we all got together and formed The Sewing Machine Cartel. We agreed to work together, fix prices, and destroy smaller companies. Even so, there were still constant hassles: what I could do, where I could go, what titles I could use for my factories. I even fell out with my brother Amasa because he was named director of one of my factories with me as shadow director for legal reasons. He somehow convinced himself that his fictitious title was reality and paid himself accordingly—my own brother, can you believe it? We never spoke again after 1856. I served in the Civil War as a mail courier, and by that time I didn't even care if I got shot. You finally achieve success, and you find it's not what you expected. Even after I died in 1867, my family kept fighting over the estate. Who gets what, who said this, who was promised that. I'll tell you the truth, Damone—you're off on some mission, I know that. But I promise, the best experience—except for having this asshole Hunt right next to me—is relaxing here in Greenwood. Especially at night when nobody is around and the moon is full and the trees are black and whispering. Isn't it wonderful?"

"Yes. Drink?"

"Thank you. Say, would you like to sew now? I did not forget your challenge."

"What are we going to sew? I don't have cloth or needles."

"Why don't we dig up Hunt and reconstruct his suit? Kidding. Don't worry, wait here."

He disappeared in the shadows. He returned carrying a large bundle.

"Here—plenty of material, and all the equipment. I propose we sew each other suits, and we must cease working before sunrise. What do you think?"

"By hand? Are you kidding me? You can't make a custom suit in that short a time, Elias. No way. The sun is going to rise in just a few hours."

"You think that attitude is going to help you persevere in your grand endeavor? Stand up. No tape measures, all by sight. That's right. No more of your whining."

We stood up and faced off. The wind rushed through the black trees. We sat down again and got to work: marking and cutting cloth, threading needles. The hours multiplied infinitely as if they were bouncing between two giant mirrors, replicating into an eternal colliding chain of black obelisks toppling one into the other like dominoes. We worked in silence. We never looked up from our racing hands. In hindsight, I suspect Howe extended the night to pick up my spirits and give me additional wherewithal to face the challenges of the years ahead, but I can't be sure. In any case, I was no match for him—even though I was focused on my work, I could see him in my peripheral vision racing with absolute mastery as if he was the personification of one of his machines. No wonder that only he could operate those first sewing machines—they were extensions of him, not separate entities.

By the time I finished his suit, he had been leaning quietly against the big black tree sipping my gin for what felt like hours. When I looked up at him, he shook his hair and smiled.

"Okay, let's see what you've got. Nice. Nice work. Very good indeed. Pardon me a moment."

He disappeared behind the tree and undressed. He returned wearing the suit I had made him. I was pleased that it fit so well.

"Very well done, Damone. Perhaps I could learn something from your leisurely pace. My work is shoddy by comparison. Here."

The suit he had made slithered in my hands with a life of its own, a quality characteristic of the finest cloth, finer than the cloth I had used to make Howe's suit despite our using the same supply. Although I didn't share Howe's modesty, I also retreated behind the tree to change.

The suit was impeccably made, an idealized paradigm of the store-bought Jim Rockford suit I had worn to tatters. Howe had even noticed that my right arm was half an inch longer than my left and had sewn accordingly. As the suit fell down my body it quivered and caressed. I felt a surge of confidence, of rejuvenation, of upward trajectory.

"Well?" asked Howe.

"Elias, it's perfect. You know that. I can't believe you made it so quickly."

"No need to flatter me. You know it's poorly made. I rushed to finish it. I won by time but you won by quality, and that's what really matters in a fine suit."

"Elias, I'm sorry for all the times I urinated on your grave. You're a great guy. I'm glad I spent the evening with you. I feel lucky."

"There's no such thing. I have a proposal, Damone—how about we stroll over to Hunt's stone and relieve ourselves? I haven't done so since before our contest."

"A capital idea, Elias. After you."

We sprayed on and around Hunt's stone. We shook off and zipped up.

"How you like these modern zippers?"

"Great, Damone. So what's next for you? I recommend you visit Leonard Bernstein. You know his father also tried to force him into the family business—I think he sold hair oil or 'spray' as Leonard calls it. It was tough for Leonard to stay the course and become a conductor. Go talk to him, you can learn nothing more from me."

I passed him the gin. He drank. I took the bottle and upended it. The gushing river of perfumed silk raced in. That sweet, slow motion blossom of heat spread from my core to the furthest reaches of the universe.

I don't remember if I visited Bernstein or not.

The next thing was a meandering stagger through an ever-widening passage that was a blend of a twisting trachea and the elongated horn of an antique gramophone; I was guided around the curves and over the chasms by a Peter's voice that was strangled under seaweed and reverberated by cavernous walls. Giant rollers of nausea coursed through me, intermittently relieved by a dry heave or dousing with freezing water. I stumbled forward, step-by-step, as the passage widened and pale light faded in.

The murky watercolors that surrounded me gained edges and purpose as the cityscape took form.

"Come on Damone, you just have to make it to the boat and you can go back to sleep."

"Drink…"

"Just a little longer, hang in there. Where's your jacket?"

"Where's my jacket?"

"Hang on, put this one on. Lift up your other arm."

"I can't wear this. No yellow leather!"

Peter took me by the arm. We marched on.

"Hi. Your name was Ice, right? We're ready to go."

"What happened to him? Here, let me help you."

"I'm fine," I said. I marshaled my forces and dragged my fragmented senses back together. The effort forced me to convert a dry heave into a slightly over-vigorous throat-clearing. I took my bag from Peter and boarded the *Paralus*.

I understood the realities of sea life because of my years on the *Banana*, so I knew better than to expect anything interesting or surprising from the *Paralus*; even though our lives as seafaring drug traders provided the occasional adventure, the vast majority of our time was spent waiting. With its purely legitimate mission, the *Paralus* would provide no excitement.

Peter on the other hand still held fast to romantic visions of wooden legs and parrots on shoulders, so when the true drudgery of sea life became apparent he grew morose. I on the other hand was glad to have a large swath of time spliced from my life where I could abdicate all responsibilities and ongoing narratives. I looked forward to lolling in my birth, drinking, and losing myself in the sway of the sea.

The trip was expected to take from one to two months. We would be docking in several ports in West Africa and Spain before landing in England. A stop in port could take a day, or it could take a week or longer if there were problems with customs. In that time, my brothers would return from Europe to the United States and perform across the country before heading to England where we'd be waiting for them. They had several dates across the United Kingdom, but with destinations as far flung as Glasgow, I decided to target their New Year's Eve gig at the Rainbow Theatre in London. This way I wouldn't get distressed over a ship's schedule that nobody could precisely control, but more importantly, the date had a certain cosmic attraction as the last day of the first year when the world became slave to new masters.

I did not know if this new era would be named by divine forces or by mathematical predetermination, but I provisionally titled it the Era of Disdain for Dust and Flesh, or the Era of Cleanliness, Xs and Os. It was the death of old New York, and by extension, the death of the olden days. I alone would engage in a torturous polemic right through the 21st Century like the Emperor Julian reincarnated as a faceless untouchable, taking my place each day in the flowers on the Park Avenue traffic island just north of 45th Street. There I'd battle the trajectory along the precise angle from whence it descended from the 16th Dimension: the only one with a scream true enough, with words cutting enough. But that still lay ahead.

The voyage passed in a haze. I refused to leave my berth—specifically, some blankets thrown on top of some type of highly refined grain that, when chewed vigorously for several minutes, resembled cream of wheat. Peter made the occasional foray to the mess for better fare which I barely appreciated, so overcome was I with weighty torpor. It made no sense—I expected the familiar rolling of the sea and the salty air to fill me with seafarer's vigor; instead, I lay on the grain and drank the days away until they became indistinguishable from hours, months, or minutes. Time was simply a clicking shutter: the dark hold to oblivion and back again.

When we docked at Libreville, Gabon, there was a problem with the ship's papers. According to Peter, we had been sitting in port for five days. I hadn't been paying attention, although I was vaguely aware we had stopped somewhere. As I emerged from a vodka-induced netherworld, I lubricated my rebirth with a sweet white Gallo. The highlight of my catatonic Atlantic crossing so far had been my reinvention of my grade-school bus driver's method of covering vomit with a pink, minty pile of chemically treated sawdust; my version consisted of pressing handfuls of the ground wheat product into my soiled ass after defecating over the edge of the shipping container that served as our stateroom on the *Paralus*. Now, sitting in the grain and loading up on the Gallo, I viewed my expedient hygiene with a certain wry appreciation, whereas until that point the act seemed to drag me further into the abyss each time I resorted to it. I was slowly turning the page. I looked at Peter.

"What? Did you just say *Gabon*?" I asked.

"Yeah, Gabon. We can't go on shore but we can't sail either. That's what they said upstairs. Some problem with the paperwork. They don't know how long it will take to fix it. Someone said it's been harder since King Bongo took over."

"He's a president, not a king. And whoever told you that has it wrong: Omar Bongo is a capable and intelligent leader. Can you get your hand out of the fucking victuals please? That's soup, Peter. Christ, Gabon."

"How far is that from England?"

"We're in the Gulf of Guinea, much further south than I expected. We're probably around five thousand three hundred miles from England."

"How long until we get there?"

"Who knows? If we sail for England this very minute, which we clearly won't, I'd say twenty days, give or take. You never know with freighters. Remember, they said we're going to Spain too."

"Oh man. Can't they drive it faster?"

"They can, but they won't."

That day I left the hold for the first time since we left New York. I walked up and down the deck contemplating memory's nature. The images and sensations of a freighter deck were of course inexorably linked to memories of my brothers—the times we conducted business on decks identical to the *Paralus*'s were too numerous to count. This led to an affectionate chuckle, precisely because these instances were not in fact too numerous to count— Johnny kept a precise record, albeit coded, of every meeting we ever conducted: the location, time, and what we exchanged. Names were the only exclusion. I felt an odd nostalgia for his precise secret history—there were never any scratch-outs or blotches despite the strenuous intellectual reach needed to guarantee that the actual meaning was impenetrable. There was zero chance of anyone figuring it out, not even those of us that had attended every meeting he recorded—all we could do was laugh as we scanned the pages of bizarre symbols, numbers, and resuscitated ancient alphabets.

Three more days passed before the crew was allowed ashore. Peter was desperate to explore Libreville, but I had no interest. When the shore party piled into the boats, the only sailors that remained onboard were the grumbling skeleton crew that had no choice, a misanthropic engineer that refused to leave the engine room, and a wheelchair-bound cook with no legs and ridiculously muscular arms. I leaned against the bulwark watching the boats head toward the bright lights of Libreville beneath a purple sunset. A tugboat passed nearby. I took out my flask and passed it to the legless cook who had rolled up beside me.

My mood continued to improve for the rest of the journey until it peaked upon entry to the Port of London after a cool meander up the Thames. Peter and I had been standing on the deck for two hours with the crippled cook, passing liquor and sharing sea tales. It was early evening. As we slowly sailed between the walls of cargo ships and docks, the scene fragmented with a soft, kaleidoscopic spasm into a spray of colored round dots. For a moment I was deaf, and the violent thrashing of colors and the spaces betwixt and between assaulted me to such an extent that I feared the resultant vertigo might induce levitation in addition to the usual panic and urges to lunge. Fortunately the colored dots raced to a proper configuration before that happened, tightening the disconcerting emptiness between them until it was nothing more than a benign and lucid backdrop.

The instant the world stabilized, I recognized our new reality: Maximillien Luce's 1894 masterpiece *The Port of London, Evening*. The violet-hued sunset—now shimmering as pointillism come to life—was a concise rendering of Gabon's blue sunset. The echo was solidified by my recollection of Libreville's skyline being slightly awry, besot with strange incongruities and anachronisms.

I realized I was gazing at the same immense radio tower now that had dominated Libreville's skyline. It was a futuristic vision that managed to be horribly ugly yet perversely hypnotic: three narrow shafts stabbing into the sky intermittently connected by clusters of giant bunkers. One of the pillars continued beyond the others, and the radio antenna itself reached further still.

Strangest of all, just as in Libreville, there were immense black babies crawling up and down the tower. At the time I had been fighting my way through a discordant condition where one's freshly anointed drunkenness coexisted badly with the remnants of withdrawal, so I assumed the babies had been the hallucinations of a tortured mind. But now my mind was clear, resting firmly on a foundation of properly maintained intoxication and swelling optimism. No, this was no vision—the babies were real. Here was the reflection of a new, rallying schism, a break in a wall between worlds that portended the righteous conclusion of my life's tale. For indeed, this tower did not exist in London or Libreville, and certainly did not exist in Luce's painting. But it existed somewhere, and although its visitation was surely on my behalf, I felt somehow incidental to its greater cause. It occurred to me that my trials and impending victory might indicate that I had been chosen by greater forces not only to deliver consequences, but also to mature into a symbol, an allegory, a messenger representing all the dark hallways of the multiverse. It occurred to me that even in the resplendence of victory, question marks would remain for me, but not, ultimately, for future mankind.

I disembarked. I directed my only goodbye to the legless cook. Peter on the other hand had apparently befriended everyone from the deckhands to the captain—I waited fifteen minutes on the dock, and when he finally emerged on the gangplank he was waving and shaking hands in the manner of a President departing a small town. I wondered what commonalities had been discovered between the foreign sailors and that landlubbing New York rogue.

December 1977. London, England. We put up in South Kensington in a narrow, rickety hotel on a beautiful street. Peter said we were extraordinarily lucky to find such a bad hotel in such a nice neighborhood. I have no idea how he could have known that, but it appeared to be the case. There was a fire alarm during our first night, and we spent most of it on the sidewalk waiting for the all-clear. The next day upon leaving a tube station a pigeon defecated on my head, much to Peter's delight. Weaving that particular incident into my narrative of good omens was difficult. I contented myself to write it off as an unrelated coincidence despite knowing that coincidence is fiction, a convenient little fairytale to fall back on whenever one event is inexplicably in accord with another.

Here I ought to relate how I aggressively explored the burgeoning punk scene of 1977, the explosion of British bands that resulted from my music and the related social impact. A lot happened that year. The Sex Pistols deemed my sound so revolutionary that they disrupted the Queen's Jubilee by performing their version of it on a barge in the Thames until the police intervened. Their version of my music—which blended the essential concepts underlying my quartets with the same atrocious mechanics promulgated by brothers—was widely understood by the British public, a fact that flattered me, and despite the Pistols' idiotic behavior and looks, they promoted my music to a broader audience. Their album had apparently been Number One the previous month. To be fair, the Pistols could not have known that the music that inspired them was entirely stolen. On the other hand, to so flagrantly imitate the original arch-imitators is both ironic and damning. In addition, their shows, look, and album had an unqualified metastasizing effect, and scores of imitators too countless to name proliferated like rabbits raised on rhino horn. It was irrelevant what topical spin they grafted onto their criminal cyborg endeavors; it was simply the same thing over and over again: my quartets ripped off anew. The Clash, The Lurkers, The Damned, The Buzzcocks, Siouxie and the Banshees, The Tripe, The Flotsam, The Surgical Remains. I made up the last three, immaterial when enumerating a bunch of conformists living la vida derivative. The only one I'll excuse is said Siouxsie of Sixousie and the Banshees since she evolved into a brilliant chanteuse in the Piaf tradition despite the dismal associations of her youth.

Here I ought to relate that I did none of those things. Any knowledge of what transpired musically in 1977 occurred in fragments strewn across the lost decades that followed. I spent my time in London drinking, sitting in the hotel, and preparing for the final showdown.

My brothers were performing on New Year's Eve in a venue called the Rainbow Theatre, a corner building that looked like the prow of a ship located on a street called Seven Sisters. I was certain these characteristics signaled in my favor. There was an absurd symbiosis between my choices and the mandates of the cosmos; it was as if two Gods from different dimensions had been placed on either side of a harp, and then they proceeded to execute a flawless rendition of Debussy's *Introduction and Allegro*, despite having lorded over two entirely separate dimensions since the beginning of time. Yes, my choices had been astute, and the end of Earth's greatest era—a devastating defeat for humanity—would be offset by what would transpire in a minor venue in London's dark streets. Eventually, perhaps two thousand years on, the London of December 31st, 1977 would take its place next to Palmyra, New York and, conceivably, the good old world would be reinstated. By then I will have transubstantiated into an ancient vapor roaming the Mounds of the Adena, but nonetheless, the new era would forever bear my legacy.

December had been grey, snowless, awash in cold dirty rain. Prior to Christmas a squall slashed across Britain like a swipe from a polar bear's claw. I pictured the blue demon with his sweeping hair of ice, his miniature prancing clones, his great blue throne. I spent Christmas sitting on the floor of our room contemplating. In the evening I joined Peter downstairs where we watched an absolutely terrible comedy show featuring two suit-clad idiots and, oddly, Uncle Dave's beloved Elton John. The show's culmination was Mr. John arriving late for his performance after a comedically dismal search for the venue peppered throughout the cretinous show. Arriving in the auditorium only to find two haggard old cleaning women, Mr. John performs nonetheless. At the song's conclusion he informs the two women it was the song he had intended on performing, and one of them says something to the effect that he's fortunate he did not. So at least there was that. In the morning the radio reported that a Danish ship had sunk off the Cornish coast on Christmas. The abyss had claimed most.

On New Year's Eve we stood across the street from the theatre waiting for the opening bands to complete their portion of the *examen rigorosum*. Listening to the opening act from the street was a system we had developed outside CBGB to minimize exposure to the musical atrocities perpetrated within. The extraordinary circumstances required me to hear the moronic thunder and the subsequent slavering shouts of the perennial followers that appreciated it; I mourned the fact that the Inquisition wasn't immediately followed by the birth of rock and roll, thus depriving the architects of the torture chambers of Avignon a chance to "go straight" as it were, and build these rock and roll disaster sites in such a way that not a trace of nightmarish caterwauling could be heard from outside.

The surge occurred, the moment when the majority of the clot outside slithered through the theatre doors to breath each other's lung filth, laying down perfectly good Pounds Sterling to hear the uniquely contemporary phenomenon of ineptitude amplified ten-thousand fold by modern technology. It was time to move.

We crossed the street. There were still substantial numbers of unoriginals outside the theatre, eyeballing each other for the latest ways to guarantee visual equilibrium and precise social leveling. They were in my way, I was not impressed by their posturing, and I had no time. I straight-armed through them like a Czarist soldier shoving malnourished socialists down Odessa's Great Staircase.

"Out of my way, livestock! Damone Ramone is late for his fated moment."

"Damone, I don't know if you should push these people, they don't look very nice."

"Quiet, fool. Look how they crumple before me."

"Hey, it's one of the Ramones!"

"That's right you fools, now avast! Save the bootlickery for my purified rising. Give me half an hour—that should give you enough time to concoct some sort of makeshift kneepads."

When Peter attempted to pay for tickets, I yanked him away and shouted:

"Damone Ramone, and he's my assistant. With the band."

Despite or perhaps because of the electric energy at the threshold of an epic moment, it occurred to me that Peter had been paying for everything—the hotel, booze, the tube, pubs. Note was made of it.

We pushed our way through the crowd until we were about five rows from the stage. The English kids continued to fawn and defer upon seeing me—it was a novel sensation after spending years and years as the Eastern Seaboard's expert vermin and non-entity in-chief.

We fixed positions among the jostling bodies. The theatre went dark. The crowd roared. They marched onto the stage. Joey mumbled some banalities, and then:

These were not the brothers I had known. It was like expecting a featherbed and birdsong upon waking only to find oneself at a Nuremberg Rally. I was terrified, certain I was in grave danger, but nonetheless wishing to submit to the authority of cold black leather and money. At the same time, this was no authority, no vaulting architecture, no articulated ideology—it was freedom as the final undiscovered element, freedom in ecstatic union with the universe's most violent examples of chaos and meaninglessness, four stars swelling at light speed into red giants of impossible girth, swallowing entire galaxies, histories, empires—as if they were nothing but klebsiellae on a burning leaf.

From the first chord, they executed with the same merciless absolutism that drove the *Banana* through nocturnal squalls on the freezing Atlantic, the same moving parts within a monolith that created a living superstructure with unknown function, a machine fueled by four personalities locking into one infrangible unit. It was like the perfectly choreographed motion that transmuted the shields of hundreds of faceless riot police into an unbroken wall that did not communicate defense, but unlimited offensive

378

capacity: viciousness backed by victory preordained. This was a structure of such perfection, clarity, and force that it made Bruckner's 7th Symphony seem like the drunken yanking of a blind hillbilly abusing a one-string bass.

Gone were the phony gyrations and gestures of the old Joey— now he was pure power: confident, aggressive, merciless. Johnny and Dee Dee, on either side, hammered their instruments with piston-like unison. Tommy relentlessly drove the machine forward, pounding with industrial precision. This was Marinetti's martial vision perfectly realized—this was chopping one's own head off with an axe, racing a ten-thousand cylinder car powered by nitroglycerin directly into a wall, shooting yourself while getting blown in a torched convertible stuck between blitzing armies.

Some barely discernible speck of objectivity realized I was witnessing their finest hour, the pinnacle of their lives, a moment so chilling and fantastical that all of its antecedents were swept into oblivion—their individualities, habits, emotions; their agendas and crimes; their scents, excrements, molted flesh; their perceived intentions, their pasts, their futures. It was over. Nothing could be done.

For over ten minutes I existed in it, pressed by the bodies until I was perfectly flat, a mirror man, an impression one atom thick, invisible from the side, but an absurd swollen pop-up man from back and front, a swirling, multi-colored liquid pressed between glass.

Fortunately the reverie had other modes of expression: a punch thudded into my cranium. I turned around. A kid hugged me, spit in my face, and then he hugged me again. I turned toward the stage and got back to the task at hand.

Now, the irrevocable aspect of my brothers' most magnificent show was that it was recorded...and filmed. Furthermore, this film is easily accessible in today's technological world. Not by me, mind you, except during library hours when there's an available workstation. But for the rest of you, I'd predict access is statistically more likely based on our respective positions in the marathon.

I came back to Earth when they broke into my quartet, *The Fluid, In Fact, Is Ponderable, Quite Ponderable Indeed*, now known as *Havana Affair*, a title which ham-handedly encapsulates the murky references to our actual biography hidden in the song's idiotic lyrics. This is the first moment of the concert where I am clearly visible on the film.

Watch from minute 10:30. Pay attention to house right—where Dee Dee is standing—when the song begins. You will notice a man above the crowd vigorously waving a cylindrical object back and forth. That's me. As soon as the song started, I leapt onto Peter's shoulders. The object I am waving is Joey's sacred spoon—you may recall it is one of the few artifacts connecting the pile of rubble at Fort Tilden with the Ramones family, and I had taken it with me after discovering the ruins.

That long wooden salad spoon was the only utensil Joey could eat with—he was terrified of all other utensils, and even if we had finger-food like popcorn or chicken legs, Joey insisted on using that spoon, as laughably inefficient as it was. By now he surely had devised a workaround, but I knew Joey—once he was attached to something, it was like a Latter Day Saints marriage: it continued for eternity. What you can't see during the song is me holding the spoon over my head with both hands and threatening to break it. I wasn't sure if Joey had noticed me by that point, so caught up was he in the otherworldly performance. But the others undoubtedly did—you will notice Johnny and Dee Dee both remove their jackets as soon as the song ends. Johnny was particularly prideful about never being visibly nervous, hence losing the coat. Dee Dee becomes visibly stressed—you will see he is soaked in sweat.

Now, I grant you that jumping up and down and waving my hand in the air in the first few rows of a punk concert might not have been an ideal differentiation strategy, but that's how it goes for me—how could I have known that English punk culture was celebrated by acting like a brain-damaged kangaroo? On the other hand, my very specific, up and down piston movement, ostensibly devoid of reason, had a character all its own, and I'm not hesitant to suggest that I may have been the source of the "pogo" dance that so characterized the British punk movement.

My brothers provide immediate rebuttal by the song they play next: *Cretin Hop* from *Rocket to Russia*. Prior to the song, Dee Dee bites his pick and flashes me a defiant look—it's quite clear on the film. It's also evident at this point that Joey had indeed seen me, but he was not intimidated by my threats to break the spoon. Although you can't see it, he sings directly at me during the entire song, firing each insulting word at me with such cruel force that they were tangible blows—my chest was covered in bruises after the show.

I took out my next weapon: *The Accommodator*. This was a Vinyl Vagina I had made specifically to cater to men who preferred assholes. Of course men of all sexual orientations can share this proclivity, however *The Accommodator* was an absurdly well-made Vinyl Vagina, and Dee Dee stole it the day I created it. I knew of course, so after a week had passed and I was sure he had fucked *The Accommodator* anywhere from, say, ten to thirty times, I told him I knew that he had stolen it and I didn't mind; that in fact, I had made it for him specifically since he preferred men. That tightness, I informed him, was not that of an inexperienced nubile ballerina or a horrifically ugly woman, but rather the tight asshole of an obese, hairy old fag from Yerevan. That, I informed him, was why he loved it so.

Needless to say, he did not appreciate the insinuation, as my smashed face during the following weeks attested. So during their show, I waved it over my head for him to see, confident it would disconcert him significantly. You can clearly see me waving it in a brief cut early in the song—my yellow leather sleeve is obvious, as is the translucent artificial skin of *The Accommodator*. Don't confuse it with similar looking arms waving miniature Ramones flags—*The Accommodator* is quite obviously different upon closer inspection. There are brief cuts throughout the song where I can again be seen waving it, and you will notice that Dee Dee's headbanging contains elements of exasperation, stress, and shame.

Having found something effective, I continued to wave the shaming device over my head—it's quite clear in several brief shots. In response, they break out the tired string of humiliating anthems: *I Don't Wanna Walk Around With You*, *Pinhead*, and so on. You will see how their performance becomes increasingly aggressive and confrontational from this point.

And therein lay my downfall: although all of them were clearly upset by my presence, the performance remained intact; in fact, it got better. The energy level increased, the crowd absorbed the contagion, the house threatened to explode. The ascending energy, the armor-plated manifestations of my genius, and the crowd's fervor were threatening my composure and resolve. It was difficult not to disintegrate as an individual and melt into the collective energy. It was clear they did not share this fear—one of them or all four of them could crumble internally, but the Ramones Empire, best represented in this, their show of shows, marched on.

The finale of this orgy of evidence begins around 19:15, after *Pinhead* and just prior to *Do You Wanna Dance*. Dee Dee and I flip each other off—it's clear on the film. The song begins. Just beyond 19:30, you will see a square object tossed from the crowd across the stage. A roadie rushes to remove it. That was František's seat flotation device from the *Havana Banana*—in addition to sitting on it during meals he slept with it, using it as a pillow and occasional mistress. He also showered with it, including when he was on land. Tossing that across the stage was breaking out the heavy guns, because it was an object for which we all shared a great sentimental attachment—it was, in a sense, František objectified. I hated to toss it so, but I knew my agony would be theirs as well.

The crowning moment occurs between 20:20 and 20:30. Enraged at my failure to disrupt their musical blitzkrieg, I took extreme action. Ironically, it was this very blitzkrieg that filled me with enough additional energy and athletic élan to create their most vulnerable moment: I leap onto the stage. Two roadies rush out. They beat me and kick me. They overpower me and toss me from the stage. It's all perfectly clear on the film. Of course, they cut out any segment that showed my face or their felonious assault. Nonetheless, that was the one and only Damone Ramone, sacrificing his body and dignity for justice in London's Rainbow Theatre on New Year's Eve, 1977.

At 20:31, a roadie returns to the stage and picks up the change that fell from my pocket as I rolled about. He darts house-right out of the frame. Then he shoves the change into his pocket. The shredded remains of a letter I'd drafted demanding compensation remained on the filthy, spit-covered stage. It was over. I had been defeated yet again.

From *Now I Wanna Be A Good Boy* right through the final insult *We're a Happy Family*, my brothers ascend in direct proportion to my monumental deflation. The energy in the theatre surpasses insanity. A beam fires from the Rainbow Theatre's roof to the asteroid belt and banishes sixteen objects from our solar system so that they might disperse the residue from the closing moment, the glorious bittersweet dénouement, of this dimension's greatest era.

Of course all of the impotent parsing above occurred many years later in coolheaded hindsight, facilitated by one of time's most cherished gifts: the death of passions and goals. During that show all those years ago, I had to flex every fiber and pray to every God in order to effect those brief moments where I waved the spoon, *The Accommodator*, or my fist. My managing to get on the stage was the absurd, one-off leap of some clumsy, doltish fish without the slightest capacity to see, breathe, catch flies, or even enjoy the feat for the sheer fuck of it; no, it was a single instance in the history of a species, a grotesque parody of the relentless efforts of the succeeders and evolvers, a gesture performed to amuse the other committed ne'er-do-wells and Darwinian non-participators, a performance like that of a vulgar bum with his low-hanging scrotum sticking out from a rotten, crusty pair of pants, pirouetting about with a rank cigar butt in his mouth while aping the mannerisms of the wealthy as he understands them: overblown gestures and nose-in-the-air disdain largely garnered from his memories of Mr. Howell from *Gilligan's Island*, a show he liked when he was just a boy. To repeat such a feat was about as likely for me as the time in 1967 when Frank Fernández hammered a line drive directly at us and František effortlessly caught it in his mouth. He stared across the field at something in his private distance, not even one of his cells actually there in Yankee Stadium in any real sense. At least František had elevated us with his genius, his incomprehensible mastery of the piano. After Britain, I had to concede—I was destined to be the swollen-tongued clown.

No, that leap into light, into resistance and rage, was an absurd anomaly, as were the other pathetic Custer's Last Stand affectations—waving around a soiled pocket pussy and threatening the physical integrity of my hostage: an abandoned wooden salad spoon. In a sense, the tepid nature of these devices was a good thing, for when I fell back into the sea, it was a more complete immersion, a total surrender to what my brothers created that night. I saw then that the end justifies the means, that Howe had in fact ripped off Hunt, that history is written by the winners. And honestly, could I have done it better? Not a chance. It was the greatest night in the history of rock and roll. It was also the final night in the history of rock and roll. Why, after that, did anyone continue on? It turns out that great works are performed not by strength, but by plagiarist assholes. I tried to keep that in mind, tried to retain one drop of my righteous venom, but the power of the performance was simply too overwhelming—my brothers had illustrated that given proper direction, they could, theoretically, receive my blessing to perform my quartets, the only orchestra so ordained.

CHAPTER XXXVI.

1978.

As it turned out, Peter had stolen thirty-six Pontiacs from a dealership in the Bronx on the night of July 13th 1977 into the small hours of the 14th. He said that another thief had arrived simultaneously, also armed with bolt cutters. Without speaking, they joined forces and cut through the fence. They threw a rock through the showroom window. They subsequently saw each other back at the lot four times throughout the evening as they returned to hotwire more Pontiacs. Peter said they drove the first few cars right through the showroom windows. Peter estimated that his cohort made off with fifteen cars at most. Peter assumed the other thief stored all fifteen in one place far away, whereas Peter stored his randomly in nearby streets; an astute estimation relative to the Great Blackout and 1977 New York: he successfully transported every car to a chop shop in the following days. He saw the other perp on the news, arrested, including a shot of his fifteen Pontiacs all parked in a row under the IRT near the 242nd Street/Van Cortland Park Station, as if he had planned on inconspicuously opening a car lot there.

He explained it on the airplane back to New York. I hadn't asked. I didn't care. When he extracted a green brick of cash at Gatwick, the only thing I noted was how I absolutely did not care how he got it or if we both went to prison because of it. Same the fake passports. I was also inured to the realization that I had travelled to England in a freighter's rat-infested hold, shitting over the edge of a weevil-filled shipping container, when Peter could easily have bought us round trip tickets on a transatlantic flight with an open bar. It didn't matter. I was an empty vessel.

I drifted into sweet folds of deafness. I carried around increasingly large numbers of plastic bags filled with talismans undefined—I planned on discerning their meanings and archiving them at a later date. In the meantime, my telepathic sensitivities dramatically increased; I could sense negative energy, positive energy, and encrypted speech coming from any number of discreet common objects. So I gathered them up: discarded newspapers, stones, forlorn playing cards. The plastic bags grew around me creating a centrifugal nest brimming with diverse energies from venerable sources such as the Nineteenth Arc between Hősök tere in Budapest and the 103rd Street Station at Broadway.[29] Aided by the accumulating energy, my work became increasingly focused on decoding exactly how it was that I had been consumed by an unknown category of misalignment. I understood that the discrepancy was specific to the aforementioned Arc, and in particular, its source in a discordant feature of the emanation points: The Seven Chieftains of the Magyars and The Tomb of the Unknown Soldier. Imre Nagy, the Hungarian leader executed for treason in 1958 because of the 1956 rebellion against the Soviets, was not reburied at the Hősök tere until 1989, so although all of these features eventually coexisted on the square, they did not in 1978. On the other hand, an estimated 100,000 people attended the reburial, an event that surely had seismic resonation in reverse.

But I couldn't have predicted such things in 1978. Fortunately, I managed to get a little ballast in the hold, thanks to a denizen of the Union Square Station with a filthy grey beard. I was resting on the next bench. His beard reminded me of someone, or perhaps he was that person. Unfortunately, when I looked over the next morning he was gone. Then it hit me: Hörbiger. He held the key,

---

[29] Arcs emanating from BrkMQ that conclude in Hungary (post-Trianon) can be considered *venerable* if the rating system adheres to Velikovskian tenets. In the same or analogous rating systems, Arcs deemed *venerable* that terminate in Hungary would still not warrant the *moderate* rating of Arcs terminating in the territories of the former Czechoslovakia (WWII-1992) that originate from anywhere in BBMQ. No Bronx Arcs terminate in Hungary. SI data N/A.

although he was also a bit of a plagiarist himself by claiming to have invented the so-called Hörbiger Valve which he swiftly patented as they all seem to do. This critical component of global gas transport was merely a dumbed-down corporeal rendition of the magnificent valves employed by the energy Arcs. Anyone with access to several dimensions who had traversed any one of the Arcs could have wrote their own ticket the exact same way—Hörbiger just happened to do it first.

Of course the interdependencies between Hörbiger's World Ice Theory or World Ice Doctrine (*Welteislehre* oder *Glazial-Kosmogonie*) and The Snow Miser immediately come to mind, along with other torturous concepts: Ganymede, Bruckner, the Ramones 1977 New Year's Show, the Neptune Avenue Platform, Prague, the mysterious tower of London/Libreville/Luce. In short, a cosmotechnical research nightmare. If I were to commit to disentangling the whole fucking mess, I'd need at least three dedicated assistants who thoroughly understood every one of the puzzle's constituent parts. Equitable distribution of tedious labor was also critical. For instance, I had a Sunday Edition of the *New York Times* that was actually a much-needed pre-World War One issue of *The Key To World Events*—having to decode *and* translate the ostensible *Times* until it was an accurate transcription of its true identity would take at least Ten Thousand Hours. I needed a helping hand.

That's when I wrote my first letter to the university in Rangoon, thus inaugurating a dialogue culminating in my 1979 performance on campus. My reasons for choosing Burma were political and personal. I was a supporter of the Burmese Way to Socialism—it had been overwhelmingly reaffirmed by the Burmese public that year: 100% of their votes went to the Burmese Socialist Programme Party. Second, there were the Nick Drake issues and the foreign mantra in my head that by then had faded into the general noise. Nonetheless, its immersion into the cacophony by no means diminished its power—it drove me to the Brighton Beach Library where I labored over draft after draft until my arguments cut like fresh razors.

By then, my pessimism was so deep and overarching that I did not expect a response. I was pleasantly surprised one day when the librarian to whom all the vagrants' letters were sent—she provided her "in care of" for a nominal fee—handed me an envelope received *par avion*. I caressed the letter with my fingers and my face with the letter for several minutes before sitting down and unsealing it. It read:

There is an assumption may be valid or - explanation for some guide---

--

--

Cosmic, with congenital ability - and be of any spectral character. Thickness comprehensive all-dimensional space --- Vti_kl with Zguet formative axles - in the center of influence waveform turning to the substance of high density - and around less and less later appears axes black-central distribution expressed in a range between large and medium spectrum of Jericho, and so after crossing the wave-shaped ██████ *grow with the rotational motion -------------------- that more accurate to say this needs to clarify ----- therefore anticipated by Hungarian formation you will find the so-called black holes - in more than one level ----- wearing a vacuum Yale high density material Konbh --- trying acquisition of all.*

They got better over time. At least it was clear they had understood the portion of my inquiry pertaining to Budapest Terminating Arcs, the event horizon, the three possible outcomes that result from crossing it, and the ever-widening accretion disc that swirled around me and kept passerby at ever-increasing distances the more talismans I retained. I had decided not to mention my compositions until their responses indicated that they were flattered by my deference to Socialist-Buddhist models.

Several days later I was back in the library staring at Volume 2 of Laplace's *Mécanique Céleste,* thinking how I'd rather read a shampoo label for eight hours than it, when Peter walked in. To the best of my knowledge I hadn't seen him since England. We said our greetings and caught up on the latest neighborhood news. These pleasantries were the usual warm-up act preceding the main event: sticking yet another knife into the Jupiter-sized pincushion known as Damone Ramone. The conversation had been prolonged only because free spaces for more knives were increasingly hard to find.

"Hey, you know, I have some bad news."

"Good for you."

"Your brothers released another—"

"Oh, for Christ's sake, you think I care anymore?"

"—and it's called *Road to Ruin*."

"Flattered, but *Arrived* would have been more accurate."

"And your brother Marky replaced Tommy as their drummer."

"They kicked out Tommy just for the pleasure. I'm not entirely unsympathetic."

"And Uncle Dave—"

"Bought the record and has endless interpretive theories he'd like to share. Does he have beer?"

"—talked to Tommy—"

"Great. Here we go."

"—and he got your sister's phone number off him. You might be able to call your sister."

Uncle Dave explained that he had seen my brothers perform in the city. He waited for them after the show. When they appeared, they all ignored him and jumped in the van except for Tommy, who had been left behind for laughs. Dave told Tommy that he needed help with Damone: that would be yours truly, the man who had become so self-reliant that something just had to be done about it.

In any event, Tommy denied he had a brother with his mouth but his eyes screamed otherwise. When Uncle Dave insisted that Tommy provide some small piece of information or an allegorical explanation, Tommy wrote Ramona's number down and gave it to Dave. He said, "Ramona's not my sister, not my real sister, but she might be willing to help this guy out, at least talk to him and set him straight. He's *not* my brother. You understand?"

Dave let me use his phone. It was a New Jersey number. A woman picked up that may or may not have been Ramona. I said, "It's me, Damone." She hung up.

Between an overall lack of energy and directing the little I had toward more pressing concerns, I didn't immediately call back. Instead, I focused on my own endeavors and furthering my dialogue with the University of Rangoon. My own endeavors, largely spelled out, were increasingly supplemented by an ongoing experiment: attempting to ride an Arc without first hurling myself across an event horizon. The difficulties of corporeal restoration while minimizing distortion upon arrival is the traditional plague of Arc travel; in the case of my new experiment, it wouldn't be an issue in the first place.

In this case, my goal was to ride the Arc without making any adjustments whatsoever. The primary objective was, of course, scientific curiosity: could it be done? But of equal importance was trying to discover a way of minimizing endless duplications and reconstitutions that resulted in slowly accumulating distortions.

The Arc I chose for the experiment was ramshackle to say the least, but the choice was by design. Its emanation point was in the flowerbed on the traffic island at 45th and Park Avenue. As I may have mentioned, it traveled to Budapest via the 16th Dimension. I hypothesized that the reception point was located in the Budapest subway. It was a certainty that an impure Arc would be the best medium for the experiment, granting that rejection based on complementarity was not totally impossible—it might be the sort of club that *would* reject me precisely because it *would* accept me as a member, if that makes any sense. By contrast, any self-respecting Prague-terminating Arc demands complete purity—you better believe your sweaty ass will not be getting any free trips to Bohemia unless you're willing to molt your present emanation and embrace whatever holographic distortions come your way.

So I ended up spending the majority of 1978—wind, rain, or shine—standing in the flowerbed and attempting to leap into the Arc. I'd attempt no more than four leaps daily, but never less than one. Between attempts I screamed every manner of supplication up the Arc along the 70-degree angle from which it departed New

York City. Imbecilic passerby christened me "The Prophet," presumably because they assumed the book in my right hand was the Bible. Granted, as the year wore on and I failed to ascend, my supplications grew increasingly fiery and my hue followed suit, flushed as it was with fury and massive daily infusions of cinnamon schnapps. The return of my long hair and beard also didn't discourage the moniker.

I spent my off-time making basic preparations. The book I held during the experiment was actually Fyodor Gladkov's *Cement*— although Hungary's Kadar regime was liberal, I thought I'd play it safe and cater to big daddy. On the other hand, Kadar's travel policy allowed me to acquire forints in advance of my trip so I'd be able to buy drinks and a paper upon arrival in Budapest. Much to my frustration, I couldn't find any of Hörbiger's blueprints or related exposition regarding his work on the Budapest Subway, which most certainly would have made the endeavor easier.

I also sporadically tried the New Jersey phone number. The woman continued to hang up as soon as she heard my voice. I was convinced it was Ramona rationally, but rejected the fact viscerally. I didn't understand how she stood to profit from joining the others in condemning me; I assumed she was acting under Johnny's orders, although I accepted this would require little coercion—the two of them had always been close. On the other hand, I was also her brother. I kept trying.

I continued to correspond with Rangoon. I, in response to a surprisingly adamant inquiry, had provided them with extensive personal details as well as more information on my musical compositions. The last letter from Rangoon had a markedly different tone than previous letters, and the English was impeccable. It abandoned our scientific dialogue in favor of broad biographical questions.

The next letter I received delighted me: it focused almost exclusively on my music relative to Burmese Socialism, and concluded with an invitation to perform at the University of Rangoon the following spring. The regime offered to pay for everything. I sent along my wholehearted acceptance and some questions to help prepare a dialectically acceptable performance. I also offered to send recordings of my quartets. They responded enthusiastically regarding my acceptance, but to my surprise they said it would not be necessary to provide recordings—my reputation sufficed. I was glad, if only because of the difficulties I'd have had finding comparable sewing machines, a location, and recording equipment.

Success parlayed into more success. I called Ramona from a Chinatown payphone on a whim, feeling spritely due to my upcoming trip and in the pink thanks to a generous[30] tourist outside *SPQR* who had handed me a fistful of change after I told him a laughably unoriginal yarn about a house fire. I slid a dime into the phone.

"Hello?"

"Ramona, it's Damone…Ramona? You there?"

"Whaddya want, Damone?"

"Finally. Where to begin? Are you aware of what's happened?"

"I'm talkin' to you cuz you keep callin' and my old man's getting weird about it. Lucky he's working. And I have my own reasons for taking the call."

"What are they?"

"They're called *my own reasons* for a reason, fuck. So shut the fuck up."

"Can I come by? I don't need money, I don't need anything. I just want to talk about our brothers."

"You seen their band?"

"Yes."

"They ain't talking to you though."

"Right."

"Where you livin'?"

"Here and there."

"You're on the streets."

"Well, I suppose you could describe it that way."

"I suppose I could. Can you come day after tomorrow?"

"Yes. Thank you."

---

[30] A gullible idiot of course, likely of Michigan origin.

"Okay, listen up…"

She gave me directions and we hung up.

I avoided 45th Street and Park before my visit to preserve my mood. My attempts to shoot through the Arc were not going well. I had initially greeted the taunts of passing detractors with complacence, because I was certain the moment would come when their jeers would be silenced by the sight of a man tilting at a 70-degree angle and shooting into the sky at enormous speeds. As the months passed and this did not happen, it became increasingly difficult to redirect my anger into my skyward supplications, and at the end of each workday I found myself tormented by lingering resentments.

So instead I "acquired" a pool lounger from Coney Island and got an early start on my Ramona visit. I went to Jersey and nested in the Secaucus Swamp, situating myself in a densely reeded, somewhat gaseous area unlikely to be penetrated by kayaking fucknuts. I spent the next day and a half decompressing among swamp sounds with two gallons of Riesling.

Ramona lived in a neighborhood outside Trenton that I had to walk to from the NJT. It was strange to be visible—in New York I could walk anywhere in any state and I remained but a whisper, an illusory shadow. In a suburb however, the suspicious glances felt like perverted hands running themselves all over my body. I walked briskly to get to Ramona's before someone summoned the police to cart off the unsightly aberration also known as an unfortunate human being, the least of your brothers.

Ramona's house was an aluminum sided bungalow. The yard was neat and there were low-key flowerboxes outside the windows. I rang the bell. I heard Ramona yelling and a child responding. She opened the door.

"Hi."

"Aw, Christ. A woman down the street called, said watch out cuz some weirdo was in the neighborhood. I thought, 'Please don't let it be him,' but I fuckin' knew it. I fuckin' knew it. Christ."

"Hello to you too."

"Come on Damone, you look like fuckin' Penn Station dog shit and you smell even worse. Whoa, close enough asshole, save the smooching for the baboon's ass or whatever you been using to groom. Fuck. So what's goin' on?"

"How about you? You look like a suburban housewife."

"Sherlock fuckin' Holmes."

"You are a suburban housewife."

"Right. So look, I'm not giving you any money."

"What happened to the house, what is going on with our brothers, and what do you know of their treachery?"

"I don't know shit about shit. Tommy calls me, says Johnny says you're cut out, nobody's allowed to talk to you. Says Johnny will explain. Johnny don't, but he calls me every year asking if I seen you. I say no. Where you been anyway?"

"What about their band, ripping me off, the money? When he called, what'd he say about me? And what the fuck happened to the house?"

"Man, I left before you did, remember? They said you ran off with some hussy from Iowa and was living there."

"Come on. Iowa? Fuck."

"I thought they might be jerking me off, they were laughing when they told me. So I don't know shit, man. Best I can do, I'll tell Johnny you dropped by looking like shit. Maybe he'll lighten up. Who fuckin' knows. Like you said, I cleared the fuck out."

"Johnny was very upset. Why did you go?"

"What, are you kidding? Fuck that place, man."

"It was a unique place to grow up."

"Had to get out, man. Fuckin' place. Moved in with a black guy. The Village. Love of my life. Mafia killed him. Lufthansa heist? He drove the van. Guys he did it with? Killed him."

"That's terrible. Unconscionable."

"Which part?"

"Your great love, murdered. Is there no justice?"

"There *is* justice, that was the fuckin' problem. Ain't gonna lie, he fucked shit up. Had it coming. Fuckin' loved that fuck."

"Sorry."

"Fuck it. Got this guy now. He's okay. Steady job. Had this kid. One over there's his. Boring. It's cool."

"I'm sorry."

"Fuckin' Montez says that too, but I know that fucker was half-glad. The fucker."

"Where is he?"

"Who cares."

"Really, do you have any idea?"

"Last I heard, back to Cuba. Or Canada. Same thing."

"Right."

"You believe someone so fucked around, a racist? We're like seventeen minorities ourselves, yeah?

"Nearly. Two, actually."

"Whatever. We're at least three. Plus half his kids retards, he's smokin' pole, still talkin' shit. Newyorican J-Dub, sees a black guy, he's John fuckin' Dean. Come on, right? Have a fuckin' heart, man. Bacardi motherfucker."

"I believe we are also Bacardi motherfuckers."

"We're all diluted and shit. Fuck it. We ain't shit. Average motherfuckers. Ancestors fucked everybody from here 'til next Sunday. Saturday too."

"We're American."

"Whatever. So where you been? And it's four: Jew, Puerto Rican, Gypsy, Hungarian. Told ya. So where you been?"

"Okay, three, I forgot Gypsy. Hungarian's not a minority."

"It ain't country club white though."

"Okay."

"Shut up. Where the fuck you been?"

"You don't know?"

"How would I?"

"You seriously don't know?"

"I'll drop this baby and cut you."

"I've been living around the city since '74 chasing down our illustrious brothers, but less lately thanks to acute alcoholism: it takes all my time to stay supplied. Before that, they imprisoned me and destroyed me. Our brothers. You were gone, this was after that thing between František and Johnny. Johnny said we were going on a long voyage, somewhere Spanish. We go on shore on Ruffle Bar, spend the night, I wake up and the *Banana* is scuttled and they're gone. There was a new tug there the night before, clearly their getaway ship. They marooned me. And that's where I was from '70 to '74."

"Yeah, but Ruffle Bar? That don't account for four years. Four days maybe, but four years? You can see the fuckin' skyline. Boats everyplace."

"I don't know. At first I tried to get back, but I had some problems. Then with each passing day I tried a little less. One day I didn't want to leave anymore. So I stayed."

"You got the Patty Hearst thing for a fuckin' island? It's a fuckin' island."

"You really didn't know about that? Honestly?"

"None of your paranoid fuck-face bullshit, Damone, I'll kick your fuckin' balls out your mouth. And none of your big-word bullshit either, trying to sound smarter than you fuckin' are, you fuckin' phony."

"They stole my music. That's why they did it. I get back and there they are, playing idiotic versions of my quartets at this bar on Bowery."

"Nah, I heard about that shit, Dee Dee told me."

"Dee Dee knew where you went?"

"Shut the fuck up. How you had them sewing machines going and you got naked in front of the entire family and sucked your own dick. On top of everything else."

"They stole my greatest works, and the music's what matters; focusing on my conducting is sensationalism, a distraction."

"They didn't steal your sound. And man, you're startin' that fake British accent bullshit. What'd I fuckin' tell you? First you, then Joey starts, we got a house full of professors and faggots on top of the rest of it. Fuckin' so glad I left."

"I had a vision during my operation, if you don't recall, and it reoriented my view toward the world, toward learning, toward musical composition—"

"What a joke."

"I rose above my own surgical table, and it transmogrified my relationships with everything; with electromagnetic fields, with art and great minds, hence my elocution...ouch, hey!"

"*Your surgery?* You were at the fuckin' dentist getting a cavity fixed, Damone. They didn't even put you under."

"They put the mask on my face, and while I was in a delirium—fuck! What is your problem, you're a mother now! My sister, Rosa Klebb."

"Don't talk shit, you won't get punished. Damone, that's your whole fuckin' problem: you turn every fuckin' thing around until it's all about you. Got it? You didn't do shit in that house, jerked off more than all our brothers put together, sat on your ass reading all those stupid books, but unlike Tommy who was another faggot bookworm, you didn't pull your fuckin' weight—Tommy'd *rumble*, man, if we needed him, and he's a fuckin' pussy, but not you. You were a dick too, talking down to everybody like you being part of the Ramone family was some sort of accident. But the worst was your laziness, man. That, Johnny could not forgive. You know he worked for two days in a fuckin' bump shop with a broken arm to feed František, Tommy, Tyler, and the rest of the freaks? That was the same day you came home from your 'delirium' where God told you never to work again, shit tulips, and beat your meat twenty times a day."

"Well, you certainly have your view."

"Called reality. That's why you got marooned, not because of music. You stay four years, that's on you, bro. You brung up that František thing that finally pushed me over the edge? How about you, your royal shittiness? What kinda fuckin' person, let alone his own brother, would be jealous of František?"

"What? What sort of utter tripe is that? Jealous of what? Ha! Ha Ha!"

"You were behind Johnny one-hundred percent, you prick. But not cuz you had to sleep cuz you worked all the time like Johnny."

"What are you insinuating?"

"You were happy when Johnny put the kibosh on it, sad when he felt bad and bought Frankie a new piano. Yeah, I heard about that. That's all I'm gonna say."

"That is completely ridiculous, I was a stalwart supporter of his right to play from the first. Why would you think otherwise?"

"That's all I'm gonna say. You're the one that's gotta live with you, and I'm sure that sucks even on the best days. So what brings you round?"

"What, what brings me around? Are you kidding?"

"I'm not, actually. Did you want to say hi, or only this bullshit about them stealing your music?"

"They didn't say anything to you, they didn't concede that they based their entire sound on my work?"

"Okay, Damone. Merry fucking Christmas: one of them might have mentioned some similarities. You repeat that, and you'll have some similarities, similarities to a corpse."

"I just wanted to know if any of those vermin would fess up in their guilt. Who said it?"

"But they do it better—it's going to make them superstars. They sound great now. But the way you do it, nobody gets it and you'll end up being one of the prisoners the other ones kill right away."

"Better that than pandering to popular sentiment."

"They aren't doing that. Not even close."

"I don't sell out."

"They don't either. And that's all I'm gonna say about it. What do you know about rock and roll? Dick. So what's next in your life? Fuck it, you coming in?"

"I can't, I have a plane to catch. I'm headed to Burma, I'm performing at a university in Rangoon."

"Ain't that a fact."

"Yes, it's a fact."

"Well, you better go then. Nice of you to drop by. Come back if you get cleaned up, but call first."

"I will definitely do that."

"Cool. And oh yeah: Cuban."

"Cuban and Puerto Rican fall under Hispanic. It's the same thing."

"Tell it to a Cuban."

"Can we settle on three and a half?"

"Whatever. See ya, Damone. Love ya, you goofy fuck."

Turn. Walk away. The fact that the plane didn't leave until March the following year seemed irrelevant relative to Ramona's face, shocking like a police age-progression made into a Halloween mask she had forgotten to take off. To be fair, Ramona still looked good—like the rest of us, she aged well. Nonetheless, the jump across time gave dooming resonance to subtleties that would have been unnoticeable had my finest years not been excised. A wispy sketch indicating where a future line *might* appear induced an existential panic in me defined by a trojan paralysis—I remained perfectly still while seizures raged within. A billion psychic tendrils flailed in darkness knowing full well they would find nothing to grab onto.

The remainder of 1978? The shouting audience waits for the inevitable encore, but the band is already back at the hotel. The first year of the new, lifeless era disappeared down a galactic vortex that was indistinguishable from the shower drain at St. Savior's Shelter. Despite my hand against the tiled wall, I listed from left to right in the boys' locker room shower as I treated myself to some luxurious holiday solitude in the spa while the others celebrated in the church rec room: seven Pall Malls, six coat-sleeved pints of mint schnapps. You really missed out, they said, as we picked our mats up from the gymnasium floor the next morning. Per policy, we rolled them up, put them in the storage closet and headed out into 1979.

CHAPTER XXXVII.

1979.

My upcoming trip to Rangoon stood out in gleaming relief against an otherwise bleak landscape. Although I approached all experiences other than physical pain with skepticism by that point, I had to concede that as of January, 1979 there were no indications that Burma's invitation was a deceitful prank designed to globalize my emasculation. For indeed, if the Burmese Road to Socialism required an absolutely horrific accident in order to keep people driving between the lines, they'd be hard-pressed to find a better example than Damone Ramone.

Doubts aside, my cautious optimism rested on a total lack of prospects, which, in addition to providing its own unique spiritual freedoms, also cleared my schedule: my only obligations until March were avoiding hypothermia and sobriety. I was therefore able to focus on my upcoming performance, and many were the winter fantasias that concluded in a bath of gymnasium light following their clamorous dénouements.

I received a letter in late February containing business-class tickets to Burma via Narita Airport, Japan. A few days later I received another letter which read:

Dear Mr. Ramone,

I speak for the working people of Burma when I state that your visit is anticipated. Your letter of January 9th listing requirements was forwarded to me. These requests are met. The systems you require are at the University. The music department will direct you. The shower curtain was made in Burma. This should offset concerns regarding the sewing machine manufacturers that arose from one People's Council.

I hope I will meet you personally and show you aspects of Burma and the ethnicities.

Best Regards,

KS

An enclosure reiterated my requests, the most important being the sewing machine models I had composed my quartets on nearly a decade earlier. Clearly the Burmese Socialist Programme Party was taking my visit seriously. To reciprocate, I prepared a preamble to my quartets that positioned them as a rejection of bourgeois materialism and the vanity of charity, the latter in specific response to Amendment 17 under the *Reorientation of Views* section of the Burmese Way to Socialism as drafted by the Revolutionary Council on April, 28th, 1962. To wit (emphasis mine):

> *17. Attempts must be made by various correct methods to **do away with bogus acts of charity and social work for vainglorious show, bogus piety and hypocritical religiosity**, etc., as well as to foster and applaud bona fide belief and practice of personal morals as taught by eithics (sic) and **traditions of every religion** and culture. We will resort to education, literature, **fine arts**, theatre and cinema, etc., to bring into vogue the concept that to serve others' interests is to serve one's own.*

I thought it suitable to focus on a pitfall of capitalism that I could illustrate with particular acuity; from that pitfall's confines I could vividly contrast the patronizing charity of beatific nuns with the surly proletarian honesty of the city-run shelters, granting that the suburban do-gooders that flocked to the latter during holidays were no different than the former in their moral grandstanding. Furthermore, my sole blessings—Lady and Burma—were surely the result of practicing every religion simultaneously, as oft was my wont during times of hardship. Of course, illustrating these dynamics via the *"fine arts"* was the raison d'être of my journey. I declined building in any allegorical references to the many times in the shelter system where I proved, *"that to serve others' interests is to serve one's own,"* because I wasn't entirely sure the methods employed[31] could be brought into *"vogue"* in the context of Burmese Socialist ethics, and in any event, they resulted from a housing problem that Burmese Socialism had long addressed.

Logistics in order, I lightheartedly squandered the days before my departure. I even agreed to Peter's adamant suggestion that I see Bruce Lee's *Fists of Fury* by way of preparation, and although I initially found his suggestion delightfully absurd, it occurred to me during the film that I was indeed witnessing true proletarian expression: working men fighting social ills with their fists alone. This reminded me that utility should be sought in all things, so when Peter later produced several gallons of what was undoubtedly the most horrific Moldavian wine ever produced under socialism— and that's saying a lot—I did not complain, but simply rolled up my sleeves and fell to. In this way, the final days were obliterated by soft moments punctuated by geysers of purple and pink.

A music student from the University met me in Rangoon. After storing my bag in a private dormitory on campus reserved for guests, he took me to the Shwedagon Temple, the Taukkyan Cemetery, and to a traditional Burmese meal. Afterwards we walked the streets of Rangoon for several hours at my request.

The brightly colored outfits, bushels of fruit, cracked sidewalks, shouting vendors, and roasting meat were oddly familiar; I realized that my brain was processing this isolated, foreign city as some hitherto unknown Little Burma or Rangoon Street, perhaps located somewhere south of Little Italy or behind a Lower East Side project that had discouraged prior exploration. It was something beyond the fact that Rangoon's journey toward socialism looked similar to New York's journey toward insolvency;

---

[31] One might, for example, want an additional blanket. Or, admittedly, one might occasionally pretend to want an additional blanket.

it was as if New York had overwhelmed my receptors to such an extent that they had muscled up, and could now process endless amounts of fresh urban stimuli, automatically breaking it down and categorizing atop the familiar cues provided by the basics: concrete, car exhaust, restaurants, men in skirts.

My performance was the next evening. I ordered a case of Myanmar beer and a case of Mandalay strong beer and sequestered myself in the dormitory. I drank beer on the balcony above dense green leaves. The campus buildings were old, comfortable.

Unlike the stress that preceded my first performance, I felt a deep stability and contentment, even after controlling for the seventeen beer stations I had visited throughout the day. Nearly a decade had passed since the stormy, ripping creative process gave birth to my quartets. The debut followed shortly thereafter, and the remnants of communing with the muse added fire and distress to that first explosive performance. I was younger then, energized by a budding composer's hunger for renown and by loins firing on all eight cylinders.

Now, the combination of Burmese Socialist decorum and my accrued wisdom lent my approach studied reserve and quiet confidence. Most importantly, the Burmese had immediately recognized the value and unprecedented reach of my Cycle; although this was not the global recognition I deserved, the quality of their recognition made up for its provinciality. These were sophisticated listeners that would not settle for commercial drivel or reconstituted platitudes. I began to realize that my youthful expectation of mass recognition had, perhaps, been naïve; in addition to the world not being ready for such an immense leap forward, the majority of listeners simply did not have palates unique or independent enough to appreciate my works. No, I would have to allow recognition to come at its own pace as my masterpieces steadily insinuated themselves into musical culture writ large.

The next day, my attitude was reflected in my preparations. I was amicable when my hosts suggested amplification. I set up the sewing machines myself, and accepted only symbolic assistance with raising the shower curtain. I chose to conduct the piece dressed in a simple green shirt and traditional Burmese skirt. Initially this conservatism was a concession to Socialist ethics, but upon donning the clothing and setting about my work, I realized a new reflective depth was afoot that would surely complement the performance.

The hall seated One Thousand. It was filled to capacity. The house went dark. A single spotlight fell on the shower curtain. I fired up the 562. The 703. The 919. Its case. I was surprised by an intense trilling in my scrotum and waves of hot needles coursing up and down my increasingly erect phallus. I had not expected such a resplendent rejuvenation. Thus primed, I leapt onto the machines. *Unsuccessfully Muffled Whimper*, amplified to disproportionate levels, blasted forth. I was immediately, irrevocably in love with the powerful wall of sound: Damone Ramone had gone electric. The Arcs shuddered, the Neptune Avenue Station quaked, and a white laser beam shot from the black clouds to illuminate Vyšehrad because...Damone Ramone...had finally arrived.

When it was done, the audience exploded into an echoing delirium of screams and whistles over never-ending monsoon thunder. They pounded the floor and beat the seats. The women sounded like they were all simultaneously delivering babies with immense heads, and the men sounded like a revolutionary army that had just overthrown a Ten Thousand Year tyranny. A student ran across the stage and pulled back the shower curtain. When I saw the howling, rapturous faces I laughed and wept. I weakly raised one arm, but immediately dropped it again.

The applause continued for ten minutes. It all stopped at the exact same moment. The house lights went on. They filed out front row to back row as if they were graduates at the end of the ceremony. I stood on stage and continued to cry. The same student that had shown me Rangoon took my arm. He led me backstage. Beers in a tub of ice awaited me. I opened two and poured them down my throat simultaneously, much to my chaperone's delight. I repeated the procedure as needed.

My chaperone brought me tea in the morning. I offered him a beer—he declined—and asked him to sit for a moment. I told him I wanted to meet the audience in order to commune with the people and listen to their critiques so that I might formulate a self-criticism based on socialist tenets. He told me it would not be possible to meet the audience because they did not coordinate who would attend—the crowd was a random group of Rangooners. He also said that I would not be expected to deliver a self-criticism—to ask this of a guest would be disrespectful. He told me that relative to the Burmese Way, I had done my duty.

This pleased me, but I nonetheless wanted feedback grounded in the social experiment, so I asked him:

"But how about you? What did you, as a music student, think of the performance?"

"But I am not a musical student, I study industrial chemistry."

"But you're a musician?"

"I am a great lover of music and your music is wonderful, so now we can discuss what is next."

"How about someone from the music department? Perhaps I could speak to the director?"

"The department is still very small, so it is overseen by the Burma Studies Department. Don't worry. Your performance was loved. Word has travelled and others wish to meet you in the north. This is important for you and for Burma. Please, we will relax in Rangoon and you will fly tonight to the Shan State."

"The Shan State? But isn't it under separatist control?"

"Beware of the half-truth. You may have acquired the wrong half. You're running out of beer. Come, we'll take care of it."

I drank, I visited Shwedagon again—forget about it—and I drank more. What a joke, I thought, those shoddy orgone jerk-booths of Reich's, veritable outhouses next to even a postcard of Shwedagon. Anyhow, Shwedagon is outside the scope of this book to the tune of a million pages.

When it was time to depart Rangoon, my original chaperone—Ko—was accompanied by a second young man—Shin. He was heavier and wore glasses. When we boarded the small plane, Shin sat next to me. We flew over green hills. Shin accepted a cold Mandalay.

"So," he said, "Ko said you're interested in reaction to your music and wish to speak to someone musical."

"Yes. Are you a music student?"

"Yes."

"What do you play?"

"Viola."

"How many years?"

"Eight."

"And you have seen reviews of my performance?"

"Yes, but understand that reviews here exist on the formal and informal level. The formal represents the state—how your music advances Burmese Socialist Realist ideas. The informal is the opinion of the *man in the street*, as you say in America. Officially, your symphony—"

"It's a Quartet Cycle."

"Of course. The official interpretation of your quartets was positive. The music was seen to represent the toiling masses of the world's sweatshops, and although the textile workers are exploited today, the thunder of your piece indicates the collective power of the proletariat and its inevitable triumph over the bourgeoisie. There was, apparently, a moment of doubt because the crowd was cheering so loudly. At this point you lifted your arm, and two very important state critics viewed this as a possible expression of cynical individualism. However, the crowd was questioned, and the fact that they had not been handpicked by your supporters cleared you of the charge."

"Great."

"Yes. So the official reviews will be positive. Expect them in a few days. Now, the complexities between the state and the masses are sometimes difficult. In this case, the informal reception is a secret as we fly high in the sky, do you understand?"

"You don't want me to tell anyone."

"Right. The crowd interpreted your piece as a statement in honor of the student protests of 1974 when a dignified funeral for U Thant was demanded. The audience cheered loudly because they perceived a hidden dissident message of support in your mockery of prescribed Socialist Realist structure. Whether it was there or not, only you know. In sum, your work was positively interpreted in two completely different ways by the public and by the official critics. This is unprecedented in history."

"Can you imagine? I suppose it's a triumph. Yes, I suppose it is."

"Of course it is. A *win-win*, I believe."

I continued reading about Anawratha, the 11th Century Emperor that fathered the Burmese nation by sticking together various local kingdoms he conquered. As far as concocting pretexts to invade, the Soviets and the Americans could learn from Anawratha—he kept it simple: he invaded and subjugated the Thaton Kingdom, but he told the Thaton king he was just dropping by to borrow a book. He invaded the Nanzhao Kingdom on the pretense that he had lost a tooth somewhere around there.

We landed in a remote airport surrounded by jungle. There was one runway and some other small planes. We had a quick beer in the terminal and then we piled into a jeep.

"Where are we going?" I asked.

"A nearby village where the governor wishes to meet you. His soldiers will be made happy meeting an American. As you know, we don't get many visitors here lately."

We bumped and jerked along the dirt road, over hills, through jungle. Brown mountains rose over plains. The driver shouted and the others laughed.

"What'd he say?" I asked.

"He say, 'Welcome to Thailand!'"

"*Thailand?*"

"Our chief lives there temporarily while they repair his house on the Burma side. It's quite common in the country for these borders not to matter."

I wasn't so sure. But the countryside was stunning, I was riding in a jeep, and I was drunk.

Forty minutes later we entered poppy fields. Workers stood in the hot sun scraping away at blossoms. Granting my family had dealt with the item further down the production chain, I was familiar enough with the process to know where we were—the Golden Triangle. For the Ramone family, it was the equivalent of the oil-filled swamp behind the Clampett's shack in the *Beverly*

Hillbillies. But these days, the Ramones were walking the straight and narrow as respectable ethics-free musicians. Meanwhile I had to contort my original musical intent to adhere to arcane East Asian Socialist-Realist strictures just to get short-term housing in Burma. At the same time my brothers were busy contorting my original musical intent to make millions and millions of dollars. The irony did not escape me.

The jeep stopped at a checkpoint. Soldiers pointed their rifles until they recognized the driver. They smiled and waved us through. The oldest one couldn't have been more than fifteen.

We entered a rustic dream-camp for similar boy soldiers: wooden houses, log fences, wooden rifle depositories. Everything had a rough-hewn, homemade quality like everyone in the camp had excelled in survivalism and wood shop.

We stopped in front of a large clubhouse. A group of men smiled and waved. One went inside. He re-emerged with another man, a tall lean man in the same drab green uniform as everyone else. He walked to the jeep. He nodded to the others and then he put his hand out to me.

"Welcome. I am General Khun Sa. Please, call me Khun Sa. Come and rest."

I followed him into the clubhouse. We sat at a long table. A soldier brought us cold mugs of beer. Khun Sa lit a cigarette.

"Are you enjoying your trip to Burma?"

"Very much. But aren't we in Thailand? And I think I've read some articles about you."

"You know who I am, but I did not invite you here to talk of these things. I wanted to congratulate you on your musical success in Rangoon."

"Thank you very much, sir. But I don't understand, I thought you were not on friendly terms with the regime in Rangoon."

"Things often appear one way while they operate a different way. Burma, Thailand, they both protest in the papers, with their diplomats to America, but we actually get along quite well. I've been in charge of the Shan State and the business since 1974, and—"

"A lot of peoples' careers really took off in '74."

"How do you mean?"

"My brothers started a rock band that year, but it's no matter."

"Mr. Ramone—you said it, it must matter to you. Anyhow, let's not play cat and mouse—I know your family, your father personally. I met your brother Johnny once. How is your father?"

"I don't know where he is."

"Do you have any ideas? But let's not talk of this. How did the sewing machines I sent to Rangoon work? Were they the correct machines?"

"They were perfect."

"Have you played this music for your family...for Johnny, for example?"

"Once."

"Good. How is Johnny, by the way? Is he happy in this rock and roll group?"

"If it's steady work, he's happy. I don't talk to him either."

"I'm sorry. A family must stick together. I will tell you, I also attempted to speak to him and he refused quite adamantly. So do you have any ideas where your father might be?"

"No. Sorry."

"Damone, let's speak freely. Right now, the American DEA estimates I provide 80% of New York's heroin. Not true. I provide perhaps 60%. When I was one among many in the Shan State, I still provided nearly 50%. Until 1972. When your father was still working. If he was still working, I'd control over 90%."

"Okay."

"So you don't know where he went? And what are you doing these days? And your sister and the rest of your brothers?"

"Not interested."

"But Damone, this is how you can have the time and resources to work on your musical compositions—creativity is possible only when the stomach is full. You will have no worries about money, a steady revenue source that will be very impressive. You surely know all the routes, the methods, the connections in the city..."

"I don't. Montez, Johnny, Danny Fields—they were in charge."

"You won't deceive me with false humility, Damone. Surely you can help me."

"Sorry, but I can't. And trust me, I could use the money. But they kept us in the dark. And Johnny's finished with that, he's in that band and they're doing better and better."

"I heard it. It's horrible."

"Everyone's entitled to their opinion."

"Damone, I entreat you, think on it: *Even as mind changes with the change in matter, so matter changes with the change in mind.*"

"With all due respect, General: *change in matter sometimes precedes that in mind; change in mind sometimes precedes that in matter.*"

"*Changes in mind and in matter are interdependent and reciprocal.*"

"Sorry, but I said no. But if you tell me where the beer is, I'll grab two."

Khun Sa kept trying. The beer flowed day and night. He sent girls to my cabin so that I might *wane and lessen* some of my *unwholesome volitions*, but I don't think my hosts accounted for the abyss between Burmese Socialism's "unwholesome" and Damone Ramones's: the girls ran from the cabin screaming as soon as they opened the door.

One morning Khun Sa summoned me to the clubhouse. He spoke one last time about reciprocity, and reminded me that *for good works good people are needed*. I responded by reminding him that *in the process of change in man, however, mental flux far outstrips the material. The flight and flux of mind are faster than light which travels at 186,000 miles per second.* Neither of us knew what that meant, which effectively put an end to his entreaties. A few days later I was transferring to a New York-bound plane at Narita. Burma was lost forever.

Back at Uncle Dave's, they were elated to see me. And I them. They had droves of dreary news regarding my brothers: they had starred in a Hollywood movie called *Rock 'n' Roll High School*. They had finished a new album, not yet released. They had released a live album overseas earlier in the year, a recording of the fateful London New Year's Eve show, my definitive final attempt to rebalance the universe. "You didn't know that?" they asked. No. I'd been gone a long, long time.

It was good to be back. Dave let me close out the '70s in his apartment, merciful and more than a little impressed regarding Burma. The autographed[32] photo of Khun Sa didn't hurt.

Still, I was left with what was left. I had to reformulate my relationship with this particular reality if I hoped to enjoy the escapist delights of others. I recalled Khun Sa's attempts to console me regarding my brothers by again referring to *The System of Correlation of Man and His Environment*, reminding me that *names are forgotten as fast as all things fade*; that all songs become obsolete the moment they are written; that founders of religions and ideologies, generals, kings, scientists, and rock and roll bands called the Ramones all must obey the universal law of transience; that when they die, an echo will remain of their existence, but in Ten Thousand Years the echo will weaken, and in One Hundred Thousand Years it will die completely; and what an insignificant fraction of time One Hundred Thousand Years is! And that after all, all of these are relative truths.

Relative truths indeed. My brothers played in front of nearly 50,000 people that year at the Canadian World Music Festival. They had "opened" for a world they had already swept into the dustbin of history: Aerosmith, Ted Nugent, Johnny Winter, Nazareth. But the mob of followers, of finger-pointing dolts, conformists, cowards—were unaware of their own myopia and irrelevance; when confronted with the end of sound, the tone of life and the space-time continuum, the end of correlation—they rejected the exposure. They threw bottles, cans, sandwiches. They booed, hissed. Johnny took off his guitar and walked to the front of the stage.

In the photograph he is wearing a yellow cut-off t-shirt. Both hands raised, middle fingers up, flipping off the 50,000-strong audience. This was Beethoven scratching out Napoleon's name from the *Eroica* dedication, Velikovsky standing alone against armies of "scholarly" detractors, this was Karl Richter's message to cowardly conformists that people make rules because they have no

---

[32] "My Dear Friend Uncle Dave, Weed is for pussies, comrade! Step up your game, lightweight! All the best, Kuhn Sa"—it was not entirely uncoached.

lives. As for the Ramones, people are entitled to their own opinion, but they're also entitled to their own facts, and in the case of my brothers, their echo would never fade or die, however I might wish it were otherwise. Vikings torch a ship. It burns on a dark sea.

☙

Part VIII.

THE LOST DECADES.

CHAPTER XXXVIII.

THE EIGHTIES.

This was the decade where bitterness set in. Perhaps some of you thought it was a decade that might grant me some malicious satisfaction thanks to the trials and tribulations of my brothers. There was some of that. But the two purgatorial years[33] were gone, replaced with a fat, sweaty 8. That overrode everything. Menace became plastic, blood became dots on a screen. The latest crop of imbeciles jumped up and down in front of the camera. The old guard did exercises on television. It all got flushed through. It might have been overwhelming, but there was the never-ending orgy of me to fight it off. My bitterness was diversifying: my brothers continued to do their bit, but they occupied an ever-lessening number of seats in my misery's parliament. I became increasingly obsessed with isolation, with hiding from the sterilized future that 1980 inaugurated.

My brothers also suspected that the new era did not bode well. They released *The End of the Century* LP in February. Therein they wrongly projected their sense of finality onto a past era: the early days of rock and roll up to and including the early Seventies. They sense something is wrong and something must be done, and they

---

[33] Mr. Ramone is referring to 1978 and 1979. 1977 was a year of transition—the old world died, the new began.

seem genuinely unaware that I already did it, they already stole it, and the final message was codified in their first four albums. They did away with "cerebral" rock, one of the more absurd Trojan horses of the idiocracy. Now it was a fallow period for the bigger world to stew in their own regurgitation until someone "heard" the Ramones as if for the first time. This would ultimately translate into a legacy, but a future legacy did nothing for my brothers in 1980.

The most important aspect of the album was not the hollow attempt to spice things up with slick production and diverse instrumentation—the most important aspect was the desperate scraping and pounding beneath the glitz, their futile attempts to maintain the basics that they had built their identities on: *Chicks With Dicks Sleep Late*. Left to their own devices, they could not even come close to replicating something that, on paper, should have been within the talents of virtually anyone. The fact that they were the ostensible inventors of this sound, yet could no longer produce it themselves was beyond their comprehension. Their sins had come home to roost: there were fast drums, thrashing guitars, blurted lyrics—but of my quartets, there was not a trace.

At the time, Pink Floyd's[34] *The Wall* was immensely popular, and I found comfort in the weirdly analogous situation: Pink Floyd was so persistently under the sway of their ostracized crazy master that they slavishly built their careers on his identity. The homage of *Shine On Crazy Diamond* simply wasn't enough to put a stake through the telltale heart. That terrible *Wall* film even went so far as to hire an actor to portray a rock star who was pretending to be someone else by aping the original person's madness and musical genius. In many respects, the clunky, ridiculous theatre piece that was Pink Floyd post Syd Barrett was the story of the miserable, pastel *End of the Century*. The expensive, embarrassing *Century* was lurking in the shadows when my brothers recorded their homage to me later that decade: *I Lost My Mind*. The obsessive focus, the liquor, the madness—it's all there. But the genius isn't.

---

[34] That's right, no "Pinchas" anymore. I started paying attention to the whole pathetic lot of them.

So I let it go—a quick flush of Nicaragua, Iran, of greed being good, and a few moronic films. The only thing keeping the beat was the U.S.S.R. with its nuclear tests at Semipalatinsk. If it wasn't for the mushroom cloud metronome, the decade would have derailed into another dimension. Women's hairstyles alone were enough to make the whole fucker shake. No, the Decade of the Airbrush did not impress me.

Lady left me. I woke up among the dunes and she was gone. Uncle Dave suggested that she had run off with a musician named Dennis DeYoung from a rock group called Styx, and even worse, he implied that their affair had been going on since before I even met Lady. On the other hand, the death of passion and hope creates excellent coping mechanisms. The decade was a green, reedy swamp baking under constant sun. One can sit very still. One simply allows it and waits.

In September 1987, General Ne Win issued a new currency in Burma with denominations divisible only by 9. I would have had to keep my money in a separate hotel room booked solely for it. Then it was the 8888 rioters and the Butcher of Rangoon. All dreams eventually relax if you move slowly enough. There'd be no selling out now.

For a few years it was the old routine: booze, shelter, beach, booze. Comfortable stays in the Brooklyn Public Library, Brighton Beach Branch depended on chance, so their blissful punctuation could not be relied upon as a true quality-of-life indicator.

It might have been a wrap had not an incident at the Library shoved me down into an even deeper layer, a place so miserable that it preserved me like a herring in brine—salvation via paralysis. It began with Peter claiming he'd seen a movie that was nearly my biography. He said it was a made for television film however, and he could not predict when it would be shown next, so I had no choice but to sit through any number of vapid episodes.

The Life of Gomez Addams was so long that it had to be cut up into parts. Peter and I watched it in one-hour increments in the library's AV room. Most segments contained only allusions to Addam's life, insinuated by a white ship. No actor appeared portraying Addams. There were also anachronisms; for example, it was hard to sustain suspension of disbelief when the relationship between the imperialist Captain Stubing and his slave Izak plays out on a motorized ship. That's a pity, because the actors explored the ironies, role-reversals, and plain old interesting moments in a close master-slave relationship. They did a great job illustrating how the human urge toward justice is perverted by a culturally imposed aberration. Their portrayal is undercut however by their ship being motorized rather than wind powered.

Ten weeks later, Addams appeared. The segment rendered one of the darkest periods of Addam's life when a promising isolation collapsed into madness. Addams had voluntarily marooned himself on an island just as I had. An actor named John Astin portrayed Addams brilliantly. Astin bore an uncanny resemblance to Addams as he appears in countless portraits. It was almost as if he was Addam's twin, somehow leaping into the future via a loophole in time. It was even possible that Addams was portraying himself.

In this segment, Addam's ongoing isolation causes a personality disorder. He believes he is a man named Dave Crothers. In this persona, he is violent, hirsute, and sexually supercharged. He inverts my role as the pursued rat by becoming a dictator. When some tourists are washed ashore on his island, he imprisons them. In the end however, he turns out to be a broken man full of salvageable passions. Of course.

That was it for me. When the episode ended, I left the library without saying goodbye—it was time to fade away. Seeing as it was the International Decade of Water and Sanitation, I thought how better to achieve alignment than to put sewage in its proper place. Of course Ruffle Bar was out of the question, not because of my original vow to return only as a victor, but because of the other things—the slow roll of the great big nothing.

And so began a cat-and-mouse game between me and the old man. I assumed, since the place was called The Arthur Kill Ship Graveyard, that the bitter old fool who chased me was said Arthur Kill. He wasn't, but let's call him that for the purpose of this. It was amazing to me how easily Mr. Kill caught the photographers, kayaking fucknuts, and the so-called "urban explorers." Granting my advantages as a survivalist and man of the sea, it was nonetheless comical to watch fit young people being captured and terrorized by the elderly Mr. Kill.

I did not have this issue. I lived in a rusted wreck that looked like something Louis Armstrong might have performed on while meandering down the Mississippi. I lived in the bow of a freighter. I lived on the madly tilted bridge of a coast guard boat. The world was auburn, nocturnal, wet. And thus it passed.

CHAPTER XXXIX.

THE NINETIES.

The lost decades weren't entirely unproductive. The Eighties served as an incubator for the monsters that finally started to hatch in the Nineties like Nirvana and The Offspring. By contrast, the Eighties and Nineties were brutal for my brothers. I'd occasionally check up on their non-progress by inquiring here and there in the city. I no longer visited Uncle Dave or Peter. I avoided Brighton Beach and Coney Island. I got my information from the record store on the Lower East Side. New faces, same stories.

The Ramones' lack of critical and financial success, their failure to achieve mass recognition, should have brought me some satisfaction. It didn't. I began to wonder if my crusade against them had been a byproduct of lack of purpose, and that once their failure seemed assured, I was robbed of my mission. I wondered about the veracity of my original, driving feelings: was my rancor the result of an asexual copulation? Had they not stolen my work, would I have simply conjured up some other crusade in order to flash off my prodigious hostility? Or were these mellow reflections merely temporary, false reassessments only made possible by the remission of my brothers' careers?

Right, it was the last thing I said. The beer commercial cleared that up real quick. I stood in an appliance store watching it blast from a wall of television sets. On the one hand, to have my quartets used to propagate crass commercialism was so paradoxical that its sheer insanity neutralized its emotional impact. On the other hand, to have my quartets marching in lock-step with beer's grand march could only be flattering, not to mention practical: every convert to beer brought more opportunities for the grab-and-dash, a critical component of my consumption economy.

But money overrode the ideological concerns: my brothers had cashed another gigantic check that should have been written to me. Ah, you say, this was surely the time to get a lawyer, when a tangible crime offered the greatest tangible reward to an attorney working on a percentage basis. But lest we forget, legalities exist between Rockefellers and Rothschilds, not between me and...well, anyone.

The beer commercial was the sign everybody had been waiting for: a thousand golden trumpets simultaneously getting blown. The unwashed masses finally received permission to imitate my brothers because they had been welcomed into the club of respectability. The Ramones had finally been sanitized by the powers that be, and the mob stormed into the shop and grabbed whatever. Scowl, get tattoos, ordain yourselves "outsiders." You threaten nobody, you stand apart from nothing, you impress no one. How are we supposed to appreciate our insignificance in the universe when you're here?

There were exceptions. Detroit produced John Brannon for example, and in addition to Peter who can be truly annoying but was grandfathered in, Mr. Brannon is always welcome to drink beer with me on Ruffle Bar, should I return. Mr. Brannon exudes true rage, he has ethics, he doesn't do it to get chicks. I even saw him once in the 14th Dimension selling multiple-blade shaving razors in the subway. There were others from that first wave that weren't the worst: Black Flag, Minor Threat, Misfits. At least they meant it.

But who could have foreseen yet another wave, a Nineties wave so terrible that if a lawyer promised I could get 100% of their royalties, I'd walk from the deal rather than admit my authorship. That's Green Day, So So Blows, The Strokes. I hereby propose a new name for Green Day: *The Faggots that Can't Shove Enough Dog Dicks Into Their Asses and Mouths Simultaneously.* In Green Day's case, I'd even support Milo Auckerman receiving a check and splitting it with me, and how absurd is that?

Part IX.

TERMINUS.

CHAPTER XL.

THE TWENTY FIRST CENTURY.

What was the author doing right before he sat down to write the final chapter? Wondering what your little entertainer, your knave, your house-fool, was getting up to? I was at the patent office where I was laughed out the door along with my Tail-Sinker blueprints. The reason given? None given. Did you forget it was Damone Ramone that darkened their door?

Yet again I stand among the ostracized Gods. But do I even fit *there?* Russia: the Great Spirtual East. I'll change my name to Voroshilov or Vinogradov. Russians making bold statements whose family names start with V are my kindred souls. Fay gunning for Volkov, Sagan gunning for Velikovsky. Velikovsky's condemnation revealed the astounding power of collective small thinkers, unable to even postulate in a completely theoretical way beyond the provincial confines of this realm. Those panicked little worms even went so far as to publish an entire series of leather bound tomes overflowing with footnoted gravitas with the exclusive purpose of undermining Velikovsky, whose supposedly laughable theories were so monumentally laughable that while they were all laughing and slapping their thighs, they were also organizing international consortiums and raising millions of dollars to smash him. The greatest dictatorship among humankind is and always will be the dictatorship of the mutually congratulating mediocre.

Velikovsky was so far ahead of all of them. For example, that utter joke Carl Sagan who is to science what the lowest pop vermin is to music writ large, a veritable John Waite attempting to ridicule and malign Beethoven, but somehow justified in Waite's mind by making some tepid and politically contemporary remarks about how those that attempted to repress Beethoven's works were wrong, that even though they were utterly troglodytic and his scores weren't even suitable for use as a food-substitute for dung beetles, that nonetheless, Beethoven shouldn't have been denied the right to note down his absurd etchings, and subsequent charlatans or adolescent morons going through a "rebellious phase" shouldn't be denied the right to "perform" such laugh-fests as, say, his Opus 131, for of course any *sane* human realizes that music simply did not exist prior to Mr. Waite's 1984 release *No Brakes*. No, everything that went before was mere chicanery, not even suitable for the carnival sideshow; the collected works of Mozart for instance were no different than other jokes like Johann Joachim Becher or Hanns Hörbiger. Ha! What fools they all were!

Well, you will reap what you sow when you "lose your battle against," and you suddenly find yourself treading anti-matter in a galactic-scale electrical discharge current racing along toward who knows what. You sure don't know, as you flail about hoping to see someone in uniform that might give you some directions. Don't come to me then Mr. Sagan, and don't try to contact Hörbiger, Velikovsky, Volkov or Becher either. See you on the other side of the event horizon, asshole. You and your pathetic calculations that verified the "impossible" nature of an actual genius's average Wednesday. To quote Mr. Hörbiger, "Calculation can only lead you astray," and embellish that brilliant statement by adding that regarding you, Mr. Sagan, at least if you were being lead astray you'd be going *somewhere*. The blind leading the blind, the sheep leading the sheep. My family never had a chance.

Phlogiston does not exist? It was thought, therefore it exists. Sugar from outer space does not exist? It is the source of life. You think those things might not be possible, or for that matter, that *anything* is impossible? If Green Day can live with themselves, than what isn't possible? What boundaries can possibly constrain us?

No boundaries constrain us. Consequently when I heard that my brother Joey had "died" I didn't concern myself. As a Ramone, I had always known that *Too Tough To Die* had not been a hubristic proclamation, but the reiteration of a simple fact. I instantly knew his death had been staged. It was simply the first salvo in yet another brilliant twist in their devious plan. I continued minding my own business until a seemingly fortuitous chain of events led to a shower in the spring of 2002 followed swiftly by participation in St. Patrick's Day festivities that, relative to the mean, appeared to be those of an average man.

The next day however I was not feeling such the average man. I used the remainder of my windfall—1200 bucks I found bound with blue rubber bands in the Queens Aqueduct parking lot—to slouch in a bar gingerly sipping vodka and sodas. The windfall's remainder, by the way, consisted of roughly 120 dollars. I hadn't the faintest idea what the rest had gone toward, although I admit taking a room at the Waldorf Astoria to get cleaned up in might not have been the most judicious first move after finding the money.

And that's how I came to witness my brothers being inducted into the Rock and Roll Hall of Fame. I had just achieved a respectable altitude and was chewing a refreshing lemon rind when the bartender shut off the jukebox and turned up the TV. There was the stage, there were my brothers, the speeches, the golden shiny thing they hand out. There was me in the bar surrounded by the enraptured patrons—the Ramones family was undoubtedly the true voice of New York. I couldn't help but preen a bit as I ordered another drink and temporarily melted into the apple-pie scent of their collective adulation.

No sign of Danny Fields, although he was mentioned. His absence shattered the ice covering my subconscious—I watched his evolving images in my mind in the manner of one flipping the pages of an animated cartoon book of yore. I thought about how the original Danny Fields—laconic, physically powerful, indelibly working class—was nothing but a pastiche of illusions that Fields had been controlling all along. His absurdly keen intelligence had always been on display; why had I so readily accepted the Fields of monster trucks, NASCAR, sleeveless sweatshirts, anchor tattoos, and screeching boatswain whistles? Throughout the years, many were the "friends" keen to show me the latest Ramones propaganda piece. There was the other false Fields: hair long, eyes ablaze. Fields the scene maker: sunglasses, sport coat, subtle grin. And what of these relations with supermodels, members of the Beatles, Ramona's beloved Jim Morrison, Andy Warhol, David Bowie? I knew he was the author of the seemingly endless false biographies that covered up my brothers' treachery, this supposed Feinberg born in 1941. I imagine all his "rock and roll manager" personas were chosen with great hilarity all around. *Our* Danny once painted the entire interior of his singlewide black, including the windows and bathroom fittings, because his wife had been relentlessly bitching at him to paint the house while she wallowed in a booze stupor. *Their* Danny roomed with Edie Sedgwick and stopped supermodel Ivy Nicholson from jumping out a window in Andy Warhol's factory. Who was he really?

I knew that what appeared to be a comedic romp to my brothers concealed Danny's true power: he traveled the Arcs. And not the shoddy Arcs emanating from New York alleys that offered cut-rate trips to Budapest aboard the galactic equivalent of a Bombay train, but the glistening blue and white Arcs that led directly to Prague. I realized that the whole mess of fragmented mirror spinning around in a glass barrel over a spotlight was some type of cosmic duping at Field's hands. I was blinded by the dazzle, but I couldn't turn away. But, rather than figure it out, I smiled at his cunning—nobody loves being sold more than a salesman.

I was rudely snapped from my Fields reverie a few seconds later. I suffered a major retreat in character evolution thanks to that little fucker Tommy, him and his *We Were Truly Brothers*. The rebirth of my rage offers no metaphor. My decision to write this tome occurred at that moment, and for one second I thought the idea had been lowered into my mind by God's benevolent hand, so spontaneous and clear was it.

Not even two months later, Dee Dee yanked the ripcord. The irony they imbued in that particular "death" was so refined that my respect for it substantially reduced my ardor. I began to wonder if the most concentrated rage I'd ever experienced was in fact temporal, the brief flash of a magician's kerchief preceding the rabbit's miraculous disappearance, the final manic elation of a man on the verge of tripping the light fantastic. An overdose? *Dee Dee?* Please.

I attended the inauguration of Joey Ramone Place. So this was it—now they had their very own Karl Marx Strasse. When I listened to some member of the Talking Heads giving his speech, it was a precise laundry list of my soul's constituent parts: my outsider status, my art's roots in violent "self exploration," my forced marginalization, my war against bourgeois hypocrisy embodied by my music and my life. Through the allegory of beautiful Joey, they celebrated the fact that I didn't *live* my life; I *fought* it, fought it against the hostility of virtually everyone on Earth excepting Peter and a few nameless saints in the shelter system that passed around smokes or a pint. I wish I could quote it verbatim, but of course that would result in more players leaping atop the litigation scrum that I currently reside beneath. Suffice it to say they spoke of him not only as a genius, but as an urban pioneer that civilized the Lower East Side with art and persistence, thereby paving the way for the high rises, restaurants, and low crime rates of the mysteriously expanding East Village.

As I looked at the assembled cast—a few of my actual brothers, some of the actors that played members of my "family," the hoard of script writers and photographers that had worked so hard to fabricate the Ramones history—I realized I had no claim, that I had been ground into the dust of history by the jackboot of victory, that I had about as much validity as some schizophrenic member of The Archies running around and around Vienna's Ringstrasse demanding compensation from Mozart for stealing the *Jupiter* Symphony.

The flood of faces waiting for the sign to be unveiled: the decrepit, the weird, the ugly. The kids that grew up being told they'd never amount to anything. I road that flood of faces backwards through time, from 2nd Street across the Burmese countryside, the streets of Rangoon, the Rainbow Theatre's Cathedral of Ice—what of the kid that spat at me and held me tight? The castaways that hung around the wicked city paying a couple bucks to give my family a chance while the symmetrical moneyed ran to their Oyster Bays and Babylons?

They had destroyed our family home only to build a far bigger house that welcomed everybody. When Marky raised his fist and led the crowd in the most famous of my brothers' chants, I raised my fist and contributed to the collective homage. Grudges and revenge—these are the most deplorable of earthly vanities. Seven bottles of Lambrusco served only to lubricate an inevitable realization. To Joey the composer I take off my hat; to Joey the man I put it back on again. I'll bequeath him that qualified nod. Let's not lose sight of it: they *did* face-fuck my life, however noble the wake.

I went to see *End of the Century*. The film is a masterpiece in its pitch-perfect amalgamation of falsehoods overlaid with a gauze of impressionistic truth. Although the film was the final codification of the Ramones fairytale, they allowed some wildflowers of truth to burst from an otherwise perfectly tended lawn. Knowing the impossibility of constantly surveilling and censoring their own personalities ad infinitum, they allowed them to remain more or less intact. If anything, they seemed mellower—maybe even wiser—than the brothers I had grown up with. Even Johnny seemed to have gained an introspective edge.

Shadows of fact come together in an abstract truth above the film's lies. Like Shostakovich's son Maxim regarding Volkov's *Testimony*, I can vouchsafe that although *End of the Century* portrays lives never led by the Ramones, the film is nonetheless *about* the Ramones deep between the lines. Why did those cocksuckers leave me behind?

Johnny taught Marky about cars—if the band flopped, he could become a mechanic. He taught Dee Dee how to rap long before Eminem emerged from Detroit. He pushed Tommy into sound production. He taught Joey investment banking. Only I had been left out, condemned to carry every brick of our destroyed Fort Tilden home and all the aberrations that had been authored within it. I had no whitewash to pour into my eyes, no bank account, no adoring fans. Nothing.

The best I could say was that by ripping me off and destroying me, the Ramones had given outcasts a tool they could actually use. In that sense, my quartets achieved their collectivist goals via the revolution of the ostracized class by granting them ownership of the means of production: a few chords and some simple rhymes. Although I hated rock and roll, this new emanation swept away the worst of it, and no matter what sort of aural mangling they concocted to throw on top of it, I could still always hear my quartets underpinning those new sounds, even in the songs of third-generation imitators like Rancid.

But despite all the Lambrusco-induced mawkishness above, my brothers are still fuckers, an unrivalled brood of bastards. But that's family, right? And don't forget, they're bullshitting the lot of you to this day.

Hence, in September of 2004 Johnny joined the others, and unbelievably the public actually believed that he too had passed, as if the Ramones had violated a Pharaoh's tomb and a laughably improbable curse was being enacted. But that wasn't all—they heaped it on so thick that their bullshit started to resemble a state-fair ice cream sundae: in a statistically impossible "coincidence," the day Johnny disappeared just happened to be the day the Ramones Museum opened in Berlin. And you bought that too.

A massive statue of Johnny erected in Los Angeles, major streets renamed for Joey, Dee Dee the unchallenged definition of a "punk" and the unofficial face of the entire movement. Tommy was still in New York keeping the beat: tending to their massive "posthumous" success. I presumed the whole ingenious escape hatch had been Johnny's idea: finish the job, punch out, disappear.

They did a beautiful job. The film, the museum, faking their deaths—everything converging at the peak of their careers, thus ensuring their story would be carved onto a mountainside. It also ensured the Ramones machine would continue full-bore for many years to come.

In hindsight you can see their foresight. The messaging was prolific and consistent: risky lifestyles, difficult tours, infighting. The strategically brilliant decision to base their never-ending fights on a false polarity based on shared family traits. Johnny and Joey indeed had their differences. At the core however, Johnny and Joey were basically two sides of the same Ramones coin, variations of the same hardwired obsessiveness. An obsessiveness designed to install order, to solve life's puzzles. Johnny got lucky, because his symptoms were highly productive whereas Joey's were debilitating. Johnny was the madly driven disciplinarian that kept the machine running, and one of his challenges was getting around Joey's implacable rituals. But Joey was just as madly driven as Johnny. He superimposed a romantic sensibility over my quartets, which were the furthest thing from tales of heartbreak and teen yearning. His vision required the anvil and hammer of Johnny to bring it to life, to pound it out and refine it until it was codified and disseminated to millions the world over.

In other words, Johnny was just as compelled to succeed, to keep on working, to be the greatest in the world—as Joey was in the servitude of his compulsions. They *had* to do the things they did. They were both loyal to a fault, but not always to the same things. But at the end of the day, the engine rooms were identical. They are, after all, brothers.

Same the rest: Tommy, the effector of intelligent solutions—a man compelled toward orderly outcomes. Dee Dee, a free spirit and seeming aberration, the imperative connection to the wild muse. Marky the jester, the diffuser of tension, the breaker of ice. Without him, our lives back in Queens would have been far more nasty, brutish, and quite possibly, short.

Impeccable complementarity like that only develops over a lifetime. I suppose it is in this respect that we ultimately got to know inscrutable Montez, the mysterious figure looming behind everything that, technically, is the person truly responsible for creating the Ramones.

So where did they go? It was swiftly becoming irrelevant. I hit the beach. I drank the wine. If I had known back in 1974 the mighty empire I was challenging, I might have done things differently. Or perhaps not at all. At the very least, I should have got Christie Love instead of trying to handle such a monumental task alone, but what good is hindsight? We live once, we live twice, we live infinite times, but the entire cycle is fueled by repeating mistakes. Stop fucking up, and your galactic goose is cooked. Eternal return rests on misery.

Fortunately I was no threat to the global supply. Although giving up my quest cast off a great weight, my overall drive had dwindled to a point where redirecting it into other pursuits was impossible. Anyhow, I was perfectly content to remain stuck in my rut: booze, shelters, plastic bags and panhandling. Switching ruts always seems to cause problems. It wasn't like I was one of the too-far-gone homeless, the ones that never came in from the cold literally or mentally. For instance, I often see a plastic bag mummy on the Upper West Side, a man who appears to have cut black garbage bags into strips which he has adhered around his body and face. So thick are the strips that he resembles the Michelin Man's dark opposite. Imagine how he feels in August. You'd have to ask him, but I can tell you how he smells—I'm a prom night rose by comparison, and trust me, that's saying a lot. I saw a similar situation on the train; this man looked like he had been in a terrible accident that required a body cast, but the accident had occurred twenty years previously and he'd never bothered to remove the cast. It was broken up and covered in filth, and was too big for his body—his head lolled in a disgusting, filthy shell that resembled those devices vicious dogs wear in public. Oversized tattered clothing covered the remainder of the cast—dirty flesh and dirty plaster were visible through a multitude of holes and gaps. And yes, his scent also lent new meaning to *Hot Time Summer in the City*. Those are somewhat amusing examples; I won't spoil your day by sharing any of the truly nightmarish visions.

Lest you think I'm playing the violin for the plight of the homeless, I'm not. I'm not interested in being told what to do and I won't change my lifestyle in any way. In order to attain that condition you can play against incredible odds and try to become the next Dee Dee Ramone or you can take the Damone shortcut and simply walk outside right now and begin a new life. Who's in charge, you or your alarm clock?

Anyhow, the original point was that I'm relatively mainstream homeless, outside my interest in utilitarian physics which for some reason really gets the goat of shelter intake coordinators, so I generally keep it to myself. Outside that, I shower once in a while, and swap out my clothes monthly. I've started going back to the Brooklyn Public Library, Brighton Beach Branch. Although the faces have changed, the culture there is surprisingly intact—for instance, one of my fellow-vagrants opened an impromptu barbershop in the stacks, and he remained in business for four months; he was only closed down when he started attracting non-vagrant customers from the community. Vodka bottles are still hidden behind the books. You can yell all you like and nobody will shush you. You can watch computer pornography all day and nobody bothers you. I composed my *Bildungsroman* there between jerk sessions. And, although I had to meet them all over again, the vagrants still gather around the same old table.

This was precisely the sort of ameliorating inventory that was taking place in my gin-calmed mind one night when I dozed off in a lifeguard's chair. My mangled contentment was nonetheless mine, I had a nearly full gallon of gin, and the waves played their serenade. My napping place was intentional—I was perfectly aware of the fall risk. I had developed a new form of galactic locomotion that I sought to refine, and elevation was a base component. In electromagnetic terms, my new system resembled a Protopopov Death Spiral executed into the murk of the time-space continuum. More accurately, I blended the original Death Spiral with their Life Spiral, Love Spiral, and Cosmic Spiral to create a new Super Death Spiral that combined the x, the y, and the x to create a spiral largely characterized by its speedy downward trajectory right through the ice of the rink, the crust and mantle, the core, and stopping somewhere down there where, technically, one can't sink any lower. Reconciling that place with a dignified concept like "the center of the Earth" was of course difficult, but therein lay the functional paradox. The spiral had an equal and opposite reaction, a shadow spiral that in addition to serving as a spontaneous pseudo-Arc, was also a remarkably beautiful structure, delicate yet powerful.

But most importantly, functional: I was certain that if I could perfect the spiral, I could travel to UY Scuti, which I can assure you is not a star, but a planet that's upper-most atmospheric layer consists of perpetual combustion, thus rendering the *appearance* of a star. Beneath that layer, it's actually a perfectly viable destination, granting hologramic form of course.

It wasn't working out. I kept ending up at VY Canis Majoris which *is* in fact a star, and hologram or no hologram, when you plummet directly into a red hypergiant, it's a little bit worse than being woken by the glare of a policeman's flashlight. Needless to say, I had upped my game and my recent revisions had been assiduous. I was confident it was my night.

It wasn't. I arrived somewhere, but it was not UY Scuti. Furthermore, it was some place that was so fucking huge that no single wormhole could traverse it—it was like boarding a train thinking it was the A, but it turned out to be the C and now you were stuck on the local. Worse yet, you look out the window and see the A racing past on the express track. That's exactly what happened. The spiral allowed me to jump from quasar to quasar, but not across the entire structure.

In relative terms, I'd been fucking around in there jumping quasars for eight Earth hours or so, and from what I could tell I was only halfway across the thing and I wasn't sure if I could backtrack along my circuitous route. I made another jump, but when I entered the wormhole I thought I'd lost my mind because I was not alone. Some beady-eyed bastard was there, and for a moment it was as if we were both sitting inside an invisible bus together, so banalifying was his presence. He kept looking over at me, and bear in mind, this is taking no time and a fucking long time at the same time—so this fucker is basically staring at me for eons and not at all, but my interpretation was erring on the side of eons because of his fuckwit looks. I wasn't sure precisely why he was so annoying—he was one of those people that just was. Then the fucker reached out like he wanted us to hold hands while traversing a wormhole. I'm sorry, but that's just gay—not the sexual orientation kind, not the really happy kind, but the gay of elementary school critiques. Then I veered out of the thing, stopping yet again in some backwater while that fucker raced on and on. I screamed in a tantrum of humiliation and rage which might have been my finest work as far as impotent gestures go— nothing beats giving yourself permission to whine in a cosmic region well outside God's jurisdiction to illuminate one's most outstanding capabilities.

Five hours later nothing had improved. I was definitely lost, and that makes it pretty hard to enjoy the scenic beauty when you're contending with a billion light years of wrong turns. I had just been coughed up into the cosmic equivalent of a West Virginia hollow, a rock on the edge of some galactic backwater ignored by the accretion disc. At least it afforded me a stunning view of an optically violent variable quasar, a cosmic vortex of blues and greens shimmering with bursts of light and sweeps of shadow; a site unrivalled and totally impossible to imagine, although it can be modeled with a penlight, food coloring, a flushing toilet, and a sheet of LSD.

"She sure is something, isn't she?"

I spun around. It was him.

"Who the fuck are you, motherfucker? You following me?" I said.

"Considering your route and mine, wouldn't it be the other way around?"

"Shut up."

"What's your problem? How can you be angry when you're looking at *that*? Isn't it human to want to share that beauty with someone else?"

"Apparently it hasn't occurred to you that a person traveling two billion light years into the middle of an obscure quasar structure might not have done it for networking purposes."

"You lost?"

"Ha! What a laugh! Think I'd be here if I was lost?"

"Maybe not, but you sure have an unusual way of getting around up here. Where are you trying to go? If you tell me where, I can tell you the best route."

"Shut up."

"How you plotting your course? Are you considering the direction of the quasars' jets? And changes in luminosity? It's an orderly system—getting around is simple if you know what you're doing. Are you accounting for feedback? Why aren't you saying anything? Even when you're not making a jump, you can still move at superluminal speeds if you—"

"Oh, that's rich. That's just great. How do you stop?"

"I can stop. Thanks for your concern."

"Bullshit. And never mind the innumerable retrocausal fuck-ups you dump all over the place as you blissfully zoom along with the wind in your hair. Nice. Very considerate of the environment."

"Doesn't happen."

"Don't blame me when the Roman Empire conquers Iowa."

"Who are you to criticize? You aren't even wearing sunglasses. Didn't think bouncing among quasars might expose you to some hyperluminosity?"

"Didn't think sticking quasars up your ass might expose you to fucking yourself?"

"You won't make me mad. Not up here. Trust me, you don't want that."

"Oooooooo, I'm so scared. See me shaking? Nothing scares me like a dwarf in a ruffled shirt. Ooooo, you have a scary tattoo. 'Joseph'? Is that you?"

"I'm warning you."

"Do I appear to be heeding? I hereby declare you an official pindick. Where's the apocalypse? Waiting…still waiting."

"You've been saying shitty things about me for a long time now; I should leave you here."

"Is that so, *Joseph*? Were you "raised differently" *Joseph*?"

"My name's Billy Joe Armstrong! What do you have to say now, *Damone*?"

"How the fuck do you know my name?"

"How do I know your name? Thanks to your in-depth analysis of my life's work. You don't know who I am, do you?"

"Let's not start that again."

"Green Day—that's me. Know me now?"

"Great. Just great. Not only will you show me the way back, but whatever money you have on you? You owe it to me, asshole."

"I don't owe you shit! What do you have to say about the things you said? Still think we should rename the band? *The Faggots that Can't Shove Enough Dog Dicks Into Their Asses and Mouths Simultaneously*, I believe was your suggestion, along with something about if I can live with myself than anything's possible?"

"Yes, that's more or less accurate. Did you think I was going melt in front of you or something? You don't know Damone Ramone—don't measure me against *your* fallibilities, Joe. Speaking of which, how do you know Damone Ramone?"

"Wouldn't you like to know."

"It's simple—you either were reading over my shoulder in the Brighton Beach Library—which I'd surely have noticed, I have a good nose for commoners—or you rifled through my papers via some low-grade skullduggery. You're here, that's all I really need to know. Anyone that can do this can break into a library or jump into a dimension where my book already exists."

"I think you're just mad because we've sold tens of millions of records and nobody even knows you or your fucking quartets exist. What, that's funny to you?"

"Go ahead, continue to play the plebian fool and pretend you don't know full well what I think of your commercial schlock compared to the creations of a defecating dog. At the very least, you've *studied* punk. You understand—theoretically—its tenets. You've studied its true practitioners in order to ape them. You therefore know not only what I profess, but also the solidity of my convictions. You respect me, and wish to earn my approval. You thought you could perhaps do so via polemics and the face-to-face grandeur of your personality. You were mistaken."

"Have you ever just looked at it practically, like a man needs a job and I happened to have landed a great one?"

"My brother Johnny was never lacking for work, but when he got into this music thing at least he had the integrity to base his project on originality and controversy rather than safe, established norms. Not like someone else I know...*Joseph*. No, there's no excuse for the things you've done. You're the Spiro Agnew of rock and roll."

"You're going to have agree to disagree with several hundred million people."

"Breaking out the masses is not going to advance your position; quite the contrary. Surely you know that. You're groping in the darkness now, opening all your holes to any old contrarian position that comes along."

"Okay, let's agree to disagree. Let's shake hands and let it rest. We're in the presence of that quasar after all."

"No. I'm bored with reconciliations and coming to terms with things. Plus you saw I'd had cathartic moments with others in the multiverse, and you thought you'd jump on the bandwagon in keeping with your traditions. And you abused my privacy. Sorry, but in this case I have to draw the line. Your cocksuckerness outweighs your nobility. You're not all bad. I thank you in advance for directing me back to New York: to Billy Joe Armstrong the man I take off my hat; to Billy Joe Armstrong the musician I have to put it back on again."

"All I get's a secondhand quote?"

"I'm allowed to plagiarize myself—can't beat them, join them. Anyway, that's as good as it's going to get. You are absolutely the most awful group that ever existed, but of the endless legions that have copied my work, you are the most fascinating; you are almost a new form of pornography. It's impossible to look away, or to stop pondering the fact that your atrocities have dramatically increased the thread count of your sheets. There's no better evidence of injustice in the universe, to a degree that definitively proves the existence of God, but certainly not the water-to-wine God we pine for. Now good day, sir. I have an event horizon to cross. Which way?"

"I happened to have enjoyed your book, although some parts are a little long-winded. But overall it's good."

"Maybe I'll write you in. Way back to New York?"

"You're a stone's throw from a supermassive black hole that takes in about a thousand planet Earth's worth of matter every minute—that much matter can't be wrong. Dive in, and you're home free."

"Okay, right. Sure. I'll just "dive in" to some random black hole because some plagiarist weirdo told me to. I'll get right on that."

"*You* asked *me*, asshole! What did you think I was going to do, hand you a map? I promise, jump in and you'll come out in a bar in Detroit called the Cadieux Café."

"Thanks for nothing Joseph."

"I'm telling you, it's the best route."

"For you—I don't have the means to get a plane ticket from Detroit to New York, and going overland down there will be a lot harder for me than traveling billions of light years up here. You know that."

"That's on you."

"Give me your wallet."

"What?"

"Give me your wallet! Now!"

"Go fuck yourself, I'm not giving—ow, what the fuck? Are you fucking crazy?"

"Where is it? Stay down, asshole. Hand it over!"

"Ow, my chest! Here, take it!"

"Shut up."

"At least give me back my I.D."

"Here, go fetch."

I threw it toward the shimmering cone of the optically violent variable quasar as if it were a flushing toilet.

My hologram's circuitous route was not mirrored by corporeal Damone resting on his perch over Brighton's black waters; he was essentially a drunken body; the hologram carried 90% of my subjective self. I woke early to screaming gulls and a pink sky. The beach was empty. I vaguely recalled my hologram demolishing a hotel room's mini-bar, masturbating over the escort ads in the yellow pages, enjoying a free continental breakfast, and having some trouble boarding the air train at Howard Beach after my flight from Detroit. It was a fading chimera. Its smoky remnants reintegrated with me around 8AM right before I unscrewed the vodka to ensure a smooth repatriation. The ensuing distortions were increasingly tolerable as they settled into the general decrepitude. They did not, unfortunately, include the remaining cash from Joseph's wallet, which had been substantial.

I let go. Finally cut adrift into freedom of the moment. The salt air, the sun, the sounds of Russian and Spanish. I dispensed with most of my accretion disc. The ocean kept me clean, I had nicked a respectable backpack, and I always managed to cadge a few bucks for booze and a chicken shashlik. I had a new begging method where I'd kneel quietly on the sidewalk on Brighton Avenue with my hands cupped together in front of me. It worked brilliantly, and made me feel like a Byzantine Stylite on a pillar rather than Damone Ramone on a sidewalk. Three elderly chess-playing Russians bought me a Baltika 9 and two shots every Saturday morning at Moscow Bar on the boardwalk. Sticking it all together made for a pretty sweet ride, all things considered, with the alcohol first and foremost assuring permanent residence inside Claude Monet's *Sur les planches de Trouville*.

I was thus ensconced one afternoon when the steady babble of waves, women speaking Russian, and children shouting was cut by a woman getting all-out aghast at some perceived social violation. I kept my eyes shut and stared at the leaping sunworms beneath my lids. She was saying:

"Can you believe it, a man his age? It's revolting. Disgusting! I've never seen anything like it. That children should have to see something like that. Terrible! He should be ashamed, ashamed! He's over fifty! Shame, shame!"

I was wholly committed to not moving a muscle, until:

"Sir. Excuse me, sir..."

Tapping my arm. Great, I thought, here we go again and I don't have the faintest clue what I've authored this time. I opened my eyes. The older woman who had been sunbathing with her husband on the next blanket looked down at me.

"I'm sorry sir, but I want you to see this revolting man. My husband refuses to ask him to leave. Will you? Right over there."

A paunchy, gray-haired man was meandering in small circles, presumably sunbathing in the vertical Russian manner—a normal

sight except for his "bathing suit," which was nothing more than a
tiny red sack that barely covered his organ, a shadow of a codpiece
held fast by red tendrils nestled in the crevasse of his ass in the
Brazilian female style. I laughed.

"Isn't it awful," the woman said; "A man his age. It's revolting.
It's disgusting. If he's not ashamed, someone needs to shame him."

It was Peter.

"Don't worry ma'am, I'll take care of it."

"Thank you, sir. Me and my husband are teachers."

I wasn't sure what that had to do with it. I approached Peter.

"Peter."

"Damone? Wow! I can't believe it's you! How long's it been?"

"I don't know. The Eighties? How long ago was that?"

"A long time, but you look just the same. How you doing? I
heard, I'm really sorry."

"What?"

"About Tommy."

"What happened to him?"

"Oh, Damone. I'm real sorry. You don't know? Maybe that's
why God put us together here for me to be the one that says."

"Let me guess: Tommy "died.""

"I'm sorry, Damone. Just a few weeks ago."

"Tommy's fine. So are the rest of my brothers. None of them
have passed."

"They didn't?"

"No. The entire thing is part of the big act. It's staged."

"Have you talked to any of them?"

"Don't need to. Peter, I can safely say that's all behind me now.
I'm simply not meant to leave this beach. How come I never see
you at the library? I figured you moved away a long time ago."

"Banned for life. Or at least until the Regional Manager gets
transferred. It's not looking good. Damone, are you still on the
streets?"

"Technically. The beach ennobles it somehow, makes me feel
more like a proverbial "beach bum" or ancient mariner. Did you
know that in Hamburg, Germany there is a sect of homeless old

sailors that refuse any sort of help or domestication, beatnik sailors that have been on the streets since the 1950s?"

"No."

"They have long white beards, many are musicians, all are drunks. From Hamburg they've dispersed to other cities, but they are still largely concentrated in Hamburg."

"Damone, I don't like seeing you down and out after all this time."

"Nice bathing suit."

"Thanks, it's new. You can't just give up. I see *your name* on at least twenty shirts a day. I mean, it's *your name*. Even if you can't sue their music, you should get something when they sell *your name*."

"Drop it. I tried everything. Everybody could see me dancing to *White Horse* by Laid Back, but nobody could see me thinking about Witkacy's *Maria Nawrocka* portraits. I'm sure you understand."

"Sure, Damone. But have you really tried *everything*? Can't you go to court? Do that thing the sewing guy in Greenwood did that you told me about?"

"Howe? I can't. Howe had the foresight to patent his invention straight away. I did not. I am definitely the Hunt in this hilarious little example of eternal return. Anyhow, even if I had, there are millions of bands out there mass-producing cheap fabrications of my original concept; how could I chase them all down? Where to start? No, I am definitely the Hunt of the situation—ripped off, forgotten, buried in a pauper's grave within feet of the man who perpetrated the crime, that devious fucker Elias Howe and his gargantuan obelisk. Don't get me wrong, I like the guy, but you have to call a spade a spade."

"You have to do something. It's not fair."

"Peter, let's face facts: rallying and old college tries apparently aren't my forte. We've been through this charade countless times, I even sought redemption in the Far East, and absolutely nothing worked out. For all my efforts I got not one shred of return."

"Damone, I'm not having it. They owe you an explanation. There's more to what happened than just music, a lot more. They betrayed you! They need to explain themselves."

"It's a little hard to take you seriously when you're wearing that scarlet change purse and your ass is bare. Look, everyone is looking at you."

"It works good. Everyone looks."

"But I don't think it's because you're an *Ocean's Eleven* type."

"That's the old type. Now it's *Outsiders* types. Did you see it? It was in the Eighties."

"I was living in the Arthur Kill Ship Graveyard."

"You gotta see it. But I can show you *Outsiders* types all over the Irish Riviera."

"Okay, let's go."

"No way Damone, it's not gonna work. I still know your tricks. Do you know where your brothers are? What about your sister? I bet she knows. If you don't call her, I will. Damone? Are you listening? Are you gonna call her?"

I told him I'd do that and no more. That's how I ended up back on the porch of Ramona's Jersey bungalow. Everything looked identical except the cars. I knocked on the door.

"Hang on a sec. Hang on…" she yelled.

She opened the door.

"Aw, fuck me! What the fuck, man. Look, I got enough fuckin' problems without this."

"Oh, not bad, thanks. You?"

"Spare me Damone, you fuckin' know this ain't a social call. All cleaned up and shit? I can already feel you jerkin' me off. Fuck, man. Look at you, you got the same ants in your pants that Montez'd get when he needed money. Stand fuckin' still or I'll kick you in the balls."

"How's domestic life?"

"Same house, different guy. I got the house, he got the bitch from the dollar store. My kid works in Albuquerque. This new guy's kids is old, so it's cool. He drinks. But he's employed so fuck it. Kinda boring though. You can come in if you want. You smell okay."

"Thanks."

"Over there. I'll make coffee. So don't dick me, Damone. Tell me what the fuck you're doin' here."

"Where are our brothers living now?"

"No."

"But they're all alive and well, right?"

"Of course."

"So where are they? Fuck, Ramona! Haven't I been through enough? Do you know anything about what's happened to me, or do you need a summary? You know what, fuck this. I'm outta here. I don't need you. I'm almost done with a tell-all about this fucking family. You'll see."

"Damone, sit back down, man. You wrote a book? Sit down."

"Thank you. Yes. It explains everything."

"Show me."

"Oh, sure. That's rich. Why don't I give you every draft plus the computerized ones too? Give them all to you, Johnny's obedient servant."

"What'd you just call me?"

"Johnny's obedient servant. Johnny's brown-nosing, frightened little worm of a servant."

"Shut the fuck up!"

"Whatever he commands, you do."

"Bullshit."

"Okay, so where are they? They can't fight their own battles? Anyway, it's over. What am I going to do now?"

"Damone, you print some fuckin' book, Johnny will kick your fuckin' ass. You better think before you do something stupid. He worked real fuckin' hard to cover up a lot of embarrassing personal shit. You don't print that shit, man. Fuckin' wrong. Why don't you run your little plan by him, man? See how that goes over. We'll see who's got no balls around here."

"I'll do precisely that. Where are they? Where did Tommy go?"

"Okay, fine. Tommy moved to Budapest. He's working at...you know that picture he had over his bed, real pretty library?"

"The Library of the Hungarian Academy of Sciences?"

"Yeah, exactly. But don't visit him, asshole. He's still stressin' down. He was fuckin' shitting himself about breaking some law. Whatever. Let him cool the fuck out."

"That's perfect for him. I could see myself working in a place like that."

"Ha! What a laugh. What a fuckin' joke."

"How's that?"

"Instead of "Jerkoff King" or whatever, your nickname shoulda been "Five Page Damone." Seriously man, you've probably read the first five pages of more books than any motherfucker ever."

"Let's move on. Dee Dee?"

"Florida. Owns a bar. Buncha girls run the place. He goes to Puerto Rico all the time. Maybe he's visiting dad."

"Dad? Are you kidding?"

"I don't know. I just got this feelin' he's out there somewhere. Dee Dee won't tell you dick. But he don't mind if you go down there. He's got short grey hair now, nobody down there recognizes him. Old Cubans in his bar, they don't know dick about records."

"Joey?"

"Paris, Amsterdam, Rome. New York on the down-low. Cut his hair short, dyed it red, grew a goatee, it's red too, lost the glasses, dresses only in suits. Unrecognizable. Not one person has recognized Joey Ramone."

"What's he doing?"

"He's into everything. Anti-nuclear shit, banning plastic bags, money for starving kids, equal access to school and shit. Everything."

"Music?"

"On the down-low. Get this, he was talkin' about forming a Ramones tribute band. You ask me, that's pushing the envelope. Johnny ain't gonna go for that. But seriously, he could probably get away with it he looks so different. Hang on, check it out."

"Holy shit, that's him?"

"Fuckin' nuts, right?"

"Wow. He looks great, actually. Great suit. Szilarda?"

"With dad or not, I guess."

"And Johnny?"

The sea was muddy, the wind was cool, and the sky was gray. We stood on deck watching New York disappear. Gulls screamed overhead. We sipped perfectly made espressos.

We got a stateroom this time. Not wanting a repeat of our 1977 voyage, I had quizzed Peter extensively regarding his finances. Although he did not have the funds at the time of the quiz, he said he could definitely raise them. In that respect, he had my complete confidence. The decision to sail rather than fly had been mine. After Ramona told me where to find Johnny, I thought it was a poetic necessity as well as the perfect vehicle to facilitate a journey into the past—in addition to bringing me back to the seafaring days of my youth, the ship's lack of distractions would allow me to burrow deeply into my soul like a crab into a hooker's cunt.

Uncle Dave, now living in Rye, had offered to send us a laptop computer for the journey. I refused. I had never been alone with a computer before, and refusing the opportunity so to do had been a major victory of willpower, perhaps the greatest of my life. I had explored today's cinema with an effervescent boyish wonder in the Brighton Beach Library—I was amazed by how far art had come. So delicious was the imagery of today, so varied and visually striking, I felt as if I had grown up with the horse and wagon. Prior to being introduced to these revolutionary films, I was quite certain my vigor had gone the way of a fractious Duma under an aggressive Czar—a lifeless organ no longer representing the people.

Modern cinema had turned that dreary notion on its head, and many were the hours I spent enjoying my rejuvenated *élan vital* at workstations 2 or 3. Thanks to their discreet location behind a wooden card catalogue retained for ornamental purposes, they allowed the viewer to massage his or her[35] genitalia through the

---

[35] "Her" in this case was an elderly Russian named Yulia. We'd assumed the hours she spent viewing modern cinema were purely sentimental journeys until one of the more astute vagrants explained the invisible wasp that always buzzed around Yulia when she watched a film.

pocket or by the covert pumping of the inner-thighs. On the other hand, many were the hours I could have spent reading up on Stephen Hawking's latest discoveries, swimming in the sea, or finishing this book in ten percent of the time.

Bearing the latter in mind, I considered how a contemplative journey, a cleansing of the soul, would be affected by having access unfettered not only to today's cinema but to one's genitalia as well. The result seemed like a forgone conclusion best avoided. There'd certainly have been no coffee on deck under screaming gulls.

And beyond that, there was no art form that rivaled modern cinema in its codification of my waning; I preferred to travel without constantly being reminded of this. In the late 1960s when I was at my most prolific, my work was unarguably revolutionary. Not only did it question all musical tradition that had gone before, it also drew a line in the sand against the collective morality of a world about to crumble. Even in 1977 when the old world died and the new was ushered in, I couldn't conceivably have imagined just how far we'd be travelling. In this respect, we must be honest with ourselves: why would someone invest the requisite time and analysis required by a sprawling work like *Chicks With Dicks Sleep Late* when they can achieve the same enlightenment in two minutes with *Sweet Plump Teen Got Her Pussy Eaten Out by an Aged Jerk Outdoors*? The answer is obvious. When I saw teenagers giggling and pointing to some brilliant piece of liberated cinema in the library, I could only smile and wish I was one of them. Why would young people with a world of fantastic art at their fingertips bother with my dusty scores and archaic philosophies? In what seemed like minutes, I had become yesterday's news.

In fact, it was at the behest of solitude that I had finally agreed to embark on this voyage. I had no intention of pursuing recognition for my quartets as exemplified in the early Ramones albums, let alone in the myriad imitators that I spawned. I hadn't just let the fight go, I had also relinquished my soul's investment in it—in short, I didn't give a fuck. Furthermore, remuneration meant nothing to me—I had no interest in material possessions or mutual funds. On the other hand, Peter had struck a chord when he said I was owed an explanation. I realized that this immense demand had existed beneath everything like the monstrous Lake Vostok, cold and forever black beneath the Antarctic ice. The pursuit of credit and money had to a great extent simply been codes representing treachery's sting. I demanded answers, and Johnny was the only brother that could adequately provide them. But most importantly, I was executing even greater punishment on myself by banning myself from paradise on Earth: Ruffle Bar. My idea of exile was a film negative that had to be flipped around.

When I picked up the remaining cash and drugs, I had never felt so filthy or spiritually underfunded—that slithering dark emotion confirmed that my former vow not to return until I was vindicated had been the right decision, although the reasons were more complex. The outcome I sought was, in many respects, more significant: hearing directly from Johnny why they had done this to me. Breaking a vow, yet again, and crawling on my belly among Ruffle Bar's magic reeds was not the image of myself I wanted to take to the grave. No, I could still return with my head held high, and spend my remaining days in glorious isolation, the unwitting Napoleon of Rock and Roll on St. Helena, inspiring the greatest works of the world's next Byron. All of these things came together in a resounding and unexpected "Yes!" that now had us on the deck of the *Inflexible*, a ship where I could bathe in my memories and in the fact that I owed my career to that French sailor's assault all those years ago. The French ships also serve excellent coffee and enormous amounts of wine.

We reached France in less than two weeks. Peter absconded to Paris. We agreed to meet in Port de Cherbourg in five days time when the *Flexible* would return to New York. I saw Peter off at the station. My train left two hours later, so I bought twenty cans of 1664—ten for the wait, ten for the train. I bought a French paper and pretended to read it while I observed passerby. This was the thrust of Peter's mission to Paris—he was convinced he'd find more *Outsiders* types there than in New York, which seemed improbable based on what he told me about the film. I also had concerns about us separating, but Peter reacted to my worry with careless amusement: "Damone, this is Europe. I can eat these people for lunch." Looking around at the choices of footwear and the innumerable pairs of bright red pants worn by men somehow managing to keep straight faces, I realized he was right. I opened another 1664.

A few hours and seventeen of twenty later, I was disembarking from the train. Winding cobbled streets, ancient stone buildings, and wonderful smells. I wandered around for ten minutes until an outdoor café caught my eye—there were only three tables, all empty. I sat down. I ordered by pointing at one of my remaining 1664s. He returned with a foamy round glass. He addressed me in French.

"Sorry, I don't speak the French," I said.

"Where are you from? England, Ireland?"

"New York."

"Ah, New York! The best city in the world."

"It's okay. Can you tell me how to get to Mont Saint Michel from here?"

"You know where the station is? There is a bus. Twenty minutes, you are there."

"Thanks."

"The God crazies walk across the sea bottom at low tide. I don't understand it. Did God forbid bridges? Many Americans. Every year these fools get caught in the tide and we must save them. Some have died."

"Thanks for the warning. I'll take another beer. And a glass of that green stuff."

When I arrived at the station, the bus wasn't there. I sat down. I observed the waiting people. Several were speaking English. They were dressed in hiking gear, as if Normandy was the Rocky Mountains. An initially cute young woman hacked her cuteness away word by word:

"Oh my God you guys, that waiter, like, totally ripped us off. He like pocketed two Euros. The bill was like fort*eeeeeeee*? He owed us two Eur*ooooooooohs*? He never came back. And like, there was already a tip in the price? And the omelette was like no big deal. I had like better in L.A."

I left. I walked through the town's cobbled streets. There was a low stone inn outside town. I went inside and drank a carafe of wine. I paid and walked west.

I entered a green vastness. There was nothing ahead except the horizon line. The sky was gray. I walked on a narrow tractor path. The imbecilic young woman had filled me with an unalloyed melancholy of uncertain origin that was perfectly reflected by the lonely beauty spread before me. If I hadn't been alone, if someone had been walking by my side engaging in witty or even morbidly introspective banter, it would have somehow raised the mood, thereby marring the sad beauty. No, without a doubt I needed to walk alone. Plus the 1664 had given me terrible gas.

A giant mound of dirt in the distance clarified into the mighty fortress I sought. Gray walls became clearer. The fortress rose sharply from the horizon, culminating in a cathedral, and beyond that a spire stabbed the clouds. From this distance the gray jumble looked like a sloppily built pyramid sitting in the sea.

After an hour, I was joined by a herd of sheep. Seagulls swooped and screamed. The earth grew softer. Sea air blew across the increasingly marshy landscape. The grass became interspersed with patches of moist sand. The sea lay beyond.

I sat down. I opened my last beer. I had achieved sufficient altitude to pretend to savor the lukewarm 1664. As I drank, gray swaths of sea slowly swept across the sandy flats, swooping and converging, burying the Earth. The massive medieval fortress dominated the Atlantic beyond.

When the tide was at its highest, I put my shoes in my backpack. I walked across the sand and into the sea. I swam toward Mont Saint Michel. A current pulled me north, the right direction if I gauged it correctly. The cold sea lent me special clarity—my thoughts came faster and my energy was restored. A propelling illumination made me feel as if I was an undiscovered wavelength, an unknown type of light that travels 186 millimeters a second, a laid-back beta light.

I reckoned it was less than half a mile. The fortress loomed above. When I got close, I could hear people shouting from the ramparts. A crowd was watching. I was very close. I tread water and looked up at them. They were reaching out, filming me with their telephones.

Shouting from shore. A lip of sand curled around the massive black walls. A group of men had come from around the corner and were rushing toward me. One of them shouted in French.

"Sorry," I yelled, "I don't speak French."

"What are you doing? Do you need help?"

"No. Do you?"

"Swim to us now!"

"Swim to *me* now, asshole."

"Take hold of this."

"Ha ha ha! Did you just throw me a ring buoy?"

"Swim toward us now or we must call the police."

I considered swimming away, but I wasn't sure what was on the other side of the island and the current could send me to England. I swam to them. I walked onto shore.

"Don't touch me. I didn't break any law. Here's your ring back. Where's the Abbey? I came to commune with God, not idiots."

They directed me up a stone staircase. I walked past the cow-like tourists. I imagined how useless they'd be if someone indeed were drowning—Kew Gardens goes on the road.

I climbed upward through narrow passages and across ramparts with stunning views of France and the sea. I asked directions to the Monk's Garden, although I had no plan beyond that. Soon I was walking in the shadowy alcove looking at the beautiful garden.

I meandered among repulsive waves of tourists. Forty minutes passed before I saw two hooded monks talking in the walkway ahead. I approached them.

"Pardon, can one of you please direct me to Johnny Ramone? He's my brother."

"Does he work here? There is no monk named this."

"Are you sure? He has long hair, he's aggressive. An American. Are you sure?"

I felt a tap on my shoulder. I turned to another monk.

"They do not know him, sir. Follow me. Perhaps I can help you."

I followed the monk through narrow winding passages. We emerged on a rampart overlooking the coast. A monk stared at the sea. My guide gestured for me to wait. He tapped the other monk. He turned.

"Hey fucker, guess who?" I yelled.

"Are you the one that just swam here, Damone?" Johnny said.

"What of it?" I yelled. The other monk disappeared down the stairs.

"That was idiotic. Did you somehow get here from south of the causeway? Leave it to you to figure out the most fucked up way possible to do something. Jesus Christ, even the religious lunatics check the tides table."

"John: there was a girl at the bus stop wearing a fucking tie-dye, okay?"

"You coulda waited for low tide. What's wrong with you?"

"A waiter told me the flats are full of quicksand, so I figured it'd be better to swim."

"Sure, okay. That makes perfect fucking sense. My mistake. Follow me. Why are you walking like that? Are you drunk?"

"Yes, of course."

"So you found me. I'm not surprised."

"You're not?"

"No. Whatever's left of your brain is still a Ramones brain."

"You're a monk? Is this some sort of joke?"

"Don't question me. This is my place, and if you ridicule me, I'll throw you over that wall."

He lowered his brown hood.

"Ha ha ha! What happened to your hair? None of the other monks had theirs like that."

"I'm of a different tradition: Franciscan. Why am I explaining this?"

"Why did you do it? You could have lived anywhere in the world like Joey."

"I'm directed, Damone. It's the voice of God. This time it was almost twenty years ago. I read that the Rainbow Theatre in London—remember it, the place we had the bouncers kick your ass right on stage and we filmed it?"

"I seem to have some dim recollection of that, yes."

"It's not a theatre anymore. It was taken over by the Universal Church of the Kingdom of God."

"The church run by murderers?"

"This church is too, whatever. Let me finish. It was founded in 1977, the same year we made our best record *Rocket to Russia*."

"You're welcome."

"Damone, you either make a *Rocket to Russia* or you don't. It's really that simple. Don't interrupt me again or I'll throw you down the stairs. Anyway, I found that out later. It was when I first heard the church had taken over the theatre: that's when I knew precisely what I was going to do—we'd stage our deaths, and I'd become a monk. That's a separate thing, but I always knew I'd end up in France."

"What the hell are you talking about, you hate France."

"That's what I said, but it's not what I thought. Now France is the last place anyone'd expect to find me."

"That's brilliant."

"Remember when you used to put your ear on the floor in your room and you could tell who was jacking off?"

"Sure."

"But you never heard me doing it?"

"I assumed you didn't have any nerves down there."

"But you swore you heard people speaking French? And I said it's because you're a schizo? That was me practicing with the French tapes. Anyway, not relevant. What do you want from me?"

"Several things. First: you destroyed my life. I'm destitute and living on the streets to this day. You became a multi-millionaire in the process. You helped our brothers become multi-millionaires. Why am I the chosen one?"

"Because it was right. Montez and Szilarda were crazy. He was into every kind of racket: rum running, pimping, pyramid schemes, drugs. If he went to CPA school and saved twenty bucks a week, he'd be set now. But you know dad—give him a billion dollars, it'll be gone in three days. And he didn't want to be square or told what to do, so he'd never take a straight job. Szilarda made some dough sewing, but she was like you, František, and Joey—she spent too much time fucking off on the accordion. Neither of them provided a shred of discipline or even cared whether or not we went to school. Did you know I took care of all that shit? They had Tyler, Terry, and František who had real problems and everyone else was crazy—you, Joey, Dee Dee, Marky. All hard to handle. With me so far?"

"Yes. Society made you do it. And the way you were raised."

"Shut up and listen. Somebody had to take charge, work, and try and figure out how everyone could make something of themselves. Even if we sometimes made a fortune selling Montez's drugs, everyone was going to end up in prison or dead. Drug dealers have short careers. So I kept thinking, what can they do? Tommy had been talking about forming a group, but I thought it was impractical. Then one day it hit me that rock and roll was the only answer—not because I loved it, not because anyone could play or write songs, but because there was *no other choice*. Dee Dee could be a rocker, never a janitor, you know? I knew if I focused and led, we'd make it and end up on top. Took fucking forever, everybody and their brother made money off our sound before we did, but we won in the end. Tommy called me and said that even in Budapest he sees ten Ramones shirts a day. Same Joey about Paris, Rome, London. Tommy said back in New York he'd see at least a hundred a day. Now everybody knows who actually invented the sound and who's truly punk: the Ramones. Not Rancid, not Green Day, not—who's another one?"

"Nirvana."

"Exactly. And Damone, nobody's more punk than you. I have more authority to say that than anyone on Earth. You cut your own path. You always lost but that was because you refused to take any shit, you couldn't be bought, and you didn't give a fuck what anyone thought. You still don't give a fuck, do you?"

"I don't."

"Good. So fuck it. It's all over now."

"You think you can jerk me off with that total bullshit, and I'm happy? No disrespect, but you're trying to get me off this island as fast as possible, right? Cheap flattery doesn't compensate for a ruined life. I mean fuck, couldn't you have let me play the tambourine or something?"

"Damone, you were a special case. You're not in the same boat as František or Tyler and Terry, but you're no nine-to-fiver either. And the band was hard fucking work. I had all those years on the boat as reference for how everybody worked. You're lazy unless it benefits you directly. You're unpredictable—one minute everything is fine, the next minute you're saying you're from Mars or you're the King of England or you're having a tantrum over something that didn't happen at all, meant nothing, or happened twenty years ago. Is that an unfair assessment?"

"Apparently not."

"I figured out something for everyone, but you're my luminous blue variable."

"I'm flattered by the term"

"Don't be. You're a major fuckin' problem, an unpredictable prick. I wasn't going to hand you a free pass. You didn't just need a trade, Damone. You needed a major ass-kicking, not just a few taps with the pink bat. You needed a monumental ass-kicking that goes on for years."

"Thanks for caring asshole, but marooning me? I could have died out there. *And stealing all my work?*"

"One thing at a time. The island: remember finding the first issue of Hustler in your cave? Who do you think left that?"

"The Christmas Miracle of 1974?"

"I checked on you. At first. I thought I'd have to take you to shore or bring more food, but that's the thing Damone—I didn't have to. You finally seemed like you came into your own. You're a genius carpenter—

"Genius?"

"That fuckin' underground house? I almost shit my fuckin' pants. That room with the thrones in the wall, that fucked up altar to chili. The dried fish and the pelts? You're like something from the French Foreign Legion. Yeah, I kept my eye on you. Who do you think paid your bail after you got pinched in Prospect Park?

We entered a cathedral. Monks were conducting a service while tourists prayed in the pews. There was a tall blur of light behind the altar that blazed white over the cross. The tall interior reached halfway to heaven. Everything was bathed in pale light. It was quiet except for the chanting of a single monk. Johnny spoke softly:

"This is the main cathedral here. So basically, when I saw that you—"

"I understand—you assumed paternal responsibilities and I became the Min Saw to your Kunhsaw."

"Damone, I'll shove a rickshaw up your ass if you interrupt me again. Understand, you fucking cocksucker?"

"You can't talk like that in here, plus you're a monk!"

The praying tourists all turned around.

"I can talk however I want wherever the fuck I want. I might be a monk, but I'm still Johnny Fucking Ramone!"

"I see."

"What?"

"Nothing. Please continue."

"Let's get out of here. Like I was saying, I was working my ass off to feed the family. Everyone fucked around on shore, but they did good on the boat. Not you. You sat around jerking off. You didn't have any excuse either. So you got what was coming. What you needed."

"You think I had a good life thanks to you?"

"No. But that's because you kept trying to be stuff you aren't, and because you left that island. That was your thing. If you had stayed there, you'd have had a base to do other shit. That's your fault."

"You'll see, I'm going to become a textiles magnate, I have new ideas that will—"

"Why do you need to be a *magnate*? Start a tailor shop or make custom decks. Or go back to Ruffle Bar."

"Easy for you to say, Mr. Rock Superstar."

"Damone, I did rock as a job—I worked my fucking ass off like any small business owner. I liked the music, but at my age it wasn't a dignified or easy road. Don't forget, I was born in 1930—I'm fuckin' eighty-four. Shit, I hitchhiked to Detroit during the war to build tanks when I was thirteen. That's why I got so pissed when people complained about how much we toured, you know, like what's their excuse? At our last gig I was sixty-six."

"Okay. Got it. You destroyed my life to help me."

"Damone, I had to make a call—my job was to figure out the fairest way to distribute everyone's dissatisfaction."

"Joey had a certain eccentricity. You made him the fucking lead singer."

"He was perfect. He was born to do that. He had a magic."

"Indeed. Joey is the rarified essence of adolescent romance, the personification of an intoxicating crush with a perfect soundtrack."

"You left out difficult motherfucker, otherwise eloquent stuff Damone. Did you wipe your jizz off the mirror before or after you thought it up?"

"That's all you have to say?"

"Yep. You're still standing, aren't you? Then don't complain."

"Where's František?"

"He's the organist at the St-Gervais-et-St-Protais Church in Paris."

"Does he play the same thing over and over?"

"It's a church. There's problems when church organists want to do their own thing. Just think how Bach used to behave."

"You know how Bach used to behave?"

"Tyler and Terry live with Ramona."

"What? Why didn't she say anything?"

"She probably didn't want you to ask their genders. Now that dad's gone it's her job to keep that under the lid."

"Do you even know?"

"František's coming in a couple days. Want to meet him for a drink?"

"Of course, definitely."

"Go to La Ferme Saint Michel the day after tomorrow at five. He'll be there. Now let's get on with it, what else do you want?"

"I have also come to receive your Imperatur. I'm finishing a book on our lives: the true story of the Ramones. I'm publishing it whether you forbid it or not, but I prefer having your blessing. Plus Ramona suggested that I might be the victim of physical violence at your hand if I did not."

"What's it about?"

"It's the entire Ramones story from start to finish, starting with our parents' backgrounds and ending at this very moment. Or maybe a few days after."

"You've got my Imperatur. Do whatever you want, Damone. Nobody's going to believe you. Even if we hadn't covered our tracks, even if you were the straightest guy producing solid proofs and utilizing robust research tools, nobody'd believe the facts—it's too fucked up a story. The more accurate you are, the less credibility you'll have.

"Your disappearing acts in quick succession, and everybody believed that? People believe anything. I have more of chance than you think."

"Touché, prick. I love our fans, but you gotta wonder. They bought it hook, line and sinker. When did we ever seem like we were slowing down, getting old, or losing it?"

"*Too Tough To Die.*"

"That's right."

"Is Montez still alive?"

"I think so. But he hasn't checked in for a while. What are you gonna do now?"

"I have a few more days. See the old town, then gotta catch a train on the mainland. I leave out of Port de Cherbourg."

"Great maritime museum down there, a lot of bars, but they're expensive. Come check this out."

We went down a spiral staircase into cool, candlelit darkness. In a small subterranean hall a group of monks and nuns were singing a slow, solemn piece.

"Know it?" he asked.

"No."

"I'll give you a hint—he was a mass murderer."

"*Miserere*, of course! Carlo Gesualdo."

"Jesus, Damone. You introduced me to him. I introduced him here. He's very big around here. It's sorta their way of being badass, doing his shit. Come on, I'll walk you out."

We crossed the ramparts and went back down the stairs. Johnny indeed looked older; he was slightly wizened and lighter of frame, but he walked up and down stairs with a new delicate spryness, as if finally casting off the mantle of responsibility had imbued him with extra bounce that would carry him through another twenty years. We reached the gate and the road into the old town.

"Good luck, Damone. You're always welcome here."

"Indeed. You can become my four great paladins and—"

"Shut up. We ain't doing that. And I don't want you to ever pick up another sewing machine again. I mean, go ahead and sew with them, but no more writing transvestite symphonies on the fucking things. Or fucking them."

"Don't worry. I'm no spring chicken anymore either."

"And no fucking wooden horses or go-carts, or anything that can't tell you it's got a headache."

"Is that classic Franciscan wisdom?"

"It's classic do-as-I-say wisdom. Got it?

"So long, Johnny. Until the next time."

Time! Forward! The never-ending story of my brothers had entered the next phase, when the volatile particle finally dispersed. Their rock story: tearing at each other's throats, beleaguered with personal problems, but still operating with perfection the full length of their careers under the leadership of my most misunderstood of brothers. In the end, their transcriptions of my works combined with the intuitive crafting of Joey and Dee created rock and roll's four greatest albums, thereby ending it forevermore. Gentleman, you are assholes in life, but aristocrats in art. Your desecration of my life ultimately fell under the latter more than the former; my life was a bizarre modern sculpture of your creation, something as inexplicable and rife with contradiction as the mysterious Libreville/London/Luce tower with the black babies crawling up and down its length. I don't regret it. At least it's my story.

I spent the following days in the old town drinking and waiting for František. I slept on the island's north side among the brambles rather than take a room, for indeed, the beers were pricey as was the food, although the celebrated omelettes were like no big deal.

František met me as planned. He was dressed in an impeccable tweed suit and maroon leather wing tips polished to a mirror shine.

His fringe had turned so white that it gave off a bluish glow. He was waiting for me at a table behind a golden globe of beer. When I arrived he embraced me vigorously, then affectionately grabbed me by the head and shook, thus nearly ending my life right there in La Ferme Saint Michel in the shadows of the ancient monastery.

Fortunately he stopped before that happened. I sat down and rubbed my neck while he flagged down the waiter and ordered me a beer in French. The waiter seemed to know him. Now that I was actually sitting across from him, I didn't know what to say. I searched my mind for the few Czech phrases Ramona had tried to teach me.

"So…František. *Jak se máš? Hudba?*" [36]

"*Hudba je nebe. Hudba je všichni svatí. Šukal jsem zdravotní sestru v roce 1973.*" [37]

"So music is good, I take it."

"*A ty?*" [38] he asked.

"*Můj život stojí za hovno,*" [39] I replied.

He reached across the table and patted my forearm. His eyes both drooped and smiled with wet, babyblue serenity. His empathy raced through the streets of the old town, up the stone staircases and into the Abbey, fusing with Johnny's implacable railroading to finally kill off any sense I had retained of having ever been cut adrift. No, they had been there all along, and I didn't even have to visit Dee Dee's bar or meet Joey in a smoky Paris café to know that unity would be reiterated by the rest because: *We were truly brothers.*

A few days later I was watching Peter cross a square to join me at a café. I ordered him a beer.[40] He told me about several brothels

---

[36] "How are you? Music?" (I retained the conversation verbatim rather than how it should have been)

[37] "Music is sky. Music is all saints. I fucked a nurse in 1973."

[38] "And You?"

[39] Literally, "My life stands behind shit," i.e. "My life sucks."

[40] French beer is the very definition of underrated.

he had visited in Paris, and how one night he had tried to break a jewelry store's window but the bar just bounced off it. He did say shoplifting was a joke, particularly food at the high-end tourist markets. I listened, but my quiet appreciation was directed more at his simply being there in front me in all his odd glory, the furthest thing from an *Outsiders type,* far better than any of the dull hairsprayed stereotypes that so enthralled him. My thoughts were still back at the lonely Abbey, the magical island Mont Saint Michel. We weren't due on the *Flexible* until the day after tomorrow, but the voyage home was already a distant memory, a puff of smoke.

I would settle my business at my leisure from Ruffle Bar. I would make my dwelling and my life there even more undetectable than before. I would be a rumor, a shadow in the night, the Ben Gunn of Jamaica Bay. At the same time I would modify my pursuits, perhaps take a second crack at the patent office. Maybe my previous dismissal had been less about tail-sinkers, and more about excrement and presentation.

Let my brothers keep the spoils. They were the ones that turned adolescence into aristocracy. I hate to even use the word "adolescence" with its Clearasil and "bad judgment," so let's allow it merely as a signal intuitively renamed so it more closely matches the facts: the most powerful feelings, the best times, endless orgasms, mad attractions, the first heavenly beers.

We sailed for America. We watched France disappear over the horizon, then we moved to the bow to watch the sunset. The water was emerald and blue, the sky was clear. As the seagulls serenaded me yet again, I realized there was exuberance inside the grayest melancholy. I squeezed my penis through my pants. I got hard. I took off my suit. I took off my underwear. I walked to the gunwale, initially planning to fire over the edge, but then I thought it better to fire upward as a mirror image of the Pillar of Creation I most resembled while in the aspirational state. I lay naked on the deck and beat with renewed fire—if my composition was my own descent, then let it be magnificent, to paraphrase Mr. Knievel in reference to a fiery demise he was fated not to author. I wish I could have spoken to him, begged the use of his Rocket to Ruffle

Bar as homage and apology, but yet again, it was too late. I thought of the girl in the red shorts all those years ago, her mouth, the pile of sad Playboys, their laughably shrouded erotica having long claimed the largest portion of my white sea. Through me, Dick Nixon provided narration: "I never profited from public life. Never get discouraged, never be petty…always remember, others may hate you…but those who hate you don't win…unless you hate them…and then you destroy yourself."

"Damone! Damone, what are you doing?"

"Come to watch the pro, Peter?"

"Damone, you always said not do that outside or to at least not in restaurants and it's sorta the same thing now! *I* learned *my* lesson. The sailors will kill you, they already said!"

"Ooooo, I'm so scared!"

"Damone, you gotta stop, they're real mad! I'm warning you!"

"Peter, the conduct of my life has been, is, and will always be the echo and reflection of my perversions. I might have matured a little, but I'm still Damone Fucking Ramone."

ABOUT THE AUTHOR

Frank Lord was born in Detroit in 1969. He died in Moscow
in 2015.

Made in the USA
Columbia, SC
12 April 2017